Elite

'Helen Liddell's new novel crackles into the sort of action rarely associated with Westminster'
Sunday Mirror

'It's witty and rude'
Observer

'A fast-moving story of sinister plot and counter-plot, realistically set in Glasgow'
Scotsman

'A good read'
Southern Evening Echo

'An exciting political novel with a frightening scenario, written by a former politician... a corker'

Me Magazine

ELITE

Helen Liddell

ROWAN

A ROWAN BOOK

Published by Arrow Books Limited
20 Vauxhall Bridge Road, London SW1V 2SA

An imprint of the Random Century Group

London Melbourne Sydney Auckland Johannesburg
and agencies throughout the world

First published in Great Britain by Century 1990
Rowan edition 1991

Printed and bound in Great Britain by
Cox & Wyman Ltd, Reading

ISBN 0 09 976360 5

For Alistair

Elite

PROLOGUE

She walked across the stage to take the microphone and
the tumult died away. Tall, with a rich fall of auburn
hair, she strode loose-limbed as an athlete. Dressed in
silk, simple, expensive, sexy and elegant; this woman,
they said, had everything. Now she reached out for what
she most wanted – power. The strength of her presence
brought a silence so still that the muted whirr of a tape
recorder grew loud throughout the hall.

Two thousand people stopped the cheering and booing
by which they had passed the long night, and which a
moment ago they had roared to its pinnacle. Here now
she stood – in all her tension, controversy and beauty.

'Mr Returning Officer, ladies and gentlemen, let me
first thank the council staff and the police for the courteous
and efficient conduct of this election . . .'

Her voice ranged on the soft side of Glaswegian, no
jargon, a polished speaker, teasing the crowd. She had
spoken these words twice before; at thirty-eight, Ann
Clarke had tonight returned to Parliament for the third
time as a Labour MP – an increased majority every time.
In less than ten years she had risen explosively from mid-
dle-class political ingénue, to radical left-wing lawyer, to
Scotland's dominant political figure. Goddess or bitch?
Both – and often at once.

In the eyes of the working classes and the unemployed
she had mythic dimensions. She had told them they
needed a Joan of Arc; and then with a single-minded zeal,
she deliberately set out to give them one – herself. Now,
from the body of the hall, they reached to her like suppli-
cants. As usual, she let them have it – power, energy,
commitment, pauses between the phrases, her body totally
still. Then she was gone, leaving Clydeside West hoarse
in her wake.

The BBC driver knew the alleyways. She sat on the fake fur of a white Mercedes, not as a virgin bride on the way to the altar, but as a woman well aware that the next few hours would change her life beyond recall. At the third roadblock on the mile-long journey, the army sergeant in charge saluted as he recognized her. Power radiates.

The BBC mandarins in their grey suits had come out in force, watching the results tumble in. Before morning new political masters would harass them and now, instinctively, they set out to ingratiate themselves sufficiently with the winners while not burning their boats with the losers. The Controller Scotland, Malcolm Thomson, excelled at this, and several other of the arts of sycophancy. He almost floored a commissionaire in his rush to open the door to Ann's car. His congratulations sounded sincere and his compliments stopped just short of being familiar, as a subtle power struggle began. In fact, Ann only finally realized she had won when she became aware that the TV executive was trying to lay down the ground rules of the BBC's relationship with a member of the new Government.

Heedless of the welter of 'good wishes', a young floor manager in the worn denim of her calling tried to move Ann into the studio quickly, but so typical of such circumstances, everyone ignored the one with the most practical reason for being there. As the girl hopped from foot to foot in agitation Ann noticed, extracted herself from the crowd, and talked cheerfully to her along the cable-strewn corridor. The moment they entered the hot, bright studio the most crucial part of Ann Clarke's campaign – the subtle and dangerous phase – began.

The executive furniture gleamed in the flickering light. The TV screen made a pool of light across the room from the expensive walnut desk where the man sitting with his feet up drank a large whisky.

He raised his glass in silent toast to the elegant woman on the screen; the gesture came incongruously from his nicotine-stained fingers, lank hair, dirty shirt and gapped

10

teeth. When the scene on the screen dissolved back to London he reached over and switched off the set. Moving his phone towards him, he punched out a number.

'The Big Fella,' he demanded. Another drink, manoeuvring the bottle one-handed. He spoke again.

'You'll have seen how it went? Are you ready?'

He listened. A slow smile spread over his face, but his eyes grew even colder.

'If people have to die, then they have to die. Do what you've got to do, just make sure she never finds out. We're nearly there.'

The pause was longer this time.

'Yes. Don't worry. You'll all have it before morning. No bother. Yes, I know, I know. Used notes, the big stuff into the numbered bank account. OK. Anyway, since tonight's gone so well, they'll probably put the first batch in tomorrow. Keep me posted. Christ! I wish I was you. A couple of weeks and you'll be lying sunning yourself with some whore on the Costa del Sol. Untouchable. Maybe I'll come and visit you!'

He hung up.

Going over to the office safe, he opened it, taking out two bundles of notes. Back at his desk he took a pile of envelopes from the drawer, filled five of them and left some spare money on the desk.

He flicked on the TV set again, within seconds realized nothing unexpected had happened, then stood up and flicked it off.

Shrugging on his jacket, he prepared to leave, stuffing the filled envelopes into his pocket, locking his desk drawer, checking the safe was secure, readjusting the rally banner that covered it. As he moved over to switch off the desk lamp he noticed the pile of Ann Clarke election posters lying on the table.

He particularly liked one – it showed Ann striding out in front of a march, the wind blowing her dress against her body, long legs clearly outlined. If you looked at it closely enough, you could see the button of a nipple through the silk of her dress. The picture had caused a

11

stir when the Party issued it; when the Party workers began to refer to it as 'the sexy poster', Ann had insisted it be withdrawn. It became a collector's item and he had just had more printed.

Picking up the poster, he shoved the other hand deep in his trousers pocket. Piggy eyes closed even further, he stared at Ann. Suddenly he swept the remaining money off the desk into his pocket and left.

His car swung into nearby Blythswood Square, the red-light district in this poverty-stricken city where the whores were plentiful now that the State had stopped paying social security.

He drove round until he found what he was looking for – no more than sixteen, maybe less, hair lank and damaged from too much cheap dye. A grubby tee shirt stretched over her bare breasts, she wore a tiny miniskirt over fishnet stockings and suspenders. The stockings were ripped and laddered. Her shoes with their five-inch heels were worn and ill fitting.

As she bent down to talk to the man in the expensive car, the vacant look left her eyes as she recognized him from the television. She'd cracked it this time. With no hesitation, she got in the car, directing him to a nearby car park.

He started the car, drove with one hand on the wheel, and wrapped his free hand in the girl's hair, dragging her mouth down to his open lap. He ignored her as she told him of an immediate price increase, forcing her on to him.

Just before dawn, another prostitute and her client found the badly beaten shell of the young girl, jaw broken, her body mutilated.

Later that day the police declared her age – fourteen – and her injuries sickened even the hardened police pathologist who gave the cause of death as asphyxiation.

Ann Clarke had not met Michael Stewart, the BBC's new political editor in Scotland. A big, tanned, TV professional, he had been transferred from the BBC's Washington bureau only days before the Government fell, and had spent the last four weeks on a crash course in Scottish politics. As she sat across the chasm of cables and monitors, she smiled a greeting.

Out of the corner of his eye, Stewart watched as the sound assistant, hardly believing his luck, pinned a personal microphone to her dress and helped her conceal the cable. Stewart, as yet unable to exchange a word with her – his ears crackled with live 'feed' – could feel her magnetism along the curved desk. A veteran of many such encounters, he now had a new challenge to make up for the slower pace of life in Glasgow.

He took the cue from his earpiece.

'And that last result from Basildon shows just how much the Conservatives are under pressure. The computer predicts a close-run result, but Labour's success here in Scotland, far outstripping anything elsewhere in the country, looks like not only putting them in the lead but deciding the outcome. I'm joined now by one of the architects of Labour's success north of the Border, and undoubtedly one of the major beneficiaries. Ann Clarke, Shadow Deputy Secretary of State for Scotland in the last Parliament, has been re-elected for Clydeside West, the seat she won in 1981 in a spectacular by-election caused by the suicide of the previous Member, Hugh Lawrie.'

He turned to Ann.

'Miss Clarke, congratulations; you have doubled your majority for the second time. Quite a personal vote of confidence?'

She smiled: 'Thank you. What I'm much more pleased with is the fact Labour's radical and caring programme struck such a chord with the voters. Not all of my colleagues shared my belief in the kind of policies we needed to win.'

Stewart saw the gauntlet – a blind man could not have missed it.

'Nor, Miss Clarke, have they unanimously approved of the highly personalized style you have adopted? Have you been guilty, as they would see it, of the cult of the personality? And how do you respond to their charge that you have been loath to condemn the violence of the past eighteen months?'

Her voice defined calm: 'Of course I'm appalled by violence. Don't forget, I would not have fought so hard to become a Member of Parliament if I didn't believe in the ballot box above all else.'

Stewart asked, 'Only this week you were accused of being the Parliamentary representative of the terrorists who have caused such havoc recently – even to the point of bringing down the Government.'

Ann hardened: 'I'm sure I don't need to remind you of clichés – the one I have in mind is that "one man's terrorist is another man's freedom fighter". I don't support violence, but I do understand what causes it. The real terrorists are this last Government who so brutalized the people of this country that violence became inevitable.'

'What are your links with the Workers' Militia, Miss Clarke?'

'I have no links with them whatsoever . . . but . . .'

Michael Stewart raised a hand and cut in.

'I'm sorry, I hate to interrupt you, but we have to go back to the Exhibition Centre, where it would appear the result is about to be declared in the Airdrie South Constituency previously held by the Shadow Secretary of State, Roddy Henderson. No surprises are expected here though.'

He intended his last remark primarily for the director in the gallery. Stewart silently vowed all sorts of vengeance for being interrupted as he tried to get the answer to the most vital question of the election campaign. And all for the ritual of a result that was already a foregone conclusion.

Sombre-suited men and nylon-clad matrons stood on the municipal stage, municipal flowers wilted in the background. The Returning Officer, his big moment at hand, cleared his important throat for the umpteenth time. He lacked Ann Clarke's talent for subduing an audience. He embarked on his forty-five seconds of stardom.

'I, the duly appointed Returning Officer for the Parlia-

14

mentary division of Airdrie South, do hereby declare the following votes cast for candidates in the said constituency.

'Allison, Rhona, the Conservative Candidate, 1,280 votes.

'Evans, Ewan David, the SNP Candidate, 11,842 votes.

'Henderson, Roderick Aloysius, the Official Labour Candidate, 27,602 votes.

'Jamieson, Agnes, Peace in the Streets, 410 votes' – Mrs Jamieson's vote disappeared in the shouts.

Voice over the Returning Officer, Michael Stewart explained that Henderson had increased his majority by five thousand and looked set to reap the rewards of thirty diligent years in Parliament, almost certain to be the next Secretary of State for Scotland. Henderson, though, did not give that impression. The image the viewers saw showed a man perspiring heavily, wiping his forehead and tugging at his collar, his shoulders slumped, distressed.

When she saw him Ann Clarke moved forward in her seat, fixated on the monitor, tensed. The director, looking at her face in close-up, could see this new strain across her mouth. What was going on? Should he cut to her? No – the journalists would eat him – but his instinct told him that the highly qualified, self seeking journalists had missed the story of a lifetime.

Stewart's commentary ran on over the traditional gratitude of the successful candidate.

Then he stopped, his instinct at last smelling a departure from the norm.

Henderson went on to pay tribute to his wife:

'Lizzie has shouldered the real burden of my years in public life. She has had to cope with the constant ringing of the telephone; often sorting out my constituency problems in my absence. And she has had to bring up four children almost as a single parent, often in the face of quite straitened circumstances, in the years before MPs were well paid. That is the true cost of a Parliamentary career, the price that has to be paid by your partner, and often I have been less than generous in expressing my thanks – and so I have an announcement to make. I know that you will be shocked and saddened to know that recently Lizzie has not been in the best of health and has endured much suffering. I can't allow her to soldier on without the kind of support and comfort she is entitled to, and therefore it is my intention to serve out this Parliament from the back benches. That way I can devote my time to the two great loves of my life – Lizzie and my constituency.'

'Bugger this,' said the director, and cut to Ann Clarke, who suddenly sat back, relaxed. Afterwards they called it 'the shot of the night'. And he cut back again to the hall in time to see Lizzie's mouth gaping open in total amazement. An unwell woman? Surely not. She looked the picture of robust good health, her complexion flushed, not just with surprise, but with the effects of three weeks' campaigning in the open air. The crowd in the hall stood in stunned silence, and as Henderson seemed to shrink on the stage, his Parliamentary colleagues throughout the country stood speechless.

Michael Stewart knew he had less than three minutes to get to grips with the story before he was back on the air. He was yelling for a biography of Henderson, his obituary even, so that he could prepare his next link. The ramblings of the politician on the way out were going on – recounting old victories, settling old scores. As he drew to a conclusion, he reminded his listeners that the Labour Party had changed its rules only months before; no longer would the Leader – or the Prime Minister, as he would be before morning – have the right to fill vacancies in the Cabinet through the power of patronage; such appointments now required elections within the Party.

'And so in the weeks that lie ahead, our colleagues in the Labour Party, MPs as well as constituency activists, will join the trades unions in choosing our new Secretary of State. I know you will wish them well in that task, and I will be happy to serve as a caretaker until the man – or woman – who can bring our troubled country to peace, can take over.'

Half ponderous, half staccato, Michael Stewart gave a synopsis of the career of Roddy Henderson. His tributes were glowing, though if events had followed their anticipated path, he had intended roasting the man once he arrived in the studio as the new Secretary of State. Stewart turned to his lady contributor.

'Miss Clarke, how much did you know of this? Surely Roddy Henderson kept you informed of his intentions – especially as you seem likely to reap the benefits.'

'No, like everyone else I am completely taken aback.' She sat forward, looking genuinely upset.

'If he had talked to me I would certainly have tried to talk him out of it. He must have realized that and kept his own counsel. From Mrs Henderson too, it would seem. This is a sad loss to our front bench, especially in what looks like a major victory.' Her face reflected distress.

'But surely you must be exhilarated too. After all, tonight's announcement could make you the youngest woman ever to serve in a Labour Cabinet as well as the first woman Secretary of State. This could put you firmly on the road to Number Ten, perhaps by the time of the next election.'

'Come, come, Mr Stewart,' she said, crisp as a school-ma'am. 'Don't get carried away. The next Secretary of State will be elected – as you just heard – and by the Labour Movement. I am too committed to that kind of democracy to pre-empt the democratic process.'

'But you will of course be standing?' Stewart interrupted.

'This is not the time to make declarations, I will speak to my constituency party, and to the union that sponsors me, before I come to any decisions. Anyway, this is neither the time nor the place for these discussions. I don't think you realize how great a public servant Scotland has lost tonight. That's what we should be talking about.'

And off she went on a flowery tribute to her erstwhile boss. In front of television screens, her Parliamentary colleagues smiled cynically as they conjured up the memory of her flaying the same Roddy Henderson at the last meeting of the Parliamentary Labour Party. Betrayed Socialist Principles. Took his wife to a Royal Garden Party.

In the studio gallery, Malcolm Thomson was having a heated exchange with the BBC Chief of Security.

'Christ man, if she addresses a crowd using facilities provided by the BBC, how the hell can we pretend we have the slightest whiff of impartiality? Who knows how long this Labour Government will last. I don't want to be marked down as a raving pinko when the next lot gets back in.'

The security chief, a retired Chief Superintendent of Police, had the knack of conveying an intimidating sense of authority; of secrets known only to him and his like. He was making the BBC Controller – who also operated on the principle of 'knowing where the bodies are buried' – distinctly uneasy.

'Look, Sir, the Chief Constable says he cannot guarantee public order if something isn't done to defuse the situation. Go and take a look out the canteen window, there are at least five thousand people out there, all of them at fever pitch. If you want to take the responsibility for a riot, or even the storming of the building, then that's up to you, but I have to put it to you straight, I'm not taking the blame for a situation that could easily be defused by using some common sense.'

The crew in the gallery pretended not to listen but the atmosphere tightened by the minute. Thomson was aware of this, and all sorts of stories charged through his imagination about broadcasting moguls caught in the crossfire of coups in the Third World.

He yelled in whispers:

'The Chief Constable cannot guarantee public order! What the hell was he playing at letting them through the barricades in the first place? Jesus, it's not as though this is a novel situation, that's why we have curfews and bloody roadblocks. Why can't he handle this one?'

The street camera which filmed arriving politicians now

looked at the crowd – Thomson never heard the director's quiet instructions to the cameraman. The crowd, seeing some action, heaved. Thomson, watching the monitor, gave in. Ann Clarke could speak to the crowd. The director, buying himself time to deploy more cameras, cut back to London.

The face on the screen had the serious good looks of a matinee hero: the dark hair, expensively tended, curling round the collar, the blue eyes that seemed to pierce, the sensitive mouth, the strong if slightly flabby jaw. Almost as much time had been given to the publicity photographs as to the election manifesto. The men and women now gathered round the television had, time after time, submitted pictures for approval. Time after time she had vetoed them all – except this one. Which is how she had conducted his career since the day they met. Everybody in the Party knew their story – Sylvia Metcalf had taken a moderately astute politician, capitalized upon his disarming good looks and husky voice, and made him Leader. Tonight she had made him Prime Minister. The BBC had just confirmed it.

His aides clustered in a semicircle around the television. At a table in the corner two armed detectives played chess, winding up a game that had kept them occupied for the three weeks of the campaign. On the sofa a man and a woman glanced at one another. Tomorrow, the real world would return – she back to her husband, he to his wife, and the adrenaline and passions of the campaign would become memories – until the next time.

Some results brought reminiscences. Despite a Labour gain in Carlisle, everyone groaned.

'That idiot who chaired the rally!' Someone else butted in: 'And do you remember how we missed getting Tony on *News at Ten* because the Chairman went on so long. The only night in the campaign. Jesus!'

They all joined in the 'worst moments' recital until, with a jaded cheer, they looked at the television image of a tired and weary man on the steps of Conservative Central Office conceding defeat.

Then they looked at one another. Quizzically. What to do? Applaud? Shake hands? Wish Tony luck? Admit it was a poisoned chalice?

No one did anything.

Except the Right Honourable Antony Metcalf, PC, MP who stood up and crossed the room heading for the bar. Constitutionally still the Leader of Her Majesty's Loyal Opposition but, with the declaration of the result in Ongar, now the duly elected Prime Minister and First Lord of the Treasury. The first Labour man for more than twelve years. The wilderness years had ended.

He slopped whisky into a tumbler, filling it to the brim. Sylvia put her hand over his on the glass. Her eyes said 'no'. Her eyes said a lot more too – worry, danger, fear. And love, always love, despite everything.

For over twenty years Sylvia Metcalf had worked their dream, that Tony would enter Number Ten, a Labour Prime Minister, able to do all the things they had argued about and which they had committed themselves to.

He shrugged, put the glass down and turned away, back to the television. He ran his hands through his hair and sighed and slumped.

Still no one spoke. The ageing commentator, bow tie askew, rasped on. More results came in. It looked like a small majority.

The silence made the room eerie. For this small band of people who for the past three weeks saw each other every waking minute, the game was over. After the excitement of the chase, the triumphs of small victories, the despair of setbacks, they now had to deliver. And deliver in a country that in the past two years had sunk deeper into violence and lawlessness; a country in hock to the Americans, a country paying off huge debts through the expedient of allowing more and more US military installations.

So obsessed had everyone been with tactics that no one had prepared for the reality of victory. What would become of the promises made in the passion of the fight? The lure of Government had kept underpaid researchers and aides loyal; now they anticipated the same perks and the crucial power that their opposite numbers had been flaunting. Would it be worth it?

Graeme Jones, Metcalf's key advisor, broke the tension. He jumped out of his chair, threw his notes, clipboard and all, at the television set and stormed out. Jones had come up with Tony from the beginning, approaching him asking for a job, any job, when Metcalf was an aspiring Parliamentary candidate and Jones the leader of Britain's students. He had gone for years living on a pittance, unable to afford a decent house, buy decent suits, all for a chance at the big one – becoming a superbly professional political manager as the years went on.

While various friends entered Parliament, Jones had stayed with the Boss, keeping his eye on the future – the day he would go into Number Ten. Offers had been made to him, some very prestigious. He could have been General Secretary of the Party if he had wanted – become a politician in his own right. But his loyalty never swerved. Not a self-effacing man, he had repeatedly shown irritation and resentment at Sylvia, but they shared a common goal – the key to the front door of 10 Downing Street. Now that the key began to turn, Jones showed the frustration they all felt.

Sylvia went over to the set and turned the sound down. In the silence that followed, the sound of cheering and singing from the street below could be clearly heard.

'Right,' she said. 'Work to be done. We've got to get on our way to London within half an hour.'

As she ticked off their jobs the Press Officer came in. Sylvia looked expectantly at him.

'The rat pack are having a bottle party along the corridor. They've got nothing to do because their political editors are lording it over them in London. But they need reaction pieces. I think they should get it sooner rather than later; they'll soon be too pissed to file copy. Is Tony going to go in to see them?'

Sylvia shook her head, but she went over to the bar and picked up two unopened bottles of Scotch.

'Give them these with our compliments.' The man smiled. 'And we'll be down in the lobby in half an hour. Tell them how happy we are. And they can snatch a few more platitudes as we leave.' Then she cleared the room.

The newly elected Prime Minister remained slumped, gaping nervously at the television. Sylvia perched on the arm of the chair. Gently she stroked his hair. Her voice was soft as she spoke.

'You'd better have some lines ready for when they ask you about the Americans.' His eyelids dropped.

Sylvia fed him the line: 'I'll be meeting the US President every second year instead of every year – and you say it with a broad grin – not a wink, that looks too rehearsed.'

He thought about it and tried the phrase out – it sounded good.

'But what if they ask me what it means?'

She put her hand on his shoulder and smiled down at him: 'You pinch the old line from Harold Wilson – "any fool can give an answer, but the real skill lies in asking the right question". That way you've got a putdown and a tease in a neat little package.'

He nodded. Abruptly Sylvia jumped up, jerked her head towards the TV screen, clenched her fists and hissed, 'That bitch.'

When Ann Clarke was escorted out of the studio, she refused to address the crowd. Then the Chief Constable told her that only she could calm them. Malcolm Thomson, shrewder, assured her the BBC would allow world-wide coverage and not exploit their unique position.

Security men raised the huge Georgian sashes on the old part of the facade. When she appeared at the window the crowd lurched forward dangerously. She stopped them with a hand – total authority, the same technique as at the count in the Exhibition Centre. Her stillness brought calm and quiet to the frenzied atmosphere. For a moment she bowed her head, in a gesture that seemed humble –

as if to give an air of meditation, appropriate to this memorable moment in history. Then she flung her head up, hair tossing back.

At first she seemed hesitant, unsure.

'The warmth you have shown me tonight has touched me. Deeply. So deeply that I am profoundly moved by the depth of your commitment.' Pause. 'Commitment to freeing this country from its chains.' A roar of approval began, she stopped it dead with a hand. 'This last Conservative Government subjected this country to slavery. Total, utter, demoralizing slavery. Four election victories became an excuse to abuse the power vested in them. They destroyed the kind of society we had all taken for granted was fair and just. Look at what they did.' She began to count on upraised fingers. 'Where is the social security network we all thought gave some decency to the worst off in our community? Look at the pensioners – sacrificed to the private insurance companies? What's to happen to those people anxious and willing to work? Who spent their best years searching but never finding a way of earning a decent wage? Where are they now? Destitute? And the National Health Service? Vandalized and then destroyed. Now only a memory in history classes in our schools. And in those schools, political indoctrination instead of honest learning.' She paused; they stood in the palm of her hand.

'But worse, much worse.' She allowed her voice to rise.

'Worse than anything else they've managed to do is the rape of our country. Against our will, they have made Britain the most densely armed country in the world. With Scotland its nuclear arsenal. Stop a second and think.' She held out the imperious hand. 'In four years we've seen tourists banned from Loch Lomond as some of the most spectacular scenery in the world serves as camouflage for deadly weapons of mass destruction. You now need to get a pass to visit the Highlands in case you disturb some of the US military. Your Highlands. Our Highlands. And the Islands. Again pillaged by those who know nothing of the rhythm of life there and the dignity of the people

– and care even less. The Clearances are with us again, not to make way for sheep this time, but for deadly nuclear submarines to lurk in the deep anchorages.' In her passion she had by now clenched her fists tight in front of her, holding them close to her chest.

'And what's it for? Are the Nazis set to return? Are there Reds under Scottish beds? No way!' A working class edge came harshly into her voice – carefully modulated. 'It's a sellout. It's a betrayal. Our history. Our dignity. Our freedom. Has been sold for American dollars. Our defences are their defences. Our economy is their backyard to play in. They call it "The Special Relationship". Special to whom? Certainly not to us. It will swallow us up. It will destroy us. But tonight we started to fight back, we pointed the way for Britain to seize back the right to determine our own destiny.'

Now the roar broke through, a ferocious affirmation that she had set their fears to rest. As she gave them their head for a second she relaxed a little at the microphone, and smiled. But as she moved again to speak, her face grew sombre and hard.

'Tonight, you have elected your own destiny – a Labour Government. I want to help you make it work. But for us all. There may be those in my Party who, even tonight, harbour hopes of backsliding. Tomorrow when they move into their elegant Whitehall offices and begin to cash in their fat ministerial salaries, maybe then the Americans won't seem so bad. What will happen when they get the smell of power? When the blackmail starts? Will the smoothies of Washington have a field day? After all, they are all boys together, giving the public what they "deserve", not what they want. Well, let them think again!'

Behind her, Malcolm Thomson knew he had been out-manoeuvred. This was no mere response to a frenzied crowd, this was a cold and calculating challenge to the leaders of the new Government. The audience knew it too, they hung on her every word. Her hands at her sides, she almost seemed to stand to attention, in deadly intent.

'I swear to you, they will not deny your mandate! Scotland will again be free! With my soul, my body, my mind, I pledge to you that I will honour the trust you place in me. I will not rest until the last nuclear weapon is removed from our shores. I will find no peace until the last United States soldier is sent back home. And every vestige of strength I have will sustain me until those black slugs of hate, the nuclear submarines, slip stealthily away from Scotland. Tonight we have given them their marching orders.' She stepped back from the window, the hairs at the nape of her neck damp with tension. Outside the roar began, the hard rhythmic chant: 'Ann Clarke! Ann Clarke! Ann Clarke!'

Sylvia Metcalf snapped the remote control to 'off' and turned away.

'She makes my flesh creep!'

Her husband argued: 'But we don't know what she said!'

'Her voice is too much for me. And the designer Socialism. Designer dress, designer hairstyle, designer voice even. She's a packaged piece of destruction. Aimed at us!'

Metcalf patted his wife's bottom. 'Don't get worked up, Ann is very easily handled. Go and make yourself pretty for your debut as Mrs Prime Minister.'

Alone in the bedroom Sylvia stood for a moment, then she began to loosen the buttons of her blouse and let her skirt fall to the floor. From the largest of the suitcases piled at the bedroom door, she took out a red silk wrap-round dress, then knelt down to pack away the elegant but restrained yellow Cache d'Or suit she had intended to wear. Her low black pumps she pushed into another bag and began to rummage for a pair of shoes with higher and slimmer heels. She had ruthlessly dieted, exercised and stretched to make herself a suitable consort for Tony; one more change would make no difference.

She was already searching through one overnight bag before she realized she had opened the Pandora's box of

Tony's dirty washing. About to close it her hand hit the vodka bottle, almost empty.

The bathroom door opened, she locked the case quickly and kept the key.

Graeme Jones came into the suite, clipboard in hand, ready to brief his boss. As he perched on the back of the sofa he handed the Prime Minister a powder compact; Sylvia tossed over a little phial of eye drops which Tony immediately used, making his blue eyes even more startling.

Graeme went through the protocol.

'As you leave the suite you'll be greeted by the chambermaids – Kate – she's the dark one – and Yvonne. The corridor will be empty save for the Special Branch lads. They'll come down in the lift with us. The drill is that once they've got out, pause for a second to make sure they've cleared the shot before you both come out – hand in hand please. Turn right and you'll be met by Maggie Fox, she a member of your local Party, now in her eighties. You had tea at her house during the last election and she sends knitted scarves to your daughters every Christmas.'

He paused to look at Sylvia, who said, 'I'll take that one.'

'You visited her in hospital last March, she had a broken ankle and she gave you a pot of her home-made jam – raspberry it was.' Sylvia nodded.

Jones went back to the clipboard: 'Once you've been given a red rose each, you'll shake hands with the hotel manager – that's Philippe, said in the French way – Todd. You know the stuff. "Always enjoy staying here, now it'll have even more special memories." Then it's out to the car through the rat pack. The Rover will be at the bottom of the steps. Help Sylvia into the rear seat then walk round to the other side. Twist your body in such a way as to face the crowd, with one hand on the car and the left hand raised above your head in a wave, but keep the shot tight, try to bring your arm over your right shoulder.' He demonstrated, Tony nodded.

'The police are complaining about you being so exposed, but we haven't got a decent picture yet for tomorrow's front pages, so you'll just have to risk it.'

Graeme straightened up from his perch and was about to head for the door. Sylvia stopped him:

'Is that all? What's been happening in the world while we've been locked up here? Is there anything Tony needs to know?'

The aide paused for a moment and shook his head: 'He knows about the sabotage of polling stations in Scotland. We've already got a statement out condemning that. Roddy Henderson is threatening to resign, but he just needs to be told how much we all love him and he'll be OK. Ann Clarke's doing the Tartan Joan of Arc stuff, but that's normal. No, nothing out of the ordinary.'

Sylvia wasn't satisfied: 'What about that speech she made on TV? What's in the transcript?'

Ruefully Jones shook his head. 'Press Officer didn't get that one, I'm afraid. Tape jammed. We'll get it when we get to London.'

As Metcalf began to blow up at that, Sylvia hustled them out the door. After kind words to Kate and Yvonne at the suite door, they all took up their positions in the lift – Jones flattened himself against one wall to keep out of shot, reciting all the while the names of the people waiting to be greeted. When the lift juddered to a halt, the Metcalfs each took a deep breath and Tony switched on his famous smile. Sylvia squeezed his hand in encouragement. They paused while the Special Branch officers scanned the crowd for their colleagues with the identifying World Economic Summit badges, then the way was clear.

Tony was about to move off when, without warning, Sylvia stood on tiptoe, pulled his face to her, and kissed him passionately on the lips. A thousand camera shutters opened and closed. The press had their pictures, and the newly elected Prime Minister and his First Lady lit up the crowd with their smiles. Sylvia and Tony both bent down to kiss the tiny Maggie Fox, overcome with emotion as she handed over the roses. The hotel manager, Philippe, got the chance to have his photograph taken with the Prime Minister – it would hang in the foyer. Then they were off through the forest of microphones. A shouted question here, a challenge there.

'What about Ann Clarke?' More than one asked that question.

'Splendid lady. Great for the team.'

Laughter and good humour got them to the door. Questions were fielded with safe banality, and Sylvia's rehearsal proved its worth.

They made their way outside, waving to the ecstatic crowd.

Ann felt a hand grip her elbow and start to move her forward to the corridor that would take her to some kind of shelter. Michael Stewart – the tallest man in the room, the impeccable public-school manners, the embassy training – then caught her round the waist and murmured, 'I take it you don't want to hang around?'

To Malcolm Thomson's chagrin, Stewart created a barrier between Ann and the crowd and moved her surprisingly quickly to the lift which a commissionaire was holding. His urbane authority smoothed the man out of the way and alone they descended just one floor, where he then took a back corridor down three flights of stairs to the basement, a clutter of broken, discarded typists' chairs and central heating boilers.

'If this is some roundabout trick to get an exclusive interview, then you're not on!'

They both laughed.

He asked, 'What do you drink?'

'I should probably go to the victory party in the committee rooms.'

'Do you want to?'

'I imagine the mob have moved on there. They'll be looking for me.'

'Do you need it?'

'Not right now.'

Taking her hand he led her round the basement looking

28

for a way out, but when they eventually found a fire door, a loud alarm sounded as they opened it. Running through the car park to Stewart's car on the street, they skirted the huge Outside Broadcast vans and slipped away.

The flat, in Glasgow's Merchant City, felt more in keeping with the upper East Side of Manhatten or Washington's Georgetown – the decor black and white furnished in the best Glasgow style with Charles Rennie Mackintosh pieces.

'Reproductions, I'm afraid. Too many debts for the real thing.'

Ann, impressed, said, 'Who cares? It's beautiful. I've never seen so much Mackintosh furniture grouped together in a room. Anyway,' she added in a mock lecturing tone, 'the problem with Mackintosh original designs is that it's much too uncomfortable to actually sit on.' Then she looked at him. 'Why does an Englishman collect it though?'

'Ancestry and stuff like that. The name. I've always had a passion for things Scottish,' Stewart said, 'and in Washington I felt it was important the Americans found out that Scotland wasn't all tartan and Kenneth McKellar.'

'So passion has brought you back here?'

'Yes and no. Obviously with a name like mine there are some roots. I went to school here and I've always felt I'd like to come back to live someday. And I can't resist a good story, and what's going on here just now is just about the best-running story since Beirut.'

He poured champagne. 'What about you?' he asked. 'Why have you stuck so faithfully to Scotland? Don't you want a bigger stage?'

'Why do you think Scotland shouldn't put me on a much bigger stage? But that's a topic for another day.'

'You're a very unusual woman,' he said. 'I've come across dedicated political career women in the States – some of them very senior. But you're different. I don't know what it is yet. But I'll find out.'

She laughed. 'You can but try! No, the truth is I enjoy

life, all the different facets. If I was a sober-sided politician all the time I'd lose touch with reality and that wouldn't help anyone, and make my life very arid.'

She waved the empty champagne glass. He poured, splashing a little on to the cuff of her dress. With the index finger of his free hand, he rubbed at the mark.

She rose from the chair, he stepped aside. She turned on her heel and walked to the bedroom. He hesitated for only a second, picked up his own glass and followed her. It was almost dawn, they had met only three hours earlier. Michael Stewart had no way of recognizing the dangerous force that had entered his life.

In a great flurry of waves and good wishes, Graeme Jones bundled the Metcalfs into the car, stage management now abandoned. The car whirled away in a screech of tyres; Sam, the driver, knew that a stranded aide was preferable to a prying camera. The aide knew that too.

Jones ran across the road and entered into the general melee as the reporters piled on to the special press bus. Minutes later the bus moved on at a sedate pace. On the outskirts of town the Prime Minister's car sat in a lay-by. The experienced driver knew he had to let the press get well in front of him so that they would be set up and waiting at the next stop. So did the press bus driver, who stopped beyond to drop Jones where no pressman could see inside the Metcalfs' car. Jones need not have worried. Drinks already flowed, the press party had resumed, supplemented this time by Metcalf's aides. As Jones got into the Jaguar passenger seat, Sam was holding up the car phone and saying over his shoulder to Sylvia: 'Number Ten. The American President says the Boss has to phone him right away.'

Sylvia said, 'Tell him "no way". OK?'

The driver hung up.

Sylvia said, 'When the police escort has reduced, stop again, say you need ten minutes – the Boss has to write something. Don't let them know he's not feeling very well – it's only the strain and the tiredness catching up. I'll have to see what I can do to help him. I reckon he needs an extra injection tonight, and I can't do it in a moving car.'

Her husband lay slumped against the side of the car, his eyes vacant and closing, saliva dribbling from the corner of his slack mouth, hands shaking. Jones and the driver exchanged a quick glance.

The new Prime Minister, in an alcoholic stupor, was on his way to Number Ten.

1

Results kept rolling in at the Scottish Exhibition and Conference Centre. The large hall was divided up into sections like sheep pens, roped off to provide some kind of barrier. The bank clerks and retired council officials who had sworn to preserve the secrecy of the ballot had to be isolated from the sombre-suited men and women with clipboards intent on seeing as much as possible of the ballot papers tipped from black boxes on to the tables. For the many faceless men and women, who nonetheless lived for politics, the next election had already begun; now was the time to spot those polling stations where the votes stacked up, and to ponder those too dismal to waste time over.

In a silence broken only by the rustle of paper, the counters thumbed on into the night. The groups who had gathered in little huddles away from the tables sent up a steady drone of noise. The defeated, still defiant in finery carefully chosen to show Party loyalty – the blue of the Conservatives wilting now – hoped for some miracle that would disprove what they already knew. Some got rid of the tension and disappointment by heckling and booing the periodic declaration of results. Some had a different kind of party time, with hip flasks passed round. Occasionally those who took their politics seriously would lose patience with those for whom it was just fun, and the police would hover. But even a fist fight tonight would prove an anticlimax, after what had gone on earlier.

The real action could be found in the corners, where men and women, haggard and exhausted for the most part, still analyzed the night's drama. Why had Roddy Henderson resigned? Did he mean it? What skeleton was about to tumble out of the cupboard? Who would he drag down with him? Many showed caution. Those with ambition knew to keep their own counsel.

Few of these bothered to look up as yet another result was declared. By now they knew all the foregone conclusions such as Monklands constituency. A few friends of Stephen Robinson near the stage gave a cheer, but it had a mechanical air, as did Robinson's speech of thanks. Robinson's face remained impassive as he heard himself re-elected for the town he had lived in all his life. At more than six foot, and despite the expensive suit, he still looked like the steelworker he had been – neck too thick for the white collar; face too rugged for the gloom of the House of Commons; hands too calloused for pressing the flesh, and kissing babies.

As he jumped down off the platform, impatient at the polite tangle around the steps, he deflected the seemingly social questions regarding the whereabouts of his wife. Other MPs drew him into conversation. The talk was all of Henderson. Who would replace him?

Who would occupy the Scottish Office?

'What about you, Stephen? You've got a good power base. Give it a go?'

He shook his head slowly. 'Not my scene! Whoever takes on that job has to sort out the Henderson skeleton.'

He went on his way, squeezing through the crowd, stopping every so often to shake hands and kiss his colleagues' wives. Most had carefully permed for the big occasion, some fought hard to hide the disappointment that their husbands had won again, and another five years of loneliness loomed. Women sought out Stephen to congratulate him, an earthy man with an unconscious sexuality. More than one lonely wife would have offered to console him. He showed no interest.

He had promised to be back in the constituency for the post-election celebrations. On the main road, he put on some speed, weaving his way through a traffic jam totally out of place after midnight. About to accelerate past a dark blue estate car, he saw the reason for the delay – a security check.

Tapping the steering wheel with one hand, he unconsciously fingered the portcullis disk he displayed on his windscreen – the Official Pass for the Members' car park at the House of Commons; usually it guaranteed a wave through. He waited his turn to be searched. From the slow way the army sergeant made his way over to the car Robinson could tell that he'd got a real bastard this time.

Most of the NCOs who supervised security duty had undergone tours of duty in Northern Ireland. For a year now they had been deployed on the mainland when the periodic violence by Workers' Militia proved such a headache for the Government. Those who supported the use of troops said it prevented the formal declaration of martial law. The sergeant pulled open the driver's door, and without speaking, gestured to Stephen to get out.

Stephen didn't move. He had heard from his constituents how people had suffered ill treatment at the hands of the security forces, but as an MP with a well-known face he had been immune. Until tonight.

'Get out or I'll drag you out!'

'Name and number, Sergeant,' Stephen barked. 'You're not going to treat me like shit!'

The sergeant didn't reply. He turned away and waved over two bear-like privates.

'Get this bastard out, and arrest him when you're at it.'

The raised voices had attracted a crowd, among them a reporter:

'Hey, Sergeant. That's an MP you've got there. Questions in the House and all that if you give him a rough time.'

'My, my. Didn't realize we'd got a VIP. Wants to be treated special, does he? Well, Mr VIP, would you please get out of your car. I have reason to believe you may be carrying dangerous materials.'

Stephen looked at his watch and got out of the car. His fingernails dug into the palms of his hands to restrain him from punching the arrogant bully.

The systematic dismantling of his car proved painfully and deliberately slow. As every nook and cranny was

34

being searched, Robinson paced up and down, repeatedly looking at his watch. It took forty-five minutes.

On the motorway, he pressed his foot down hard on the accelerator, leaving behind the few vehicles out on this curfew-free election night.

He left the motorway at the Shawhead flyover. Almost there, tightening up his collar with one hand, then running his hand through his hair. Flagged down again. Another roadblock. Meek and humble this time, it took three and a half minutes.

By the time he got out of the car he had the look of someone on a short fuse. Disco music blasted from the box-like social club. Desultory applause broke out. The small group of drinkers in the foyer of the club felt they had to do something to mark the return of the victor. They gave him a sporadic cheer then reminded him that the drinks were on him.

More genuine applause came when the other revellers saw he was back. As he started to make his rounds, thanking the workers, making sure everyone had a drink, a commotion broke out at the bar. Two boys in their late teens and dressed in cheap imitation army fatigues shouted at one another, obviously the worse for drink. They squared off. Nobody stopped them. The men around them looked embarrassed, staring down into their beer.

In half a dozen steps, Stephen reached them. He got both boys by the scruff of the neck, lifting them off the ground, then dragging them forcibly into the little office he borrowed from the club steward to hold his advice surgeries. With his foot he banged the door shut, throwing the boys aside. One missed his footing and landed on the floor, the other cowered in the corner. Then both simultaneously whispered, 'Dad.'

'Home! Now! Out! If you're going to show me up, don't show your faces back here. I'm ashamed of the pair of you, two useless drunks and neither of you nineteen yet. Freedom fighters! That doesn't make you men. Little boys playing soldiers. Out of my sight!'

As his twin sons scurried away, Stephen sat down at

the battered little desk, fatigue and disillusion on his face. He loosened his tie and undid his collar, sighed a deep sigh and let his head fall back, his eyes shut. He stayed like that for a full minute, then stood up, splashed his face with cold water from the chipped sink in the corner, and braved the party.

Everyone had crowded round the twenty-eight-inch TV screen. Stephen squeezed his way in to see what they were watching.

Ann Clarke was addressing a crowd through an open window. As her words and their implications sank in, a vein twitched in his neck, his fists clenched and unclenched.

He turned away, facing a man who looked as angry as he felt. Joe Black, his election agent, had never been known to raise his voice or lose his temper in his life. Tonight he looked livid. The others who had noticed the change in his expression stared at him awestruck. When he saw the answering anger in the MP's face, he said in a strangled voice:

'She's got my son, Stephen. The bitch has got my son. He's joined her Workers' Militia. He scares Maggie half to death by staying out all night, and talking about preparing for the Revolution. He's only fourteen! She's going to destroy him!'

Those nearest could see the horror in Stephen's expression and the tears in the eyes of his oldest friend. Joe Black had bullied and cajoled Stephen into going to night school and getting an education. Joe Black had seen him in danger of getting into the grip of the hard men of politics, the agitators out to destroy rather than build. Joe Black had shown him a better way, had fought every election at his side. Joe Black's quiet strength had kept everyone going.

Without saying a word, Stephen took Joe by the arm and led him to the office. Quietly, two more men got up from their seats and followed. Once inside, Stephen took a bottle of whisky and four glasses from a filing cabinet.

'So how are we going to stop our little Miss Eva Perón?' he asked.

Even as Mary opened the door, even as she called out, she knew Ann had not come home – the emptiness echoed round the elegant rooms still in darkness.

Mary wandered around, checking these rooms that resembled a magazine layout. Ann had bought this part of her image off the designer shelf. Yes, it had restrained elegance. Yes, it had obvious good taste, and high value – but it was all fake. Not that Ann hid that – she had even made it clear to the interior designers that she wanted a showpiece, not a character reference. She need not have worried about giving away too much of herself – apart from the cleaning woman and her election agent, Mary Connolly, Ann Clarke kept her home to herself.

In the event the interior designers created the perfect backdrop for the beautiful and intelligent woman politician. They advised cool and muted colours set off by riotous Mediterranean flowers. Shelves of books ranged from dignified antiquarian investments, through political theory and biography to classics and bestsellers; the record collection covered every taste from opera to jazz, with eclectic Celtic folk music thrown in. Anyone who walked in here saw a careful, even impeccable, piece of faultless image-making, tailored and manicured, all spontaneity carefully planned.

Mary switched on the imitation Giacometti lamps in the main reception room, which ran the length of the house; French windows at one end opened on a small patio with a table and chairs; these made by an Ayrshire blacksmith in stark clear lines with the initials AC woven into the only embellishment. The flowering red geraniums gave the place festive, continental colour.

Two huge sofas flanked a wall-mounted coal fire, positioned facing each other across a marble coffee table on which sat a magnificent arrangement of yellow lilies and orchids. A double door helped to divide the room into a dining area with a rare, early American circular pine table and six chairs around the large circumference. A floral arrangement dominated the table, this time of roses in peach and yellow shades – Socialist high priestess or not, Ann Clarke had fresh flowers delivered several times a week – Scottish Colourists hung around the walls, one or two of which came from the top bracket of Scottish art.

Mary Connolly and Ann Clarke had birthdays within days of one another. On their first morning at university, Mary had stared at this cool and poised young woman, so plainly dressed but so stylish in black slacks and red shawl, and immediately felt shabby in her carefully saved for wardrobe. In the Fife mining village Mary's family wondered whether she had gone mad going to university rather than out to work, as any decent girl should. The clothes represented an effort to throw off her background – but now she felt she had wasted her money.

Ann had smiled at her, and they had started to talk, making an instant connection. Each supplied what the other lacked. Ann needed Mary's drab stability, Mary needed Ann's dangerous whoosh! of glamour – not for the first time did lifelong friendship exist on such dependencies. Each recognized it, never acknowledged it outwardly. Instead, they began to share a flat, eking out their tiny grants to live in what Mary saw as great sophistication – tins of beans, acres of toast, lemonade bottles filled with cheap wine, student style. For all her chic, Ann had as little as Mary, from a family fallen on bad times of which she never spoke. Unlike Mary's, Ann's determination included a passion to avoid poverty.

Slowly – though inevitably – Ann began to lead and their lives revolved around what Ann wanted to do. Mary went along, the willing handmaiden, grateful for the glamour and excitement.

They had only parted once. Ann won a scholarship to Harvard for her postgraduate year. During her absence Mary went off to take a secretarial qualification – so that she could run the law office Ann planned to open. Within weeks, Mary could tell that something important had happened. Ann wrote fewer letters – and those felt secretive.

Then one night, Mary answered the doorbell of her father's house to find Ann on the doorstep, distraught, a touch away from hysteria. When she did come in and relaxed, she crumpled. Mary never got the full story; Ann muttered words between tears and exclamations. 'Brainwashed . . . frightened . . . out of control'. Mary could make no sense of it. A man? Married perhaps? Some kind of wrong company, certainly. Ann's eyes hid something.

From that night on the relationship changed. On the one hand Mary became an emotional mentor, seeing Ann as her brilliant charge, more vulnerable than she pretended to be; on the other hand Ann thereafter kept something profound hidden from Mary, from everyone.

Ann then went back to Harvard, and when her year was up, in place of the briefly glimpsed hysterical and frightened girl, a sophisticated, aware Ann Clarke returned. She gradually emerged as a woman with a mission, a mission to lead, to drive, to succeed, to revolutionize. Someone somewhere had motivated her – it was as if she had been fitted with a powerful, hidden force. Soon Ann had become an MP in a rough and tumble election; by her side Mary had set about learning how to become the best political organizer in the business. Together they had achieved their joint ambitions; Ann was the leader, Mary her indispensable agent.

And that one occasion, the night when the shell had cracked and Ann Clarke had been peeled open and raw, was never repeated. Once Ann, in a moment of confidentiality, tried to find out exactly what she had said in Mary's front room; Mary, though she began to tell her, suddenly stopped, seeing Ann's alarmed stare, and said she could remember no more. The event produced one lasting side effect: the merest hint that Ann had a vulnerable side would provoke the famous Ann Clarke rage.

This morning though, plumping up cushions, picking up damp towels in a tangle on the bathroom floor, Mary looked like a proud mother whose child had just done something brilliant. In the bedroom she turned down the satin comforter on the lace-fringed bed. She arranged the robe on the blue silk chaise longue by the patio window. The Darvel lace hanging in swathes at the window came from the lace workers, a gift acknowledging their gratitude that Ann had fought for their imperilled industry. The room had no personal mementoes, no photographs, no ornaments, not even a hint of Ann Clarke's extensive travels.

Once when Ann had been in bed with flu, Mary had visited unexpectedly. She had a fleeting glimpse of Ann hurriedly putting a silver-framed photograph into the drawer of the bedside table and locking it. The drawer had remained locked ever since. Ann also kept her answering machine locked away.

A light still shone through the study door. This, the only room in the house in which Ann had become personally involved, felt like the office of a high-powered business executive; the huge black ash desk held a word processor and a telephone and nothing else. Six filing cabinets sat immediately behind the matching desk, so that Ann could swing round in her high-backed leather chair to get at anything she needed. At the other side of the desk sat two leather and chrome Bauhaus chairs, and against one wall a soft black leather sofa bed behind an oversized black coffee table covered with carefully arranged piles of papers. The room had only one personal touch – a portrait of Ann's father on one wall. Two identical televisions each had a video; both had been taping election programmes all night.

The scarlet and black Marimekko curtains covering one wall had not been opened, a sign that Ann had worked all through the previous night. Mary shook her head in irritation; where had Ann disappeared to after her TV appearance? The word processor flickered on, discarded notes littered the floor. Ann habitually wrote and rewrote her speeches, then worked entirely without notes, preferring to appear spontaneous despite being exceptionally well prepared.

Mary bent down and started gathering up the paper,

ready to put it into the already full waste paper basket. She recognized the wrapping paper round an obviously discarded box, paper she herself had spent days looking for, weeks looking for the Swedish rose bowl it covered, a campaign gift to Ann after the eve of poll rally. 'To Ann, a memento of the best election yet. "And she shall have roses where ever she goes". Your devoted friend, Mary'

She shook the unopened package – it rattled badly. The tears began to spill down her face. Over and over she said to herself:

'It was an accident. She didn't want me to know she had broken it. It was an accident.'

She turned the little gift over and over again in her hands, keening to herself. Eventually, putting the package back in the waste basket, she scattered the papers around the floor again, leaving the room as she found it.

Going back into the bedroom, she took a notebook and pen from her handbag and scribbled a few words:

'Came to see everything was all right. You were wonderful tonight, we were all so proud. Ring me in the morning. Love, Mary.'

She left it on the pillow.

Sunlight brightened the room sufficiently for him to see her. She lay spreadeagled on the bed beside him, face down, her hair tangled and free.

His eyes roved over her body, tall and slim, yet too rounded to be boyish. Tempted to touch her, instead his hand hovered over her buttocks, almost fingering the small brown mole on her inner thigh, near to the damp patch of hair peeping out beneath. He wanted her, but he dared not wake her – in any case, he was expected in the studio within half an hour, and regardless of the woman, regardless of the circumstances, he had never been anything less than professional.

A month short of his fortieth birthday, Michael Stewart already had the reputation of one of the foremost economic thinkers and communicators of his age. The son of a diplomat, his education had been broadened by contact with some of the most prestigious embassies in the world. Already poised and confident when he went up to Oxford, long before he left it had become clear that he had uncommon intellectual ability. He matched it in sport as well – sailor, rockclimber, boxing blue: he hardened his body as he honed his mind. As a student he wrote an acclaimed book of legends and photographs of the Himalayas. *Fortune* magazine picked him out as one of Europe's 'Fifty Most Promising'.

After graduation, both the Civil Service and academic life beckoned – the Civil Service won; within five years he had flown high as one of the youngest and most influential Under-Secretaries in the Treasury. His papers crystallized the most difficult and complex issues, his remedies combined sharp daring with the eminently practical.

He had, however, an Achilles heel – an addiction to adrenaline. Intellect and body always had to stretch to the limit: he worked hard – punishingly so, often for days on end without a break. Played hard too: women proved his passion, the brighter and more challenging the better, especially if they belonged to someone else. One affair ricocheted into another; lunchtime raids of passion on some Mayfair bed, nights on aristocratic silk. Not infrequently he ran more than one affair at a time. And when they started to cling, or take his attentions seriously, he moved on. He needed constant challenge, with a sex drive as formidable as his intellect, as energetic as his sportsman's body.

One morning, leaving the bed of a talented and sexually inventive sculptress, the wife of a prominent peer away on a Foreign Office trip, Stewart walked down Whitehall towards the Treasury – bored. His adrenaline, he realized, had begun to slow down. He had been replacing the charge he used to get from his job with new and more daring sexual adventures, and if he didn't do something new soon, even the sex would become jaded and the great promise the world knew he had would go unfulfilled. By coincidence he lunched that day with the iron Scotsman who edited *The Times*. This man, who had shaken that dignified edifice to its roots by calling a writing implement a pen, now told Stewart he was throwing himself away.

'Get out of that bloody ivory tower and into the real world. D'you fancy Economics Editor?'

The Editor recalled for him the example of Peter Jay who fifteen years earlier had left the Treasury for journalism and had gone on to become British Ambassador to the United States. Stewart decided the excitement of the media might compensate for the knowledge that no Minister would ever ask him a question he could not answer, and so he accepted.

Inevitably, television found him.

On the box Stewart's sexuality proved even more potent than his brain. His face had that kind of lived-in look which thrilled women, and his sexuality came across even more magnetically. The regular guest appearances on TV current affairs programmes grew into a series of his own, and millions of women who thought that John Maynard Keynes was a street name in a new town became hooked on late-night dissertations on the money supply. They moved Stewart to peak viewing, and his bank balance stretched to a house in Canonbury Square and a cottage in Argyllshire.

And then he blew it. Seconded to Washington at a huge and undisclosed salary, he was given a mission to help explain to a perplexed public the growing dependence of Britain on the United States. This came at the same time as the US President saw in Britain's economic weakness an opportunity to get all of Western Europe in a stranglehold. Stewart's lucidity and physique soon attracted a following among the glitterati of American politics, and he revelled in it. Senators' wives, Congresswomen, even a couple of beautiful and talented Supreme Court Judges, queued up to get into his bed – a place to which he did not, to his undoing, confine his athletics.

His reputation as a major economic thinker in his own right had won him the only one-to-one interview granted that year by the President. They networked his live interview across the US and Europe. After the interview, and informal drinks with the President and the First Lady, he left the White House still on a high. At the office he found the stunningly sexy wife of a Senator waiting for him; he had met her at a party the week before and had promised her a tour of the studios. Now, having just seen him on TV, she had decided to remind him of his offer. As they walked around the studio from which he usually broadcast, she began to loosen the buttons down the side of the pink cheongsam she wore. She was naked underneath. Stewart didn't need much encouragement, the warnings forgotten about caution near a microphone – or, in this case, a remote control camera.

Certainly no one remained in the building, but three miles away, in the network headquarters, the crew maintaining the remote control facility had an unexpected lesson – on the floor and on the desk – from the great British economic guru, but not about the balance of trade. Inevitably someone pressed the 'record' button, and America's most popular home video went into production. Stewart's luck had run out. The Senator, from the deep South, owed his advancement to Moral Majority – and his friends in organized crime did not care for this attack on his honour. Stewart's work permit was questioned, but, more sinister than that, he learned on a dark night that he had just made a laughing stock of the next Presidential running mate, destroying his career. To say the least, the Administration frowned. The BBC, fearful of the threatened retribution, recalled him. As he left, an anonymous and authoritative caller told him not to return – ever.

Stewart sold up in London, embarrassed by the sniggers and by the knowledge that his father had felt shamed into premature retirement. He moved to the west coast of Scotland, to a desolate castle near Ardnamurchan, to set about its restoration and to write a history of contemporary economic theory, amusing himself sailing and walking. Until one day a pinstriped mandarin from BBC Scotland had braved the mud and single-track roads to come to lure him out of retirement. The scandals had blown over – certainly by contrast with the BBC's need to have an authoritative voice as chaos spread. Stewart took possession of his office in the Corporation's Glasgow headquarters on the morning the election was called, grateful for the opportunity to apply his mind to the problems of the country, and vowing to remain celibate until he had publicly rehabilitated himself. And then he would have to tread carefully, in chauvinistic, Calvinistic Scotland – where in any case he expected to be safe from the kind of beautiful and intelligent woman who turned him on.

And now, Ann Clarke exploded into his life, the most powerful and important woman in the country. She had aroused him, not with deliberate seductiveness, but with a straightforward sex drive equal to his own. He could not pass this up – besides, as the running story of the moment she added extra spice.

Under the shower, he heard movement outside. He called out to her:

'Coffee in the cupboard, orange juice in the fridge. I'll be out in a minute, but I'll have to run.' The bedroom was empty as he left the bathroom. Naked, he walked through to the kitchen, towelling his hair as he went:

'Two questions – when can I interview you today? And where would you like to eat tonight?'

Before he had finished speaking he knew she had left. No note, no greeting, nothing but a flat bottle of champagne and two untouched glasses, and a very untidy bed. She had put the boot on the other foot. He dressed quickly.

At the office his PA had already clipped the newspapers. 'What's our main priority for the day then?' she asked.

He swept the papers off his desk into the waste paper basket:

'Screwing Miss Ann Clarke!'

Smiling sweetly she turned to him and said:

'Again?'

Stephen Robinson spent the night on an armchair in his

living room, sleeping badly. Just after six o'clock and a couple of aspirin he stood under a cold shower; the icy water cut a path through last night's fog.

The local news led, not with the election of the first Labour Government for twelve years, but with Henderson's resignation. Commentators asked why the man, who had fought for three decades to become Scotland's first citizen – had given up just as he won. They floated every imaginable explanation; until it became glaringly obvious that no one had a clue what lay behind it.

Next they discussed the tortuous procedures through which Labour would elect a successor. All agreed that an election would merely turn into an exercise in gesture politics; Ann Clarke would be made Secretary of State for Scotland, probably unchallenged, certainly by popular acclaim.

When he heard Michael Stewart in the voice of the *éminence grise* predict that, Robinson threw his towel at the mirror. Tiptoeing naked into the bedroom, the politician glanced quickly at the bed. In the old days Stephen had joked that his wife didn't like him strutting about naked in case the saints in the myriad holy pictures on their walls had impure thoughts about him. In those days he had been allowed to joke – when he spent six days out of every seven in the backbreaking and soul-destroying heat of the steel furnaces, before night school, before university, before he had added the letters MP to his name, before his wife had embraced martyrdom.

All her martyr's sacrifices hung around the room – the shirt she had left out the night before sparkling in its whiteness, the fresh suit, pressed and brushed, outside the wardrobe. His shoes sat underneath, gleaming in the early sunlight. On the few occasions Stephen had tried to talk about the poison destroying his marriage, she gave him a litany of all the work she put in to send him out 'a credit to the family'.

'I wanted a wife, not a valet,' he shouted; this she was determined not to understand.

Close Party colleagues told him more than once that

she was pulling him down. He recognized her hurt and disappointment that the steelworker she had married had changed; politics made her uncomfortable, uncertain, it was a world she could not grasp. Where they both came from, you married for life. The mere fact that husband and wife had become total strangers gave no good reason to part. His closed-in face would have told anyone interested enough that he missed his wife, for all her faults he felt her absence.

He always wore long-sleeved shirts, even in the hottest summer, to hide the steelworker's tattoo, blue ink in the shape of a heart with 'Mother' engraved on it.

He replaced the passion of his marriage with the passion of politics. He cringed now to remember how innocent he had been, sure he could change the world. Luckily old hands sorted him out in time. Once on a union delegation to East Berlin, he had offers of money. Joe Black whipped him away, though he never told Joe about the money which materialized in his – Stephen's – bank account. At least he had found a way to give it back.

Leaving a cup of tea and a slice of toast on her bedside table, Stephen bent down and kissed his wife on her forehead. Her eyes were tightly closed – too tightly for someone asleep.

Already at eight o'clock in the morning, cars lined the street outside Roddy Henderson's house. Newsmen huddled together, some of them speaking into portable telephones.

After twenty years of visiting the house, he knew Roddy and Lizzie's secrets. Parking two streets away, Stephen walked down a lane and climbed a stile into the field running behind the tidy thirties houses. He walked along until he came to the gap he was looking for, and groped until he found the edge of the chicken wire.

As he began to squeeze through he heard noises in the neighbouring garden. Over the fence he saw a reporter and photographer working quickly to set up a camera with a wide-angled lens, the photographer, on a small metal ladder, attempting to focus his camera on the Hendersons' bedroom. Stephen pushed his way through the hedge as quietly as possible, then crashed deliberately into the ladder. The photographer fell, his camera smashing to the ground. The reporter, hanging on, lost his balance; a push by Stephen floored him. The rage on the MP's face convinced the two pressmen they should move – they left camera and ladder behind.

Stephen pulled back the chicken wire, easing his large frame through into the Hendersons' garden. Roddy had made this hole in the hedge to save him having to take the dog for a walk. Stephen frequently teased him that the Shadow Secretary of State preferred not to damage his macho image by being seen walking a grey poodle.

Sprinting up the path, he knocked gingerly at the door, silently praying that the stupid dog would not yap. The house remained quiet. A curtain fluttered. In seconds the door was opened, and Lizzie Henderson fell into his arms, the deliberate control of the past few hours crumbling at the sight of someone she knew would care.

Stephen half carried, half dragged her into the tiny kitchen. She spoke and cried incessantly as Stephen made her a cup of tea, but he could make no sense of her incoherent bewilderment.

He did learn though that in the past week she had hardly seen her husband, but the same would be said in the home of every Parliamentary candidate. Lizzie and Roddy had campaigned together for more than thirty years. He had said nothing to her, not even in the final stages of the campaign. She had thought his preoccupation had to do with taking on the political leadership of five million Scots.

And then he had managed to shock her. About to leave for the count, an undemonstrative man, he had taken her in his arms and held her close. No other sign, no other gesture.

The reasons he gave in his announcement shocked her as much as the decision itself. She had never been ill for a day in her life, and even if she had been, she would never let him give up what they had both struggled and planned for.

Stephen questioned her closely; she could only point to a phone call Roddy had taken at the count. He had certainly been more subdued after it, but on his way back from the phone he had been told his friend Emyr Evans had lost his seat. They had entered the House together, and she had put his quietness down to that.

Stephen reached out and held the hands of this ugly, gentle woman:

'You've got to make him talk to me, Lizzie. We've got to get to the bottom of this. Will you try to get him to see me?'

But she broke down again:

'He won't! He won't! He's been sitting in the same chair since we came home last night. He hasn't moved a muscle. He won't talk, he won't eat. He won't tell me what's happened. He won't even tell me what to do about the press. It's as if he's dead.'

This strong woman had come very close to full-blown hysteria.

Stephen pressed her: 'Forget the politics. Let's just help the man. Get me in to him, and whatever it is, I'll find a way to help.'

He said this with more confidence than he felt.

Half an hour passed. She stood at the door and, without speaking, beckoned him him into the room where for most of his adult life, Roddy Henderson had plotted and planned the path to the only seat in the Cabinet that mattered to him. The one he had given up hours before.

Henderson had not changed his clothes since the previous night. The grey stubble on his chin added to the ghastly pallor of his complexion. A one-bar electric fire heated the room, drawing the oxygen from the atmosphere and causing Stephen to catch his breath.

Henderson never looked up as the younger man came in, he sat as he had all night, staring down at the faded carpet. Saliva had dried to a crust at the corner of his mouth.

Stephen got down on his knees in front of him, trying to force his friend to look at him:

'Who's done this to you? Tell me. C'mon. Tell, Roddy, tell. Whatever it is that's happened, you can't carry it alone. Please let me help you!'

No response – Henderson was deaf to him. The younger MP kept up his monologue, begging, cajoling. Still no response.

Stephen's patience, never long, snapped:

'You're being blackmailed, aren't you? What is it? Planning permission for some pub? Money from a Swiss bank account to you in the Co-op Bank? If you don't tell me, Roddy, you're going to make us all vulnerable. No matter what you've done, or what you've been set up with – you have to tell somebody, because if it's as big a skeleton as you seem to think it is, then you could bring down the Government. Is that how you want to get into the history books?'

Henderson flickered. Stephen pressured – reciting a catalogue of all the dreams they shared, the late-night confidences in the House over a whisky, the power their union affiliations would give them, the changes they would make.

In mid sentence Henderson raised his head and looked up at him. He had dragged his lips across his teeth. What he said – the last option Stephen might ever have imagined – stopped the tough MP, shocked.

Glasgow's world famous Burrell gallery gleams in surroundings as stunning as the Collection it houses. The setting is the middle of Pollok Park next to dense woodland, where swaying trees shade its long glass north-west wall; the tapestries and stained glass displayed inside reflect the themes of sunlight and leaf. The doorway comprises the first of a group of Romanesque, Renaissance and Gothic doorways and window embrasures that Sir William Burrell bought from William Randolph Hearst.

The intricate stonework draws the eye in, past the dark and sinister interior of rooms reproduced exactly from

Burrell's castle in the Scottish Borders, to the enormous Vase from Hadrian's Villa at Tivoli, its huge size dominating the indoor courtyard with its fig trees.

Each day coachloads of tourists relentlessly wander round the Egyptian, Chinese and Mesopotamian art, overawed. But when they confront the familiar Degas *Rehearsal*, with its young ballerinas striking poses – familiar from its mass reproduction – to the even more familiar Rodin sculpture of the *Thinker*, they relax, refreshed at spotting something they can claim to identify. Elderly ladies exclaim over the lace collection, telling the uniformed museum assistants how their mothers used to make intricate lace too.

It normally took the museum assistants half an hour to get everyone out at closing time; that day, however, the Germans and Japanese had arrived in force. Two women assistants – one a grandmother looking forward to retirement, the other in her thirties recently widowed, glad to be learning a job – checked the Gothic Domestic Room and returned to the entrance later than the others who also attended to the final chores of the day. The unique silence of an empty gallery had begun to fall.

The first news flash only reported an explosion. By the six o'clock bulletin, the extent of the destruction had become clear – two women assistants missing, the building almost totally destroyed. A post-mortem countdown began: the anonymous phone call to the *Daily Record* left ten minutes to evacuate the building. Confusion when the message had been received had cut this to eight minutes; the alarm had been sounded in the outer gallery, but whether the women heard it and reacted, or didn't have time, or thought it routine or accidental, caused by someone locking up, would never be known. As the BBC transmitted the first pictures, a phone call from the Workers' Militia claimed responsibility; all those who exploited the Scottish working class – as, they claimed, had Sir William Burrell whose treasures were housed in the gallery – were now legitimate targets.

Next afternoon, the salvage squad found the bodies of

the two assistants. The younger woman's four children, all under ten, appeared in the main bulletins being taken into care by the local authority.

2

Secretaries already leaned from the windows of the union offices, an hour before, watching the cameramen and reporters arrive. Cheers went up as her red Volkswagen Golf GTI came round the corner and pulled up at the front door. She flushed with delight as she got out of the car and felt the warmth of the welcome. She waved up at the windows, getting another cheer in response. In her beige Max Mara linen suit, the skirt six inches above her knees, showing legs glistening in silk stockings, chunky gold jewellery weighting down the green camisole she wore, she looked every inch the soap opera queen – with the extra edge today of power.

The film crews, Australian, American and national, surged forward; smilingly she had nothing to say. The pictures they took made the statement she wanted.

Nobody held the cameramen back as she was walked into the foyer of the high-tech union building. Genuinely moved by the impromptu reception committee, she thanked each individually, with a special hug for the elderly office worker who presented her with a posy of roses. Down the corridor to the lift door, workers applauded; she shook hands and reached every one, then she disappeared.

Harry McGregor did not look up as she came into his room – just continued reading his newspaper. Ann pulled up a chair opposite his desk, carefully choosing one of normal height. McGregor, a smaller than normal man, discomfited visitors by seating them on couches so low he towered over them. Still he read, his attention insultingly held by a ripe pin-up page.

Ann took off her jacket, draping it across the back of the chair. She sat patiently, her hands clasped loosely in front of her, her eyes never leaving his face. His eyes remained glued to the page as he spoke:

'Where the hell did you get to last night?'

She remained silent and totally still.

After a long second, McGregor looked up. A smirk twisted his face:

'Whoever he was he must have been good. Keep a glow like that about you and we'll walk it!'

Her voice was soft and pleasant, a faint huskiness betraying the rigours of the election trail. Her eyes were cold.

'*I'll* walk it, you mean. You've got a job to do and I'm here to make sure you stick exactly to plan and don't indulge in any of your little freelance tricks. What's the latest on Henderson?'

McGregor shrugged. She had never changed her stare, had she?

18 August 1971

A small man of about thirty with thinning dirty blond hair stood, waiting, outside Queen's Park. He allowed himself to be jostled by the excited crowd. In rumpled grey suit, with shirt and greasy tie, he stood out from the others in summer dresses and short-sleeved shirts.

An elderly lady tugged at his sleeve: 'Will they be long, son?'

There was a faint colonial twang to his voice as he answered: 'Shouldn't think so. I can hear the pipe band.'

'You'll not be local then? Are you from the papers?'

But Harry McGregor was not to be drawn into inquisitive small talk, even with an old woman seeking respite from loneliness. He crossed the street and stood on the opposite corner.

He watched as they drew closer. Tens of thousands stretched behind the head of the march; bright banners depicting scenes of Labour history fluttered in the light breeze, garish behind the main banner – simple words on a white background – 'Upper Clyde Shipbuilders. The Right to Work.'

Jimmy Reid, the young Communist shop steward with the silver tongue and dark good looks, marched at the front talking to the tall aristocrat and Labour MP Anthony Wedgwood Benn. Occasionally he would puff at his pipe and turn to listen to Vic Feather, the now elderly and grey-haired General Secretary of the Trades Union Congress, whose benign paunch testified to his love of good food and fine wine.

As they marched past, a cheer greeted the giant banner of the Transport Union – 'Unity is Strength'. McGregor moved out and fell into step among the men behind the banner, asking for the union's Regional Secretary. Spotting him, he forced his way across the column, tapping him on the shoulder.

'I'm Harry McGregor, your new Education Officer. I know I'm not due until next week, but I thought I'd come up early and join the demonstration – give myself a chance to get the feel of things. Head Office said you wouldn't mind.'

The portly union official stretched out his hand: 'Welcome to Glasgow, son. We'll show you the right way to run a union up here. Call in tomorrow.'

Five years later, Harry McGregor had lost his South African accent, replacing it with the harsh guttural tones of the West of Scotland. He had also become the most powerful man in the Scottish Labour movement; within a year of his appointment he had formed a powerful breakaway union, well financed, but with no obvious benefactor.

McGregor had come to Glasgow as a missionary, with power his cause. He believed in Revolution, read Trotsky as diligently as a priest his breviary. With equal dedication he had set up the kind of network the Old Man had decreed as essential to prepare Britain for the Revolution.

His vehicle, the newspaper *Struggle*, began as a four-page duplicated effort circulating in the cells of the Revolutionary Party that had existed in Britain since the years before World War Two. Effective business planning had built it up to a full-colour sixteen-page tabloid with a circulation of more than 50,000 every week. Luck played a part. The new Labour Government in 1974 quickly became entangled in a major economic crisis which could only be resolved by the International Monetary Fund. Harsh public spending cuts and widespread austerity bred an atmosphere of suspicion and unrest, exacerbated in Scotland by the discovery of North Sea oil which the Government had seized on to pay off the country's debts. McGregor, watching how the Nationalists capitalized on Labour's misfortunes, identified the base from which he could further his aims. He belonged to a network of Revolutionaries throughout Britain, setting up more and more cells, building up the cadre of key activists Trotsky had decreed as a prerequisite to breeding the chaos essential to Revolution. This work had been going on for years, anticipating just the kind of economic crisis the country now faced. McGregor ran 1,500 cells in Scotland, usually with ten or a dozen members each, mostly young, and all convinced that the collapse of capitalism lay just around the corner.

A financial network supported the cause. Every member of the Revolutionary Party – who described themselves merely as newsvendors for *Struggle* – committed fifteen per cent of their income – salary, student grant, unemployment benefit or pocket money – to a fighting fund. Always in arrears so that they began and remained in debt, they further raised monies from others – to reach targets set by McGregor and his small band of assistants. They attended meetings twice a week; each member had to recruit two more members each month. Anyone drawn into the tight discipline of the network had very little time or money left to think about breaking free. To leave meant clearing the debts. Failure to pay could bring a visit from one of McGregor's lieutenants who had graduated from Peterhead or Barlinnie prisons. In any case few wanted to leave – they belonged to a heady crusade.

McGregor worked ceaselessly and ruthlessly towards his aim. As he dominated the cadres, so did he begin stealthily to dominate mainstream political activity in Scotland. His union had the most power, and without often breaking the surface of publicity he exploited to the full his role as kingmaker – making and breaking politicians at will.

From time to time he disappeared – to congresses abroad where he worked on building powerful contacts, but most frequently to Liverpool. There, in a terraced house, at the centre of the growing network of Revolutionary activity, lived McGregor's guru – the elderly man who had been ignited by a boyhood meeting with Trotsky and who had gone on to become President of the British cell of the Revolutionary League.

Five years to the day since he had watched the UCS demonstration surge through the streets of Glasgow, McGregor received a phone call calling him immediately to Merseyside; his guru lay dying, the mantle of power must pass.

In the fetid air of the overheated little bedroom, McGregor approached the bed. The desiccated, yellowed man beneath the covers, who seemed asleep – or already dead – opened his eyes and smiled a little. McGregor, turning to the minders to look for a chair, saw one other visitor in the far corner of the room. She stood up as he looked at her; even in flat shoes she stood easily six inches taller than the union official. Plainly dressed, in skirt and navy sweater, she still exuded style and composure. Too much to begin with for McGregor, the hazel eyes, the auburn hair, the full breasts and long legs – but the eyes had a sharp intelligence, and in the set and determined lips, in the overall stillness of her, he felt a challenge.

'Hello, I'm Ann Clarke.'

McGregor ignored the hand she held out. He turned back to the bed: 'I've come all the way from Glasgow to see you. We'd better talk alone.'

The dying man smiled again: 'Ann's come from Boston. And she's going back tonight. I needed to be sure you had been brought together at last. You've got to carry on the work. Together. You've got what it takes to be a great organizer, Harry, but she's got what it takes to be a great Leader.'

57

He stopped. McGregor got a chair for himself, leaving Ann where she stood. She kept her eyes on the old man; McGregor openly examined her in minute detail.

The old man spoke again. They both leaned forward. 'I'm going to tell you what you must do. Don't interrupt. Ann has been groomed by our American comrades. They spotted her at Harvard, and they knew I needed someone. Harry, make this young woman the most powerful politician in Britain. The workers need Leaders they can look up to, have confidence in. Ann is being trained to provide that. Do you understand what I'm saying?'

McGregor nodded.

The man went on: 'Next, control the Labour Party. Make sure that every Cabinet Minister has to be elected by conference. You won't get anywhere until Labour loses an election, but once that happens, you'll have plenty of ammunition. And as the crisis of capitalism deepens, you will need to train our cells to be workers' militia. As unrest grows – and it will – the State will turn to violence. That is when we will strike. We must be ready for it, our people properly trained for the time when law and order collapses. It doesn't matter who starts the violence, by that time no one will really care. And by then the Labour leadership will be so discredited that the workers will look elsewhere for their Leaders. That will be our time.'

His eyes turned to Ann: 'Always remember Chile. Allende tried to build a reformist socialist State, and the Americans destroyed him. When another Labour Government is elected, it will be reformist too, and the workers will not stand for that. You must take over.'

McGregor interrupted: 'What about resources? Money to train the militias, weapons, propaganda.'

The authority in Ann's voice allowed for no contradiction: 'I'll make sure you have all the money you need.' She stared him out. '*We* need.'

McGregor looked away first.

The old man spoke again: 'Chile must always be your example. There can be no half measures. Use everyone and everything you can. Go to the vicars and liberals in the anti-war movement. They are all old women of both sexes. You should find it easy to make them think you are on their side, but use them to get control of the means of war. Once you have that, you have power.'

His voice was gaining passion. 'Get control of the Bomb. Make it the Workers' Bomb.'

But the passion exhausted him, and his eyes closed again. McGregor opened the door and spoke to the women outside. Ann quietly gathered her belongings and left the room.

McGregor stood at the window as the wife and nurse bent over the old man in the bed. The tall woman walked unhurriedly down the street, her step long and determined.

Polystyrene coffee cups littered every surface in the newsroom. No one had managed to ease up long enough in the forty-eight hours since election night to tidy up; the cleaners had retreated, yelled at. The Burrell explosion had added to the chaos.

The editor's office, all tinted glass walls and dimmed spotlights, looked like an extraterrestrial oasis of order in the midst of the open-plan chaos.

The Burrell notwithstanding, decisions had to be taken, and fast, about how the BBC could maintain the momentum they had gained on Thursday night.

Editor of News and Current Affairs – ENCA – Donald Ross called in his key political staff. Anyone who got it right on this one had done his career a major favour.

Stewart lounged in a large leather armchair opposite Ross, without his jacket, collar open, long legs thrown over the arm of the chair.

Also in a leather armchair, Peter Watson slouched less elegantly, legendary drinker, gifted news director. The fog of his hangover kept him quiet. In any case he always had to wait until the others had cleared in their own minds exactly what kind of programme they wanted. He usually looked miserable, as if counting the hours until opening time.

The fourth member of the team, Clare Edmonds, thirty-four, petite, dark, clever, sexy, had been researching Ann Clarke's life for weeks. Her own body, to Clare's fury, inevitably came into the reckoning when major jobs came up, and in this story she recognized in Ann Clarke some of the drive a good-looking woman needed to beat the chauvinist odds. The arrival of a distinguished professional like Michael Stewart was too good a chance for Clare to miss. She assigned herself to him as apprentice; that he was sexy as well was a bonus she had no intention of ignoring.

Clare had suggested to Ross before the election that the BBC should prepare a 'warts and all' profile for transmission on the network, but at the time Ross backed off, dismissing the idea to his colleagues as misplaced feminism. By now he had, of course, bowed, seeing this as a window of opportunity to start getting into focus what had really begun to happen in Scotland.

Clare settled down with her notes and began to read:

'Ann Clarke is the daughter of David Montgomery Clarke who was a senior Scottish Office official charged with fraud and corruption in the early seventies. He was found not guilty, but the judge's summing up accused him of all sorts of incompetence – so bad that he was forced to resign and no one has ever employed him since.'

Ross interrupted: 'Was she close to him?'

Clare nodded: 'Only child. Adoration both ways. And they spent almost all their free time together. After the trial, he developed a drink problem, and Ann seems to have been the one to sort him out.'

Ross stopped her again: 'The mother?'

Clare screwed up her face. 'Off the wall. And a bit of a bitch. Took to her bed after the trial and has hardly left it since, although no one can find anything wrong with her. Hasn't attended any of the big events in Ann's life – graduation, entry into Parliament, anything. A Disapprover – with a capital D, seems to increase the pressure on her daughter the more famous and successful Ann

Clarke becomes. If she's getting a lot of publicity, Mother has a relapse.'

Stewart cut in: 'Ah! Is that what drives our power lady?'

Clare read on: 'Ann Clarke and the Metcalfs; he lecturing in history at Glasgow for a while, just before he went into Parliament. Ann, one of his students. Sylvia – now she's going to be worth a close look soon – quite a talent-spotter in those days, made sure there was a ready stream of acolytes to shore Tony up. Ann was a natural for her. Both Metcalfs were very good to her when her father was in trouble, Sylvia even seems to have groomed Ann. Through them Ann met Barbara Castle, Ann herself claims Castle got her started.'

Michael Stewart perked up. 'When you think about it, they're two of a kind,' he said to Ross. 'Not just the red hair, and the good looks – think of Barbara Castle in her young days. Glamorous; determined. Passionate. Committed.' He thought, still commanding the conversation. 'So that would make it early seventies that they met. Just after Barbara was Secretary of State for Employment.'

Ross laughed. *In Place of Strife* – remember? That was Barbara Castle, wasn't it? Wasn't she the one who put the Labour Party and the unions at each other's throats to start with? If it hadn't been for that, the unions might have been a bit less bolshie and they might not have been such a bad influence on the Labour Party. How old is she now? Put her on the list – we should talk to her.'

Clare took a note and read on: 'Then came the States. Scholarship to Harvard, friends with the Democrats. Worked on one of the congressional campaigns, got close to the Kennedy dynasty. Corrupt Boston politics at the time – she must have felt at home!'

The men let out a groan. Peter Watson looked up to heaven: 'The gentle sex. That was about as gentle as a hand grenade.'

'Well, we said "warts and all"!'

'She came back from the States a changed woman,' Clare continued. 'Really elegant – highlights in the hair, teeth capped, the regulation ten pounds lighter so that

61

she would look good on TV. A wardrobe of designer clothes a lesser woman would have got from some rich sugar daddy.'

Stewart cut in again: 'Who paid for them? She had no earnings.'

Clare waved him aside. 'I'll come to that, spell as a lawyer, then a determination to get into Parliament. A seat came up when Hugh Lawrie – remember him? – committed suicide, and the Clarke machine was on its way. She also seems to have teamed up with McGregor by then, and he started systematically building her power base in the Party.'

Stewart's eyes narrowed at that: 'Ye-es. We need more on the tie-up with McGregor. He's got funny friends.'

Watson came out of his slumber: 'Hang on. Hang on. Lawrie. The suicide. Can we do anything on that?'

Ross said in a voice just the safe side of sarcasm: 'Peter, you've been working on drama too long for your own good. We needn't go over the top.'

'No. Hang on.' Watson shook himself. 'Trust my nose, Donald.' In the pause, Stewart and Ross studied their notes.

Watson sank back; Clare returned to her theme: 'McGregor's an odd one. Whenever I bump into him, Party Conference, press conferences, whenever, he makes my flesh creep, and it's not just that he looks like he needs a good bath.'

The editor snorted: 'He's a Trot. He started *Struggle* – if ever there was a seditious rag. He's up to his ears in the Workers' Militia. It's all classic Trot destabilizing stuff.'

'Is Clarke involved?' from Stewart.

'She doesn't seem to be,' responded Clare. 'But she dances a bit to his tune. Wouldn't you – if you were her – make sure you had the most powerful union on your side? They'd make or break you. I figure those two are together out of mutual self-interest. But we do need to show what exactly McGregor is about, even if that does make a programme on its own.'

Stewart, restless, heaved his long legs over the chair and stood up, running his hands through his hair. 'Loose ends. Loose ends,' he muttered. Then he spoke, enumerating with his fingers. 'One. The Lawrie suicide. How come the timing suited Ann Clarke so perfectly? I'm not happy about what happened there.'

'Oh, for God's sake,' said Ross, 'this is real Reds under the beds stuff, that died out in the seventies.'

'Two. The father. Something's running that gal. The bitch of a mother isn't enough.'

Ross opened his mouth and shut up. Stewart in his stride always impressed.

'Three. Where did Clarke get her money in the States? Look, Donald, there is something rattling in this cupboard.'

Clare flicked back over her notes: 'Lawrie. There was no suggestion at the time that his troubles were anything other than financial. He'd been involved in some scandal about a research paper he was alleged to have plagiarized, but he seemed to be riding that one. He was a bit bitter about never having the chance of office – regarded himself as one of the finest thinkers of his time. No, I'm sure his suicide was just coincidence. After he died it was revealed he was a serious gambler.'

'Who revealed it?' said Stewart. 'Check where the blackening of Lawrie came from. Go back to his university, find colleagues who knew and/or liked him . . .'

'That'll be difficult,' said Ross.

'Check the source of everything said about him,' said Stewart.

Ross got up from his seat and began to pace the room. 'But is any of this telling us what Ann Clarke is really like? God, we're not bloody muckrakers!'

Stewart said: 'This isn't muckraking. Too many things about her clash – they're too neat and too vague.'

Ross said: 'OK. So she's fascinating. A cool, ruthless politician! Taken the Labour Party up here by the scruff of the neck and made it into what she wants it to be. May well do the same nationally. Bent some rules maybe on the way.'

'Bent them!' hooted Watson from his depths.

'What about Roddy Henderson?' asked Stewart. 'He retires as conveniently as Lawrie committed suicide.'

Ross went on: 'OK. If you want it that way. She's put the screws on Scotland's most senior politician and forced him to take early retirement. There's every suggestion she can grab the Prime Minister by the short and curlies and squeeze whenever she wants. She's the sexiest woman I have ever come across. Are we going to make this programme?'

Watson asked softly: 'Does she like violence?'

Ross only paused in his flow, then: 'Michael' – he stopped and leaned across – 'Forgive my terminology, but this is an inside job. First, get to the States and talk to the people there. Somebody backed her, emotionally as well as financially – could it even be ideologically? We *need* that kind of knowledge, even if we never use it.'

'Come on, Donald,' said Stewart. 'You know if we have it we'll use it.' Clare could see the growing discomfort in Michael's face. Even Peter squirmed a little. Michael's disappearance on election night was the only topic of canteen conversation; with his record, that story's embroidery would become very intricate.

Stiffening with irritation, Clare interjected: 'Why is it that every time a woman makes it into the big time, it's assumed there is a lover somewhere – a Svengali. This woman is brilliant intellectually, she's a loner – completely self-sufficient. She knows what she wants, and if that means she has to put up with thugs like McGregor, then she will, but I'll lay a bet she'll dump him as soon as possible. OK, so she was given some gloss and glitter in the States, that just shows how shrewd she is, she spotted how campaigning was going in this country and made sure she learned to make the best of it from the experts. I do not think there is anything remotely sinister about an ambitious woman playing the game by the men's rules. You lot can't take it because she leaves every man she comes across looking like a quivering inadequate – that's the real reason you're dredging around for some dirt – suicides and Trots and McGregor! Surely you can be more original than that!'

Her neck was stained with red, and she was shaking. Stewart and Ross looked at one another.

Ross turned to the researcher: 'You mustn't get so emotionally involved. We have to look coldly at the fact that Ann Clarke is involved with one of the most prominent and dangerous underground Revolutionary leaders in the country, a man we know has helped encourage the setting up of the Workers' Militia. Don't forget, he was the one who said the Queen should be sent to the gas chamber, and when social security payments were phased out, openly encouraged arson attacks on the homes of Ministers. And he's no fool – thug McGregor may be, but he's clever enough not to go too far and get himself arrested.'

It was Michael's turn. He reached over and put his hand on Clare's knee and spoke quietly, holding her gaze: 'And you forgot to mention, Ann met Lawrie in the States weeks before he died. There may be nothing in it, but we've got to know. And she's made no secret of her contempt for Metcalf; she may not have said it on the record, but she's undermined him at every turn – you would have to be blind not to see that it's really his job she's after.'

The young woman stood up. 'I saw Ann Clarke the day she stood in the snow outside Killoch colliery when the men were trapped, she stayed with the women there in driving snow until they knew their men were all right. I saw her take her coat off and wrap it round a woman with just a thin tee-shirt on. That was no publicity stunt, I saw her shiver. Remember that young girl with leukaemia, the case she took up because the kid's doctors had gone public and said the girl was dying because she lived near a nuclear power station? Well Ann Clarke paid out of her own pocket for that child to go to Disneyland and swore her family to secrecy.'

'So how do we all know about it?' asked Peter Watson.

Ross shouted at her: 'Why the hell do you think you saw all these things? Because you were with a film crew – every bloody time! This lady lives her life according to photo calls and camera angles.'

The phone rang – Ann Clarke had arrived at reception, fifteen minutes early for *The Michael Stewart Interview*.

As they walked along the corridor to the studio, Stewart slowed down to talk to Clare.

'Don't get so emotionally involved. We don't know what we'll find on this one, and if we find dirt, then you'll hit the ground with a thud.'

Clare raised an eyebrow as she responded, but her voice was gentle. 'You're telling me not to get too involved! Be careful, Michael. Even you could get hurt on this one.'

He smiled down at her, but the bleakness clouded his eyes. He opened the door and disappeared into the studio.

Any who watched the transmission sat – as the gallery crew had done – on the edge of their seats. The two crackled – always courteously, always with the undertone of savagery. He asked what she was going to do about the Leadership election; she, point blank, refused to answer him. He probed on her attitude to Metcalf: would he be a good Prime Minister, one of whom she would approve? How big a stage did she want for herself? She said the people would decide. She matched him point for point. They fought to deadlock. Finally he asked her for her reaction to the Burrell bombing. Wasn't she giving legitimacy to terrorists who took lives? She answered, harsh and solemn at once.

'That, Mr Stewart, was a regrettably cheap trick. You know as well as I do – or perhaps you don't – that the taking of life is never justified. One of those women had family in my constituency. To associate me with violence, or the condoning of it, is less than worthy of you. The poor families bereaved tonight deserve better than to be used for point scoring!' Sorrow dimmed her eyes.

He lost, as he admitted in the post mortems. She had

long gone, swept off by minders. 'But did you notice,' said Donald Ross across his desk, 'that she never answered the question?'

The civil servants, out in force from Permanent Secretary down, stood up as the Prime Minister came into the room. From experience they knew that the first twenty-four hours of a Labour administration would prove the most crucial; Harold Wilson, they remembered, had changed the rules. He brought in his own appointees into Number Ten to keep the civil servants under control. The formidable Marcia Williams they could cope with, and even the irascible Press Secretary Joe Haines, but the dangerous new appointment had been an academic, Bernard Donoughue. Wilson gave him the job of setting up a Policy Unit in Number Ten as a direct rival to all the advice the Civil Service traditionally gave to the PM. Initially, the Civil Service had been obsequious, suggesting to Donoughue that he would find more space in the Cabinet Office for his Unit rather than in the crowded Number Ten. The Cabinet Office, entered round the corner in Whitehall, linked by a door into Number Ten, was technically very close; in reality, it represented Siberia. Donoughue would have none of it. Outmanoeuvred, the civil servants developed new and ever more sophisticated techniques to ensure they could run the country without interference from the politicians.

Fearing the first meeting with Metcalf might not go according to plan, the civil servants looked to the Permanent Secretary for a lead. Each of them clutched a large buff folder, the fruits of many weeks' work by the entire Civil Service machine. As soon as the election manifestoes had been published, orders went out for bulk purchases of Labour's document; and every Department set to work to find means of implementing it in ways that would not greatly impede the government of the country. As ever, they hoped to capitalize on the natural instinct of any politician to win an election, then worry later about what to do with victory. Today, the moment had arrived to lob the proposals into the middle of the floor; in the vacuum of the election and the changeover, here came the helpful Civil Service, full of ideas to implement the election promises. No one would have time to read the fine print.

This time, it looked as if it might not go to plan.

Instead of deferring to the chief civil servant present, the Prime Minister had ignored them and gone over immediately to his political advisor, Graeme Jones, who had already caused enough trouble the day before, nipping into the building during the PM's photo call outside Number Ten, and commandeering the office next to the Cabinet Room. In this, the key office in the building, any occupant could hear all the corridor gossip among Ministers both before and, more importantly, after, Cabinet. Jones, they concluded, had to be watched.

Old hands had entered with Metcalf.

George Jeffries, who minutes before had been formally confirmed as Foreign Secretary – having been elected to the Shadow job – watched the silent exchanges between the civil servants, recognizing from past experience what they were up to. He could also see from Metcalf's face that the new PM would give short shrift to civil servants he neither knew nor trusted.

George had been around before, a large, shambling man, a distinguished academic. Minister of State in the Foreign Office during the last Labour Government, and possessor of a considerable intellect, he lacked the ability to reach out to the public – too much the intellectual, not enough of the common touch. All recognized him, though, as the most formidable brain of this new Government. As a tough man, he would supply the steel in the spine of the Prime Minister – working in harmony with Sylvia Metcalf, the arch strategist when it came to what would be best for Tony. Many rank and file Labour Members regretted Jeffries' lack of charisma – without it he could never lead the Party or the country.

Over the years, as it became more obvious that Metcalf – a man ten years his junior – would be Leader, Shadow Cabinet colleagues feared that Jeffries might abandon politics for the common rooms of Oxbridge, or even that he might become Secretary General of NATO, where brains, not good looks, could still triumph. Jeffries had stayed, though – some said because he feared the consequences of leaving Tony Metcalf to run the country unaided.

When a Party has sat in Opposition for many years those with memories of having served in previous Governments become both rare and valuable. Jeffries' knowledge made him indispensable. He knew that everything being discussed by the new Government would be the subject of detailed analysis by the key Permanent Secretaries over lunch in the Athenaeum or the Reform Club. They would shred Metcalf's reputation by nightfall if he showed any sign of the weakness known only to his close colleagues.

Raising an eyebrow to Graeme Jones, George Jeffries stood up:

'Prime Minister, I know there must be a lot you want to discuss this morning, but perhaps we could get Party business out of the way first. I'm sure the General Secretary will want to get back to Walworth Road as quickly as possible, after all, he has to work out what we do to pay for the last few weeks. Would it be acceptable to do that?'

The inscrutable civil servants looked down at their note-pads and shuffled their papers. After a barely discernible pause, the Permanent Secretary got to his feet. The mandarin's mandarin smiled obsequiously at his new masters and led his colleagues from the room. As he passed George Jeffries, the faintest film of anger crossed his eyes. Jeffries had played his trump card, civil servants would always absent themselves from Party political discussion.

When only the Prime Minister, Jeffries, Jones and the Party General Secretary, David Fredericks, were left in the room, Metcalf threw himself down in a chair and ran his fingers through his hair; collar loosened and his shirt sleeves rolled up, he looked, after forty-eight hours in office, shattered.

'Conway wants a summit!'

Jeffries and Jones, not natural allies, looked at one another, confirming what they had feared.

Not for a century had the United States been run by a man of the strength and determination of Patrick Conway – elected on a pledge to finalize US/Soviet disarmament. When he achieved this, while remaining a hawk he turned the pressure on the British who needed huge loans to keep out of economic crisis; Conway had forced a huge pay-off through a massive rearmament programme in Britain but with the Americans, behind the scenes, calling the shots. The previous PM had gone along – he had little choice. A dummy run like this had been tried before in the seventies when Denis Healey as Chancellor had been forced to go to the International Monetary Fund for help to get out of debt; as a trade-off, the Labour Government had been made to introduce unpalatable domestic policies. This time a more astute US Administration had been able to exact a more useful price.

The Soviets had, on the surface, been powerless to act to counter this, but they too had 'encouraged' their satellites to pursue rearmament programmes that merely resited nuclear weapons in obscure corners – and the rulers of the USSR wrung their hands and declared themselves powerless to act in the face of emerging 'democracies'. In effect 'disarmament' treaties between the Soviets and the US, while purporting to do the opposite, had made the world immeasurably more dangerous.

The American approach wasted no subtleties. Britain 'purchased' US weapons systems, installed by US military 'advisers' and 'paid for' by loans from American Aid funds. The techniques that had destabilized much of Central America had been transported to Britain – with the same consequences – civil unrest and growing economic chaos.

The recent General Election had been brought about by a sense of outrage at the weakness of the previous Government which stood accused – principally by the Labour Party – of lying down and allowing the Americans to take over. The election finally ran on this theme, but in the closing stages of the campaign, it had become clear to senior Labour figures that they too might have little power to resist the might of the United States. Britain's economic chaos had increased, the Balance of Payments crisis caused by so much foreign debt led to hyper-inflation; many British companies weakened by the crisis found themselves taken over by American conglomerates.

Throughout, Workers' Militia had formed, across England, Scotland and Wales, a series of small revolution-ary cells. They had the greatest strength in Scotland, where the constantly simmering distrust of the English had been raised to boiling point by the strategic decision to site all the new nuclear installations north of the Border. Huge parts of the country had been cordoned off for security purposes and whole communities dispossessed. Escalating violence against the 'invaders' and their pos-sessions had led to a state of virtual martial law, with curfews and extended power of arrest to police and armed forces alike.

Had these armed bands been without leadership they would have settled down into little factional fights among themselves and been contained. But they had a Leader, and a very plausible one at that, even though she would never publicly acknowledge the role or put on record any support for violence. Ann Clarke put into words what hundreds of thousands of ordinary Britons, especially Scots, had been thinking: that this couldn't go on, that the Americans had to be got under control; the British Government had to throw off its lapdog status.

Suddenly it became apparent that her articulate and popular opposition to the Americans was the catalyst which had forced the US President to flex his muscles with the brand-new British Government even before a full Cabinet was in place.

'Conway saw Ann Clarke on television and he says he's not going to put up with it. Somebody had better get me a recording of what went on.' Metcalf looked over at Graeme Jones, silently accusing him for not keeping him

71

informed. Not for a second did Metcalf acknowledge, or perhaps even recall, his own election night oblivion.

Jeffries voiced his worries about the implications, long- and short-term, of an early summit. Until the Government had been able to measure the full extent of the chaos in government departments, they could not even think of devising a plan of action. Therefore, if the British did not table some ideas of their own at the summit, the Americans would have no hesitation in telling them what to do – by force if necessary.

'We've got to stall,' Jeffries said. 'We need a couple of months to plan a strategy. And we have to ensure that the summit takes place here. If there is one thing we can count on Ann Clarke for, it's to stir up so many demonstrations that Conway will be in no doubt about popular opinion here.'

Metcalf looked at him for a long second, then slowly shook his head:

'We've got a month. And it's to be in Washington; the preliminaries start next week. A team's been waiting in readiness in the State Department since the start of the election campaign. Horowitz is going to head it. We need a team ready to meet with him in London on Monday.'

Sharp intake of breath: Horowitz, the US Secretary of State, had an even tougher reputation than Conway. Beginning as a Senator, he had assumed a role so crucial to the long-term strategy of the Conway Administration that he had abandoned electoral politics in exchange for the power of being Secretary of State. One of Washington's open secrets said that Conway had already nominated Horowitz as his successor. Horowitz had never concealed his contempt for the British – he would eat alive an ill-prepared Metcalf Government, especially if the new British Government did not have a solution to the crisis by which it was elected.

Jeffries rose, walked to the door and opened it, signalling courteously to Fredericks and Jones to leave. Fredericks did so willingly; he knew that in this cool-headed strategist lay the best hope of guiding the erratic Metcalf through the trauma of the days leading up to and during the summit. Jones, Metcalf's closest aide, seemed less pleased; now that they had achieved real power, he was even more wary of being usurped. But for now he would go along with Jeffries. He left.

Standing at the tall elegantly draped window, Jeffries allowed the silence to grow, then he turned to face the man who had been elected Prime Minister.

'This summit could bring the Government down if it goes wrong. We raised people's hopes that we could sort things out. If, after a month, we are seen to be as powerless as the last lot, then we'll be out too.' He walked to the dishevelled Metcalf. 'Something else – you'll have to be careful of Ann Clarke. I don't think it's Henderson's job she wants at all. She may say she wants to run Scotland, but I think she wants more. A wrong move and we could face a Leadership election here. If we blow the summit, she could take you on.'

Metcalf, who looked as though he had not been listening, did not respond. After a few seconds, Jeffries spoke again:

'We need to know who is behind Ann Clarke?' the remark contained more inquiry than assertion.

Metcalf looked up at that:

'You mean one of the big unions? I thought Fredericks had them sewn up behind me?'

Jeffries shook his head. 'No, I mean the Russians. Or someone else who could benefit from the complete collapse of everything here – the economy, democracy, you name it. She's friendly enough with that psychopath McGregor, and he's been keeping the security people in jobs for years.'

As Jeffries spoke Metcalf leant back in his seat and listened with a raised eyebrow. The Foreign Secretary elaborated, reminding the Prime Minister of all the stories there had been about the British Security Services and the South Africans trying to bring down the Wilson Government, stories subsequently claimed to be the fantasy of a fevered imagination.

Metcalf stood up, looked his Foreign Secretary up and down, then spoke:

'George, I know you and Sylvia think I've lost my marbles. But have you thought that I could be the only one who's sane?'

At that he left the room. Jeffries lifted up a newspaper, crumpled it, and threw it at the wall, dismayed that he had no influence over Metcalf. He picked up the phone and asked for Sylvia.

She waited until the flat quietened. The night, sleepless and exhausting, spent wrestling with the ghost that haunted Tony, his fear of failure, had left her drained. She lay back down on the bed, curled up in a search for emotional comfort. There was no one to hold her until the panic passed, as she had done with the man she loved, trying to hush the sobs that racked his body. Not for her the luxury of shared tears, her strength was what he needed most, so her tears must wait for solitude.

Even solitude was now beyond her reach. She longed for privacy. Here, though, in the second-floor flat of Number Ten, dozens of people worked within a few yards; the walls had ears. Her first post-election lesson told her that their privacy had disappeared – she had not yet dressed yesterday when a man from the Department of the Environment walked through the door to wind the clocks. When Tony reached for her in the night, she stiffened, the half-forgotten adolescent fear of discovery, of being overheard, stifling her sexual responses. Tony had blamed himself, another scourge with which to punish himself.

Slowly getting out of bed, she wandered round the flat. It would cause her no grief at all to abandon their plans for 'living above the shop' and go straight back to the cosy home she had created in Highgate with its warm chintzes and lovingly restored Victorian fireplaces. There she had built a cosy nest, a bolt-hole for him where he could feel safe. Other Prime Ministerial wives had suffered the same shock at the shabbiness of the private apartments in Number Ten, contrasting with the carefully maintained splendour of the State rooms. The previous Prime Minister had left the rooms unused – he found the flat too small, as had some of his predecessors. If you had grown up at Chartwell or Malborough, then it was small, but with its multiplicity of bathrooms and bedrooms, sitting room and dining room, it was almost as big as any home Sylvia had lived in. The state of it, not the size, depressed her.

She let out a sigh at the condition of the sitting room, where bulky sofas sagged in the middle under bilious green loose covers. The curtains with their huge scarlet cabbage roses had lost whatever life they had ever had, and clashed vilely with the depressing yellow of the walls. The carpets had the faded elegance of the once valuable, but who would take responsibility when someone tripped over the frayed edges? The philistinism of some recent Premiers was all too obvious in the tasteless private rooms. She should overwhelm the furniture with vases of flowers and silver-framed family photographs to hide its monotonous shabbiness.

No question of spending money on the place, the Metcalf overdraft had reached epic proportions with the election campaign; spending the taxpayers' money brought the risk of bad publicity.

Yesterday had filled her with gloom; she had learned the rigid rules about Government hospitality and what had to be paid for out of the Prime Minister's own funds. If a colleague dropped in for a drink or a working lunch, the Metcalfs would have to pay. If Sylvia had to see her daughters or go shopping, security obliged her to take a Government car, but the mileage would be charged to the Prime Minister. And even on a sizzling June morning, Christmas loomed – official cards to be ordered, lists drawn up. The tactful civil servants had told her of the restrictions on the cards that could be sent by official mail.

It had, she learned, once been worse, and might have continued so but for Mr Edward Heath. As a Conservative Prime Minister without independent wealth, he had brought in huge improvements allowing Premiers to offset many more of the prohibitive costs of life at the top. He had, for example, arranged that fresh flowers throughout Number Ten could be provided out of the public purse. In the little notes she had received from Lady Wilson, Lady Callaghan and Glenys Kinnock, they had made tactful – and blunt – reference to the inevitable overdraft that went hand in hand with life at Number Ten. All her married life, Sylvia had shouldered the financial burden, careful to keep from Tony their straitened circumstances lest he be deflected from their campaign, or blame himself for their poverty. She had succeeded in building around them an image of success, power and style, often by doing without herself.

Poverty or not, she had to sort out the antediluvian kitchen. The caterers who came in for official functions had the use of the gleaming stainless steel kitchen on the ground floor. The first floor had another 'official' kitchen; here, even the most august civil servants – or the Church of England Commissioners, lodgers in Number Ten – could sometimes be found making beans on toast. And in the Garden Room, the typing pool for the house, staffed by pretty girls in the pie-frilled collars and single-strand pearls of the Sloane Ranger, she had spotted a little cooking area. But the kitchen in the flat had all the charm and efficiency of an unsuccessful summer holiday house.

Number Ten generally – not unlike Doctor Who's telephone box, deceptively small on the outside, but a working village inside – seemed to empty at lunchtime as the senior civil servants disappeared through the door into the Cabinet Office to eat, and more importantly gossip, in the Cabinet Office Mess. The political staff disappeared to the House of Commons canteen for their daily dose of gossip. The Prime Minister most likely lunched officially most days, leaving Sylvia untypically to twiddle her thumbs. She mentioned her intention to invite people of interest – and of use to her husband and his Government – to lunch, but the ever tactful civil servants pointed out it might prove less inconvenient if she limited her personal entertaining to afternoon tea, as had previous wives. Sylvia resisted the temptation to ask about Denis Thatcher and she chose instead to show some steel – she successfully insisted on the right to set up weekly luncheon parties. For these she moved a small table she particularly liked into the window area in the White Drawing Room, with superb views out over the garden of Number Ten to St James's Park, and also out on to Horse Guards Parade. Her sense of victory dimmed a little at the knowledge that its cost would add to the Prime Minister's overdraft.

She eased herself into the bath; the hot water bringing womb-like comfort. Still tired, she dressed in the sort of sensible Jaeger suit that she felt befitted a woman of her status and then set about tidying her husband's desk. He always left the clutter of his personal papers to his wife, no one else had the patience to follow the stream of consciousness of his notes taken during meetings. As she was sorting through his notepads she came across the page of doodles. He had written Ann Clarke's name over and over again, sometimes with a drawing of a stick figure holding crown and sceptre, at other times dangling from a gallows.

Tony was becoming obsessed with Ann Clarke. Anger built in Sylvia at what this woman was seeking to do to her husband. As his kingmaker, she had to decide whether there was a real threat to Tony, or if this was a politician who had not yet learned how to control her ambition. If the latter proved the case, a few perks of office would do the trick; the former needed more attention.

Taking a leather-bound address book from a drawer. Sylvia looked up a number and started to dial, but put the phone down before it could ring. She picked up a pen instead and began to summarize what she knew about the woman whose very name so distressed her husband.

15 January 1971. Wilton Street, Glasgow

Downstairs, she could hear Tony ushering people into the lounge, the laughter, the clink of glasses. Her daughters also heard the guests arriving and rebelled, even against the bedtime story. Sylvia had anticipated them; even if it took the rest of the night, she would make sure Tony had no screaming toddlers to contend with. These students, in his charge over the six months of his visiting lectureship almost certainly constituted his last teaching appointment. He had clinched a seat in Manchester to fight at the next election; then stage two of the Metcalf master plan, towards leadership of the Labour Party, would swing into action.

They had all arrived by the time Sylvia joined the party. Tony, completely encircled by admiring students, gave full reign to his talents as raconteur, charming his impressionable audience with his good looks, his humour and his thoughtfulness. Every student left his class convinced he had singled them out for special treatment. She checked drinks and conversations – then sought out the 'useful' people – those who were too far from the epicentre of Tony's glow to fully benefit from it. While these trips round universities helped Tony broaden his list of acquaintances, ready for the time when he would need them, they also gave Sylvia the chance to meet and groom the politicians of tomorrow. Tony had particularly mentioned one girl, a tall redhead with incredibly long legs, father a senior civil servant, albeit under a cloud at the moment; of the girl Tony had said: 'Very bloody bright'. And as a law student, ideal for cultivation. Even if politics as a career did not appeal to her, she had such outstanding talent, she seemed set to make her mark in whatever field she chose – perfect for the Metcalf Christmas list.

Sylvia spotted her immediately. She stood with a group, but a shade apart. A stunner indeed, hair auburn rather than red, falling to her waist, no back-combing or sculptured cutting. They made legs like hers for black suede miniskirts, and whereas nearly every other girl in the room wore boots, mostly of shiny white plastic, this girl had low-heeled black leather pumps. She wore a blouse in a simple black and white stripe, buttoned high at the neck, long red beads and a couple of chunky red bracelets – she had natural style.

Another girl, small and plump and a little dishevelled, said something and the tall girl laughed, quite a husky, mature laugh for someone so young, though her eyes still seemed to remain grim. Ann Clarke – Sylvia's gift for names linked her with the father: the papers had the story again today. An architect had been arrested for massive fraud in relation to a planning application for a luxury leisure complex. A senior Scottish Office official – this girl's father – might also face charges.

'I'm Sylvia Metcalf.'

They shook hands. 'Thank you for inviting us, Mrs Metcalf.'

'It's Sylvia, please. I want to stay young! She turned to the smaller girl: 'And you're Mary Connolly? Yes? Tony told me you two were inseparable.'

Mary blushed as she shook hands with the Professor's wife, and covered her confusion by handing on the plate of sausage rolls and then taking them round. Sylvia and Ann Clarke settled on the bright sofa, resting glasses on the wide teak arms, and Sylvia asked Ann what kind of year she had enjoyed.

'Not the best, I'm afraid. Some problems at home. As you probably know. Bit of a strain.'

Sympathetically, Sylvia said: 'Yes, I've heard. I'm sure you'll find it difficult not to let your worries affect your studies. If you do find yourself in – well, problems – come here and see us.'

The girl looked startled: 'Oh, no question of me getting behind in my studies. That would upset my father even more. He studied here as well, took the same course, so I've got to do at least as well as him, and he got a first.'

Tony had mentioned how single-minded and determined the girl seemed. As Sylvia watched Ann, she could see a woman emerging who would always get what she wanted. She had about her a maturity far in advance of that of the other nineteen-year-olds in the room, and when Sylvia remarked on this, Ann laughed, showing for the first time some genuine mirth: 'Oh, I'm not nineteen yet, Mrs Metcalf. Sylvia. I won't be eighteen till next month.'

Sylvia's eyebrows rose involuntarily – not yet eighteen, and in her second year at university.

Mary plucked up the courage to join them and the girl relaxed enough to let Sylvia ask them both one of her most useful questions. 'Tell me about your childhood. Where do you come from?' People rarely resisted. An only child, Ann Clarke had been brought up in the exclusive little village of Gifford outside Edinburgh. Music and good books, evenings spent with father, mother and daughter in companionable reading. Mary Connolly came from a miner's cottage in Fife, with seven loud, and often bullying, brothers. The only books to which Mary had access came from the public library. The more the two talked, the more Ann gave the impression of someone slightly embarrassed by her sheltered background, as if she had missed out on part of her education by not having to fight every bit of the way. Afterwards, as she told Tony about the conversation, Sylvia mentioned that she felt Ann saw Mary as a way into the real world. In return, Mary basked in the reflected glory of being the only friend of the class star student, who also had a posh background.

Ann became a regular visitor to the Metcalf house. Tactfully Sylvia made sure that Ann did the lion's share of any babysitting they needed. Ann, her privileged background means-tested, got little in the way of a grant; pocket money had shrunk in anticipation of her father's potentially enormous legal bills.

Tony and Sylvia frequently discussed the tension building up in the young woman. She never opened her heart, but as the trial drew nearer she lost more and more weight. In an attempt to divert her, the Metcalfs tried to interest Ann in politics, but her bitterness about how politicians had abandoned her father, whose innocence she insisted on, made her less than receptive.

One weekend the Metcalfs went to Manchester where Barbara Castle, former Secretary of State for Employment in the Labour Cabinet, was to speak in support of Tony. The children went too, for the happy family photographs – taken with the Minister – to be used in Tony's election material. Ann travelled with them to help with the children.

Barbara Castle mesmerized the young student. Dressed in her pretty sea-green suit, the skirt daringly and fashionably touching her knees, with pearls round her neck, pearl studs in her ears, Barbara looked like a well-groomed fashion plate. A redhead too, Ann had never thought a Secretary of State for Employment – or indeed any politician – could be glamorous and attractive. And the woman's passion and intelligence made an enormous impression on the hitherto embittered girl.

At one point, when the group had gathered at a drinks party in someone's house, Sylvia nudged Tony. Barbara Castle had taken Ann into a corner and in her fiery but charming way, spoke to her at length about the need to get women, and highly intelligent and attractive women at that, into politics. For the first time since they had met Ann Clarke, a spark appeared in her eyes. In bed that night, the Metcalfs talked about the incident with gratitude. The passionate left-winger, a veteran of many a bruising political battle, had conveyed the excitements of politics to a mere girl. They might yet mould Ann into the winning team around the rising star of Tony Metcalf.

Ann joined the Labour Party; and Tony promised her a summer research job with a young Labour MP drafting a Private Member's Bill about changes in Scots Law. In one step she could expand her legal knowledge and get to know the House of Commons. It would also keep her occupied immediately after her father's trial. 'You know . . . in case.'

The last vestiges of girlhood left Ann during her father's ordeal in court. Though he was found not guilty, the judge destroyed his future by graphically condemning him for gullibility and incompetence. Sylvia had slipped into the back of the court the day the verdict was declared, determined that Ann should have someone there just for her, but realized too late, as Ann recoiled on seeing her, that the young student had wished no one to witness her humiliation.

Ann's father resigned – he had no alternative, and although it became glaringly apparent during the trial that the true blame lay with the politicians in whose service he took orders, no charges were brought against them. Labour politicians too, and in Government – colleagues in her adopted party had destroyed her father. Ann went to see Tony Metcalf, ready to resign; he sat her down and showed her how to use the Party to destroy the careers of the guilty men. Sharing her outrage, he explained that any constituency Party unhappy with their MP could force him into another selection process, and in that way unseat him. It only needed a majority opposed to the MP on the management committee of that constituency. It worked best using the trades unions; they could easily pack a constituency committee and insist that all their delegates voted the same way – all they usually wanted was a favour in return.

On that day, too, Tony revealed to her that he intended to become Leader of the Labour Party, and ultimately Prime Minister. Given the current Party organization, he would have to wait too long; he and Sylvia had identified others similarly impatient for power. Disenchantment proved easy to find in the wake of a crisis-ridden Labour Government; any dedicated person could easily mount a strong campaign to change the Party constitution and seize the power base. Metcalf wanted to ensure that every MP, regardless of status or popularity, should go through a re-selection process between elections. That way every MP would have to toe the line. Some people, to give more power to the Party activist, planned to ensure that the whole Party, not just the MPs, should choose the Leader, and therefore any Labour Prime Minister. They had approached him to seek his support for this policy – in return they would back him in any future Leadership election. He decided to go along with them, though less than happy about their plans to have every Cabinet Member elected. That could work against him when he reached Downing Street, but the prospect of such wide-spread support for his candidature outweighed his fears. He could compromise later. When Metcalf noticed Ann's scepticism about the possible success of this plan, he pointed out that her heroine, Barbara Castle, had lain the groundwork. Her plans to attack the trades unions meant that the unions could be counted on to back any proposal that increased their own power.

He, Tony Metcalf, was determined to become Prime Minister. He had, he told her, identified already that she, Ann, had the potential to go to the top with him.

'This isn't the time to leave the Labour Party; this is the time to go for more power. Not only will you be building a marvellous career for yourself, but if you help me set up these changes, you'll have created the weapons to use to avenge your father.'

She left him, intending to think about it. They never discussed his plans again, never ever mentioned the conversation. Gradually, though, Ann became more active in the Party.

Life grew very hard personally. Her father, drained by the trial, in despair of getting another job, had begun to drink heavily. The lovely house in Gifford had been sold; her mother, always demanding and snobbish, had developed a full-blown case of hypochondria. Ann worked harder, almost manically; to forget, and to indulge her passion to be the best. That might wipe out the shame of the constant tittle-tattle behind her back; she never noticed that like all such gossip, it soon waned, and the colour of it made her seem more fascinating.

The Metcalfs went back to London and resumed their search for young talent to build a court around Tony. In less than a year he had entered Parliament, but as Labour had lost the last General Election, his route to Government was slowed. The discontent in the Party helped him make others see change was necessary. Ann worked a couple of summers in the Commons, quickly catching on that the only reason to devote yourself to the twenty-four-hour-a-day job of politics was for power. With power there was nothing you couldn't do; with power no one could hold you back. Astute enough to know that power eluded those who sat on the back benches, she determined that if she entered politics she would never be lobby fodder – the foot-soldiers of the Parliamentary Labour Party who had little role other than to troop through the lobbies to vote in the way the Whips told them. She began to warm to the attractions of Tony Metcalf's plan.

Respite from the depressing tangle of her home life came with the winning of a scholarship to Harvard. From the aircraft window she sighed with relief as she saw the coastline of Scotland recede; the immediate prospects thrilled her, especially the armful of introductions to US politicians provided by the Metcalfs and their friends. Ann, still bitter about the men who had destroyed her father, determined more fiercely than ever to beat them at their own game, and planned to use her time in the US to learn the skills for doing that.

Her impact in the American university was considerable. Faced with the determined competitiveness of the American system, Ann came into her own. Here everyone was striving to win – Ann Clarke more than most.

The Democrats fascinated her. She had expected to find a political party like the one she knew at home, with policy debates and endless meetings planning a better tomorrow, but here she found the Democrats were like a Bedouin tribe – they packed up their tents between Presidential contests; the lawyers and PR professionals would go back to their practices and only the pollsters retained some semblance of continuity, constantly monitoring changes in public taste and opinion. But with the start of the race to the White House the Democrats revealed themselves as a true electoral machine. Here in Massachusetts, she saw that machine at its best, honed to perfection by Kennedy money and ambition. She met the legendary Tip O'Neil, one-time Governor and now a Congressman. The bluff Irish American struck her as familiar, he was out of the same mould as the power brokers of the trades unions and local government back home.

Just as Ann watched the Democrats, so did they watch her. There is a long tradition of links between US and British politicians, links usually formed when the aspiring politician is young. Ann was quickly absorbed into the inner circles of Democratic politics, singled out for her obvious talent and extraordinary commitment to being a winner – the acid test for success in politics.

And that is how she met Senator Richard Johann Horowitz.

On a blank sheet of paper Sylvia Metcalf listed the options in her campaign to safeguard her husband, and the dangers he would have to face. She ringed the words 'health' and 'stability'. At the top of a page she wrote 'Ann Clarke', pen poised to write 'destroy': but might Ann Clarke as an ally be a much more potent force? The first question, though, had to be whether Ann really was a rival to Tony. Getting to the bottom of that would take a great deal of subtlety. Therefore it became important that no hint of official approbation be given to Ann until every skeleton in her cupboard stood revealed; any scandal, any dubious connections, could rub off, and maybe even destroy Tony if he was again cast in the role of mentor to Ann Clarke.

Taking her jacket, Sylvia left the flat and entered the working part of the house. She still had to ask directions from obsequious messengers and condescending typists before she could find her husband's study.

Graeme Jones was reading a print-out from a telex as she came into the outer office; in what seemed like an automatic movement he shifted over so that he blocked the entrance to the Prime Minister's room. With civil servants all around pretending not to look, the hostility between the two had to be masked, but the air between them chilled as they looked at one another.

Sylvia drew herself up to her full five foot two inches. 'I'd like to see my husband.'

Graeme's tone was patronizing: 'He's with the Foreign Secretary and has made it clear he's not to be disturbed. By anyone. Isn't that right?'

He looked over at the Principal Private Secretary, who by this time was also standing, for once a useful ally.

'He was most insistent, ma'am,' said the young man. 'Perhaps if you left a note?'

Sylvia gave him the benefit of her most disarming smile. 'Not to worry! I'm just off for a walk in the park. After all, I've got the entire evening to talk to him!' And with that she walked away, trying not to flounce. As she approached the front door one of the detectives stood up ready to accompany her, but he was favoured with such a cold look that he felt better of it, contenting himself with leaving thirty seconds behind and tailing her to St James's Park.

The park was crowded, young lovers lay on the grass, some kissing long and passionately, others just gazing silently into one another's eyes, others horseplaying. Mothers sat watchful as their children giggled at the ducks. An elderly couple passed, their hands as tightly clasped as any of the youngsters', bringing a smile to Sylvia's troubled face.

About to turn back, she saw a familiar figure loping towards her, Stephen Robinson. A favourite with Sylvia, for his natural charm and enormous energy, with the fierce integrity she loved in her father and brothers. She found his tenacity exciting, and despite his immaculate dress, he had a rough earthiness she found attractive.

He lengthened his stride as he caught sight of her. Smiling, he put his hand on her waist, drawing her to him that he could more easily kiss her on the cheek. As he did so, he could feel her shrinking from him, as if afraid. She blushed. Exchanging warm greetings, they fell into step until they found a bench they could sit on. Once settled, Sylvia gave him one of her long hard looks. Something was wrong, she could feel an anger in him that in a more sophisticated man would have been better concealed.

'Are you going to tell me about it?'

Startled by her words, he said: 'I wasn't aware I was so transparent.' Then – 'What the hell,' and with a great rush of words he told her what was happening in Scotland.

Joe Black's outburst in the club, the tortured face of

Roddy Henderson, the youngsters, some as young as thirteen, enrolled in the Workers' Militia (though he kept from her his own sons' involvement) – they all tumbled out. He hesitated before he explained his theory that Ann Clarke had either carefully planned the events of the past few years, or had at least been in on the planning, and that her position in the election of Secretary of State for Scotland could shortly become dangerous, even unassailable. Robinson could see that Sylvia's interest was total, and she of all the people he had spoken to did not dismiss his ideas as fanciful. So, with a careful pause, he then told her that he thought Ann was out to either remove all the power from the Prime Minister, or take his job.

As Sylvia's jaw hardened Robinson knew he had connected. For years she had fought to get Tony into Number Ten when the entire Labour Party knew she was the better politician; now she was not going to let anyone take the prize from them.

'We're going to stop her. Aren't we?'

He did not even need to reply. They both knew that they had formed an alliance. The full battle plan, they agreed, would come in due course: for now the election of a new Secretary of State for Scotland would have to take priority.

'Should I stand against her?'

Sylvia, thinking, nodded, and about to talk of how they could join forces to get him elected, she saw the cloud pass over his face:

'What about your wife?' As he shrugged she involuntarily touched his arm. She looked away and when she looked back at him could see the colour had suffused his face.

Simultaneously, they stood up, almost jumping apart, each embarrassed by the strange moment of intimacy. They made plans to meet again the following day, this time in the safety of the Harcourt Room in the House of Commons. The sight of the two of them lunching together would spread a rumour like wildfire: was Sylvia Metcalf set to back Stephen Robinson as a direct snub to her former protégée, Ann Clarke?

At the end of Birdcage Walk they turned, ready to go their separate ways; they stood briefly at the bottom of the steps that would take Sylvia back to Number Ten. The detective a few feet behind knew he would have to log the meeting in the duty book. He would make no mention of the longing so plain in the eyes of the MP. New instructions had been issued that morning that a particular watch was to be kept on Mrs Metcalf – for her own safety.

3

The office, on the ground floor of a red sandstone ten-
ement, in the midst of cluttered newsagent and hardware
shops, was distinguished by the large single portrait of a
smiling Ann Clarke. Inside, political strategists turned
cleaners for the day began to remove the debris of the
General Election – to make way for the next campaign the
Ann Clarke team would fight. This would be the nerve
centre for what the staff called 'the big one' – Ann's
bid for the Leadership of the Scottish Labour Party, the
launchpad, for those in the know, for a fundamental
assault on the nature of British politics.

The cheap furnishings still showed a certain style –
white-painted walls framed by a scarlet picture rail, office
furniture in white with a red rim, a chequered red carpet;
all contributed to a businesslike but breezy atmosphere.

The image seemed to fall apart somewhat in the office
occupied by Mary Connolly, who from a tiny room littered
with cardboard boxes guarded the entry to the inner sanctum. Her desk overflowed with paper, the year planner
was almost invisible behind a cluster of yellow stick-on
memos. It remained a mystery to those who respected
Mary's prodigious organizational abilities how she could
be so efficient amid such clutter.

Normally Ann Clarke's office seemed a haven of tran-
quillity, blue Laura Ashley curtains matching paler blue
walls, deeper blue carpet. The squashy leather chair sat
behind a habitually clear pine desk, facing two hessian
director's chairs. Around the walls the bookcases held
green bound copies of *Hansard* the official record of
Parliamentary debates. This morning, however, many of
the *Hansard*s were scattered on the floor, some of them
showing little yellow stick-on memos as page markers.
More of them had been spread on the desk, piled high

one on top of the other, odd bits of paper sticking out of them.

Ann walked into the middle of the empty room, her expression incredulous. Her lips narrowed into a thin line. She put her bag down on a chair, and without turning round shouted for Mary, the anger in her voice reverberating off the walls. The election agent came into the room, her face flushed, hair dishevelled, blouse parting company with her skirt, a run in her stockings. Next to the superbly elegant younger woman she looked a mess, and her embarrassment showed in her face.

'I'm sorry, Ann. I didn't think you'd be here for another hour. I was trying to put together some stuff for your campaign literature . . .'

She rushed on, her words tumbling over each other as she sought to excuse herself, hands trying to smooth her hair into some semblance of order. The ringing of the phone saved her from further shame.

Ann picked it up, and as she listened red blotches appeared on her neck. Mary could see the knuckles on the hand clutching the phone turn white, the other hand clenched in a fist. When Ann spoke her voice was low and vicious, each syllable perfectly enunciated.

'I have no intention of coming to London. I will be there when it suits me, certainly not to give Tony Metcalf some delusion of grandeur as he lectures me about not rocking the boat. And don't call him "the Boss" to me. He couldn't run a bath. My boss is the elector. They need me here, and if you haven't the courage to tell Metcalf that, then get him to call me himself. Goodbye, Graeme.'

She smashed the phone down, shaking. The colour that had stained her face now drained away, leaving her white. Mary's mouth gaped in shock. It was one thing to make passionate pleas on public platforms, quite another to insult the Prime Minister on the first day of a new Government. Metcalf could make life very rough indeed, if he had a mind to.

Mary put her hand on Ann's arm.

'Why don't you sit down and I'll make you a cup of tea?'

Ann whirled round to face her and spat: 'The day they drop the atom bomb you'll make everyone a cup of tea. I don't pay good money to you to make endless cups of tea. I should have left you to your squalid family after all, then you could really indulge yourself as a mother hen. Now get the team together. And get this place tidied up. If you're incapable of running an office efficiently, then say so and I'll find someone who can. Now get out and let's get some work done!'

Mary went out, head down to hide the pain. Total silence fell in the outer office. Only one old timer who had been with them from the start took Mary aside.

'Why do you take it from her?' she asked. 'She wouldn't be where she is if it wasn't for you. Why do you let her treat you like dirt? Walk out of here and you'll be in a job paying twice as much by tomorrow morning.'

Mary, smiling ruefully, came to Ann Clarke's defence. 'Oh I wouldn't worry about it. Ann's always on edge before something major. She's not like the rest of us, you know – she really is someone very special. Special people are difficult, but they're worth it.'

The older woman shook her head in wonder. When it came to Ann Clarke, Mary remained incapable of seeing any flaw in the woman she idolized; it was like talking to a brick wall.

Nevertheless Mary remained subdued all during the planning meeting. As details of speaking tours were worked out, receptions for leading trades unionists planned, direct mail shots to Party members listed, she made no contribution. Eventually, Ann asked her if she had done anything to get features on Ann into women's magazines. Mary looked startled at the question, she obviously had not heard a word of the discussion. The research officer and press officer shuffled, anticipating another explosion. Walking to the door, Ann opened it and signalled to the two young assistants to leave. They did so quietly, as Mary sat with her head bowed.

Returning to her desk, Ann sat still for a few seconds, then in a voice as crisp as frost, inquired what was going on. As she sat she saw the tears begin to roll down Mary's cheeks. Despite her tension and bad temper, Ann softened.

'I'm sorry, Mary. But I can't afford for you to have a fit of the vapours. I didn't mean to be so hard on you. I suppose I'm under more strain than I realize. But if I can't let go with you, then who else is there? You're the only one I've got. Please forgive me!'

Mary looked up and shook her head.

'It's not you, Ann, I don't blame you for being angry. Today of all days I should be making sure everything goes like clockwork. But I've been so worried!'

And then the sobs came. Ann took a box of tissues from the drawer and went round the desk. She handed them to Mary, then put her hand on her friend's arm.

'What is it?'

She waited as the sobs subsided.

'It's a lump. I've found a lump, Ann. Just like the one that killed my mother, on my left breast too.'

The time of Mary's mother's death was etched on both their memories. Ann had never before seen such cruel chauvinism in men as she had in Mary's father and brothers, who had put all the strain on Mary and had expected her to leave university to look after them. All this at a time when Mary had lost the only person who had ever shown her any affection and tenderness.

She put her arms round Mary's heaving shoulders, rocking her gently.

'When are they taking you in to see to it? Whenever it is, you mustn't worry about work. I'll cope. Somehow.'

Mary didn't reply at first. When she spoke, her voice was hesitant.

'I haven't been to see about it yet. I only found it on Monday, and I was too busy to do anything about it until after the election. I had decided to go today, but with Henderson resigning and everything, I had to come in here and get everything started for your campaign. But I just couldn't concentrate. I've not had much sleep since I found it.'

Ann almost lost control. She shook Mary. 'You stupid, stupid woman. Nothing is more important than getting you well. All the elections in the world won't matter if I lose you. You should have told me right away!'

She dialled a number, which was answered on the first ring.

'Ian! It's Ann here. I need a very big favour, and I can't afford to have you say no. My best friend has discovered a breast lump, and she's been ignoring it for a week. Her mother died of breast cancer, and I know that makes you people all the more suspicious.'

She listened for a few seconds, then spoke in a much gentler tone. 'Have I ever asked you for anything before?' She listened then answered. 'Yes, even more important than the election.'

Another pause.

'Half an hour?'

She put down the phone.

'Get your coat, we're going to the Royal. Ian Meldrum will see you right away, and if he thinks you need surgery, you'll be first on his list tomorrow morning.'

Mary looked shocked. Ann was famous for never seeking favours, never wanting to be treated differently from anyone else.

As she began to protest, Ann hustled her out.

Suddenly she stopped. 'But you can't come with me, I've agreed you'd do an interview with Michael Stewart for the tea-time news. And I think he's arrived.'

Ann sat Mary down behind her cluttered desk and went out. Michael had indeed arrived. She could tell from the sharpness of his expression that he was far from pleased with her. Oh well – he was about to be less pleased.

She walked up to him.

'Michael. You're angry, I know. Can I explain later? This isn't exactly the easiest time of my life. And now I'm going to make you even more angry. Can I come in and do the interview live? Something very important has come up that involves a friend of mine, she needs me and I can't let her down.'

Stewart snarled at her: 'I suppose if I don't agree to do it live I don't get any interview. Right?'

He saw that she was much too preoccupied to take in his anger – she fidgeted with her rings, obviously very much on edge. His irritation eased, his interest reawakened.

'All right – six. Not a minute later.'

Without another word, she rushed out with Mary.

In the quite little village of Swanick in Derbyshire, well away from the hurly-burly of the larger world, two clerks worked behind the counter of the only bank. In a back office the manager drafted a letter in longhand. Two men opened the door, came in, and approached the counter, the cashier looked up and smiled – into the muzzle of a gun which blew most of his face away. The raid happened in minutes, the total haul comparatively small – a little under £50,000. They also left two bullets in the head of the manager who had tried to get to the silent alarm.

An identical raid at exactly the same time, at a bank in the Wirral, netted over £100,000, with one casualty. The Press Association received a call from the Workers' Militia claiming responsibility for both raids.

McGregor had taken up Ann Clarke's suggestion. He drove two of the younger girls on the staff to the street corner nearest their homes. House to house, CID men had begun questioning: a massive manhunt for the murderer of the young prostitute, Carol Copeland, was under way. A bored constable came over to ask what he was doing. 'Errand of mercy,' said McGregor. 'Safety, you know.' The policeman congratulated him and volunteered some details of the young girls murder. The force, he said, 'even the hard nuts', had been shocked at the brutality.

As the two members of his staff got out of the car, McGregor called after them: 'D'ye hear that? Avoid strange men, there's some right animals about!'

He drove off, heading out of the city, to Barrhead, where he looked around for the pub he had been told about.

Inside, his eyes adjusting, he looked round the room. At the back a man was sitting with a pint of beer and a whisky in front of him. In a black leather jacket, his stomach flat beneath his blue jeans, he had a scar from the corner of his mouth to his chin, dragging his face to one side. In the thickly matted hair showing through the neck of his checked shirt was a large gold crucifix.

He looked up as McGregor approached him. A frisson of excitement made the union leader shiver as he looked into the cold cruel eyes of the man, yellow like a cat's.

The man held out his hand, not in greeting but in demand. McGregor took the envelope out of his inside pocket, but he hesitated: 'Is it done?'

'An hour ago.'

'She says there's to be no killing.'

The man shrugged as if that was of no concern to him. McGregor smiled. He handed over the money. Taking it out of the envelope, the man counted it, unconcerned about the watchful eyes around him. 'Once the money's in the bank for the other one, we'll deliver.'

A frog in his throat, McGregor croaked. 'They transferred the money this morning. Phone Dublin anytime, they'll confirm it's there. So when you're ready . . .'

There was contempt in the man's voice as he answered: 'Oh, I'm ready all right. I've been ready for years. I'll deliver, so you'd better too. And her. Oh – and let her know we'll be watching. Not that we can protect her from now on, but if she thinks she can start doing things on her own, tell her not to be so stupid. She wouldn't be this close if it wasn't for us, she must know that. If she doesn't we'll tell her.'

Then he leant over to McGregor, his huge calloused hand gripping the union official's hand. Without changing his expression, he squeezed. McGregor went white with pain. 'And you. I've been told to tell you that you'd better behave.'

McGregor stuttered, the pitch of his voice varying. 'But two women killed at the Burrell . . .' he gasped.

The man released his grip. 'Sometimes people get hurt in a war,' he shrugged. 'But we don't do it for fun.' He made as if to grab McGregor again, who quickly got his hands out of reach.

The man stood up and laughed, but the sound he made caused a hush to fall in the pub. No one spoke till the door closed behind him.

McGregor went to the phone and dialled. 'It's started.' He didn't wait for a reply as he hung up.

Above the noise of the bath she could barely hear the voice of the newsreader. At the mention of her own name she turned off the taps. 'Labour's Scottish Executive meets today to finalize arrangements for the election of a new Secretary of State. Early indications are that Clydeside West MP Ann Clarke will be unchallenged for the post. Speculation is mounting that newly elected Prime Minister Antony Metcalf will overrule his Party's constitution and appoint the new Secretary of State without an election to allow the Government to begin its programme in Scotland immediately. Informed sources expect an announcement today.'

Ann laughed and switched it off. She sang quietly to herself in the bath, and dressed with her usual care – from now on she moved on a massive public stage, high profile. The practicality of her clothes must henceforth take second place to their impact. Watching that first heroine of a lifetime ago, Barbara Castle, had taught her that. The public didn't want jeans and wellies – they had those already. They wanted glamour. From now on, the TV cameras came before comfort.

She chose a dress of aquamarine silk, high at the neck and falling straight to just below her knees. To lift its classic plainness she dressed it up with gold chunky jewellery and matching, important-looking earrings. This she topped with a patterned jacket, a kaleidoscope of blues and greens, also in silk, but heavier, a souvenir of a holiday in the Far East.

Before leaving the flat she switched on the answering machine. If the news had got it right and an announcement was imminent from the PM's office she had better make sure she was ready for the summons.

Reaching her car, she groaned. Still covered in election stickers it needed a wash, and its conspicuousness bothered her. She removed the most glaring posters; the rest could come off later. As she drove west out of Glasgow towards Loch Lomond she hummed happily in tune with the cassette – James Galway playing Mozart. Before eight o'clock, the Saturday morning had little traffic. This was the time of day she liked best.

The cheerful flute added to her good spirits. At Balloch she turned away from the loch, heading towards Aberfoyle. She had chosen the long route, looking round with pleasure at the peaceful scenery. She turned off the highway before the village of Gartmore and took her speed right down, the state of the unmade road making her more cautious. The dogs had been barking and yelping long before she reached the end of the road. As she got out, she did a little jig to avoid their muddy paws jumping up to slobber all over her. The two chocolate biscuits she had slipped into her bag calmed them.

Then her face clouded when she saw the man at the door. The bitter set to his lips and the droop of his shoulders suggested that he hadn't had a good week in this apparently idyllic retreat.

The worn cardigan and carpet slippers jarred again – they always did – with the memory she carried of an elegantly suited, prosperous and powerful man. She walked up to the door.

'How are you, Father.'

She could hear the self-pity in his voice.

'Your mother hasn't been too well. She's still having trouble sleeping, so she wants to talk during the night. I find I haven't much energy after that. Breakfast? I was just about to start it.'

She reached up to kiss him. 'You sit down and talk to me and I'll make it,' she said, taking off her jacket and covering her dress with an apron.

He replied: 'Go in to see your mother first. Or that'll be another complaint!'

Ann went through to the extension that housed the bedrooms. When she had bought this cottage, captivated by its whitewashed walls and tiny windows, she had expected that her parents would sort out their lives reasonably quickly. Once they were back into their busy social life, she would make the cottage her own. Her desk at home still contained the plans for redesigning it – walls knocked down, old fireplaces opened up. In storage the early American pine bed waited for the bedroom. It had never happened.

Her mother lay staring at the ceiling, no sign that she knew her daughter had come into the room.

'Hello, Mother. How're you feeling? I'm sorry I couldn't get here last week.'

Her mother eased herself up on her elbow and smiled weakly: 'Oh, I'm as well as can be expected. You looked nice on television the other night. I'm glad you remembered to wear peach, your colouring isn't good enough to take anything stronger. Where did you get it?'

'In Harrod's,' replied her daughter absently. Her mother's voice held a constant martyred whine.

'I used to spend lots on clothes before your father disgraced himself. I always believed that it was the duty of the wife of a successful man to make the most of herself so that people could see that he was a man to be respected and admired. And of course I had such good bones. Pity you didn't inherit them.'

She settled herself more comfortably on the pillows. 'You're going to avenge him now, aren't you? When you're Secretary of State for Scotland you'll repay those men who brought your father down. Oh, anything for him! That's why you're doing it, isn't it? You don't care that the old scandal will all be reopened! It'll kill me, you know. Then the two of you can be together without me being in the way!'

Ann recoiled from the hatred in her mother's bitter face.

This conversation had been taking place off and on for most of the past ten years. Ann opened her mouth to say something, decided against it, and left the room.

In the kitchen her father had perked up somewhat. An able, intelligent man, he found his frustration at his 'invalid' wife sometimes boiling over, more this year than ever before. Retirement year – if he had still been in the Civil Service. Had all gone well he could be lined up to join the board of some major Scottish company. The most recent Honours List had contained the names of his contemporaries; he might even have expected a knighthood. Eve would have been Lady Montgomery Clarke.

But David Montgomery Clarke had sat at the wrong desk at the wrong time, and so carried the can for his dishonest political masters. Labour masters. Trying to clear his name of charges of fraud cost him every penny, and although he had been found 'not guilty', the judge's summing up had been scathing in accusing him of negligence. And the two year wait for the trial had depressed and demoralized him.

While the truly guilty men had walked away without a mark on their characters, he had been ruined. Some satisfaction had come from the defeat of that Labour Government, and his successor at the Scottish Office had eventually managed to get the new Secretary of State to reinstate his Civil Service pension. But the scandal lived on in people's minds, and he had long since given up trying to get a job.

Now he spent his time worrying about the vigour with which his daughter had dedicated herself to a career in politics when she knew what politicians were capable of. He had argued with her that she should not get involved in politics, especially Labour politics. Nor did he believe that dropping the Montgomery from her name would sufficiently distance her from him – and his disgrace, he warned, would return to haunt her.

But Ann had been determined, and he had to admit that it looked as if she had been right. She would be a courageous Secretary of State for Scotland with a good head on her shoulders, even if he didn't agree with some of her more radical policies.

They chatted as she prepared breakfast. He may have been out of the mainstream of Scottish government for a long time now, but he still knew how the system worked. She laughed as he demonstrated how the civil servants would hijack policies they didn't approve of and make them their own, subtly altering them on the way. Ann realized again that her father had also influenced her attitude to men. She was attracted to men with his bearing – like Horowitz, to whom her mind now turned.

Second-generation immigrant, determined, elegant and ruthless, even on the day she met him he made it plain he intended to fill the vacuum left by the Kennedys. Her initial reaction to Horowitz had been physical – when he came into a room, he exuded such energy, such drive: permanently tanned, the firm body of a sportsman dressed by Brooks Brothers in wool and cashmere, hair glossy and well-maintained, flopping boyishly over his forehead. His charm wrapped her in a warm glow and, somewhat regrettably, he made the string of escorts she had already acquired seem mere boys by comparison. Add the power factor he so clearly possessed and he also answered the private questions inside her about her feelings for her father, who now set off to carry the breakfast tray in to her mother. When he returned, she sat down opposite him, having shivered a little as he touched her cheek on his way to the table.

'I heard the radio,' he said. 'Can Metcalf appoint you Secretary of State today? And if so, should you be here?'

She laughed. When it came to plotting, she left him far behind.

'He'd like to! Even though the rules say he can't. It would make life much easier for him. But if I accepted

100

his blandishments, I would lose a lot of power in Cabinet. If I'm an elected member of the Cabinet, I don't owe Metcalf any favours. He won't be able to demand obedience because he put me there. Nor can he sack me. So I'm going to hold out for the election, and hope that someone stands against me.'

He asked, 'And if they don't? They're not fools, I suppose?'

'If no one volunteers,' she said, 'I'll make sure one of my supporters has a go. It would be better for me to be able to point to a derisory vote for my opponent than to have it said that my election was a fake.'

Her father shook his head. 'Much simpler in my day,' he sighed. Then hesitantly, he raised again his fear that his own fall from grace would be recalled – to damage her.

'I'm glad you raised that, Father.' She took his hand, knowing the risks. 'Two weeks today, I'll be Secretary of State. On the Monday I'll walk into New St Andrews House to take office. I want you there. I want the world to know who my father is and that I'm proud of him. Never forget the jury's verdict: "not guilty". Will you?'

He lowered his head to hide his eyes. As a little girl Ann had followed him around like a puppy dog. On that horrible day when his life had been destroyed, his first thoughts had been panic that he might lose his daughter's adoration.

That fear soon evaporated, to give way to his new worry. Ever since Tony Metcalf had told her how to unseat the men who had brought him down, she had steeped herself in politics, working single-mindedly to build her power base and change the Party she had joined so that she could use it more effectively, as if gaining the Scottish Office might simultaneously blot out the past and give her revenge.

'I can't, Ann. I'm touched but I can't. It would detract from you. And it would bring the story all back.'

Ann began to interrupt him, but he went on:

'And your mother. Forget her hypochondria, she's ill.

101

Ill mentally. She never came to terms with what has happened. She blames me.'

'But Father, I did so much of it for you. Please.'

He shook his head. 'No, dear, you may have started out doing it for me, but along the way you obviously found commitment. Besides – you mustn't give your enemies a chance to say that the only reason you've gone this far is for some kind of revenge. You'll know, and I'll know what lies behind all of this. That should be enough.'

She had no alternative but to accept what he had to say, but the disappointment lined her face. On the drive back she tried in vain to recapture the good humour of her early morning journey.

Mary, still groggy, had some discomfort but no cancer. She cried as she thanked Ann for getting help for her so quickly. Ann, in her turn, had shifted several times in the past twenty-four hours at the memory of many little cruelties to this woman who not only adored her, but had helped her carve out her success. Ann kissed her cheerfully and with relief.

Back at the flat, she checked her messages. McGregor had phoned to say 'everything going well. See you tomorrow? We've got things to talk about.'

Two press calls asked was she going to make a statement about her plans. And a call from Michael Stewart.

She ignored it too.

Indefinably uncomfortable after parting from her father, she wandered aimlessly around the house. She took a glass of wine and a book out on to the patio into the hot early evening sun. The book did not hold her attention. Next she dead-headed the geraniums in their tubs and repositioned some pots to give them a better chance of the sun. Still, she looked around for something else to do. In the bedroom she took out the silver-framed photograph from the bedside table – lying down on the bed she reached for the phone. No reply. She tried three times, letting it ring eternally.

For a long time she lay on the bed, looking at the

ceiling, hand on the photograph. After a while she rose, shrugged off her clothes and pulled on the tight second skin of a leotard over naked flesh. Stretching and bending her body, she let her muscles adjust to new demands. Then, setting up the sound system with Dvořák's Sixth Symphony, she opened up the double doors to a small mirrored exercise room dominated by a weighted exercise machine. She sat down, spread her legs wide, adjusted the weights between them, then reached up and began to pull on the heavy weighted levers above. For twenty minutes she worked out, thighs and shoulders mostly, letting the music waft her with each crescendo to greater and greater effort. Her body was drenched with sweat before she finally let go, warming down to let heart and body adjust back to relaxation. She stripped off the soaked leotard, prepared a bath with potent, luxurious bath oil and lay back until the water began to cool. She towelled, then smoothed creamy lotion over her skin, slipped a beige silk camisole over her head and matched it with tobacco-coloured silk trousers, finishing off with strappy high-heeled sandals. Hair piled loosely on top of her head, she confined make-up to lip gloss and mascara, touched her pulse spots with perfume. Was this carefree, glamorous young woman the elegant professional politician feared by the most powerful in the land?

At the door she stopped, went back, collected a bottle of champagne from the fridge. Then she switched on some lights so that the place would look occupied when darkness fell, and headed out to her car.

Michael woke from his television doze when the entry-phone buzzed. Life in New York and Washington made the flat's video security system second nature.

No mistaking his caller, even if she stood with her back to the camera. He hesitated. If he ignored her, he could go on with rebuilding his life; if he let her in, he ran all kinds of risks. He pressed the button.

When she came out of the lift she was already smiling.

As she passed him, where he stood in the doorway, she reached up and kissed him on the mouth.

'I was just about to leave; I thought maybe you had someone with you.'

Still he stood back: 'You knew for sure I was alone. Otherwise you would have phoned first, Miss Discretion.'

She laughed at him: 'If you behave as if you had something to hide, people jump to all the right conclusions. If there had been someone here, I would have given you this champagne to thank you for helping me out the other night, and gone on to a dinner party with friends who live in the next block.'

Walking over to him, she held out the bottle:

'As it is I'll give it to you and suggest we have the drink we missed out on the other night.'

Michael took the bottle and stroked the foil top. 'Where did you go the other morning?'

'You mean – why did I go?'

'Well, yes. I felt like some kind of stud.'

Irritably, she replied, 'Look Michael, Thursday night was great. The perfect end to quite a special day, but I didn't think we were in the business of making commitments. The logical thing seemed to be to get out of the way. There is nothing worse than strained silence the morning after or, for that matter, synthetic romance. If I've offended you, I'm sorry.'

She turned to leave.

'Why did you come back tonight?'

She stopped in her tracks and turned to face him. 'Because I want you.'

He reached his arms and stopped her. This time she picked up the champagne.

Afterwards, as they lay in each other's arms, she asked him about Washington. She was the first person to speak to him openly about the scandal he had caused, and for the first time he felt he could speak about his anger with himself at his own weakness.

She raised a hand and touched his face, exposing a nipple that he brushed gently with his fingers.

104

She pushed his hand away.

'And what about you? Why are you here? What brought you back from the States when you seem to have taken Harvard by storm?'

She didn't answer immediately; a wariness came into her eyes, but soon passed: 'I'm very ambitious. I saw in Scotland a chance to change the way people live, to improve things. I was also very angry at the way the country was being run. Like most politicians, I decided I could do it better.'

She held his gaze as he asked: 'Why politics?'

'Power, Michael. Power. And don't let any politician fool you that they're in the business for any other reason. They may want power to do great and wonderful things for mankind, but at the end of the day, the only reason to get into politics is because you want the power the other guy's got.'

'And who is the "other guy"? Tony Metcalf?'

She laughed and changed the subject. 'I'm hungry. Any food in this house?'

Moving on to his elbow, he looked down at her: 'You're not getting out of my bed that easily.'

With arched eyebrow she asked, 'And you've never left someone's bed quietly to avoid any fuss?'

He started to get up, and was pulling on a robe as he said to her: 'But you hurt my pride.'

He looked shamefaced when he came back. 'I was about to astound you with my cuisine, but all the fridge will yield is one egg and an ancient lettuce. There's a delicatessen on the corner that's still open. Don't move!'

When the door had closed she went into the other room, intending to set the table for two.

Going up two steps to the dining area, she noticed his typewriter sitting on the desk in the corner. Every bit of its surface was covered with election stickers, many from American Presidential campaigns.

His notebook lay on the desk.

Her name was at the top of the open page:
Documentary: Ann Clarke.

Transmission: to be decided.

She let out a low whistle. Obviously the BBC were doing a major investigation of her, and Michael was to do the digging.

Everything was going to plan, but with a bonus no one could have planned – a reporter who was becoming sexually obsessed with her.

Going back to the bedroom, she quickly undressed again, and pulled on his robe. Finding her bag she sprayed herself and the robe with perfume.

In the living room she draped herself on a chair, arranging the robe so that it gave a tantalizing glimpse of flesh.

She was barely settled when the door opened, and he came in. She looked hard at him.

He dropped his bags and came over to her, pulling off his clothes on the way.

The sunset stained the sea orange, and the hills of Arran, in varying shades of grey, seemed etched against the sky. The huge Hunterston nuclear power station seemed abandoned, but the few hundred people who worked nights were settling inside for their shift.

In the security lodge two guards made supper. Bloody slow, the night shift, no deliveries or visitors; it was rare too for someone to leave the plant – no place to go. One made toast as the other brewed up. Engrossed, they never saw the four black-clad figures crawl on their bellies past the lodge and under the barrier. No windows at the back, so they couldn't see the four running figures make for the shelter of the administration block. Here they removed their overalls to reveal the uniform of a private firm working in the plant, giving an estimate of the cost of a new, tighter security system.

Two of the men clutched clipboards, one a stopwatch. The fourth carried a long sports bag hoisted over his shoulder, obviously very heavy. Not a soul passed them as they made their way to the control block. In any case, they had nothing to fear from a casual encounter – the security review had been going on for weeks and no one thought anything of new faces in the middle of the holiday season.

Without obstacle they entered the control block. Once inside, the man with the sports bag got down on his knees and quickly assembled two sub-machine guns. He passed one to the leader – a tall muscular man with a scar on his face running from the corner of his mouth to his chin. A silent signal passed among them, and the door entry buzzer was pressed. One of them stood under the video camera and held up a badge. After a moment, the door bleeped then clicked open.

None of the three technicians even looked up as the armed group silently entered the room. The only sound was the gentle whir of the high-tech equipment, punctuated by the occasional bleep.

The oldest of the three engineers looked up – a man in his fifties with an open-necked cotton shirt and light blue summer trousers. 'Jesus!' His two younger colleagues gasped. For a long second the room seemed suspended, then suddenly the older man dived for the main control switch. As he did so, a burst of machine-gun fire ended the silence, and his body was thrown up into the air, blood and brains spraying over the computers and the stench of death immediately filling the room.

No emotion was shown by the three invaders, but terror suffused the faces of the two remaining technicians. Slowly, a wet stain grew on the front of the trousers of the youngest; he whimpered. The leader prodded him in the ribs with his machine gun, directing him over to the control console. The man edged past his dead colleague, afraid to touch the body, avoiding looking down.

'Switch it off!'

The engineer hesitated, but a savage poke in the stomach with the gun muzzle convinced him. He pulled the central red lever, and a piercing siren filled the air, fading after a second inside but still penetrating the sound-proofing from outside. The huge power plant shut down; the reactor rods retracted to safety. The dead engineer had been trying to do that when he had been shot. His death had been for no reason other than to show that the invaders were serious – his killers had no intention of letting the plant continue to operate.

Simultaneous with the sirens, steel shields had closed across the doors in the control room, making it safe from invasion – bolting the stable door as it were. The gunmen forced the two technicians into a corner and tied them together. Silence descended, no longer broken by the electronic chatter of the computers.

From the capacious sports bag one of the men coupled electronic equipment to the phone network, an entire communications system. A second joined him, the third man guarded the hostages, and the fourth carefully checked the computer, looking for signs that some kind of override had been used to keep the plant contributing to the grid. His checks completed, the man smiled.

The night editor in the *Daily Record* stretched in satisfaction; the last edition of the paper under way, he could relax. When it came off the presses he would be able to go to bed; the only decision left was – whose bed?

As he headed for the coffee machine the phone rang. He almost ignored it – at this hour only cranks came out of the wookwork; anyway, only for something really major would he hold the paper now. The newsman in him won: he picked up the phone – and jer：.ed. 'Hold on! Hold on! A pencil.'

He took down whatever was being said to him. When he put the phone down he reflected for a second or two, then he left his seat and ran yelling down the newsroom, forgetting new technology in favour of the need to feel he was actually doing something to stop the presses. The little huddle of exhausted journalists round the coffee machine suddenly broke up, tiredness forgotten as the adrenaline surged to meet the needs of a late story.

The news editor started yelling out facts, pointing to people to check on different parts of them. 'The Workers' Militia have occupied Hunterston. It's gone off the grid.

It's no longer supplying fifteen per cent of the country's electricity. And it's nuclear!'

He wanted a check done on every power station in the country. Was this a concerted attack on the nation's source of electricity? The country would grind to a halt – the miners had proved that in the seventies, and everyone had been confident they had been so weakened that would never happen again. But the miners had shown how a Government could be brought down. It built and built until he screamed: 'Get the political editor in. Get the editor. Get the publisher. This could be a world exclusive . . . This could be a coup!'

Facts began to emerge: one engineer dead, he didn't do as he was told. More could follow. The plant to be completely evacuated. Radioactive material had been removed under cover. It could be abandoned in Central London if demands were not met. Details of these demands to be revealed in due course. Now the English could get a dose of what it was like to be a nuclear dustbin. Generations would pass before they would know how many cancer deaths the radiation would cause. Scots lived with this every day of their lives.

The managing director of the British Electricity Company had begun the climb to orgasm after long and delicious foreplay. The phone jarred. Fingers removed from the blonde curls of the beautiful girl with the flicking, ecstatic tongue. Voice shaky, one hand still trapping the lover's head below. But the telephone made Audrey Cavendish jump up, her knee catching the chin of the younger woman, who, bewildered, watched her companion throw on clothes. Was she going to be paid? She would still have to pay her twenty-five per cent commission to the escort agency. Her eyes scanned the elegant Barbican flat looking for something to take in lieu of payment, but the woman took out a pigskin wallet and removed a pile of ten-pound notes.

'Darling, leave me your telephone number.'

The Incident Team grew restless waiting for the Prime Minister to join them. All had been dragged from their beds, red-alerted to Number Ten, and all had arrived inside half an hour. The Prime Minister only had to come downstairs and still he kept them waiting. With so many dummy runs behind them to bring together this special team, the men round the table now looked at one another in some doubt. Was this a real incident – or just to show the Prime Minister how the system worked? The doubt evaporated when a tense woman was ushered into the room, instantly recognizable to the team. Ms Cavendish had made quite a mark as the managing director of the largest privately owned power-generating company in the country. A very tough lady, they said – therefore her worried look said something had to be seriously wrong. Before they could quiz her, the Prime Minister arrived, elegantly dressed, clean shaven, but with red-rimmed eyes and trembling hands.

The Principal Private Secretary made the introductions, pointing out that the procedures for major incidents had been set up many years before but constantly updated. This group could expect to be called out six times a year, though real incidents rarely occurred. When he got to Ms Cavendish, the Private Secretary indicated that she should sit at the end of the table; even the seating plan had been prearranged.

Five men and one woman gathered round the coffin–shaped Cabinet table opposite the Prime Minister and his staff, the blotters in front of them bare, except for the file before the Metropolitan Police Commissioner. This contained full, updated details of every key individual identified as a potential threat to the State. A further hefty dossier lay on the floor beside the Private Secretary's chair – the file to which he would refer if the Prime Minister chose a course of action less favourable to Civil Service wishes.

The Metropolitan Commissioner, like the three service chiefs and the SAS officer present, had come through to Downing Street from the Cabinet Office in Whitehall in case subversives had mounted a watch on Number Ten. As the Prime Minister settled himself everyone watched him, silently waiting for him to start the meeting. Suddenly he took charge, turning towards Ms Cavendish and Commander Davies of the SAS. He seemed to have no interest in any of the others. To Cavendish he spoke first, anxious for an outline and an evaluation.

She ran through the facts as she knew them – nuclear power station occupied by unknown terrorists, the supply cut off, one engineer killed.

Metcalf asked aggressively: 'What kind of security do you have in these places? How come someone can just walk in?'

Not waiting, he turned to the civil servant: 'Contingency plans for evacuating parts of Britain in the event of a nuclear incident. What are they? Where do we put people, and for how long? Do we evacuate the whole of the West of Scotland? Tell us the truth, just how serious is this? What are the potential fatalities?'

Audrey Cavendish sighed, inflating her bosom, running fingers through her thick hennaed hair, and answered for the Prime Minister's aide: 'Depends where you're coming from. It is very serious for my company because the only way we can supply our customers is by selling them much more expensive electricity. Devastating for our revenue. We also don't know if any damage was done to the plant when it was taken over – and that, as much as anything else, will ultimately determine when we are likely to be back on the grid again.'

Metcalf's face turned scarlet. 'Bugger your company – and your profits. In case you hadn't noticed, there's been a change of Government. No more profits before public safety. What's the nuclear risk?'

'Prime Minister, there is no risk. We know that within minutes of the invasion, the plant was shut down and the rods from the reactor retracted.'

The men in the room looked at one another. What the hell was all the fuss about if it was just a normal siege that would be ended eventually? Screed upon screed of contingency plan existed for something like that.

'But what about the contamination of Central London?'

Despite her better efforts, the executive looked annoyed. A physicist, she was fed up with the hysteria among Labour politicians about things nuclear. They had been getting in her hair for years.

'The only radioactive material they could possibly have is something so low level as to be totally harmless – something like a pair of gloves. You've more risk of contamination sitting next to someone getting treatment for thyroid trouble. For them to have anything higher grade than that would have involved such a complicated transport operation, we'd have known about it. The only way a nuclear installation is of any use to terrorists is when they can get their hands on the kind of technology only governments have access to. So if you are confident we haven't been invaded by the Russians, you can stop worrying about another Chernobyl!'

Metcalf was silent for a while, thinking this over. He was suspicious enough not to believe the woman, but if the scientist was telling the truth – and what she said could be checked – then his Government had only a minor crisis to resolve, rather than the very serious one he had anticipated. His face relaxed.

Seeing the change in the Prime Minister's expression, Commander Davies spoke up. A tall man whose uniform gave him great presence, he had a voice with the kind of quiet authority of someone who is totally confident that what he says is accurate and will be acted upon. He dominated the room:

'Don't let's relax too quickly. The threat here isn't the risk of nuclear contamination. It's hysteria. Once word gets out that there's a nuclear risk in Central London, we could have an uncontrollable situation on our hands. Think, sir, of your own worries about a major nuclear accident – everyone in this room, with the possible exception of Ms Cavendish, shared it – and multiply it by millions. People just do not believe that the nuclear process is safe.'

The Police Commissioner nodded, agreeing. 'We have to stop word of this getting out!'

At that, Graeme Jones came in: 'Too late for that! The papers all have it and the BBC have been on asking for the Prime Minister to go on Breakfast TV.'

Depression fell like a pall. Everyone looked to the Prime Minister for an indication of how he was going to handle it – he seemed to be in a daze.

Cavendish looked over at Commander Davies; a frisson of dislike hung between them, but each recognized that the other had a true grasp of what was happening, and its significance. The soldier was looking at the Prime Minister, hiding the exasperation in his eyes at the indecision of the man. The Private Secretary shuffled through his file, presumably looking for an entry marked 'hysteria'. The Police Commissioner began to spread out a map of Central London on the table.

Cavendish spoke up: 'Sir, I think you should go on TV to reassure people that the threat is a minimal one. After all, you're known as one of the arch opponents of nuclear power. We could put together a little presentation that explains the kind of nuclear material they're likely to have and contrast it with luminous watches, granite, X-rays, all that kind of thing. It is important that people are reassured. One of the trendy science presenters could front it.'

Metcalf clutched at the straw being handed him. He nodded. Without warning, he got up and left the room. A way out had been shown, he didn't need the meeting any longer.

Six more people now knew that Britain had an ineffectual Prime Minister. Six key people.

Michael Stewart could not get enough of Ann – nor she him. Words became unnecessary; they spoke in the exquisite language of skin against skin.

They slept for a little, and as he, intent on waking her,

flicked his tongue across her groin in tiny butterfly kisses, the phone rang.

Seconds later he shook her, motioning her to listen in; she pressed her ear as close as she could to his. Together they learned about Hunterston and as they hurriedly dressed, Ann agreed to be interviewed on the network breakfast programme – in case, as she put it, Metcalf said something that needed contradiction.

She went home and while changing telephoned Harry McGregor, telling him of the television appearance. Circumspect on the telephone, she spoke angrily of the death of the engineer, whose body, said the car radio, had just been thrown out of the control centre.

Then, as she sat in the Glasgow studio, Metcalf in London gave a vintage performance. Calming, reassuring, his charisma given full relaxed reign. He dismissed attempts to get him to admit he was changing his views on the nuclear industry out of mere expediency with a very sober reply saying that he had consulted the country's greatest experts and he was convinced by their reassurances:

'If the greatest sceptic can be convinced, then I don't think anyone needs to be concerned.'

His interview was followed by a detailed explanation of all the different kinds of nuclear waste, measurements were taken from common household items. From a previous science programme a Scottish reporter was seen with a geiger counter going down Aberdeen's Union Street, the white granite buildings sparkling in the sunlight, the meter readings going off the scale.

In Glasgow, Stewart looked over at Ann Clarke, miked up and ready to go, her presence not revealed to Metcalf, no decision yet taken as to whether she should be used. In his earpiece Stewart could hear the debate going on between the gallery in Glasgow and the programme's producer in London. Was she likely to say something that would give another dimension to the story? Stewart's view was sought – he looked straight to camera and nodded.

Stewart turned to the woman who had raked her fingers in passion down his back a few hours before:

'Well, Miss Clarke?'

With a wry smile, Ann responded: 'Fine, if you can believe him, but this is a man in office only days, who has already sold out his principles. Despite being the architect of party elections to Cabinet and Shadow Cabinet posts, he has been trying since election night to bribe me to join the Cabinet without an election.' She turned it on, Stewart gave her room.

'A couple of days in office and he's prepared to turn tail on everything he claimed to have believed in. How can you believe a man who only last weekend devoted a speech to describing in graphic detail the horrific consequences of a nuclear accident – and a week later claims everything is hunky-dory? I'll tell you this, I wouldn't be travelling in the London tube today. What if radioactive material has been planted in London?' She let the question hang. Suddenly the picture on the screen changed to a furious Tony Metcalf getting out of his seat in the London studio, yelling obscenities at the camera, knocking over the coffee table in front of him. A Tony Metcalf totally out of control, a side of him carefully concealed until now.

The picture went to blank as the mandarins' nerve failed.

Detective Superintendent Hamish McLean paced up and down the corridor outside the Chief Constable's office. Like a Guardsman, he swivelled on the balls of his feet with every turn. In the corner, his partner Frank Ryan rapped out a tattoo on the chair arm with the fingers of his left hand. Irritated glares came from the grey-haired secretary who presided over the entrance to the Chief's domain. Her annoyance almost spilled over when McLean bent over her desk to verify that the light still glowed on the switchboard, proving the phone call hadn't ended. As the light went out, secretary and police officer simultaneously jumped for the door, the grey-haired woman getting the edge on the equally grey-haired but pot-bellied man. A major confrontation was avoided when the door was thrown open and a scowling Chief Constable Alexander Morton bawled 'In!' to the two officers.

Plans of Hunterston littered the mahogany-panelled office. Detailed maps of Ayrshire covered every chair, fighting for prominence with charts of anticipated aircraft traffic from the international airport at Prestwick.

The pent-up frustration of Scotland's senior police officer burst to the surface as he bent down and brushed his arm across the desk, dumping everything it contained on the floor.

The subordinates remained standing to attention, their eyes fixed on the middle distance. Ryan tried to hold in his belly, McLean was past such vanity.

Morton looked at them then turned his back. He paced the room, stood at the window, then spoke, his voice clipped, professional and furious. 'The Carol Copeland case is closed.' He slapped his hands together. 'There never was a prostitute called Carol Copeland, d'ye hear? There was no murder. There was no red Ford Granada seen in Waterloo Street. There will be no inquiries about the whereabouts of certain . . .' He paused, turned to them. 'The files are to be destroyed. Do I make myself clear?'

When the full implication of what he had said sank in, the two officers half-yelled, 'But sir . . . !'

'Shut up. Anyone who wants to contradict that order can have their resignation on my desk in fifteen minutes.'

Red flowed into the bull neck of Detective Superintendent McLean as he opened his mouth.

The Chief got in first: 'Back to work. I've got a siege to handle. And no one is to be told of this conversation. Right?' He grabbed a file, turned to a map of Hunterston. Ryan turned to go, but McLean remained standing. The Chief Constable looked up. Ryan went, closing the door.

'Does it have to be in writing? The resignation, sir . . ?'

Morton got up and checked, then locked the door. He opened a cupboard with a key from his belt and took out a bottle of whisky, handed a tumblerful to McLean, poured another, then settled himself in one of the two huge chairs. McLean, unbidden, also sat.

'Not long till your pension, Hamish?'

'Not long.'

He drank, the Chief sighed.

'Wish I could say the same! You've no idea what it's been like. The pressure. Some of the orders from on high just don't make any sense.' McLean did not react.

'Look, Hamish. We *know* who murdered that girl. But I've been told there are to be no more inquiries. And in case I decided to turn a blind eye to my orders – I've been told there is to be no more police overtime. So – I don't have enough men to do normal duties, plus stop the scum who call themselves Workers' Militia, and investigate the Copeland case. What puzzles me – these orders are coming from the highest possible level.'

Both men sat silent for a moment. When Morton spoke again, he sounded weary: 'You're sure you feel strongly enough to throw up your career?'

'Oh I feel strongly all right! I had to look at that poor kid's body, remember. You've a daughter the same age. So have I.'

Morton stared into his whisky as he spoke: 'As of now, you're off the force.'

McLean drained his glass and stood up to go. 'Do you mind,' he asked, 'what I do about it?'

'You mean – freelance? I'll help if you want to go solo – but discreetly. OK?' Only then did McLean offer a handshake – the familiar Masonic one. The Chief looked bemused – that was usually used when you joined the force, not when you gave it up.

A telex chattered outside as Graeme Jones worked his way through the pile of correspondence the Prime Minister would sign. Absently getting up from the desk, he went out to rip the message from the machine. His attention focused quickly when he read it. Turning on his heel, he went through his own office, into the Prime Minister's study, tossed the flimsy paper on the desk and watched as Tony Metcalf read it.

The PM scanned the paper twice and looked up, smirking and cold: 'What does she take us for? We'd be mad to let her anywhere near Hunterston. Tell her to get lost!'

Jones threw himself down on a chair. 'Think again, Tony, she's counting on you reacting like that. She has no intention of putting herself at risk. Call her bluff, and if she goes ahead, then, when she's cooped up at Hunterston, we've got a breathing space to make some progress with the Americans.'

Metcalf threw up his hands in horror. 'Have you gone mad? If she succeeds in getting the siege ended, then we're all finished.'

The aide interrupted: 'No, no, no! If she wins them round then we can accuse her of complicity with the terrorists. It's a great chance to really stitch her up. And if she doesn't pull it off, then she's a failure.' His knuckles were white as he held his fists tight, so determined was he to convince Metcalf to follow his advice.

'And if she's killed . . . ?'

'Dead martyrs we can cope with. Living challengers are harder. She'd leave the Militias leaderless. Think of that!'

The Prime Minister began to pace the room, obviously hesitating. Jones allowed him his silence, then he spoke.

'If you don't trust my judgement, talk to Jeffries.' He nodded towards the telephone. Metcalf hit the pre-set button, and in seconds the Foreign Secretary had got the gist of the dilemma. His booming voice on the broadcast telephone filled the room.

'Go for it, Tony! This is the bit of luck we've been waiting for.'

Metcalf nodded and gave his agreement. His two most trusted advisors had told him what to do, he no longer needed to make a decision.

Jones went back to the outer office to instruct the civil servants, a definite spring in his step.

'Ms Clarke has put out a statement offering herself as a hostage or mediator at Hunterston. She's made a plea for calm so that there is no further loss of life. Tell Commander Davies that the PM has said she is to be taken up on the offer, but that he is to do nothing until he has consulted us. Oh, and you might as well put out a statement saying the PM welcomes the ready way Ann Clarke acceded to his request!'

The fast official drivers, using escorts, can get from RAF Northolt to Whitehall in half an hour. The Prime Minister's Private Secretary stood in the Cabinet Office, waiting to escort Commander Davies through the private route to Downing Street. The posse of journalists outside Number Ten had doubled.

Audrey Cavendish, with a strong scent of Mystère de Rochas, was already with the Prime Minister when the officer was shown into the study.

Ms Cavendish looked up as he came in, but bowed her henna-coloured head back to the plans. The Prime Minister followed her finger across all the vulnerable parts of the plant, and listened to her theory that the control block housing the terrorists might yield to a seaborne assault.

Eventually Davies waited no more: 'Prime Minister, there is no need for an expensive and dramatic military intervention. If we sit quietly and wear them down, the terrorists will come walking out in time to maximize the publicity for this Loch Lomond rally the unions have called for to condemn the Americans. From experience we feel the safest thing to do is to play them along.'

Before Metcalf could reply, Cavendish jumped in: 'Nonsense! We can't allow these people to disrupt the business life of this country. At the end of the day, my shareholders aren't going to be too impressed with a Government that takes the easy way out when their pockets are suffering. And don't forget, Prime Minister, many of my shareholders are ordinary people who bought into the company when it was privatized.'

Davies began to speak, but the Prime Minister silenced

him with a raised hand: 'Miss Cavendish is perfectly correct. The siege must be ended.'

'But Prime Minister, consider the consequences . . .'

Metcalf's face was growing red. 'Are you challenging me, Davies?'

The soldier sighed. 'No, Prime Minister.' And then, to salvage something from the exchange: 'Do I have your permission to plan the "liberation" of the station in my own way, sir?'

'Up to a point, Commander, up to a point. Whatever you do, make sure it's good television. You know the Iranian Embassy siege years ago, that sort of stuff. Good bit of publicity for you, eh?'

Davies looked horrified: 'But I could lose men, sir.'

Metcalf spoke as if to a deranged child: 'Commander Davies. I would have thought that you of all people would have been aware of the extent to which the people of this country have been shaken by the events of the past few days. They have to be convinced that there are no lengths to which their Government, their Prime Minister, will not go to safeguard them. They've lived through months of periodic violence and terrorism with a Government that was only prepared to lock them up in their houses at night and disturb them with security checks. We're going to show that we are not afraid to act.'

The soldier asked to be excused, 'a lot of planning to do'.

Metcalf called him back.

'I think you should use Ms Clarke in some way in the liberation.'

Surprise ringing in his voice, Davies said: 'That could be very dangerous, sir. I couldn't guarantee her safety as a civilian.'

Metcalf was smiling as he said: 'Of course. I understand, Davies. I will not hold you responsible if something goes wrong. But I want her used! You may go.'

Just before six the phone rang from Hunterston itself. 'Commander Davies. You *are* serious?'

Quick and alert, she said she was.

She showered then grabbed trousers and a sweater, a larger than usual handbag, with toothbrush and some toiletries as well as a notepad and books.

Less than an hour after she left her Glasgow house, her car stopped at the main gate of the Ayrshire power station a little past seven-thirty. The press encampment had retained a grumbling life all night, and Ann's unheralded arrival brought back the sense of excitement that had abated through the long cold night.

Her timing, as ever, was impeccable – the radio and television reporters began to update live into their bulletins. In homes all over the country, the nation left breakfasts and baths to see the unfolding drama. Police swarmed round Ann's car, ordered to make sure that she should not speak to the press. Ann insisted on going over to talk to the reporters. A Chief Inspector urged her not to, giving terrific pictures to a press now hooked on the idea of a cover-up.

Ann won. She walked away from the police officers and over to the barrier. The shouted questions were incoherent. She stood silent until the reporters caught on that she wasn't going to be part of a rabble. By some unspoken decision, an elderly reporter from the Press Association got to ask her the simple question – what was she doing at the plant?

'The Prime Minister has suggested I might be of some assistance. There could be negotiations, I don't know. There isn't much more I can tell you, other than my determination to see this thing over and done with as quickly and as peacefully as possible.'

She turned to walk away.

A reporter shouted after her: 'Are you going into the plant?'

She stopped. 'That's up to whoever is in charge here. If they want me to go in then I will.'

She made to move away. Before she was out of earshot, a woman reporter called above the hubbub: 'Miss Clarke, are you scared?'

Again Ann paused. 'What do you think?'

The woman noticed the puffiness, the signs of sleeplessness around the normally cleverly made up eyes.

Davies had made a detailed study of Ann Clarke's files. Nevertheless, her power when he walked into the makeshift conference room startled him. She stood at the window, looking out on to the complex. She hadn't heard him come in, giving him a moment to appraise her. In navy sweater and trousers she stood in clear relief against the window, tall and slim, though certainly not boyish. Davies greeted her. She turned round.

Each weighed up the other. Davies' eyes were hypnotic, light blue, piercing, with an inner light, in a deeply tanned face – cruel eyes, but exciting too. He had large and blunt hands, the nails cut short, a thick down of blond hair on the backs. He followed her eyes, looking down at his hands, and slowly looked up again, holding her glance.

WIth a brisk knock a corporal brought in a tray with two cups of coffee, and the moment passed.

'Miss Clarke, I'm Commander Davies. I spoke to you on the phone this morning.' He gestured to her to sit down opposite him at the scratched and battered table. Pulling out one of the green camouflage chairs, she accepted the coffee mug. 'We don't know if we can use you, or if it would be safe to use you, but I wanted you here just in case. We know they are prepared to talk to you, but they say you must come into the plant alone before they'll do that. It may come to that, and you could end up a hostage. The decision to go in will ultimately be your own, and you will have to take the responsibility for the consequences yourself. We know who these people are, and they're dangerous.'

Her eyes widened in surprise at that, no mention even hint of identity had come across in the media reports.

'Who are they, Commander?'

'Their leader is a man called Peter Shaw – a Scot from Aberdeen who got used to the big money on the oil rigs. It wasn't exciting enough for him though, so he went abroad. Turned up in Angola, via West Germany where he had some dubious contacts. He became a mercenary. He came back to Scotland about six months ago and began recruiting a terrorist force from the cream of the finishing schools of Peterhead prison and the IRA. He's been behind some of the big raids recently. Organized the attempted kidnapping of Prince Harry, we only stopped that because one of Shaw's accomplices lost his bottle. His body was found in a burnt-out car a month later. Shaw won't do anything rash, and we know he has a crack squad with him this time, all highly disciplined. We don't expect him to make any mistakes.'

Ann reflected on his words. 'If he's so clever,' she asked, 'how is he going to get out of here? If he's taken alive, he'll be in prison for a long time.'

Davies laughed, as if at the silliness of a child.

'Because, Miss Clarke, someone is paying him a lot of money to have a spell in prison.'

'But where has the money come from?'

He looked hard at her, then away before he responded: 'You tell me, Miss Clarke, you tell me.'

He stood, picking up his coffee mug, and walked towards the door. 'When we have something to tell you, I'll come back. It could be a long wait.'

She stood up. 'I've brought some work with me.'

Just before he opened the door, he seemed about to speak but changed his mind.

At Oxford Street tube station no one knew how the panic spread. At first it was thought that a bomb had been found; others rumoured a fire. One man told of a guard getting on the train and shouting that someone had planted radioactive material on the London tube. Within seconds, fear engulfed the tube station, and as people rushed to get out the weakest were trampled to the ground, some pushed on to the track in front of incoming trains. The pictures from the disaster were graphic, uncensored because of the speed of their transmission: TV companies had been able, within minutes, to get their most up-to-date equipment on site to beam the scenes of carnage into homes throughout the world.

When the news reached Number Ten, Metcalf and his aides unanimously decided that he should go to the scene. By the time they arrived the rescue workers were lined up outside the station. Seeing the lights of the television crews, some youths had gathered. Inflamed by bravado, they pushed forward. As the Metcalfs moved along the line, the young people started to chant:

'Metcalf is mental! Metcalf is mental! Out with the bastard! Out with the bastard!'

Their cruel jibes could be clearly heard as they were hustled away by the police. Sylvia Metcalf noticed the embarrassment of the men and women she and Tony had come to thank. None looked them in the eye. A thin pall of unrest hung over the exhausted but still well-disciplined group – a silent recognition that the hecklers had a point.

At the Middlesex Hospital the Chief Nursing Officer and the hospital administrator met them on the pavement and escorted them round the wards where the injured were being cared for. At the last bed they visited, the young man in traction, his arms plastered and his ribs taped up, moved his head to the side and shut his eyes as the Prime Minister approached the bed. In a stage whisper the doctor in charge of the case mentioned the shock all his patients were in, and not to take their reactions too seriously. When the young man heard this, he opened his eyes, and turned to stare at Metcalf. His voice filled with contempt, he said:

'I wouldn't be here just now if you weren't so stupid! Christ, you've only been Prime Minister a couple of days and the country's in a worse state than it ever was. Pack it in now before something worse happens. You're not up to the job.'

Metcalf was hustled away, but as he approached the next bed a gob of spittle, well aimed, hit his jacket. The one photographer allowed to follow the Prime Minister's progress got the shot and managed to run like hell, fast enough to escape the security men trying to grab his camera.

Time passed very slowly for Ann. She tried to keep her attention on the reports she had brought to read, occasionally jotting down a few notes. Her eyes kept straying to the window. She paced the little room.

Meals had come in with great regularity, the only activity, and each time she asked what was happening, but learned nothing. She asked if she could go out for a walk, but that, referred to a higher authority, had been turned down. She asked to see Davies, but was told he would get back to her whenever he was free.

Eventually she could stand it no more. She pulled open the door with considerable force, marched down the corridor, irritation obvious in every sinew, and at the end of the corridor a sergeant sprang to attention.

'Can I help you, ma'am?'

Ann pulled herself up straight, matching the soldier inch for inch, and outweighing even his carefully developed aura of authority.

'The commanding officer, please. I've had enough of being kept prisoner.' A sound from behind interrupted her and she spun round. Davies stood there, the smell of fresh air reaching her from his clothes.

'I'm sorry, Miss Clarke. I've not been able to get back to you, but we've had a lot of planning to do today. We're just about finished and I was going to come to see you in about half an hour. If you can bear with me until then, I'll be able to fill you in.'

He smiled, suddenly transforming his face and looking much younger. 'We've both got a lot riding on this, so it's best to get it right, OK?'

Ann was mollified: 'OK, another half hour it is then. Are you going to use me?'

His face became serious again. 'If you agree, once I have outlined the plan, then we'll use you.' He didn't look her in the eye.

Back in the little room she had come to think of as a

cell, she again began to pace up and down, this time deep in thought. She jumped when the door opened and Davies came in. He held up a bottle of whisky and a couple of paper cups, his face a mute inquiry. She nodded.

She sat down at the table, gathering up the work she had been trying to concentrate on, he sat opposite and passed her the cup of whisky. Each concentrated on their drink, avoiding looking directly at the other, the tension of the morning still faintly tangible.

Davies looked her straight in the eye, fixing her gaze.

'Anything you do here, Miss Clarke, has to be your own choice. You have to weigh up the pros and cons of what I'm going to ask of you, and if you decide the risks are too great, then you must say so.'

She gestured to him to continue, her face serious, her drink forgotten.

'I've spent the day working out a very detailed plan. We know every blade of grass in this place now, and we know these men are no fools. There is only one possible way we can invade the plant, and that's from the sea. It's their only blind spot, and they know that all the safety devices in the control block make it a virtually impregnable fortress. That's why they were so careful about getting inside and set up before the alarm activated the security cordon. The only chance we've got is if we can get them to open the door. That's where you come in. We want to use you to create a diversion so that we can get the doors open, and once that happens we'll storm them. I've got a trained squad all ready to move round the coast, they can scale the outer wall and be ready for you doing your stuff. But there could be shooting, and all we could do is give you some basic advice on keeping out of the way of the bullets. We couldn't guarantee your safety.'

She ran her fingers through her hair, obviously analysing the meaning of what he had said. 'When would you do this?'

'At dusk, in about an hour. My men are ready, as soon as it's dark enough from them to be undetected we'll bring them round the cove. There's always the chance there are lookouts posted. But we're pretty sure there are no more than four of them inside, maybe less.'

Again she paused. 'Publicity?'

A cloud came over his face and his voice was cold as he replied: 'I suppose you politicians always have to think of that! Yes, we'll have cameras at the back and the front. We could even make a virtue of showing you walking into the plant, we know there's a television in there – they could see you were completely unaccompanied and unarmed. What do you think?'

She led him in detail through his plans, asking questions and in a very businesslike way ensuring he had every angle covered.

'Why would they agree to open up for me?'

He raised an eyebrow. 'Can you think of a better hostage?'

Her answering smile was without humour. She again began to pace, he respected her silence. Then she looked at him and nodded. She would do it. He stood up, concern on his face, but said nothing, merely put his hand on the door handle, ready to go to finalize the arrangements and to convince the terrorists to speak with her. She asked to speak to them first on the phone, he refused.

'No, there would be no hope of getting you to them if they could speak to you on the phone. The line we'll use is that you are offering yourself as a hostage in return for information about the whereabouts of the nuclear material. Is that OK?'

She nodded again, preoccupied. He turned to her, his voice suddenly gentle:

'You can call it off right up to the last minute, you know. You'll be taking a hell of a risk. My men are paid to take risks, you're not.'

Her response was a perky: 'You want a bet?'

The networks broke into their schedules. Television arc lights lit the front of the building as she began the long slow walk into the plant. The country watched in suspended animation as the beautiful young politician took what could be her last journey. In the closing light of day the orange sunset made the atmosphere surreal – the sea to her right was calm, the sunset reflected in it, and mirrored again in the windows of the power plant's office block to her left. In the distance, the hills of Arran, dominated by Goat Fell.

To cover the seven minutes the carefully paced walk was expected to take, commentary being beamed throughout the world concentrated on a résumé of her career. It would have been impressive for a politician many years her senior, but for one so young and so attractive, it was even more remarkable. Lawyer, MP, the politician who had, almost single-handedly, changed the direction of her Party. In ten years in Parliament she had emerged as a passionate defender of her country, on occasion at considerable risk to herself. Now, in the midst of the greatest political battle of her career, she was prepared to sacrifice it all – perhaps even life itself – to save people she had never met.

As she neared the control block the silence became complete. The cameras focused on her face, white and tense, her eyes huge with fear, making her all the more human and vulnerable. Not some mindless heroine, but one with a very real idea of what could go wrong. And then she turned towards the door, the stiff set of her shoulders the only clue to her feelings as millions realized they may have seen her face for the last time.

The arrangement with the invaders was that the door would be opened as she approached the outside of the block. They could plot her progress on television. Everyone watching, not least Davies, had a sharp intake of breath as very slowly, the door opened. The gun microphones had now lost their range, and as Ann had refused to be miked up, in case she was taken hostage and had to prove she wasn't some kind of Trojan horse, the sound became untransmittable. The cameras picked up a faint hesitation in her walk, then she seemed to pull back her shoulders and go on. No one could be seen inside the plant, but it now looked certain that she was going to succeed in talking to them.

Ann started to call out to them as clearly and distinctly as she could without shouting, trusting to the inadequacy of the microphones:

'Listen to me. I'm a friend, I know who set this up. I also know that there is a crack SAS squad coming round the building now. They'll shoot all of us, me as well. Walk out with me now and they can't shoot. It would be seen as murder all round the world. Come out now and we've won.'

There was no response to her words, and she was getting closer and closer to the door.

'If you do as I ask, each one of you will get an extra £100,000 into your account in Dublin. And you'll be alive to enjoy it. Your sentence won't be that long, we can do something about that. We can make you into heroes, insist you are treated as political prisoners. Please!'

She thought she had failed. She stopped walking. The viewers wondered if she might turn and run. But then they saw her move again. No one but she could hear the muted voice from inside the building. She whispered a word – just one – only the men inside heard her.

The door opened wider and she saw a figure start to come out – black in the shadows, but as he emerged she could see the strange yellow eyes, and the scar twisting his face – Peter Shaw, the leader. She threw both arms in the air, frantically waving her lace handkerchief in the air. She turned round and began walking back to the perimeter fence, her arms still above her head, unmistakably signalling surrender, a mixture of fear and elation in her face as she came into camera shot – not daring to look back to see if the men were behind her. The cameramen zoomed past her to pick up the straggling band of men leaving the building.

A cheer went up from the press encampment as it became clear what was happening, especially at the sight of the terrorists solicitously helping their hostages back to the real world. In the BBC outside broadcast van, Clare

Edmonds reached out and held on to the hand of Michael Stewart, the sinews in his neck stiff and prominent as he watched Ann's gradually more triumphal progress, his eyes on the monitor holding her in close-up, watching the fear in her face give way to joy, then relief.

Then even his eyes could not resist the new pictures on the screen. TV companies had been offered an exclusive vantage point at the back of the building to record the dramatic storming of the plant by the SAS. No signal had been sent them to abort, so in the midst of hysterical joy at the peaceful ending of the siege, soldiers with blackened faces and armed to the teeth looked and sounded faintly ridiculous as they hit the building – in the face of the heroism of one young woman.

The director cut from bewildered soldiers to Ann Clarke, helped now by paramedics, her legs weakened by the relief coursing through her body; tears of joy pouring down her face strengthened the image. That was the picture for the morning's papers, and in pubs, clubs and private homes, the cheering had already started that would accompany her wherever she went for a long time to come – except in Downing Street.

4

Ann sat mesmerized in her study, watching for the umpteenth time the video of Hunterston. The remnants of the speech she had been working on were spewed around her. Startled by the sound of the doorbell, she wondered for a moment if she had heard it or if it was some subliminal sound on the screen. It rang again.

The two women stared at one another across the threshold. Ann, elegant and feminine in turquoise silk, Sylvia tailored in a navy jacket and scarlet dress. The Prime Minister's wife looked stern and determined – her eyes unsmiling, her chin held high, looking up at her taller one-time protégée. Standing aside, Ann made way for her to enter, gesturing to the main room.

Neither spoke until they stood facing one another in the middle of the room. The pleasantries forgotten, each knew this was a showdown anticipated for years. Each with a strong will, determined not to back down. Ann, power-hungry, who had chosen the path to power on her own, Sylvia the king-maker – neither could leave room for the other to flourish.

A clock ticked away the seconds, the traffic droned outside, the silent exchange continued.

Slowly, and with great emphasis, Sylvia scanned the tastefully furnished room – appraising. Her eyes came to rest on a Cadell original above the fireplace, with a value way beyond the entire Metcalf wealth.

'You've come a long way,' she said, conscious of the bitter tone even as she said it.

Ann never moved, not head, nor face nor expression. Then she lowered here head in silent acknowledgement, her expression unchanging.

Sylvia again, with more control, spoke: 'I've come here to ask you as a sensible, intelligent woman, why you have set out to destroy Tony, and the Government. I can't believe what you're doing. You've fought like the rest of us for a chance at government, and now you seem determined to destroy us! Why?'

The control began to slip. 'You're costing lives! Haven't you done enough?'

Ann turned her back, slowly moving to the window. Her silence infuriated Sylvia more:

'I can't believe you're the same girl we first met. We tried to give you warmth and comfort when you needed it, and now you're trying to destroy us. But I'll never let you. Tony is worth ten of you!'

As Ann turned to face her, the movement taking an eternity, she smiled. Smug and in command, Ann's very stillness lent her contempt greater impact. When she spoke, Sylvia had to strain to hear her, but every word was carefully, deliberately, spoken.

'What right do you have to come here? To invade my home to call me to account? What gives you the right to think you can lecture and moralize at me! You're little better than a whore, selling yourself to Tony Metcalf to get your hands on power even if it is at second hand. I'm a Member of Parliament. I've let the people decide if they want me. They know me – they know what I stand for, and every time I ask they give me more and more support. You're just the other half of a photograph, frightened that the world might find out about the inadequate you married to manipulate into Number Ten. Do not presume to judge me. And get out!'

Her face, transformed by venom, aged her. She walked to the room door and held it open for Sylvia to leave. But the older woman, shocked by the malevolence of the outburst, stood still, unable to move.

The impasse was broken by another ringing of the doorbell. As Ann eased the door open, automatically checking who was there, it was suddenly thrust from her hands, and a florid and very angry Stephen Robinson burst in. He grabbed Ann by the shoulders, shook her and yelled:

'You stupid, stupid woman! You're evil, really evil!'

Ann did not move – he took his hands from her shoulders. Sylvia, hearing the commotion and the familiar voice, rushed into the hall, grabbed Robinson by the arm and led him away.

'Sylvia, what are you doing here?'

'Much the same as you, so it would seem.'

Both looked at Ann. She looked back, an eyebrow raised, a slight smile, taking in the rapport between the MP and the Prime Minister's wife. Stephen's anger boiled up again:

'It's all a game to you! Look at the tube disaster. There are at least eighteen people dead because of you. And your Hunterston antics. Families are living in terror because of you. Young lives ruined. Who's backing you? What evil is behind it?'

She smiled, silent, inflaming him even further. He turned as if to grab hold of her again, but Sylvia stood between them, pushed him back and got him to the point of leaving, when suddenly he turned again to Ann who visibly stiffened, as if anticipating a blow. But this time his voice was soft:

'You're going to destroy yourself, Ann. I've watched you change over the years. You were always ambitious, but you're now so determined to get power it's become like an obsession. People will only take so much, and then it will all be over for you. They'll hate you yet.'

For a fraction of a second she looked as if he had got to her. Pain flickered across her eyes, but the vulnerability soon passed, and insolently she closed the door.

Her solitude restored, she leaned back against the door, her eyes closed. her sigh came from the depth of her being. Holding on to the wall for support, she made her way back to the study and threw herself down on the couch, drawing her knees up beneath her. As she lay there, huddled, the doorbell rang again, but she covered her ears with her hands, shutting out the painful sounds of the world. This time it was Mary, able to come in with her own key. The election agent was pale and haggard. She walked gingerly, conscious of the deep incision above her left breast. As she walked along the hall, she called out:

'It's me! I'm on my way back from the hospital. You know, I saw Stephen Robinson drive away with a woman I could have sworn was Sylvia Metcalf . . .' Her voice trailed away as she came into the room. She crossed the room swiftly, taking the shaking Ann into her arms, wincing involuntarily at the pain.

Feeling the unquestioning affection, Ann relaxed. Mary soothed her, cradling her as she herself had been cradled only a few nights before. Stroking her hair, Mary murmured:

'They don't understand. None of them understand. They should be here giving you all the help they can, not upsetting you like this. But no one said it would be easy. You're not an ordinary woman, you're a great woman. One day they'll see that!'

Sylvia and Stephen strolled through Royal Exchange Square, mutually subdued. They had left the art deco splendour of the Rogano Restaurant where they had dined on smoked salmon and crayfish, washed down with chablis. The indulgence helped them both to calm down after the confrontation with Ann Clarke. They had gone on to talk of happier things, stories of election campaigns long forgotten, bizarre candidates, journalists who almost got it right. They laughed together at apocryphal tales of the eccentricities of colleagues – politics in the good old days.

Inevitably, Ann Clarke reappeared in the conversation. She had played such a big part in their own political life that it was hard to leave her out of the reminiscences. Sylvia asked the question that had most troubled her:

'When do you think she turned against Tony? They were very close when she was a student.'

Stephen shrugged. 'I didn't know her in those days. But I don't think it's really Tony she's getting at. It's his job she wants. It's the logical extension of everything she's done so far. I sometimes feel she's playing a part but she's always got to be number one.' He looked down at Sylvia, and hesitated before he went on. 'Tony's changed too, don't you think? He doesn't seem to look as fit as he used to.'

They walked on in silence, through the streets with shop windows boarded up and the occasional personnel carrier roaring in the distance. The enormity of the problems Tony had to handle were inescapable. As they got to Stephen's car, she turned to him:

'What's the point of pretending? Tony isn't well. He's got a bit of a drink problem. It started when he hurt his back, the whisky would dull the pain. But now it's pressure. The more it builds, the worse his drinking gets. I keep trying to get him to stop, but he can't. I'm sure it will get better once everything settles down.'

Stephen looked embarrassed.

She sighed. 'But, if I'm honest with myself, a lot of it is just plain terror of taking the wrong decision, that's why he takes fewer and fewer. He's a historian, remember, he knows too much about what can happen when leaders get things wrong.'

In the glowing dusk she looked tired and very sad. 'Ann knows what he's really like. You can't be as intelligent as she is and not spot it. In fact when she was helping him in the Leadership election, she must have seen the start of it.'

She laughed bitterly. 'Isn't it ironic, if Ann hadn't run such a brilliant campaign to get Tony elected Leader of the Party, with all the American-style razzamataz, and the daily polls of the electoral college, and the deals struck, he'd never have won. Whyever did she do it?'

The MP shook his head: 'Maybe as a dummy run for herself, Sylvia. Now she knows what works in that kind of campaign, and what doesn't. And it does mean Tony owes her one.'

'You really think she's that devious?'

He nodded. 'She's that devious all right. Look how she's stuck with McGregor. That's an evil man if ever I met one, and everyone knows the Militias are controlled by him. Ann is using him and them for her own ends, despite all her protestations about hating violence.'

The depression dulled her eyes and made her shoulders slump. He put his hand on her shoulder. 'Why don't you stay overnight?'

As soon as he saw the confusion in her face, he felt embarrassed. 'I didn't put that very well, did I? What I meant was that you shouldn't force yourself to put up with the discomfort of the sleeper when we could book you into a hotel. I was going to suggest you might like to come out to the constituency and meet some of my folk.'

She smiled, a mixture of relief and regret. 'All right, I have to admit that I hate the sleeper, and it would be good to meet a few normal people.'

In the busy social club bingo – usually sacrosanct, never to be disturbed – had given way to a football match on the large screen TV, but the women still lingered at their tables in little groups nursing sweet martinis or lager and lime, relishing their one outing of the week. They kept their voices down as they gossiped – after all the men were entitled to their enjoyment too. As Sylvia walked in, however, someone spotted her and stood up to cheer. When the realization spread, the television was first ignored, then switched off out of politeness, and the party stalwarts surrounded her, jostling for the chance of a few words with her and to shake her hand.

The women told her how much nicer she looked in the flesh, bolder ones asked how she was settling down in Downing Street, and how were her daughters coping with seeing so little of their mother?

The warm affection of these people folded over Sylvia like balm; Stephen could see her visibly brightening under their kindness. Despite the warmth, the impression grew of a community near to despair. Their eyes, in faces filled with character, showed that none of them really believed that the good days could come back. Too many mothers looked haggard and worn, not just with poverty, but with fear. As she and Stephen got a break in the group she murmured to him:

'What's happened to all their resilience? Do they think we can't do anything to make things better?'

He looked at her for a moment, deciding how to explain it, then led her into his little office. 'Sit there – back in a second,' and returned with Joe Black. The election agent, overawed at meeting the Prime Minister's wife, had the fidgety dilemma of trying to hide his grimy hands, despite a need to hold the buttonless collar of his working shirt closed. With prompting from Stephen, Joe told Sylvia:

'D'you know what it's like to be a father when your only child is in the grip of hysteria? We raised him with years of love and respect – gone. When my son's out, I don't know if he'll be found dead after some stupid bandit raid – or if someone else will be found dead at his hands. We're terrified of every knock at the door.' He came near to breaking down as he spoke of his wife, almost a junkie now on tranquillizers prescribed by doctors as distressed as their patients.

A barmaid brought in a tray with a lace mat and tea in three fine china cups. There were little home-made cakes on a plate, and home-made shortbread. Sylvia exclaimed in gratitude at the trouble she had gone to. The barmaid blushed and explained that someone had run over to one of the houses opposite to ask for help in view of their unexpected visitor, and the women in the houses had come up trumps. Another woman crept in carrying a crystal sugar bowl and silver-plated sugar tongs.

The phone rang, Stephen answered it. He stood up.

'Sylvia, I have to go to the police station. Two children have been taken in for suspected assault and robbery. That was one of the fathers, in a terrible state.'

She stood up. 'I'll come with you.'

Outside in the foyer, dozens of people had crammed in. They began to applaud when she emerged. Sylvia saw that the women, who had all been wearing overalls as they sat round the tables with their drinks, had removed them. Lipstick had been hurriedly applied, in some cases without the benefit of a mirror. Despite her anxiety to get to the police station, Sylvia went round shaking hands. An elderly man thrust a little posy of roses into her hand, hastily wrapped in aluminium foil – he had grown them in his garden.

Although she had only been in the club twenty minutes, the streets outside were lined with people. Stephen called over one elderly lady:

'Maggie, was that not your wedding china we were using? I'm sure I recognized it.' He turned to Sylvia; 'This lady here is eighty-seven. That china you used was nearly seventy years old, and it has probably touched no lips other than yours. It's her pride and joy.'

The woman was beaming with pride. Impulsively, Sylvia leaned over and hugged her, and the tears began to course down weatherbeaten, liver-spotted cheeks. The old woman smelt of a mixture of soap and decay. As the Prime Minister's wife got into the front of Stephen's car, a rousing cheer went up. Very slowly, Stephen drove down the street. Sylvia kept the window of the car down so that she could be seen more clearly. In some windows she saw mothers clutching bleary-eyed babies, got out of bed to be shown this important lady. As Stephen picked up speed away from the crowd, he handed Sylvia a handkerchief. She blew her nose. They travelled in silence. As he stopped the car, she turned to him:

'Thank you. That made me feel quite special. And if ever I had doubts about why we've got to sort out Ann Clarke and her type, that got rid of them.'

The police station formed the basement and ground floor of a Victorian town hall, a small building for a town of sixty thousand inhabitants. No crime wave had struck here since World War Two when local young bucks, anxious to be in on the act, broke the windows of every Italian ice-cream shop in the town. Summary justice had seen them locked up for a night and then put to work for the next week replacing the windows at their own expense. In a town like this, the police were respected, and the indignity of having a child in trouble devastated families.

The anguished fathers rushed over. Sylvia and Stephen tried to calm them, while piecing together the facts. The boys had disappeared two days before; their families had scoured the town for them, not daring to tell the police and have their fears confirmed about the extent to which the children were out of control – disappearing night after night, wearing semi-military uniform, lionizing the violent. Despite the words of Joe Black, Sylvia recoiled when she realized that the boys were twelve and thirteen, not as she had been expecting, carefully nurtured thugs of eighteen.

Stephen, temper fraying, had to make a fuss to get in to see the Chief Inspector.

Chief Inspector Laing, an old school friend of Stephen, sat calmly listening to the MP's tirade about the law and young children. He remained silent as Stephen, whom he respected – and vice versa – threatened to make an official complaint that the children had been kept in custody for thirty-six hours without access to either parents or lawyers. When Stephen ran out of steam, the policeman spoke.

'I took a chance here by breaking every rule in the book. I will almost certainly be thrown out of the force, and that'll be the best I can expect. But tonight I got the information I need to set about proving that there are organized terrorist cells in this country. That they are being heavily financed by an outside source, that weapons are being brought in from abroad, that prominent people are backing it – and that Ann Clarke is in it up to her neck.'

He let this sink in and was about to speak again when Stephen interrupted him:

'Sylvia Metcalf is outside. Do you mind if she joins us?'

Laing looked concerned at this. Stephen was sure the policeman was worried about whether he could trust her, or if by telling her he would be escalating the situation beyond his control He relented, and Sylvia was brought in.

At the end of the tale, Stephen and Sylvia could scarcely acknowledge, let alone accept, the enormity of what had been going on.

The two boys had been picked up after a midnight break–in at a newsagent's: the elderly proprietor heard a noise and came to investigate. In their rush to escape, the boys knocked him over and he broke an arm as he fell. In the ambulance, he admitted he had known the boys, but he hadn't wanted to get them into trouble, having watched with growing horror as two pleasant and courteous children, just out of primary school, had turned into political fanatics, endlessly talking about 'freeing Scotland from the chains of oppression'.

It had been an easy job for the police to track down the boys; in the station they 'leaned' on them, especially about the Workers' Militia.

Both had been recruited into the Militia by older boys at school. At first it had seemed like a club – a very exciting one, a secret society, two nights every week, classes in a derelict scout hut near Hillend Loch. At first only the illicit thrill kept them going, because when they got there it became just like school. The men in charge gave them lessons in Scottish history, not the dry schoolbook stuff, but exciting tales of bravado and recklessness in places all the boys knew well.

With the boys' imaginations captured, the lecturers brought the history up to date, with tales of miners' strikes, of the fight to save the shipyards, of the American invasion and the siting of secret army bases. A story of oppression and invasion was built up, of a proud nation and people ground down by an empire more evil than it seemed – the United States of America.

Then came the videos. One featured Ann Clarke, documenting some of the campaigns she had led, picturing her in horrible slums, fighting with landlords to improve conditions. It showed her outside steelworks and factories and shipyards fighting for jobs. It showed her in old folk's homes laughing and joking with the residents. Marches led by her, speeches made by her, elections won by her – all built up a picture of a great popular heroine, fighting for, with and beside the people.

The video, with stirring music, ended with Ann

addressing a rally, looking as though she was speaking straight to camera in a very tight close-up, her eyes alight with conviction, talking about how Scotland could be free again – just by showing strength. Her passion and anger inflamed them. Here they had a leader who would make them proud to be Scots again, not downtrodden lackeys of the English and the Americans.

Next week the weapons practice began, then training in covert activity. All their instruction led to membership of the Workers' Militia in which they would become true Freedom Fighters like the young people of Northern Ireland, Central America, the Middle East, grenade-carrying, gun-bearing. No turning back, and by way of apprenticeship they would do what all freedom movements everywhere did, raise funds from robberies, to get workers money to finance the struggle. They knew the example of the IRA, ETA in Spain, and the history of the OAS in France.

The two lads had been caught on a raid they had themselves set up for practice, determined to impress their commander. Now they were scared, no longer Freedom Fighters but terrified children.

From the description of the weapons they had handled, the police could identify a Russian-made Kalashnikov submachine gun, impressive, effective and expensive. Sylvia cried out involuntarily when the policeman went on to describe how commitment was rewarded with drugs, from cannabis to amphetamines to heroin.

'So where political passion fails, addiction keeps them loyal?' she asked.

'Precisely,' said Laing.

'The source?' asked Stephen.

Laing flinched, then in a what-the-hell tone of voice told them it was almost certainly Harry McGregor. His 'friendship' with those who made up the shady world of Scotland's drug culture had been under surveillance for a decade.

Facing up to what they now knew, Laing, Robinson and Sylvia each had to decide what to do next. Laing had

141

to tell his superiors, but 'face to face, rather than submit a report'. His unspoken fear hung in the air. No one knew just who backed the Workers' Militia, their resources appreciably greater than anyone had remotely realized. There had even been fears about the police themselves recently – not as vigilant perhaps as they might be. Too many guilty men and women had been left unchallenged, too many questions unanswered.

Sylvia looked at Stephen, each reading in the other's eyes the realization that the stakes in the political battle had suddenly become infinitely greater. Would they be believed when they told of this? Would they be effective in stopping Ann Clarke joining the Cabinet? If they were unsuccessful – what then?

Sylvia invited Stephen into the hotel for a drink, this time both too preoccupied to assume a hidden meaning. Over and over again they discussed the events of the night, unable to decide what to do.

Stephen kept repeating: 'But she has said over and over again that she's not part of the Workers' Militia.'

And Sylvia reminded him over and over again that what they had learned brought them to an inescapable conclusion – Ann Clarke was up to her ears with the Workers' Militia, and money, big money, was coming from somewhere to fund what was happening.

'It can't just be the profits of a few robberies – that network is too huge, too expensive.'

Exhausted, they decided to sleep on it, and to meet in London to plan strategy. As Stephen stood up to take his leave of her in the deserted lounge of the railway hotel, he bent down and kissed her tenderly – his lips no more than brushing hers. For a moment it looked as though he might say something, but he turned and left, not looking back.

Michael had worked hard since her phone call. Dozens of candles blazed throughout the flat giving an inviting, restful glow. He threw open the door on the first ring, smiling happily in welcome, but his smile turned to concern as he saw the obvious signs of her exhaustion, the drooping eyes, the slumped shoulders, the lopsided smile. As he bent down to kiss her, he felt the tense set of her shoulders. Without a word, he drew her into the bedroom.

She protested: 'Not yet Michael! I need to unwind.'

But he stopped her protests with a kiss. Putting his hands on her shoulders, he pushed her down on to a leather wing chair in the corner of the bedroom, then left her to go into the bathroom. For the first time she had a chance to look round the very masculine room. The wall-coverings seemed like suede in a rich tobacco brown. Oil lamps converted to electricity gave a warm glow to the room and a rich brown satin comforter glimmered on the bed. Her toes nestled in the deep pile carpet. The room of a man who knew the power of touch.

When he came out of the bathroom he opened a cupboard and took out a large fluffy bathrobe. Slowly he undressed her, as he would a child. Gently he loosened her stockings from the suspenders, rolling them carefully down her legs, unfastening her bra and letting her breasts fall free. Carefully and slowly he folded her clothes, leaving them in a neat pile – throughout resisting the temptation to kiss her skin, still faintly perfumed. Finally, he lifted her up and carried her into the bathroom, placing her gently in the bath, where the warm, foaming water engulfed her. He left her then, returning a few minutes later with a glass of champagne.

She almost fell asleep in the bath. She felt cared for and safe. The world outside was miles away. Had he not come back, she probably would have slept. He ordered her out of the bath then wrapped her in the robe which by now he had heated. He carried her again into the bedroom, deposited her on the chair and began, very gently, to brush out her hair, with methodical, rhythmic strokes. She now felt unbelievably relaxed, and was almost disappointed when he took her back into the living area.

He had set a low table between two large sofas, and placed cushions on the floor for them to sit on.

She laughed when she saw oysters as the first course

and teased him with his lack of subtlety. Next, he served salmon in a light hollandaise, accompanied by a well-chilled chablis. All the time he kept up almost a monologue, telling her of his schooldays, amusing her with stories of his exploits as a fledgling correspondent – lulling her into a greater and greater sense of peace. She was almost asleep before her salmon was eaten. He watched her eyes droop, and the start she gave as she tried to keep awake. He moved beside her, pulling her head down on to his shoulder. It was she who asked to be taken to bed.

Again, he carried her through, gently putting her on the pillows.

Quickly he undressed and slipped in beside her, he stroked her gently, lightly circling her nipples. His fingers traced a line over her belly. As he looked at her face, in the half life before sleep, he could see the imperfections: the lines around her eyes, the creases where frowns of worry and concentration had left their mark. They made her more beautiful to him. She had worked for everything she had achieved. He sensed more than a little pain. She was never more beautiful than when she was vulnerable. Gently kissing her eyelids, he knew that this woman was unlike any other he had ever known. With his tongue he stroked and teased her body, flicking lightly across her belly and down across her abdomen. Finally he found the centre of her sex. Hardly touching her he flicked and sucked, watching her respond, until, in shudders, the tension finally left her body. As she drifted into sleep, he heard her say something. It sounded like 'Johann'.

Harry McGregor settled back in his seat on the Trident as it took off from Glasgow. He looked smug as he sat, musing, a faint smile playing around his lips. The 'fasten seat belts' sign switched off and he reached up to buzz for a stewardess. The young tartan-clad woman moved down the aisle of the plane, a solicitous smile on her face. As she bent across McGregor to switch off the call button, he was smoothing his hair and his fingers brushed against her breasts. Unsure as to whether or not it was an acci-

144

dent, the girl stepped back, pointedly ignoring the incident.

'A large whisky, no ice, no water.'

The stewardess remained civil: 'We'll be round with the bar in a minute, sir, then we'll be happy to help you.'

'Not in a minute. Now.'

'Certainly, sir.'

The memory flooded back, of April 1970, April 12th.

The young man who waited to go through customs at London Airport studiously read his copy of the London *Times* as he waited for his luggage to be searched. When his turn came he kept his answers to the customs officer's questions monosyllabic, conscious of the colonial drawl of his South African accent, anxious not to appear in any way out of the ordinary. He had drunk steadily from his duty free whisky on the flight from Amsterdam, but now, courage stocked up, he knew he had to be unobtrusive. He had no idea if the British police had joined the search for members of the Trotskyist gang who had assassinated a leading Dutch politician – but he couldn't take any risks, he had been given his next assignment, a big one. As he walked away, he ran his fingers through his greasy blond hair. He was almost clear when he heard his name called:

'Mr McGregor?'

He paused, undecided as to whether to run or turn back. He turned.

'You've forgotten your paper.'

McGregor smiled, and the stewardess managed a professional smile as, balancing two small bottles and a glass in one hand, she again had to lean across him to release his table.

Across the Gatwick terminal, McGregor made it to the Brighton train with seconds to spare. He found his seat, and got himself another double whisky to help pass the half-hour journey.

The taxi driver didn't try to make conversation with the taciturn man with the Scottish accent as he drove him to the Regency terrace. Some instinct warned the driver: this looked a rough one.

The door was opened before McGregor had a chance to knock. A huge thickset man with greasy black hair and an enormous paunch blocked off the light from the hallway. With his head, he gestured to the visitor to come in. Slowly, McGregor stepped over the threshold, and waited until the door was closed behind him before he spoke:

'Couldn't have got me to come any further, could you? It's a wonder I didn't fall off the fuckin' end of Britain!'

He looked round, expecting a response. The huge man seemed not to have heard.

'I said, you've brought me far enough . . .' The contempt on the other man's face made him shut up.

The silence grew as McGregor stood in the middle of the room. He looked around. The walls were lined with books, and two sofas faced each other across the fireplace, each covered with a plaid rug. In the bay window was a bar table with decanters and spirits bottles. The Scot looked pointedly at it, but no offer was made. The big man sat down on one of the sofas, looking McGregor up and down as he did so. The Scot sat opposite him, visibly squirming now in the growing silence. Eventually the man spoke. His voice was strangely soft for such a large man. He spoke with the clipped precision of someone for whom English isn't the native language, and there was the faintest hint of a mid-Atlantic drawl.

'So far, so good. Everything seems to have gone very well in Scotland.'

McGregor made as if to preen, but the other man held up his hand.

'Now you've got to deliver elsewhere. That won't be so easy. The real test. Are you ready for it?'

The union leader looked hurt. 'Of course I'm ready! Do you want me to run through everything I've set up?'

He cleared his throat, ready to begin. The man across the room held up his hand.

146

'I'm not interested in the detail, just the results. Where is the first incident going to take place?'

'Liverpool. Next week.'

The man nodded. 'And London?'

'Two days later.'

The man sat silently, nodding his head as if mentally agreeing with himself. McGregor spoke again:

'It'll take a hell of a lot more money. We'll need to have some more little helpers, and I've decided to export some of our Scottish friends.'

At that, the man raised his eyebrows quizzically.

McGregor stuttered: 'Only if you agree.'

'It's of no consequence.'

The man heaved himself out of his chair and crossed the room to a Turner reproduction on the wall. He moved it aside to reveal a safe. Slowly he opened it, taking out a large black pilot's bag. Coming back to his seat across from McGregor, he placed the bag on the floor and flicked it open. It had been packed in a most orderly way with twenty-pound notes, thousands of them. McGregor swallowed hard. He reached out to touch the money, but the man bent down and closed the case, flicking a combination lock.

'You'd better get back north with this. And no more planes.' He gestured to the bag. 'We don't want this going through airport security!' He smiled to reveal blackened teeth, his eyes ice cold.

'You're booked on the ten fifty sleeper. One of my people will be coming with you.'

McGregor made to object: 'Don't you trust me?'

'Do we want you combing your hair again as the stewardess bends over you?'

McGregor, flabbergasted, began to speak but stopped when another man came into the room, who gestured to him: time to leave.

The Scots union leader stood up and held out his hand to the man sitting opposite him. It was ignored. The other man shut his eyes, turned away and said no more.

McGregor was hustled away. He had been in Brighton thirty-five minutes.

The Foreign Office car already stood outside the Gay Hussar in Greek Street. The Foreign Secretary's security man, standing guard outside the fashionable political watering hole, rushed forward to open the car door for Sylvia. He and another detective scanned the half empty street as she went through the door into the small restaurant and straight to the window table, the one where conversations couldn't be overheard. Sylvia responded to various greetings with a preoccupied wave. As she sank into the plush seat George already had a large gin and tonic waiting for her, and had already ordered wild cherry soup and ham with lentils, to get the mundane business of eating sorted out.

As she took a drink and let out a sigh, visibly willing herself to relax, George raised his eyebrows:

'That bad?'

She nodded.

Jeffries and Sylvia had formed an alliance years before out of a mutual desire to see a Labour Government again, and one that would feature each of them prominently, but soon a friendship had grown up between the brilliant academic strategist and the woman who had honed her gut instincts to cutting point in the quest to get her husband into Downing Street. They spoke each other's language, often without saying a word. Jeffries knew that Metcalf didn't have the intellectual firepower to take on the Americans, and Sylvia, despite her loyalty to the man she had moulded to win the election, had been forced to accept that he lacked the emotional stability to cope with the campaign Ann Clarke was waging to destroy him.

Sylvia looked Jeffries straight in the eye: 'I've been to see Ann Clarke.'

Perpetually calm, Jeffries merely inclined his head to indicate his surprise; he gave no sign whether he approved.

Sylvia went on: 'A heavy scene. She seems to think I

have no right to reproach her for trying to destroy my husband!'

Jeffries allowed the silence to grow. Sylvia gave him an account of the interview between the two women, playing down Stephen Robinson's intervention but revealing the extent of her own determination to take on the other woman and win.

'There can't be any doubt now that I'm right – she is now out to get rid of Tony and move into Number Ten herself. If I hadn't seen the venom in her eyes about Tony, I wouldn't have believed it.'

The waiter arrived with the soup at this point, giving Sylvia a chance to calm down. Once they were alone again, Sylvia went on with her story of the visit to Glasgow, especially her impressions after her trip to the Labour Party Social Club in Coatbridge. She didn't mention the interview with the police officer until they got to the coffee. Before she started, she took a deep breath. Jeffries knew that what was coming was very important to her and, valuing her judgement, he listened carefully. She gave a little self-deprecating laugh as she started:

'You're going to think I've flipped when I tell you the next part, but Stephen Robinson was with me, and he can back me up in everything. But it does sound rather fantastic!'

She told him of the discovery by the Coatbridge police of just how sophisticated the terrorist recruiting operation was – the money that seemed to be available, the deliberate effort to brainwash children. She told a story that had the hallmarks of insurrection seen in numerous countries throught the world, almost always sponsored by a major power.

Jeffries made no response. He sat looking into his coffee cup. Eventually, Sylvia broke the silence:

'Put like that, it does sound as if I've got carried away doesn't it?'

The tension between them grew as she waited for his response. The Foreign Secretary drew his hands across his eyes, and as he looked up at her, he seemed terribly weary:

'I honestly don't know what to believe! I tried to get hold of you the other day because I had spoken to Tony about the danger that another government might be trying to destabilize Britain. He more or less accused me of being off my head. And I've thought about it lots of times since then, and I just don't know what any government would hope to achieve. The only superpower with any interest in Britain is really the United States, and they've got us by the short and curlies already. What could they hope to achieve by making things worse?'

Toying with her cup, Sylvia asked without looking up: 'The Russians?'

'They've enough trouble with their own satellite states without wanting to take on another bag of tricks. What could possibly be in it for them!'

Sylvia shrugged, self-doubt written on her face. 'So you think we're just talking about Ann Clarke manoeuvring a popular front to further her own ends?'

Jeffries nodded.

They both sat silently thinking, then Jeffries spoke again: 'If this is really just domestic political game playing.' He held up his hand to stop Sylvia as she made to interrupt him. 'OK, OK, I know lives are being put at risk and the Government is in danger, but if we are just talking about the rampant ambition of one politician and her sidekicks, then we've got weapons to fight it with. We can either do a deal with her, or we can discredit her.'

Her voice heavy with suspicion, Sylvia responded: 'What kind of deal?'

'We get Tony to endorse her in the election for the new Secretary of State for Scotland.' Seeing her scepticism, he went on: 'It could be done through me or one of the others known to have Tony's ear. We find out what her price is and we negotiate. It could be if we give her a more senior role in UK matters in the Cabinet she'll be bought off. Promise to groom her for the job next time round.' He sniggered. 'I never really wanted to be PM anyway, and if we get over this first crisis, there is no reason why Tony can't be Prime Minister indefinitely. And we could let her loose internationally – she'd like the glamour of that. If she's carrying the can abroad, it will be very hard to rubbish a Cabinet in which she has a senior post.'

Seeing that Sylvia remained patently unimpressed, he changed tack:

'Or we destroy her. We have the security people take her apart – her sex life, her finances, her past, her contacts. What we don't find we plant. It may take some time, though, and that could be something we don't have. In the meantime, we put pressure on the unions to pull back on their support for her in *this* election and we get the whole party machine into gear behind Stephen Robinson. Which strategy do you want?'

She stared out of the window for a long time. When she turned back to him, her eyes were cold, her lips narrow.

'Both! We cultivate her, and as we're doing it, we destroy her. She's not going to destroy my family!'

Sylvia didn't notice the slim black tube on the window sill, almost covered by the lace curtains – nor did she notice the transit van parked down the street, opaque windows hiding recording equipment which a few minutes later, even as her official car passed by, replayed the conversation with the Foreign Secretary. Once the black Rover was out of sight, a tall blond man jumped from the back of the van and hailed a cruising taxi. He asked to be taken to Grosvenor Square, the US Government's embassy in London.

5

The young Scottish student's friendship with Horowitz grew; gradually he revealed to her how he planned to be President, and in the face of his ambition, her own was nurtured. He convinced her that she too had the necessary ingredients for success in politics, and gradually he unfolded to her the tricks American politicians used that made them such expert campaigners. Here the emphasis was on the psychology of the voter rather than the nuances of policy.

During intimate suppers in his apartment he so completely devoted the time to talking politics that she thought he had no interest in her other than as a potential British politician. And she tried not to be disappointed.

He quizzed her about what was happening in the British Labour Party. She told him about Antony Metcalf and his plans to be Prime Minister. Horowitz dismissed him as a weak man who had no vision of what he wanted to do once he got power. Horowitz possessed no doubts as to what he wanted – complete US domination of every major country, and that including Britain; only in that way could the American people feel globally secure. He worked hard at justifying his point of view, overcoming Ann's rejection of his vision with hard facts. Britain had missed so many chances that the country's economy was stagnating; the life style of the people lingered generations behind their American counterparts; Britain scarcely registered progress. Gradually he enthused her, slowly convincing her that democratic freedoms could only be maintained with a strong, and well-armed US presence in Europe.

Her attraction to Horowitz intensified, though he maintained the role of teacher. Unaware that this attention constituted exceptional treatment from a senior American politician, she never realized that in order to spend time with her he made additional journeys back from Washington, often flying in solely to have supper with her, then back overnight. She rewarded his efforts by responding not just to the proposed foreign policy of a future President – and she soon had no doubt that he would succeed – but absorbing the techniques of getting a country's electors on your side.

The inevitable change came in the relationship without warning. One night, as they rose from the table after supper, he took her by the hand and led her to the bedroom. Warmed by the love of a mature man, she began to blossom. He convinced Ann of her exceptional qualities, inspired her – she could do as much for her country: together, they could change the future shape of the world. She merited more than a role as handmaiden to Metcalf.

Next, Horowitz introduced her to his image makers. No conscious decision had ever been reached – or even discussed – that they would work on her, yet she found she was having subtle highlights put into her hair, her teeth capped, her body worked on to make it lithe and firm – Horowitz gave her a gift of membership of his exclusive sports club. Already slim, she was encouraged to diet to compensate for the ten pounds she would gain through the optical illusion of television. Posture classes changed her businesslike gait to the fluidity of a catwalk model. The best speech coach in Hollywood trained her voice, making the Scottish lilt more musical while deepening the pitch – making it more husky, more intimate. She learned how to project her voice so that she could be heard in an auditorium without having to strain and sound harsh. In the techniques of crowd control, a drama coach showed her the value of stillness, how she could use her body and her eyes to subdue a crowd. She spent time with speechwriters, watching how they developed memorable lines and throwaway asides. Just when she thought she was finished, she found herself being seriously trained in the techniques of using television – how to make eye contact with a metal camera, allowing the viewer to feel singled out, how to control an interview, how to look, what to wear, how to gain sympathy in the face of the aggressive interview, how to appear authoritative instead of strident.

With Scottish practicality she began to worry about what all this must be costing. Stylists brought her clothes to wear, elegant but young, almost always in primary colours, with no fussiness, just superb cuts in beautiful and expensive fabrics – but they never presented their bill. When she mentioned it, and the other obvious costs to Horowitz, he dismissed her concerns. A token of his love, he said.

When they had been lovers for six months he pronounced her 'ready'. Ready for what? He took her to Washington to find out. Ann was disappointed to discover herself booked into a service apartment round the corner from the State Department; did this mean her time was likely to be lonely? Horowitz could hardly risk visiting her in Washington, what chance could there possibly be for contact with other people? She needn't have worried; by the time she fled this company town a week later, not a waking minute had been spent alone.

Day one, expecting to visit the State Department, she had just finished dressing when the phone rang. A man identifying himself as a Labor Officer in the State Department, at Horowitz's request, would like to call on her – the first of many.

By the end of that day, Ann had been shown incontrovertible proof of a heavy infiltration of British Labour politics. An organization called the Revolutionary Socialist Party, operating in small well-disciplined cells throughout the country, had stealthily grown immensely powerful in the white-collar unions near to the seat of power – and at both national and local level. Photographs and slides were shown to her from a dossier of men and women prominent in public life; then she learned of their precise involvement with this Trotskyist party, so left-wing that the Soviet Union had made it plain long ago that anyone who gave them a safe haven deserved all the trouble they got. Trot-

154

sky, one-time Leader of the Red Army, believed that the end justified the means. The end for these dedicated people was total domination of Britain – by violence if necessary. Ann in Washington was being shown evidence of how close they had come to taking over the main Opposition Party.

Day two, the man from the State Department showed her a psychological profile of Tony Metcalf. It revealed astonishing, disturbing traits. For a start did Ann know that he had been involved in a homosexual relationship as a student? That therefore constituted a straightforward target for blackmail – the most damning condition for any potential leader. In an aside she heard that he had 'received money from a Middle Eastern country', and the relevant dossier, proving meetings with known agents of that country, was 'accidentally' left behind on her table.

The British economy occupied all of day three. Ann had no idea of how deeply Britain had plunged into debt and the potential scale of the hardship just ahead – real poverty, massive unemployment running to twenty, perhaps even thirty per cent, making Britain little better than a Third World country.

On day four they told her how she could fit in.

Certain 'people' in the US administration were worried about the strategic importance of Britain. As a country in hock, a major world power could easily dominate it in exchange for economic assistance. The Soviets and Chinese had begun to cultivate a number of key British figures – and not just on the political left. They referred to Cuba, Angola, Mozambique – convincing examples of how it could be done.

This would prove devastating for the free world, worse than anything the Nazis could have done. To prevent it happening, the United States sought to enter into a partnership with the British Government, though obviously a proud nation so rich in history might find that difficult to accept. And the repeated policy changes coming after frequent elections exacerbated the country's instability.

Which, they told Ann, was where she came in. She had the potential to be a great political leader, one who fully understood and agreed with the policy position of senior US politicians – Horowitz's name was never mentioned. Given the right kind of power base, she held the key to leading Britain to the kind of prosperity she had seen in America; it was felt – though by whom was never revealed – that considerable resources should be put behind promoting her to that end. Her Scots nationality proved an added bonus, unrest lurked never far from the surface in that country, where for centuries people had felt colonized by the English; their resentment had been heightened at the prospect of sharing North Sea oil.

First, though, Ann had to become accepted by – they almost said 'infiltrate' – the Labour Party and play a part in moulding its policies; before Labour was forced to see that American 'aid' was the only way, they had to see how bad the alternative was.

A plan was shown to Ann of how she could infiltrate the Trotskyists as an *agent provocateur*. The CIA could provide her with excellent credentials linking her with American Militant and make her perfectly acceptable. A seat in Parliament was also needed, she could be helped in that, and Metcalf would be neutered to rid the scene of the only viable alternative candidate.

They left her to think about it, leaving yet another 'background file' for her to read. When, recovered, she got round to it, she found how thoroughly they had researched her past. The men who had destroyed her father had been dependent for their political power on the Revolutionary Socialist Party, and the money raised from the kind of corrupt activity that had ruined her father was the Party's principal source of finance. Shocked, Ann read the name of the eminence grise behind their activities – a well-known academic and Labour MP, Hugh Lawrie. His seat had been singled out for Ann to fight.

She paced the floor all night. Shortly before three in the morning, Horowitz came to her. He inflamed her again with his idea of a crusade, to rid British politics of the second-raters and to build the kind of wealthy, free society she saw here. As they made love he kept telling her over and over again how they could forge a magnificent place in history, presiding over two of the world's major powers, because with her Britain would be great again. But when he left she was still confused and undecided. Panic welled in her as she recognized that she was being brainwashed.

The men who visited her on the fifth day came not from the State Department, but from another, unnamed Government organization, and very subtly they let her know how much they knew of her affair with Horowitz. When they left her, confusion had turned to fear. Within three hours she had taken a plane back to London, and a day later stood knocking, incoherent and hysterical, at the door of Mary Connolly.

Calmed down and faced with the prospect of sharing her burden, Ann became vague. She hinted to Mary of a relationship at once shocking and exciting. She mentioned no name, but an implication hung in the air that the man was married. Mary diagnosed a bad case of rejection, and made a fuss of Ann, revelling in feeling needed for once.

After a day of tears and strong sweet tea, both girls felt exhausted, content to flop in front of the television. Ann had spent so much time immersed in the great issues of British political strategy that she had quite lost track of day-to-day events. Suddenly she jumped up in her chair when the news came on. The British Conservative Party – that bastion of fusty tradition and exaggerated chauvinism – had appointed a woman to lead it. Margaret Hilda Thatcher, grocer's daughter from Grantham in Lincolnshire, lawyer and scientist, wife of a millionaire and mother of twins, stood an excellent chance of being the next Prime Minister. Anger and resentment showed in Ann's face. Had that honour not been reserved for her? They must have known in Washington about the probable elevation of Mrs Thatcher, so why did they massage her ego by suggesting that she could take that place in history as the first British woman Prime Minister.

As the profiles of Mrs Thatcher unfolded, Ann perceived for the first time the amateurism of the British political machine. The woman's voice hit her first, sharp and hectoring with an unpleasant edge to it. The well-scrubbed face was so typically British middle class, so suburban, that the yearnings of tens of thousands of British women for some glamour in their lives was ignored. Why did film star magazines sell so well if a ready market for glamour did not exist? The British image makers, or what passed for them – had obviously decided that this woman should be given as homely an image as possible. TV pictures of her in a shapeless tweed suit with a pussy-cat bow at the neck going to the shops to buy the family groceries, must have been felt by some to be reassuring. But, ludicrous thought, how could she resolve the balance of payments crisis if she was worried that she'd forgotten to take something out of the freezer?

And the hair! Ye Gods – proof positive that Ann had been given an exceptional training in the Horowitz camp. Carefully bleached and teased at the front, in every shot of Mrs Thatcher from over the shoulder it was flat and uncared for at the back. Ann could think of one or two people who would be in paroxysms of laughter at the complete denial of the significance of TV – if there is a shot you would rather not have taken, the cameras are sure to capture it – the rule they had drilled into her.

Mary observed her friend's fascination at the election of Mrs Thatcher rather irritatedly, noticing how politically committed Ann had now become.

Next morning Ann had gone – she left a note:

I don't know how to thank you. You were so kind yesterday, you helped me more than you will ever know. I came to a lot of decisions last night. You only live once and it's time that I stopped preparing for life and started living it. I'm going back to the States, I'll write soon. Your friend, Ann.

They were waiting for her at the airport, not the least bit surprised that she had returned. Ambition, especially for power, remains one of the strongest motivating factors of all. Ann knew now that Horowitz and others had not been talking about a pipe dream. They had prepared her to be ten years ahead of her time, and with Richard Horowitz, they could do it all. Together.

The rest happened in a rush. She returned to Boston to finish her studies. A few days later Horowitz joined her, bringing with him a dossier on Hugh Lawrie, MP and academic – and architect of her father's disgrace. Lawrie, a clever man but greedy, lived way beyond his means and maintained three households – wife and teenage daughter in one – mistress in the other – and London residence the third. He dined well and enjoyed fine wines, yet had no source of income other than occasional lecturing and his MP's salary. This had alerted the British security service – always wary of the unexplained. What they found proved so interesting, their deep plants in MI5 had passed on the information to the Americans. Lawrie's finances came from Gaddafi's Libya; in return for the money, he helped to establish Trotskyist cells throughout Britain.

Ann shared Horowitz's contempt for Lawrie's treasonable activity, and it fuelled her growing belief that something very rotten had taken root in Britain. Together, the Senator and the aspiring MP set about destroying Lawrie. An invitation was concocted to get him to the States, and at the same time, the machinery to infiltrate Ann into American Militant swung into operation.

Lawrie jumped at the chance of an all-expenses paid trip to the United States, with the added bonus of an admiring audience at the Militant Rally he would be able to address. It was after that Rally that he 'bumped into' the remarkable young Scotswoman whose name had been fed to him as someone worth watching. She was all – and more – that he had been told about. He wrote a coded letter to Jimmy Cane, leader of the Revolutionary Socialist Party, telling of his find, and recommending her in the highest possible terms. When he returned to Britain, he boasted of his discovery, not just within his own Revolutionary sect, but in the broader Labour Party as well – this woman, he insisted, would prove a real winner and he prepared everyone for her return from the States. It was a source of great joy to him that he had been able to introduce Ann to the great father of British Trotskyism before his death.

But, apparently accidentally, scandal began to attach itself to Lawrie. First came his exposure for having allegedly stolen – from a Dutch research student – the data for his most recent paper on the British economy. Then the tabloid press revealed the identity of a mistress – a well known society call-girl. An implicit suggestion of living off immoral earnings lurked. Those who knew best, though, now made it plain to Hugh Lawrie they knew where his cash was coming from.

It took almost four years before Hugh Lawrie's body was found in the bath of a seedy hotel bathroom in Plymouth, a bottle of vodka lying on the floor, several chemists' prescription packs empty by his side, and water red with the blood that had drained from his cut wrists.

Three months later, the victor of the by-election caused by his death, the young woman who had over the past three years made such a name for herself as a radical lawyer and firebrand politician, was introduced into Parliament as the new MP for Clydeside West. As Ann Clarke stood at the Bar of the House of Commons with Tony Metcalf as her sponsor, Sylvia sat in the privileged cubbyhole under the Gallery to watch her protégée walk, confident and beautiful, onto the centre state of British politics.

Michael Stewart found the school without difficulty. He had phoned ahead and asked Maureen Tumilty to meet him, hoping his fame would overcome her misgivings. When he got there, charm would do the rest.

At the gate, to his relief he could see plenty of distracting activity – boys playing football in the yard, the sound of Scottish country dance music and the pounding of feet from the gym hall dance classes. Familiar smells of cabbage and lavatories called up his own school days. He waited in the dingy corridor for a women he hoped would lift some veils from a much more interesting past – that of her father, the late Hugh Lawrie MP. Entering Parliament in the first Labour Government for thirteen years, in 1964, already a distinguished academic, he quickly shone among the time-serving local councillors and trades union officials. His abrasive challenges to the then Prime Minister, Harold Wilson, had however, kept him firmly tethered to the back benches. Lawrie had recognized that he had little chance of office, and rather than run the risk of the corrosive effects of bitterness and thwarted ambition, had dedicated himself to becoming the Labour Party's major thinker. His amusing delivery and inexhaustible energy, combined with his natural brilliance made him a darling of the rank and file of the Party in a very short time.

Stewart could remember how every new book on political and economic theory produced by Lawrie had engaged the highly vocal rising generation. He himself had abandoned a sick bed to listen to Lawrie at the Oxford Union, which was the first thing Stewart mentioned to Donald Ross as he pulled up a chair in his office to tell him what he had found out. Lawrie had kept undercover his involvement with the Revolutionary Socialist Party – the organization that started the Workers' Militia, who had only a few hours earlier burnt down the Town Hall in Motherwell – Ross was, even as they spoke, putting together more and more coverage of the Militia's violence.

Stewart ticked off the main points. Lawrie had gone to America ostensibly on an academic lecture tour, but he had managed to juggle his timetable to ensure he would be available to address a major rally for the RSP's US organization, Militant. In the States he had met Ann Clarke. His daughter could well remember his enthusiasm for the young woman whom he was certain would become a key player in his crusade for socialism in Britain. He had helped her get into a radical law practice on her return from her year at Harvard, even getting her friend Mary Connolly fixed up as the office manager so that they could be together. He had arranged speaking tours, often standing down himself to give her the limelight. Her father had seldom seemed happier, with real hopes now of bringing

161

about a fundamental change in the Labour Party. And then it had all started to go wrong. He was accused of being a cheat and a womanizer, and his links with radical movements in the Middle East were made to look little short of treason.

When he could take no more, he had taken his own way out. No note explained his reasons, but the thoroughness with which he had prepared his suicide made it clear it was a coldly determined act.

Ross asked: 'Did he leave his admiration for Ann Clarke on the public platform, or do you think they were lovers?'

Stewart shook his head: 'With the wife and the mistress, I doubt if he would have had the energy! Anyway, the daughter says he was always open about his affairs, and he never mentioned Ann in that way at all.'

'So what about all the other mischief he was up to? What about these "radical links" with the Middle East?'

Stewart picked up: 'Libya. He was a consultant to the Libyan Economic Planning Agency.' Ross's expression identically matched his cynicism.

'So he was bent. Who was going to expose him?'

Stewart shrugged – Maureen Tumilty didn't know. He sat back as Ross thought aloud: 'Could Ann Clarke have targetted Lawrie, maybe innocently at first, knowing he was a flamboyant character who was quite capable of deciding to quit politics and leave the field open for her. When this looked too slow a course of action, she helped things along by setting him up for blackmail. It went too far and he killed himself. But still she got what she wanted – his seat in the House of Commons?'

Michael shook his head, not convinced: 'How could she have got the information to set him up for blackmail? I don't think she's ruthless enough to get involved in something criminal.'

'You've got to go to the States, find out where Lawrie and Clarke met. Find out where exactly it came from that he was getting money from the Libyans. Presumably our own Security people knew?'

Stewart laughed: 'Lawrie told his daughter he was doing work for MI something or other!'

Ross sighed: 'We're going to get a mini series out of this if we're not careful!'

'But what do you think of me going to the States? Will it be . . . safe for me?'

For a lot of reasons, Michael Stewart was plainly unhappy.

Ross said: 'Memories are short.'

Behind his desk Chief Inspector Laing tried to conceal his restlessness. He avoided looking Stephen Robinson straight in the eye. The more the MP probed, the more evasive Laing became. Eventually, the policeman leant across the desk to him:

'Look, this isn't an easy time for the police. We've got all the problems of trying to get things back to normal after the election, all the violence, vandalism. Be realistic. Our resources are stretched to the limit.'

'But the leaders. You know who they are.'

'We've no evidence.' His face told Stephen that Laing himself was unconvinced. The MP knew there was no point in staying, but was taken aback when Laing said he would walk him to his car. As they walked through the police station they made small talk about mutual friends, but as they got out into the deserted yard at the back, Laing looked around before turning to speak:

'Look. I've been trying every conceivable route to get to the Chief Constable. I've let him know what it is I want to talk to him about. But I'm being blocked at every turn. And that's not the worst of it. You and Mrs Metcalf couldn't have been out of the building the other night when I got a phone call from the Assistant Chief to say I had no authority to speak to politicians. Strictly speaking, I should have got clearance from HQ before talking to you, but it has always been force policy that we maintain a good relationship with the local MPs. Not this time, it would seem.' He let out a sigh. 'The thing that really worries me – who phoned to let them know that you and

Mrs Metcalf were with me?' Stephen could see Laing's genuine concern.

'I wish I could help but I've got no power whatsoever. If there is a cover-up going on, obviously it's in my interest to get to the bottom of it. But, let's face it, I'm the one person they would make sure never found out. All we can do is keep trying, keep asking questions.'

After a silence Stephen, reaching out to shake hands with the other man, was startled to find his hand grasped in the familiar Masonic grip. Laing smiled, but without much humour, as Stephen recoiled a little.

'So you're not one of them? I wondered, I never knew how honest they were about allowing Catholics in nowadays. Don't worry. I'm not one either.'

As Stephen turned towards his car, Laing took hold of his arm. 'We need to talk. Take us for a drive over the lochs.'

Both men stayed silent until Stephen drew into the car park at the small loch, switched off the engine and turned to face Laing who cleared his throat as if to give evidence:

'Know anything about Freemasonry?'

The other man shook his head: 'Only that it's a secret society. I used to think it was just a way of men currying favour to get jobs, and in this town to keep the Catholics out – but now they're supposed to have Freemasons in the Vatican. I'm not too sure about that.'

'Freemasonry is a very powerful force in this country, has been for hundreds of years. It extends down through the Royal Family, into the Government, the Civil Service, the police. They've been trying to root out Freemasonry in the police for over a hundred years. It all started in the City of London because the police force there was paid for by the banking community, and the banks owe more to Freemasonry than anyone else. In the seventies, there was a major purge on the Masons. But I've seen the power of the Masons growing again in the past two years. For some reason, the Masons in the police are protecting a lot of the terrorists. The day I went to report about the Workers' Militia, I kept being given Masonic handshakes, and when I didn't give the right response, people started to clam up on me. I thought nothing of it, I'd been told hundreds of times if I joined the Masons I'd be guaranteed my promotion, but I've always been opposed to secret societies and jobs for the boys. I'll get ahead on my own merits or not at all. Then I heard another story. Remember the young prostitute murdered on election night?'

Stephen nodded.

'The murder investigation has been called off. There was a rumour somebody important was involved, and the officer in charge was drafting in more troops to help nail the man, then he was told to drop it. He resigned, and no one else has been given the case.'

Confused, Stephen asked why.

'An order from on high, either the Scottish Office or the Home Office – or the Grand Inspector General of the Masonic Order.'

'You've lost me. Why should the Masons be interested? It was a sex murder, was it not?'

Laing nodded. 'Everyone knows about the sex side of it, but the mutilation has been hushed up. Remember Jack the Ripper?'

The MP nodded.

'His murders were the same, carried out in accordance with Masonic ritual – "the breast torn open and the heart and vitals thrown over the left shoulder". That was another murderer who got away because he was a Mason.'

Seeing that the confusion in the MP's face had not cleared, Laing told him a history story, about the way the police are organized in Britain.

'We know for a fact that well over half the senior police officers in Britain are Masons. And that's been the case for the last twenty years. In some forces it has helped cover up corruption, in others it has had no effect at all. But think what must happen when a criminal, the arresting officer and the judge are all Masons and can signal to one another that they are. All three have sworn solemn oaths to help one another as Brothers, oaths that carry the most dreadful threats if they're broken. Much of Masonic

ritual centres on murder. That would be enough to concentrate the mind.'

Stephen was sceptical: 'Why should sensible intelligent
men agree to be part of it, though?'

Laing shrugged. 'That's a question people have been
trying to answer for hundreds of years. But if you know
the only way you can get on is to be a Mason, you'll put
up with a lot, and the approval given to it by so many
powerful, untouchable people sort of legitimized it.
They're also scared to back out. Those threats would
curdle your blood.'

Stephen attempted to make sense of what the policeman
was telling him: 'You think much of the covering up of
the activities of key people in the Workers' Militia can be
put down to Freemasonry? You must therefore think that
somehow the Terrorists have managed to key into the
Masonic network.'

'Spot on.'

'Can you prove any of this?'

'Not a word, the evidence is all circumstantial. But I
would stake my life on it. I know the police, and I know
how deep Freemasonry is dug in. The Masons have been
somehow convinced that their cause and the terrorists' is
the same.'

Stephen was still unconvinced: 'What could that be?'

'I'm guessing, just guessing, remember. But if the
Masons thought that the increased hold the Americans
were getting on Britain was going to jeopardize the Royal
Family, then they would be duty bound to lay down
their lives if necessary to protect the Monarchy. And
remember, necessity makes strange bedfellows. The Trots
and the police may look pretty ill suited, but the Trots
and the Masons both believe the end justifies the means,
even if the means are violent.'

Laing could see that, despite himself, the MP was
beginning to accept what he had to say. Stephen made no
response, merely started the car and drove back to the
police station.

*

Harry McGregor had set up a special team to undertake all the planning and coordination. At least a quarter of a million people were expected, from all over Britain, to the Loch Lomond demonstration. His union had volunteered to take on the organization out of a sense of public spiritedness, anxious that as many as possible should be able to take part in this major protest against the nuclear industry, the Government and the Americans. That McGregor was Ann Clarke's campaign manager had not been missed by the press. His intervention was hailed as having her touch of genius; not only was his candidate the only politician who took any action towards ending the Hunterston siege to get the country back to normal, her team was developing a major platform for her, guaranteeing publicity throughout the world. Who therefore would be the star speaker at Loch Lomond? Few energies were required to convince people that they should take part. Improbable bedfellows such as the Women's Institute, the Church Army and the British Legion nationwide planned to join the growing band of 'professional' demonstrators from the political parties, the churches, environmental groups and others. Coach and train bookings boomed. McGregor's problem changed into straightforward logistics, how many people would fit?

As he pored over ordnance survey maps, trying to find suitable pathways that could be used to get all-terrain vehicles to and from the head of the march in an emergency, his secretary interrupted. 'A Mr McLean' to see him. He cursed the secretary for disturbing him, and smashed down the phone, refusing to be diverted. It rang again, he ignored it. After a couple of minutes, she came timidly into the room.

'He refuses to leave. He's making a bit of a scene. There's no other man in this afternoon.'

'What does he want?'

'He claims it's personal.'

With a sigh McGregor threw down his pen. Hamish McLean, in Harris tweed jacket and flannels, a checked shirt and tartan tie, had the unmistakable look of a police officer. McGregor, ready to roast the intruder, kept quiet at the malevolent contempt in the eyes of the large Highlander. He remained seated. At six foot two inches the other man towered over him. McLean's first tactic had him prowling round the room, even going so far as to turn round a pile of letter on McGregor's desk.

McGregor nipped this – or tried to. The taller man ignored him.

'What do you want? Who are you?'

McLean leaned over the table. 'I want to know where you were at about two a.m. on election night?'

McGregor recoiled. 'What is it to you? Who are you? Are you the police?'

'I didn't give you permission to ask any questions, did I?'

McGregor reached for the phone. 'Then I'll make this a police matter.'

McLean grabbed his arm. 'Where were you?'

McGregor, turning purple, said: 'Get you out of here.' The grip tightened.

'I was with my girlfriend. You can ask her. Her name's Mary Connolly, you'll get her on 249 3331. She's Ann Clarke's election agent. Now – your name?'

McLean's eyes never blinked. He put his pen and notebook away.

McGregor dialled: 'Police? I have an . . .'

McLean slammed down the telephone cradle. 'I'll be back.'

McGregor said suddenly: 'I know who you are,' and McLean left. The union official's hands were shaking as he again picked up the telephone.

'Trouble, you'll need to help me.'

As Stephen, preoccupied, passed the open door at the bar, Kathy called out to him:

'You've had a phone call! Mrs Metcalf was on. Hold on and I'll bring you out her message. I wrote it down.'

Stephen didn't realize that his face had lightened. A slight smile lifted the corners of his mouth. Kathy noticed it: 'Well at least we've found something to put a smile on your face these days!'

But he frowned as he read the message. 'How did she sound, Kathy?'

'Oh, very businesslike. But a bit worried. She asked if I knew when you would be coming down to London again, but I said I didn't. You've to phone her, but she'll not be free for another couple of hours.'

Frowning, he went into the office and closed the door. He sat at the desk wondering why it was so important to Sylvia that he should come down and talk to her. She knew he was in the middle of the Scottish Leadership campaign, so it must be something vital to cause the ultimate politician, Sylvia Metcalf, to ask him to abandon it, however briefly.

The club steward, Bobby, was clearly unhappy; normally an ebullient 'mine host', he couldn't even raise a smile.

'Stephen, I hate having to do this, but the brewers have been on. The directors have decided that we could be in infringement of our drinks licence by using the club for political purposes.'

Stephen let out a laugh. 'But it's a Labour Party social club. What else would we use it for?'

Bobby shrugged his shoulders: 'That's exactly what I said, but there's a by-law about using licensed premises, apparently it has something to do with corruption in the last century. I phoned Party headquarters and they told me it's true, but usually everyone turns a blind eye to it. The Party will have to go to court on it because if the brewers start getting strict, it'll affect more than us. Until then, they say I can't let you use the club for meetings or for your surgeries, and I'm afraid they've said you can't have the use of this office either.'

Jumping up, Stephen yelled: 'That's a load of crap. You know it too, and don't pretend you don't. If you were fed up with me using your office, you should have said and I'd have got out.' He glowered at the other man. 'Or the club could have got a new steward!'

The man looked embarrassed and a little sad. 'You should have let me finish. I said I would have nothing to do with such a stupid instruction, and I offered them my resignation.'

This calmed Stephen down. The steward had been out of work for three years before he got this job, and had worked tirelessly because he was so happy to be employed again. He would find it hard, probably impossible, to find another job, and if he resigned he would get no unemployment benefit.

Stephen picked up his chair and slumped back into it. Wearily he looked over.

'I'm sorry. I know you've always been very loyal to me, and it was terrible of me to doubt it. There's no question of you resigning. Tell me who I speak to at the brewery and I'll tell them you didn't mean to resign and I'll be out of here by tomorrow.' He held up his hand as the other man made to interrupt. 'We'll get our own legal advice, after all there's no point in having these premises just as a drinking place if it's useless for the Party. But until then, I'll just have to work at home.'

Both men sat in silence. Although nothing had ever been said, it was well known that Stephen's wife had made it clear he wasn't to bring politics home with him.

'Maybe the Party could rent offices for you?'

Stephen shook his head. 'No chance! The election cleaned us out, and now that I've got this Leadership thing, we'll need to use even my union sponsorship for that.' He stood up opposite the steward. 'Don't worry. There's plenty of room at home. I'll cope. But we'd better get things sorted out for you. Get me the name of who it is I've to speak to at the brewers and we'll get that out of the way.'

Stephen was alone but still sitting on the end of the desk when Joe Black came in. Joe had taken holidays from the steelworks to run Stephen's leadership campaign, and he looked very businesslike as he bustled into the office. But Stephen could see the worry in the face of the small man. He assumed he had heard about the eviction.

'Cheer up, Joe. The wife is always saying she sees nothing of me, now I'll be under her feet all the time. It'll teach me to be tidy!' He smiled and gestured at the clutter on his desk. But Joe didn't respond.

'OK! Spit it out! What else is wrong?'

Joe looked out of the window for a while before he answered.

'I went in to see your union today to ask if they'd give us your union sponsorship money a month or so early. They looked a bit shamefaced, then they told me it had been decided to remove you from the list of union-sponsored MPs. You won't be getting any more money.'

Stephen was genuinely taken aback. 'But they can't do that! I've been a union member for over thirty years. Every union member who's an MP gets sponsorship. I'll get on to them and tell them that!'

Joe shook his head. 'It won't work. They've had a full executive meeting about it, and they're removing sponsorship as a disciplinary measure. They say you're campaigning against union policy and they can't allow the members' money to be used against the best interests of the union.'

Stephen was aghast: 'What policy?'

'Support for Ann Clarke.'

Again, Stephen slumped in his seat. 'How much?'

'We lose seven thousand pounds for this coming year.' He paused, there was obviously more. Stephen waved to him to go on.

'They've also decided to withhold the ten thousand pounds we're due for the election.'

The colour drained from Stephen's face. The Party was broke; if he couldn't find the money to pay his election bills Joe could be declared bankrupt as his agent. If because of that an inquiry into his election expenses found them to be over the legal limit, as he knew they were, he could lose his seat and Joe could be sent to prison.

'Do they know the consequences of that?'

The election agent knew the inevitable track of Stephen's thoughts: 'Yes, they know that the Government's reduction in the legal spending limit for candidates put everyone over the limit, but that there was a nod and a wink that, provided there were no grounds for individual inquiries, a blind eye would be turned. I told them we had no money to pay, so there would be an inquiry. All I got was a shrug and told it was my problem.'

Stephen, too worried to be angry, sat quietly for a moment, composing his thoughts.

'Let me try to think of a way out of this, Joe. Meantime, go and look through the accounts and try to work out how much we owe.'

Before Joe left the room, he stopped with his hand on the door. 'You've probably forgotten that as a union MP, you get a union car. They want it back tomorrow.'

Stephen stood up and picked up a pile of *Hansard*, throwing them across the room to try to get rid of his frustration. His election agent left him alone as he went to investigate how much trouble they were in.

Once Stephen had calmed down, he tried to get hold of all the senior officials of his union, but none would speak to him. He asked for appointments with them, they were refused. He phoned London to speak to the General Secretary, he too was unavailable; but phoning London reminded Stephen he had to speak to Sylvia.

By her voice he knew she was in determined mood but would say nothing on the phone. He told her what had happened to him, but she seemed apparently uninterested. She insisted that he come to London immediately, unconcerned by his protests.

He agreed on the overnight sleeper and to meet her in a hotel for breakfast, hoping she would suggest something more intimate. She didn't.

Now he had to go home. It would be bad enough telling *her* he would have to work from home, but now that they would be strapped for cash, his wife would be even less pleased.

He felt the crisis as he opened the door; his wife sat in the living room, her eyes red from crying.

'It's all your fault! They've left! The boys have left!

172

They've got a flat in Glasgow and they're going to help in Ann Clarke's campaign.'

Stephen's face flushed with anger. He stalked the room trying to get a grip on himself, but his wife's accusing looks pushed him over the top.

'Well that's one problem solved! I need a place to work. I've been thrown out of my office in the club. And they won't be getting any more money from me either, I've none left to give.'

He sat down and told his wife what had happened. Recounting it brought home the full force of the opposition he was up against, opposition that could destroy him.

He sat with his head on his hands, despair threatening to overwhelm him.

As he sat oblivious to her, his wife's face softened with compassion and she reached out her hand to touch his bowed head. But her face suddenly clouded over, and she quickly withdrew. She went to make tea, leaving him feeling that no one gave a damn what happened to him.

Harry McGregor rang his opposite number in the General Workers' Union – Stephen Robinson's union.

'At the end of the day, you've done the best thing for Robinson and the Party. We can get this election out of the way and I've heard on the grapevine, Robinson is going to be offered a junior ministry. You can reinstate all his privileges then and this will all be forgotten about.'

He hung up abruptly and rubbed his hands with self-satisfied glee. Another problem out of the way. It was time to speed things up. After Hunterston, she didn't need phony challenges.

The bustle of the Leadership election campaign went on around him as Hamish McLean sat in the middle of the committee rooms. Computers churned out direct mail shots while an army of volunteers stuffed them into envelopes. The excitement was infectious.

Against one wall, at a bank of telephones under noise

hoods, calls were being made to key activists asking for their support. A supervisor sat at the end of the line ready to take on anyone who seemed undecided. Through a slightly open door, McLean could hear a television, but it was playing and replaying a video which looked like some kind of election broadcast; whoever was watching it didn't like one shot and was insisting it be re-shot to put Ann Clarke in softer focus.

Even in the short time he sat, two members of the public came in to ask for posters; they were given them and a note was taken of their names to follow up if more help was needed. Two men sat opposite a printer that spewed out lists – obviously the names of firm supporters, as they were being removed from a mailing list. An elderly lady asked if she could help, was given a cup of tea and pointed in the direction of the envelope stuffers.

Absorbed, he failed to notice the small woman who came out of the back office. Her brown hair, lightly flecked with grey, was severely pulled back from her forehead and anchored at the nape of her neck with a tortoiseshell clasp. She wore a navy blue suit and a white cotton blouse with a lace Peter Pan collar; her low-heeled navy court shoes were scuffed. She looked prim, but a woman not overly concerned with her appearance – a spinster. McLean saw the quick intelligence in her eyes, however, and the hesitant smile that revealed her nervousness. His answering smile was genuine. He liked Mary Connolly on sight, and it took only a glance to know that this woman would have nothing to do with Harry McGregor if she could help it. It would be interesting to see if she would admit that, though.

She ushered McLean into her little cluttered office, hastily removing a pile of envelopes from a chair so that he could sit down. She offered him tea, he declined. Nervously she chattered on about how sorry she was to have kept him waiting, but it was a very busy time. He shrugged it off as of no consequence. Having run out of small talk, Mary had to let McLean get down to the reason for his visit.

'Miss Connolly, what did you do on election night after Miss Clarke's result was declared?'

Mary hesitated before she answered him. Without realizing it, she glanced quickly at the door into the inner office. McLean followed her eyes. The door was slightly ajar, and he knew instinctively that someone was listening. The election agent cleared her throat.

'Are you a police officer, Mr McLean? I notice you gave no rank and you didn't show me any identification.'

McLean raised a quizzical eyebrow and smiled wryly, but made no comment other than to confirm that he had only days before retired from the police.

Mary's voice shook a little as she continued: 'What right do you have then to question me about my whereabouts?'

McLean's liking for Mary was beginning to diminish. 'As you know, the police are greatly overburdened at the moment, and I had started on a specific line of inquiries. I'm just carrying on to help out.'

'That's a bit unusual, isn't it?' Mary's voice was getting stronger now.

McLean was running out of patience. 'Miss Connolly, when you've looked down at the broken and battered body of a fourteen-year-old with sperm dried around her mouth and blood covering her vagina and rectum because a hard metal object had been forced into her, then you would be prepared to do the unusual. And that's without the mutilation. A young girl who had no other way to escape grinding poverty, was forced on to the streets, probably by some pimp, and she meets her death at the hands of a sadistic psychopath. Somebody has to bend the rules if that young girl's killer is to be found – before he does the same to someone else!'

Mary couldn't look him in the eye; she stared down at her desk. 'How does my whereabouts help to find her killer?'

'You let me work that one out, Miss Connolly. Now are you going to answer me?'

A meticulous description of all the places Mary had visited on election night was given to McLean. Throughout her catalogue, Mary kept her eyes averted.

'Was anyone with you?'

Again, Mary treated him to a long list. McLean visibly cheered up when she didn't mention McGregor. He stood up to go. Mary spoke again:

'I should have mentioned that after about two o'clock, Harry McGregor drove me around. He's very good about helping out with his car.'

'You mean, you don't drive?'

Mary blushed as she answered: 'Yes I drive, but I was very tired. Miss Clarke and Mr McGregor were worried that I was too tired to get behind the wheel of a car.'

Still she couldn't look at McLean, but the bitterness was so plain in his voice that she didn't have to see his face.

'What a very considerate employer you have! I didn't think thoughtfulness was a trait common to too many politicians. And McGregor seems to be a man of hidden depths.' He stood up to go. 'I won't take up any more of your time, I know how busy you are. Don't forget what I told you about that girl, will you? What it must have felt like to have a tyre wrench forced up you.'

He saw Mary shiver, his message had got home. He left her.

Ann waited until the door had closed behind the former policeman. She had been affected too by the picture he had painted of the murdered child, and she could see that Mary was very upset. She signalled to her to come into her office. Going to the little fridge in the corner, she poured them both a glass of white wine and gestured to Mary to sit down.

'You did well. It couldn't have been easy.'

Her words caused the anger and resentment to boil up in Mary: 'Why did you ask me to lie? Why did I get the job of covering up for McGregor? What if he did kill that girl? I'm as guilty as he is now.'

'Don't be silly, Mary. Of course he didn't kill any prostitute. The police are trying to frame him because he's a key figure in my campaign. This is all a plot to discredit me.'

'So why couldn't he be honest about what he was doing on election night?'

Ann brought the conversation to a close: 'Don't be stupid, Mary! You know that as soon as Henderson announced he was going, contacts had to be made so that everything was ready to move the next day. Do you want McGregor to admit we had advance knowledge of what Roddy Henderson was going to do? Don't you think people will start to wonder about how we knew and no one else? I told you this campaign was going to get rough. Dirty tricks. We're playing for enormous stakes here. Don't you think Metcalf and his pals are going to want to see me discredited?'

Fearing she was going too far, she softened her voice: 'Come on, Mary! You know me better than anyone. Do you think I would ask you to lie for a rat like McGregor if I didn't think there was good reason? It breaks my heart to think of what happened to that poor kid. But you've got to think the whole thing through. If there was a genuine chance that McGregor was in some way connected with her death, would the police have sent some old guy who had just retired?'

She walked round the desk, put her hand on Mary's shoulder and kissed her on the cheek. The election agent, looking sheepish now at her fears, went back to work.

The Ambassador stood outside the embassy to welcome the Prime Minister and his wife. The windows of the elegant Berkeley Square house blazed with light, and Sylvia could see that the party was in full swing. With the deference Sylvia had come to expect from East European diplomats, she was offered the arm of the tall and distinguished white-haired man. Moving graciously up the stairs into the drawing room, she acknowledged the bows of the embassy staff gathered in the foyer to welcome the Metcalfs. Despite the worries that seemed to constantly weigh her down these days, Sylvia had to work hard to suppress a grin as she caught a glimpse of herself in a mirror in her black velvet Frank Usher evening gown with ruched white peplum and long pencil skirt – far cry from the dingy committee rooms and draughty halls, the milestones to Downing Street.

Tony Metcalf had been her first love. Students together, they had grown close campaigning in the University Labour Club – she from a comfortable working-class background, secure and loving, he from a home split by bitterness and divorce. Tony had always looked lost and lonely, but his startling handsomeness had made him much in demand with the women who studied alongside him. Sylvia had felt sorry for him, had often taken him home to her parents to be fed and looked after, and he had come to depend on her, openly yearning for the security he saw around her.

Out of that, love had grown. And passion had linked with ambition. Sylvia, a doer, became irritated by endless debates about philosophy; she wanted power. She knew early that a woman had limited chances for herself – and if she wanted Tony, her job would be to build around him the security and the family he had lost.

And so it began. Tony and she set about planning his future, always keeping clinically in mind the ultimate goal. They made friends with the people whose support they needed, sometimes giving their young married dinner parties two or three nights a week. The charm of Tony and the warmth of Sylvia soon made invitations coveted. Graeme Jones had joined them, and soon justified the cut they had to take in their income to pay him. He provided the first professional back-up, building up detailed file indexes on everyone of importance, hustling for speaking engagements and TV invitations for Tony, making nationwide Party contacts. They marvelled at his unshakable commitment to get Tony Metcalf into Number Ten, when he could have been building a thriving career for himself.

In those days of the Kennedys and Camelot in the United States, all three perceived how powerfully television would shape the future of politics. Metcalf had a natural talent for the small screen, handsome and rugged, a husky voice and startling blue eyes, infectious charm –

and enough intelligence (or maybe too little patience) – to leave the detailed planning of strategy to Sylvia.

When they analyzed where best Tony could get a seat, they moved from London to Manchester. From there, via lectureship after lectureship, they tapped into the fertile source of working-class students going to university for the first time, unsure youngsters needing reassurance and leadership. Sometimes they came across someone from a different background with the kind of talent they wanted to harness to their own campaign rather than see a new force emerge on the political scene – like Ann Clarke.

Now it had paid off. The effort to be in the right place at the right time had brought them where they had always wanted to be – Number Ten, their turn to be feted and cultivated, like tonight.

The duty introductions over, Sylvia scanned the crowd for the union dignitaries she had been told to expect. Ceremonial though the occasion was – the Hungarian National Day – the dinner party gave her an excellent opportunity to buttonhole the powerful men of the trades union movement, whose help she would need to halt Ann Clarke.

Eddie Barraclough made his way over to her, and she smiled in delight. This genial son of a Blackpool landlady was now the General Secretary of Britain's largest and most powerful trades union – Ann Clarke's power base.

Barraclough stood between the improbable duo of Clarke and McGregor, when they first tried to take over a major part of the Labour machine. They might, in the process, have learnt the skills they would need to influence internal elections, but Eddie Barraclough was his own man, and had been unfailingly kind to the Metcalfs over the years. Without having to be told, he had realized how financially draining the long years in opposition had been, keeping up the trappings of the Opposition Leader. Entirely without prompting, a car and driver had been provided for Tony, and his entourage had been accommodated in the best hotels during the past two arduous election campaigns. The union leader had been obviously moved when Sylvia had regularly visited his dying wife over the long months she had spent in a London hospital.

Only three weeks ago Barraclough stopped a national dock strike – the adverse publicity could have cost Labour the election. Commentators credited him with bringing down the previous Labour Government by calling his road haulage drivers out on strike right at the start of the campaign. His support had clinched Metcalf's Leadership – and Ann Clarke had been Tony's campaign manager. At the time Sylvia had been grateful to the woman who had been her protégée. Now she had to accept that Ann must have wanted Tony to become Leader in order to oust him – defeated Leaders never rise from the grave.

Barraclough had just been appointed Chairman of the Economic Planning Board, the first of the post-election quangos – £15,000 a year for two days' work a month. Tonight he was likely to be in receptive mood, and without his help, her prospects of success were remote.

He abandoned the protocol expected when publicly greeting the wife of the Prime Minister, and smothered her in a bear hug. Tilting up her face to his, Eddie looked long and hard into her eyes, and she could see the great well of affection and concern he had for her:

'Well, girl. You've made it at last! You look a million dollars, so why aren't you feeling a million dollars?'

Sylvia took hold of his arm and led him into a corner where they could speak without being overhead. She rambled a little to cover her nervousness, talking of Tony's anxieties about the US summit, her worries about the strain he would be under, the need to make sure the Queen's Speech at the opening of Parliament didn't promise too much whilst at the same time not dashing people's hopes, but she could see from his expression that the union leader knew she was leading up to something. Taking a deep breath, she launched into it:

'It's Ann Clarke. I need your help. I think she's out to destroy Tony. I'm sure she's going to challenge him.'

Although his expression never changed, Sylvia sensed Barraclough moving away from her; although he gave every sign of listening intently, she felt him recoil from what she was trying to say. Fearing that she sounded like an over-anxious wife, she tried to toughen up her story with the detail of her experience in Scotland, but he wasn't listening. When she stopped speaking he patted her on the arm.

'I've monopolized you too much. Back to the Ambassador's wife with you, then maybe she'll give us some food.'

He gripped her arm firmly and led her back to the centre of the company.

As she tried to make small talk with the coterie of rather jaded diplomatic spouses she saw Barraclough cross the room quickly to one of his union cronies and the two men slipped through a door. A chill passed over the nape of her neck. Her hostess noticed the change in her, and with the composure of decades as the wife of a diplomat, took Sylvia off to the guest suite to 'freshen up'.

Safely alone in the overwhelming splendour of the bedroom, Sylvia leant against the door, pulling the collar of her gown away from her neck to help her breathe more deeply. Frantically blinking, she kept tears at bay, then the panic began to grip. Her one golden opportunity to enlist serious and powerful help, and she had blown it.

With the backs of her hands, she felt her cheeks burning up. Looking round the room, she saw light streaming out from a bathroom. She left the door open and ran the cold tap, holding her wrists under the icy water. Suddenly both the bathroom and the bedroom were plunged into darkness.

Sighing in irritation, conscious now that she had been away from the party for longer than was polite, she fumbled her way to the door. The handle would not turn – the door was locked. Assuming that a servant must have thought the room was unoccupied and had used an external switch to put the lights off, she raised her hand to hammer at the door. A hand grabbed her arm from behind, and a stronger grip, gloved, closed her mouth. Fear engulfed her, paralyzing her. As she stood rigid, trying to hold her body away from her captor, she felt a breath on her cheek, and a rough woolly fabric rubbed at her face. A man's voice penetrated her fear:

'Leave Ann Clarke alone! If you value your husband's life more than his power.'

As she tried to say something, ask what he meant, the hand clamped tighter. He forced her down on to the floor, making her kneel. She felt something as soft as a feather run down her back. 'Move and I'll kill you!' Then silence. It must have been minutes before she realized he had left. She knelt huddled near the door, too scared to move, until she was almost startled to death by rattling at the handle. Suddenly the lights came on. Stumbling to her feet, Sylvia discovered that her dress fell loose – he had used a knife to cut down the seam of her dress.

Seeing the key again in the lock, she turned it. A shocked and distressed Ambassador's wife stood outside:

'Oh, Mrs Metcalf! I'm so sorry! There's been a fault in the electrical circuit on this floor, and the security system automatically locks all the doors. You must have been very frightened, you should have called out!'

Conscious of the woman's embarrassment, and with the realization that this could probably finish the Ambassador's career, Sylvia made light of it, saying that she was more distressed at the tearing of the seam in her dress. The diplomat's wife summoned a maid, who stitched the couture creation back together.

Making no mention of her attacker, Sylvia repaired her make up, chatting to the Hungarian woman about the problems of the electricity supply in old houses.

The damage repaired, the two women walked downstairs. Seated next to the Ambassador for dinner, Sylvia felt the relief of being free mingled with the fear of what the masked man had said to her; she drank too much of the strong Hungarian wine, until she almost began to think she had imagined the warning she had been given. But even through the fog of the wine, she could still distinguish the chilling look on the face of her old friend Eddie Barraclough.

6

The day of the demonstration dawned bright and sunny. Ann stood at her bedroom window and watched the tiny white clouds scud across the sky. The phone rang a few times, but she ignored it, pausing only a second to listen to who was leaving a message on the answering machine.

McGregor phoned to say that he was off to Loch Lomond to make sure everything was ready for her. The next call was from Michael Stewart. The message was very businesslike – a request for an interview. But seconds later he phoned again, this time voice low and husky, a throb of passion in it. He wanted to see her. His arousal was obvious.

Picking up the phone, Ann dialled Stewart's number; he answered on the first ring.

As she spoke, she made it obvious that though anxious to be interviewed, she had other thoughts on her mind. Her voice dropped to a murmur.

'I can't see you, I've got to work. Ssh, don't be disappointed. I'm coming in for an interview, we'll get some time alone.'

She smiled as she listened to the frustration in his voice. 'Even if you can be here in fifteen minutes, I've got to leave in half an hour. I'll see you this afternoon. Be patient.' She laughed, hung up, and walked back through the bedroom to run her bath.

The group in the Cabinet Room stood up as the Prime Minister came in. Jeffries and Graeme Jones sat together opposite the fireplace with their backs to the window. Further along was John Downes, the Home Secretary, and next to him, David Fredericks, the Labour Party General Secretary – on the green leather blotter in front of him, a copy of the Party constitution. No civil servants were present, although the Principal Private Secretary had unsubtly grilled Jones to find out what was going on. He had learned nothing.

Metcalf wasted no time in coming to the point: 'Ann Clarke is getting out of control, and the delay in getting someone in charge in Scotland is not helping anyone. I'm going to sue for peace with her. Another week of this phony war before she is elected will help no one. I'm going to offer her the job right away.'

Jones jumped in first: 'You've already offered it to her and she turned you down and publicly humiliated you into the bargain. Why should she accept you now?'

Metcalf looked over at Fredericks, who was studiously avoiding his eye. 'Have nominations closed?' Fredericks nodded. 'Robinson is the only challenger?' Again Fredericks nodded. But this time he looked up. He was beginning to put two and two together. Maybe it would work.

Metcalf spoke with more decision than they had heard him use in months: 'We get Robinson to withdraw, so there is no need for an election. We insist we cannot again open up the nominations because the requirements of the constitution have been satisfied, and she can move into the Secretary of State's office on Monday.'

Jeffries put the next question: 'And if Robinson doesn't agree?'

Metcalf dismissed the thought with a wave of his hand: 'He'll accept. We offer him the number two job. Guarantee it in fact. We'll need someone like him in the Scottish Office to keep an eye on her.'

Jeffries was unconvinced: 'She won't wear it! She'll want one of her own placemen in there. Probably she's offered it already. She must have been doling out quite a lot of sweeteners to get this far without any opposition, and she'll know that if you get Robinson to withdraw, you're getting desperate.'

Again Metcalf dismissed it: 'If he doesn't get the Scottish Office, we can guarantee him something else. He'd jump at the chance to go to Industry. He can look after the steel re-nationalization.'

Again Jeffries came back to point out the weakness of that: 'You've just offered that job to someone else. You announced it yesterday.' Metcalf made to butt in, but Jeffries held his ground. 'Again you'll show her just how desperate you are, and that is exactly what she wants.'

Metcalf retorted angrily at Jeffries: 'OK, Smart Aleck, you're the one with all the answers. You tell me what you would do!'

Jeffries had remained quiet, impassively doodling on the notepad in front of him until Metcalf had stopped. Then he spoke. Those who knew him well could see that he wasn't totally convinced of what he was suggesting, he had probably wanted to mull it over a little longer but his hand had been forced by Metcalf's madcap plan. He set the scene.

'Let's review where we are. Ann Clarke is causing a very great deal of trouble not just in Scotland but in the rest of the country, and she's making things harder for us with the Americans. She has a massive power base which is likely to grow even bigger if she gets a popular mandate with this election. It looks as if her hidden agenda is to get Tony's job.'

He looked round the table to see if anyone was going to object to his analysis. No one spoke, although he could see the warning red film in Tony's eyes. A swift glance at Jones revealed that he realized the risk Jeffries was taking – Tony was well known for blaming the messenger who brought the bad news.

The Foreign Secretary and Deputy Leader of the Labour Party went on: 'We buy her out. We make her the offer she can't refuse. Her part of the deal is that she backs us – in return, we catapult her into the big league.'

Much to the irritation of the others, he paused. Metcalf told him to get a move on.

Jeffries took a deep breath, ready for the bombshell: 'We make her Deputy Prime Minister.'

He tensed his shoulders as if waiting for a physical assault. Looking round the table, he saw that the others were sitting open mouthed. No post of Deputy Prime

Minister currently existed, but it had been widely suggested that the job should be created, largely because of Metcalf's erratic behaviour. There had only ever been one name talked about to do it – George Jeffries.

Suddenly everyone spoke at once.

No one seemed to think it was a good idea. Jeffries held up his hands and tried to shout above the others. The hubbub subsided. But before he could say anything, Downes jumped into the silence.

'This is such a radical suggestion, we need time to think about it, and to test the water. Let's reconvene on Monday and by that time our thoughts should be clearer.'

Shaking his head, Jeffries went on with what he had been about to say: 'It is now eight forty-five a.m. Ann Clarke is to make the speech of her life to a quarter, maybe half, a million people at Loch Lomond in just over six hours. If we don't head her off before then, we could have real trouble on our hands. Don't forget why this bunch around her wanted a demonstration in such a strange place as Loch Lomond. The place is surrounded by US military installations. What if some of the nutcases who follow her around decide to storm one of the sites and come face to face with a rookie American marine with a sub-machine gun? What happens then?'

He let the thought sink and knew from their faces that he had scored. His colleagues now recognized they had somehow to stop Ann Clarke using her speech to aggravate anti-Americanism, and even, perhaps, formally launch a challenge to Metcalf.

The questioning started. Meticulously and logically, Jeffries responded. As he saw it, Ann Clarke had exploited the troubles in the country out of ambition. That she was a brilliant and charismatic politician remained without doubt and no way would she be content with being Queen Bee in Scotland. It had to be assumed that the Scottish Leadership fight was a minor skirmish on the way to Number Ten. With a popular mandate in the Cabinet she would be uncontrollable. It was Metcalf himself who asked the obvious question – would she not be more uncontrollable as his number two?

Jeffries was ready for him. No real constitutional base existed for the role of Deputy PM, it could be as much – or as little – as Metcalf wanted it to be. But the job was one central to the Administration, and would leave Clarke no room to distance herself from the decisions of the Cabinet.

Her ambition would draw her into a stranglehold. The dream of being only a heartbeat away from the top office in the land, would effectively make her give up much of her power. And she would still be Secretary of State for Scotland – giving her, all told, the heaviest portfolio in the Cabinet, and not much time to spend as a troublemaker.

And as for the Americans, they would soon accept that the minute she was brought round the summit table, she could no longer afford to peddle her irresponsible and patently unworkable anti-Americanism.

Would she swallow it? No one would know until they tried. This discussion went round and round until they could get no further. Surprisingly Metcalf asked for a vote, forgetting that convention decreed the Prime Minister sum up at meetings. Without exception, they all decided to give it a go.

Now all that was needed was to get Ann Clarke to agree. Jones went off to contact her.

A few hundred yards away from the discreet splendour of the Cabinet Room in Number Ten, in the back room of a souvenir shop on Whitehall, two men sat across from one another at a table, headphones on, a tape recorder spinning in front of them. Simultaneously they removed the headphones and looked at one another. The older man spoke.

'Looks like it's going to plan. You'd better sort things out here while I get back. We'll get a signal off as soon as possible.'

At that, he picked up the lightweight anorak that had

been hanging over the back of his chair and went out into Whitehall to hail a taxi.

The dining room of the St James's Court Hotel was filled with Japanese tourists festooned with cameras – and the inevitable Americans, shouting at the tops of their voices and planning another rape of London's fashionable stores.

Stephen Robinson felt irritated by the noise and the overly ornate splendour of the room. Nursing an orange juice, he waited for Sylvia Metcalf to arrive. She was late. He stood up as she approached the table. Her face was grim, and her skin seemed to have lost some of its luminous quality. In the few days since he had last seen her, this lady had been through the mill.

For her part, Sylvia saw a man with shoulders slumped in the subconscious attitude of defeat. His shirt seemed rumpled, his morning shave less effective than usual. The brave declarations of war against Ann Clarke seemed a bad joke now. As she settled herself and took in the full evidence of his weariness, she apologized for her delay.

'Tony woke up this morning full of resolve. He's decided the Ann Clarke problem has to be got out of the way once and for all. I tried to get him to tell me what he intended to do, but he refused to speak about it. He summoned the Inner Cabinet, so I'm counting on George Jeffries to keep me informed. I'm seeing Jeffries later today. That's why it was so important we had to talk. George and I have decided the Security people need to look at who's backing Ann Clarke. And not a minute too soon!'

Stephen's eyes widened at this, and he listened intently as Sylvia told him what had happened at the Embassy. Startled to hear of her shocking experience, he reached out and took hold of her hand. A camera clicked, just another noise among the Japanese tourists loading their film for the day. 'You've got to take care! I've seen what these people have done in Scotland, they'll stop at nothing to get what they're after, and it would be terrible if something happened to you.'

As it sank in how he would feel if Sylvia did come to some harm, he repeated himself: 'It would be really terrible. And you don't even seem to have a full-time detective. You'll need to speak to Tony about that.'

Sylvia smiled but looked away. Stephen was a good and dear friend, but she could not be diverted from her campaign to protect Tony.

'I've got a detective now. He's sitting outside the dining room. I got such a fright the other night that I won't be taking chances again.'

As she said it she looked at him and saw that he realized that her increased protection would remove for ever the chance of repeating the intimacy in a Glasgow hotel lounge, and she saw the regret.

Sylvia broke the short silence: 'But I didn't bring you here to cry on your shoulder. Something else happened at the Embassy and it's as well you're here, you should know about it right away.' And she told him about her conversation with Barraclough. She tried to break it as gently as possible that she thought his challenge was now totally pointless, but he stopped her.

'My challenge was a bad joke. I now have an idea what I'm up against.' He looked thoroughly miserable as he told her how he had been let down by his union, how he had lost his office, his car and even his sons.

It was her turn to reach out to his hands, to cover them with her own.

They were both startled by a cough. Guiltily jumping apart, they looked up. Sylvia's detective had come up to the table:

'Mrs Metcalf, the Foreign Office has been on the phone, the Foreign Secretary wants to see you immediately. Could you come right away? Oh and sir, I overheard the switchboard at Number Ten putting out a search for you. You might like to phone to let them know where you are.'

Sylvia hurriedly collected her belongings. Stephen rushed to pay the bill, too preoccupied to object to being charged for two breakfasts when all they had got round to was one glass of orange juice.

Within fifteen minutes Stephen was walking up Downing Street to Number Ten. Before he reached the door, it had opened, the doorman attracted by a discreet ring from the policeman on duty outside. As he passed, the police officer greeted him by name. Stephen was startled, then he remembered that all the police on Parliamentary duty and outside Number Ten spend the election looking at photographs of the candidates so that they can identify them immediately they arrive in the House.

He had stood in the foyer of Number Ten for only a few seconds when one of the Private Secretaries arrived to take him to the waiting room, but he had time for a quick look round. The floor was tiled in black and white, and a well-worn hooded porter's chair sat at one side of the fireplace. As this was high summer, the grate was filled with fresh flowers in bright amber and gold. A square Georgian clock sat plainly in the middle of the mantel, ticking slowly away. A corridor led off to the left, and he knew from reading the newspapers that it led to the room occupied by the Press Secretary. It had been pointed out to him that the window looking directly onto Downing Street, to the right of the door, was the press office. At the other side of the fireplace was a little room where he could see the detectives playing chess to pass the time. The doorman checked off his name from a list on a highly polished console table in the window embrasure, and his escort arrived.

As he was led along the corridor by the civil servant, he kept on looking, trying to be discreet, but also trying to commit to memory details of his first – and maybe last – visit to the most famous house in the country. He was left to sit in a little waiting room at the side of a rectangular hall, opposite what he took to be the Cabinet Room. He was to sit there for over an hour before he was summoned to the presence.

As Stephen paced the little waiting room with its elegant Georgian furniture, pausing occasionally to look at the books in the glass-fronted bookcase – all gifts from previous Cabinet ministers honouring the tradition that a

donation should be made to the Number Ten library –
Sylvia was with George Jeffries.

George took five minutes to tell her what had happened
at the Number Ten meeting. She immediately recognized
it as a high-risk strategy, but she saw its potential. But
like George, she shared a fear that Ann wouldn't swallow
it. They didn't have too much time to debate the consequences; soon George's intercom buzzed to announce the
arrival of another visitor.

The tall, slim, prematurely grey-haired man was shown
into the room. George hadn't had time to explain his
presence to Sylvia, so he filled her in through his
introduction:

'This is Colin Warrender, Sylvia. He used to be with
Number Ten Security when we were in Government
before, but he's been in special projects for the past few
years. He's going to help us with our vetting of Ann
Clarke, and I thought he had better hear what happened
to you in Scotland and the other night at the Hungarian
Embassy.'

Although Sylvia had agreed with the need to put together a dossier on Ann Clarke, now that she was confronted
with the reality of what would be involved she was a little
nervous, and this showed in the abridged version she gave
to Warrender. George sensed her reluctance and its cause,
so he asked if he could be left alone with the Prime
Minister's wife for a little while.

Once Warrender had left them alone, George wasted
no time in strengthening Sylvia's resolve.

'You're the one who told me in the Gay Hussar that it
was essential to rein in Ann Clarke. You know she's out
to destroy Tony, I suspect she's out to destroy a hell of a
lot more than Tony. So you can't afford to be squeamish.
If we're going to take on Ann and win, then we have to use
every weapon at our disposal. Especially if she becomes
Deputy PM. Now you have to tell Warrender everything
you know, and don't forget her student days either. There
might be something there.'

Sylvia still looked worried. 'Exactly which branch of the Security Service is Warrender from?'

'Let's just say he's doing this as a little freelance job for me. If he does it well, he knows I'll consider him for a project I have.'

The worry was still in her eyes. 'He's not connected with any foreign service, is he?'

Jeffries laughed. 'You've been reading too many thrillers!'

But Sylvia was ready for him: 'It's not thrillers I've been reading! I'm old enough to recall some of the things that happened before to Labour Governments. Remember Wilson and the South Africans? And are you convinced MI5 wasn't out to bring down the Wilson Government?'

Jeffries laughed. 'The South African story was the invention of fevered imaginations close to Wilson, and I never really swallowed all that stuff about MI5. Still, we can find out about it now. Must ask the Home Secretary to dig out the files.' He buzzed for Warrender to return, and he was still smiling and shaking his head as the man returned.

Sylvia was with them for an hour and a half. Despite her misgivings about this particular development, she felt a sense of satisfaction as she walked back to Number Ten; at least now something was happening.

As soon as she walked in the door, Sylvia could sense that there had been developments: an air of celebration, missing since the day the new Government had taken over, hung in the air. A message had been left at the door for her to go straight to the Prime Minister's study. She was shown into the room where Graeme Jones wrestled with a bottle of champagne. Tony Metcalf crossed the floor in a couple of steps, grasping his wife in a bear hug. She looked from one man to the other. At last she got the feeling that they had won the election. This is what it should have been like on election night.

'What's happened? Why the celebration?'

Even Graeme Jones gave her a hug: 'Ann Clarke's been bought off! She's agreed to be Deputy Prime Minister.

The election in Scotland's being called off, she moves into the Scottish Office on Monday.'

Sylvia hadn't expected things to happen quite so quickly, and her thoughts immediately went to Stephen Robinson.

'What about Stephen? Has anyone told him?'

Metcalf waved his arms in an expansive gesture. 'Just appointed him Minister of State at the Scottish Office.'

Sylvia's eyes widened. 'What will Ann have to say about that?'

'Oh, she suggested it. I was about to beat about the bush, try to bring her round to the idea, but she jumped in and said she wanted him as Minister of State. I've just packed him off back to Glasgow. He's to have a meeting with her at lunch time, then he's going to accompany her to this rally. We'll make the announcement at half past two, just as the speeches are about to start.'

Metcalf lifted up his glass of champagne in a toast: 'To the Metcalf Administration. We're in business at last.'

Even as Sylvia joined him in the toast, worry gnawed at her heart. It had all been too easy. Why should Ann Clarke agree to be bought off as easily as this? What stunt was she going to pull next? Rather than saving himself, had Tony dug his own grave? After all, Ann Clarke was now only a heartbeat away from real, unrestrained power.

After the call, Ann sat, immobilized, at her desk. A slight flush stained her neck, the only visible sign of her excitement. She picked up the phone, dialled an international number, then hung up before the exchange would have time to connect. Leaving the desk, she went through to the bedroom, collected the silver-framed photograph and took it with her back to her desk. She dialled the number again.

Disappointment clouded her face as the phone rang out. She was about to hang up when it was answered. Her face lit up, her eyes sparkled.

'Oh, darling, I thought you weren't there! I had to speak to you!'

She listened intently to the voice on the line. When she spoke again, the warmth in her voice was laced with joy:

'The Scotland job is mine. Unopposed. He offered me the other job this morning. As you always said he would. I've accepted. It'll be announced in about four hours. I thought you'd want to know right away – professionally as well as personally.'

She listened again. 'Does that mean I'll see you soon?'

Disappointment again took possession of her face. 'Well, at least we'll be in the same room! It's just that there are so many things I want to tell you. I love you.'

She hung up. As if willing herself to put sad thoughts behind her, she pulled forward her notepad and telephone book and set to work.

Mary was summoned with no explanation given. McGregor was contacted by radio pager and asked to phone her immediately. A quick phone call to her parents warned them what to expect, but she kept the conversation brief, fearful that she could no longer keep a check on her emotions.

As she waited for Mary, she switched on her word processor and started to change her speech. She was deeply engrossed in putting down the ideas that had filled her head for months when the doorbell rang. Surprised and a little irritated that Mary hadn't used her key, she bustled to the door.

A tall man stood on the doorstep, broad shouldered and heavily muscled, with quick intelligent eyes. He pulled out a badge from his pocket.

'Detective Sergeant Macdonald, Secretary of State. I've been assigned to see to your protection. May I come in?'

She stood back to allow the policeman to come into the flat, pointing to the reception room. Sergeant Macdonald went in, immediately scanning the windows, going over to check their clasps.

As he turned to speak to the Minister he could see that she was a little flustered.

'I'm sorry, ma'am. I should have phoned first. I thought

you would realize we would be here as soon as you were appointed.'

Ann smiled: 'Certainly, Sergeant, but at some stage we're going to have a talk about how we handle my protection. I've no intention of being a bird in a gilded cage. But if you'll excuse me, there's something I must do urgently. Make yourself at home.'

Ann went into the bedroom, closing the door behind her. She threw herself on the bed. She lay for a while looking at the ceiling, but as a few tears escaped the corners of her eyes, she got up and stood at the window, looking out on to the little patio, her face pressed against the glass.

That was how Mary found her.

'My God, Ann! What's happened? Why is that policeman here? Has someone tried to attack you?'

The election agent crossed the room to her charge, but before she could reach her, Ann had turned from the window. The triumph in her eyes stopped the other woman in her tracks.

'Mary, meet the new Secretary of State for Scotland.'

The two women fell into one another's arms, tears now freely coursing down their cheeks. When she had taken in the information, Mary stood back and looked at her friend quizzically. 'But I thought you would never accept that without an election. What made you change your mind?'

Ann took both Mary's hands in hers. 'Because I'm now also the Deputy Prime Minister.'

Mary sat down on the bed with a thud, speechless.

Ann told her what had happened, the call from Metcalf, the bargaining to make sure she wasn't sidelined, the guarantee that she'd be on the team for the US summit, the decision to appoint Stephen Robinson as Minister of State. Still Mary couldn't take it in. Ann sat beside her.

'I didn't fully grasp it until the policeman arrived and called me Secretary of State. It all seemed like a dream until then, now I know it has actually happened I feel like a stranger standing outside myself looking in. But a very happy stranger!'

She pulled Mary to her feet and together they did a little jig around the room. The women were giggling happily when they heard a knocking at the bedroom door. It was Sergeant Macdonald.

'I took the liberty of answering the phone, ma'am. Mr McGregor is replying to your message to contact you.'

Ann stifled her grin and smoothed her dress and hair. 'Thank you, Sergeant. I'll take it in my study. Perhaps you could help Ms Connolly make us all some tea. I think we could do with it after the excitements of the morning. You two had better get to know one another, you'll be working closely together. Ms Connolly will be joining my personal staff at the Scottish Office.'

Ann couldn't resist a quick look at Mary's face to see how she took this news: confusion, delight, fear, all crowded into her eyes at once. Ann went off with a laugh to answer the phone.

Despite the bad connection on the radio telephone, Ann could tell McGregor was ecstatic. She had quite a job calming him down. It was very important he told no one.

After an argument he saw the point of what she was saying. She would be the one to tell the crowd, his job was to make sure there was massive international coverage, and that there would be a helicopter available to take her away at the end. She needed to get back into Glasgow to do TV interviews, she couldn't afford to be out of touch.

Finally, she told McGregor that she would be accompanied by Stephen Robinson. McGregor wanted to know why. When he was told, Ann could feel the force of his blind fury come down the crackling telephone line. Only a promise to do something for him got him under control.

As she hung up, she jotted down on her pad:
A job for McGregor – one that keeps him out of the way.
She tore off the memo and put it in her briefcase.

As Mary and Ann settled down to do some work, the

police officer positioned himself by the entrance door. It was he who brought Stephen Robinson to her. Immediate awkwardness materialized between Stephen and his new boss. A lot of insults had been exchanged recently, and now he had capitulated by agreeing to come and be her assistant. Ann noticed that the other MP was so tense he missed the policeman's formal introduction:

'The Minister of State to see you, ma'am.'

Ann went round her desk to him, smiling and holding out her arms: 'Congratulations, Stephen. I'm so grateful to you for agreeing to work with me. We'll be a great team.'

She reached up and kissed him on the cheek. Sheepishly he responded.

Ann turned to Macdonald: 'Could you manage to squeeze another cup of tea out of the pot for the Minister?' As she used the expression, she saw Stephen jump back, his emotions not unlike hers a short time before. Once the door had closed behind Macdonald, she turned to her old enemy.

'I was like you when I heard my new title. I felt like looking round to see who else was in the room! But we'll soon get used to it.'

Hesitantly Stephen began to congratulate her, but she waved him aside: 'Have you had a chance to phone home to let them know what's happened?'

Stephen shook his head. Ann gestured to the telephone, then signalled to Mary to follow her, leaving the man to pass on his news in peace.

Before they left they both saw the cloud descend on Stephen's face. Each looked at the other, acknowledging a sympathy for the man who would have to apologize for his success.

Hamish McLean had been questioning people all day. He knew now about McGregor's frequent use – and abuse – of prostitutes. An old friend – a retired Special Branch officer – had seemed to be on the point of telling him something about an investigation of the union official that had been going on for years – then he had clammed up. That had been the problem, every time he got close to some hard facts, a fog descended. But he was sure he could come up with a positive identification of the car; if only the tart who had plucked up the courage to admit having seen it didn't lose her nerve, that would be enough; they would have to reopen the case then.

Turning into his own street, the retired police officer was surprised to see two police cars parked outside the block of flats. Both cars were unoccupied. Wondering what could be going on, he raced up the stairs to his door.

A uniformed constable was standing guard outside. Without looking him in the eye, the officer opened the door and gestured to the bewildered former colleague to go in. The flat had been torn asunder, drawers emptied on to the floor, couch and chairs ripped apart, books pulled out of the bookcase.

He walked into the living room, and Divisional Chief Superintendent Andrew Morrison stood up.

'You're nicked, McLean,' He held up a clear plastic bag filled with a white powder.

'Possession of an illegal substance. I have to caution you that anything you say may be taken down and used in evidence against you. And God help you inside. No one hates anything more than a crooked cop, and a drug dealing one is the lowest of the low.' Still speechless, McLean was handcuffed and hustled out to the car.

Three hundred thousand people looked up into the sky at the circling helicopters. Most would carry film crews, but one would carry Ann Clarke. Men, women and children had come from all over Britain to hear her speak. Some had travelled for days, others risked losing jobs, taking time off where they had already been refused. For what she was trying to do for them, they reasoned, this was the least they could do for her. Throughout the crowd stories were recounted of what people were doing, what they were thinking, when they saw Ann Clarke walk into that power plant. Admiration swelled into adoration.

Some spoke of what it had been like for them over the past couple of years, living with the constant threat of violence from the Workers' Militia. The daily poverty, the food shortages when the dockers went on strike, yet the Americans could always get the best. Parents spoke of their despair that their children had got caught up with the Militias, how frightened they were. Every discussion came to one conclusion – now they had someone who would sort it out; Ann Clarke would take on anybody. The world had to be told the people were behind her.

The sunshine added to the excitement and the air of expectancy. The police grudgingly told the media how well-behaved people were. A buzz had gone round that something was going to happen. A young police constable had let it slip that the security cover had been upgraded. Maybe someone even more important was going to come? Some speculated it was going to be Metcalf. That set off the first rumble of discontent of the day.

The main press team had started to push its way to the front as the time for the helicopter arrival got closer. McGregor had set up a marquee for the press with mobile telephones, anxious that no part of the day's events should be concealed from the world just because of inadequate communications, but the heat in the tent had driven the reporters outside. One elderly reporter from an agency stayed on, filing crowd stories.

The others had gathered around the edge of the helicopter site, hoping Ann might have an advance copy of her speech with her so that they could get it over as quickly as possible. The banter of the reporters was keeping everyone happy when the elderly keeper of the tent came running out.

Immediately, everyone knew it was a story. The man was breathless when he reached the pack. Panting, he told them the news from Downing Street. Ann Clark had been appointed Secretary of State for Scotland and Deputy Prime Minister.

Robinson was Minister of State.

After a stunned second, the press pack dispersed, falling

over one another as they raced for the tent to check with their news desks. Was it true? If it was, what were they to do?

Phones were abandoned as the rotor blades of the helicopter chopped the air. Back raced the newsmen and women, still unsure of the story's accuracy.

The first person out of the helicopter was Macdonald, which confirmed the story. Macdonald was Special Protection Squad and only the top-liners got armed protection: Ann Clarke had made it into the big league.

She came out and raced clear of the rotors, closely followed by Stephen Robinson. Mary brought up the rear, carrying the briefcases. As if from nowhere, a police team surrounded Ann, and even above the clamour, she could hear the groans of discontent from the press. She stopped in her tracks and came over to them. Everyone shouted their questions at once. She laughed at them:

'Hold on, hold on! Have I ever let you down? Yes it's true. I'm Secretary of State and Deputy Prime Minister.'

Above the racket, she heard one reporter ask why she had taken the appointment without an election:

'Because it is the ultimate recognition for the policies I fought the General Election on. No one can relegate Scotland to the sidelines now. And as Stephen Robinson withdrew, there was no one to fight an election with!'

Robinson quickly covered up his confusion – it was news to him that he had decided to withdraw. He had thought Metcalf had called the election off, but he kept his mouth shut, other than to give a ringing endorsement of his new boss:

'It's time to put the bickering aside. There is much to be done for Scotland, and together the Secretary of State and I will make sure Scotland's best interests are served with determination and compassion.'

The two politicians departed for the speakers' platform.

The speeches were already under way, the crowd listening respectfully to various clerics and trades union leaders. Only one pop singer, well known for his passionate radicalism, managed to raise a cheer, but that was forgotten when Ann walked on to the platform.

Standing in the wings, Stephen had to admit she looked magnificent. Ann had changed into a Marimekko cotton dress. Its white background was enlivened by brilliant swirls of red, orange and yellow. Round the discreetly low-cut neckline she wore a necklace of bright red stones, huge and eyecatching. Her hair hung free about her face, and large red earrings mingled with its auburn rich lines. Her high-heeled shoes gave her extra height, and those close to the platform could see that her breasts were free, the nipples hard as the adrenaline coursed through her.

The crowd went mad. The cheering was ecstatic, thousands jostled for a better view of her, and the nondescript speaker who had the microphone was ignored. Suddenly Ann saw a surge forward in the crowd; concerned, she raced to the front of the platform, holding up her arms to the crowd to be still. Beckoning the speaker, she took hold of the microphone:

'Be careful, there are small children in the crowd, someone could get hurt, and then the great news I have for you will be spoiled for all time.'

She stood silently until the crowd had quietened, using again the powerful force of her stillness. But the strong woman whom they revered had tears streaming down her face as she was embraced in the powerful wave of their emotion.

When the hush was total she began, her statement blunt and devoid of any embellishment:

'At eleven fifty-five, the Prime Minister asked me to become Secretary of State for Scotland. Tell me what to do!'

The ecstatic response was deafening, leaving no one in any doubt of what the crowd wanted.

Again she held up her hand, again in complete control of them.

As the silence deepened, she smiled: 'He has also asked me to be Deputy Prime Minister. Should I take it?'

A roar swept through the crowd, until they noticed

that she had begun again to speak, then they subsided. Hundreds of thousands, people of all hues and passions, stood in the sunshine. It could have been Latin America, not the blue shore of Loch Lomond.

'I am your servant. My life is you, the poor, the disadvantaged, the oppressed, and all who fear what the future may bring. Together we need have no fear. We have come this far hand in hand, no one can stop us now. We are going to be free!'

She punched and punctuated her sentences – carefully, powerfully, clearly. Captivated, the crowd simply cheered and cheered and cheered.

Michael Stewart stood at the front of the platform, watching her and wanting her. Behind him he heard a cynical hack snigger and say to his companion: 'Eva Péron out of Adolf Hitler!'

He almost spun round, but Clare, never far from his side, caught his arm, warning him with her eyes.

In the melee of press behind the platform, Ann caught the eye of Stewart; Clare saw the signal passed between them and it reverberated through her own body.

The helicopter was ready to take Ann back to Glasgow. Unexpectedly, she asked Mary and Stephen to wait behind to keep an eye on how the day developed. To Stewart and Clare she offered a lift.

Clare and Macdonald sat together at the front of the chopper, Ann and Michael immediately behind. Out of the corner of her eye, Clare saw Ann's hand reach out and stroke the inside of Michael's thigh. Switching her position, Clare used her body to give the politician and the journalist the privacy they needed.

At the BBC, Ann asked for a dressing room to enable her to do her own make-up: a well-known requirement of hers so no one was surprised. Unexpectedly, she asked Michael to join her as she prepared – she wanted time to think of the answers to the questions he would ask. No one thought anything of it as the door closed.

Alone, they fell on each other, Michael forcing his hand down the front of her dress, squeezing her breasts and

202

forcing her back on to the dressing table so that she was bent backwards. Ann fumbled with the belt of his trousers. Neither could wait. Forcing himself inside the silk of her French knickers, he entered her. Their climax was quick and deep. When Ann rejoined the others before going into the studio, the Controller was waiting to congratulate her. He was to tell his wife that evening of the almost incandescent glow that had settled on Ann Clarke now that she had the power she wanted.

Police outriders overtook the official Jaguar at the Maybury roundabout, west of Edinburgh. They led the driver away from the congested Corstorphine approaches to the city and through the well-heeled suburb of Barnton. At every junction motorcycle officers stopped the traffic, allowing the small convoy to sweep through.

Within minutes the car passed the rear of Bute House – the official residence of the Secretary of State for Scotland. Few Cabinet ministers could boast such an elegant residence, part of one of the most beautiful Georgian terraces in Europe with a view over the Charlotte Square gardens to the brooding hulk of Edinburgh Castle. The house, magnificently furnished for entertaining, had an intimate flat at the top – Ann's home, if she chose. The very existence of Bute House testified to the unique role which the Secretary of State for Scotland played in the British Cabinet, to begin with, the office bore the responsibility for the equivalent of more than a dozen English departments, each with their own Cabinet status. But the Secretary of State was heir to the Act of Union, when the Crowns of England and Scotland had been joined, Scotland had been left with her own Church, legal system and education. Out of that had grown a system of government that gave immense power to the man or woman who controlled it – and a deep feeling of dissatisfaction to the people ruled by it.

The car neared a modern office block, workplace to six thousand civil servants, current home of the British Government in Scotland. As government had grown more complex, these same civil servants had assumed more and more power. The woman in the limousine would challenge that power.

The crowds had been gathering since early morning; but many had been disappointed, as the police held them back, allowing nobody nearer the office block than the narrow public road facing the main entrance, some 250 yards away. Nevertheless, almost a thousand people had managed to squeeze themselves in, anxious to have a bit part in the making of history. Reporters and film crews had been allowed into the small car park, but were kept behind barriers.

Just before the car came into view, the crowd knew something was about to happen; Sir Edward Grierson, Permanent Secretary at the Scottish Office and Scotland's premier civil servant, came through the bank of glass doors to stand in the bright sunshine. His patrician profile, slicked-back grey hair, pinstriped grey suit and pink candystriped shirt with white collar, seemed to mock the cheerful exuberance of the crowd.

The chant began: 'Ann! Ann! Ann!'

A lone piper, there to pay his own tribute, began to tune up. When he saw the outriders, the unmelodic wailing became 'I love a Lassie!', an anthem much loved on Scottish charabancs for generations. The crowd joined in; when they saw the car the excitement threatened to go out of control. A crescendo of cheering broke out, taken up by the many junior civil servants, relegated to watch the event from their office windows. Though it didn't seem possible, the noise increased further as she stepped out of the car. Wearing a dress of red silk, enlivened by white flashes and silver jewellery, she looked like a successful model off to a showbusiness lunch, or the pampered pet of a rich man. But the outfit, chosen as always for impact and its effect on the TV cameras, made her stand out against the background of the grey men whose power she had to curb in order to succeed.

Leaving the car, she walked up a few of the steps. For a second the crowd thought she wasn't going to acknowledge them, and their cheers became more frantic. But she turned to give them a better view, and the photographers better pictures. She raised her arms in the air, clenching them in a salute of victory, rewarding the photographers from the less politically conscious papers with a picture showing more of her long slim legs and a much better profile.

Secure in the adoration, she turned away to meet the men against whom she had to join battle. As she moved along the line, she sized them up while they appraised her. They saw in the wariness of her greetings that she would never underestimate them; in the challenge of her eyes they knew they had a fight on their hands to keep her under control.

She had met Sir Edward Grierson before; he was the 'normal channels' through which Her Majesty's Loyal Opposition communicated with Government. Now, as they greeted, each knew the other to be a worthy adversary. As she began to turn away from him, he raised his eyebrows involuntarily. She turned back and held him in a stare until he had to lower his eyes.

Her personal office staff was small, just the Principal Private Secretary, Jonathan Browning, two assistants, one female – Fiona Cockburn – who kept the diary, and two shorthand typists, again female – Lesley and Karen – who would seldom need to take dictation from Ann. From now on her conduit to the outside world would be Jonathan. The letters he dictated on her behalf would appear every night in her ministerial red box; if he was unsure of her wishes they would be in draft form, otherwise all she had to do was sign them.

As long as Ann remained a Minister in Her Majesty's Government – which she would soon learn to call HMG in the jargon of the Civil Service – she would have to live with the tyranny of the ministerial boxes. Just as the civil servants filled her days with official meetings and delegations, they would also fill her boxes with memos, position papers, letters, advice notes and draft bills, occasionally hoping that exhaustion might let something slip through which the Minister would otherwise refuse to initial. The real work of a Minister went on through these boxes, and they would follow her wherever she went. As one box was filled, another would be opened. The department would have to know where she was at all times, and through grief or joy, she would have to be prepared to work on them, ready for the next day when they would be emptied and filled all over again.

As an elected Member of Parliament, Ann would also have her constituents to serve; in that she would be helped by the unmistakable impact that a letter on official departmental notepaper would have on any authority or individual.

Jonathan would be forever at her side, only the plea of 'Party business' would earn her some respite. For these young men from the best schools, and with some of the best brains in the country, the route to high office in the Civil Service was linked to running the Private Office of a Minister. Some said it was because it gave them high administrative skills – others that it was a testing ground to see how well they kept the Minister under control. He would be the siphon through which everything would go – listening in to her telephone calls, sitting unobtrusively at her meetings.

Jonathan had been trained to switch allegiances from one Secretary of State to the other without anyone being able to see the join. His loyalty was not to the Government in power, but to the Service he was part of. His promotion was much more a function of how well he got on with the mandarins who controlled the Civil Service than the benevolence of a Minister who could be here today and gone tomorrow. To ensure that he remained in good grace, he would keep his superiors informed of what the Minister was up to, and they in turn would mull it over, either in the Cabinet Mess or in a discreet club over lunch. If they decided they could live with a Minister's policy position, they would let it go unchallenged; if they didn't, they would close ranks to thwart every initiative, using the might of the Treasury with its control of spending, if they

206

encountered a Minister lucky enough or shrewd enough to outmanoeuvre them.

Ann was under no illusions – one person would get more loyalty than the Secretary of State; the Permanent Secretary, Sir Edward Grierson. Jonathan, by the very nature of the job he had been given, was a high flyer, his future promotion prospects tied not to Ann Clarke but to Sir Edward. Getting the upper hand from the first encounter was crucial.

Before she had even looked round her new office, she asked Jonathan to arrange for some coffee to be brought in, and that he should join her.

He had anticipated her request – a tray was already set with the white government-issue china, shallow white cups with a silver rim. The biscuits on offer suggested this was a special occasion.

Jonathan, despite being only a few years younger than Ann, reminded her of all the students she had met at university, and whom she knew at a glance even then would go into the Civil Service. Of medium height and build, with curly brown hair and gold-rimmed spectacles, he wore suits in a tweedy blend of blue and green – he had not yet graduated to the pinstripe brigade – and brown highly polished brogues. She imagined him going home to a nice semi-detached in the suburbs, and having the odd bridge night with the boys. In ten years' time, with his hair showing flecks of grey at the temples and with the aplomb of promotion, the ugly duckling would have become a suave and cultured swan.

Without yet showing it, Ann regarded him with respect; anyone who had prospered in the cut-throat world of the British Civil Service had to be bright, cunning and a consummate political operator. He waited until Ann was seated before taking his own seat across from her, but it was he who started the discussion:

'Minister, the Office would like to welcome you and congratulate you on your appointment. We've looked forward to you coming in, and I hope we are able to do the kind of job for you that you want. Anything you want

207

done, regardless of how small, you only have to tell us. If you are agreeable, I will travel with you most of the time. But you can request a change of Principal if you want one. I've still got eighteen months of my assignment to run, but Sir Edward can always arrange for you to look over some others if you wish.'

Ann smiled at him, the perfect Civil Servant to the end. She knew if she did indicate she wanted a change, Sir Edward would to go exceptional lengths to talk her out of it. After all, the process of government could cope with a new Secretary of State every other week, but there would be havoc if the Civil Service changed.

'No, Jonathan, I don't think there will be any need for that, but we'll see how we get along. I'm going to be very dependent on you to keep me right. After all, you know your way around this place in a way that I don't. But there are some changes that I want to make immediately. I have appointed a Political Advisor who will enjoy the same Civil Service grade as you, but she will handle all of the politically sensitive aspects of the job. She will determine whether or not a subject is a matter of significance, and you will cooperate fully with her. Her name if Mary Connolly and she is my election agent. She will arrive after lunch with all my files, and you will have arranged for a desk and cabinets to be made available for her in the outer office.'

She stood up from the armchair she had been sitting in, and moved behind the desk, her voice growing in authority as she did so. Looking from beneath her lashes, she could see that the carefully cultivated poise of the civil servant had been punctured.

'There are also one or two minor things I would like seen to. I know it is your job to listen in to my telephone calls. I will tell you which calls it is acceptable for you to monitor, and you will make sure you do not listen to the rest. Do I make myself clear?'

She watched as Jonathan relaxed a little; he was used to this response from ministers. It would last until she forgot something she had promised to do during one of her phone calls – and then she would ask that her calls be monitored again.

Ann went on: 'And I want a direct line installed. And I don't want any tales about how difficult it will be for the phone company to get one in before the middle of next year. I want it installed and operational when I return here from London on Friday. Similarly, I want a direct line in the official residence. Both phones must have scrambling devices.'

Ann sat back in her chair and waited for his response, an appraising look on her face. Jonathan stood up and moved over to the desk, trying to steal back some authority for himself.

'Minister, I'm not in a position to process your requests, that is a matter for Sir Edward. But I should say, ma'am, that it's just not possible to appoint someone out of the blue to a senior Civil Service job. There are exams to be sat, vettings to be completed, boards to be gone through. I'm sure we could fit Ms Connolly in on one of the temporary ad hoc grades.' Warming to his theme, he made to go on with his litany of why Ann's demands could not be met. But he stopped when the Secretary of State stood up. Her voice was soft but firm:

'I wasn't *asking* you to do this for me, I was *telling* you. If you are unfit for the job I expect of you, then I am prepared to accept your resignation from the Home Civil Service . . .'

Taken aback, Browning interrupted: 'You have no authority over the Civil Service. We must get Sir Edward.'

This time her voice had an edge to it: 'Never interrupt me again! I will decide what I can do and what I cannot. If you intend to go and whine to Sir Edward, then also tell him I want to see him. The good old days are over. I run this Department, not you or Sir Edward. And I will remind you that I am Deputy Prime Minister.'

She glared at him, then her face relaxed and her voice became softer:

'Don't be so frightened, Jonathan. Once you accept that I'm the boss, we'll get on well. And if things go as well as I think they will, I'll remember your name when I'm running another department.'

His expression changed as he worked through the implications of what she was saying. This woman would either destroy herself in weeks, or go right to the top. He had to be careful. Resignedly, he lowered his eyes.

Ann relaxed back into her chair. 'Now that we've agreed the ground rules, let's get some work done, shall we? I want an immediate instruction to be given to all the chief constables to end the curfews from a week today. I want that information telexed to them immediately, and a press release sent out. I also want to see all of them this coming Friday to discuss the future shape of policing in Scotland and the anti-terrorist laws.'

A group of technicians clustered round the monitor in the edit suite as the pictures of the Secretary of State's arrival at the Scottish Office flickered across the screen. A couple of times they ran through the triumphal wave on the steps. The way the sun and the wind had caught her dress had etched her body in clear relief. A tangible aura of desire clogged the atmosphere of the darkened suite. One technician broke the silence: 'Christ. Half an hour on my own with her!'

A sharp cough from one of his colleagues shut him up. Michael Stewart had come in with Donald Ross. Quickly the room emptied.

Wryly, Ross remarked: 'I didn't know our engineers were so obsessed with technical excellence they were prepared to spend their tea breaks checking video tape!'

Stewart laughed. 'You're one to talk! Since when did you find it necessary to check I chose the right clips for my reports?'

Shamefaced, Ross shrugged his shoulders, then pointed to the screen: 'Do you blame me?'

Stewart turned to look at him: 'You're asking me!'

Ross bit off the flip remark he had been about to make. Stewart had the look of a man who found that things weren't all going his way.

210

Silently the two men worked until Stewart was sure he had all the shots he wanted for his script and Ross had decided how long he would run the item. Both were aggrieved they had been denied an interview on the day Ann took up office – Stewart more so, because he could have used a longer piece than a news item for his documentary. Added to that, he was off to the States in the morning, and he wanted her before he left. They hadn't exchanged two words since the passionate scene in the dressing room days before. His calls to her answering machine went unanswered.

As the two men walked back along the corridor, Ross reviewed the bits they had been able to fill in about Ann Clarke so far – the brilliant academic career; the father who had gone off the rails, plunging his family from wealth to poverty almost overnight; the early friendship with the Metcalfs; the spell at Harvard; Lawrie's suicide; the passionate espousal of nationalism. All had undoubted interest, but none filled in the vital spark of motivation. Was something still missing?

They stopped outside the studio. Ross turned to the other man: 'You realize, it is possible that she's totally straight. Surely it's not too much to expect that once in a lifetime a politician comes along who is a genuine idealist and who gets to the top on merit rather than manipulation!'

Stewart shook his head ruefully, and put his hand on the other man's shoulder; 'Don, you'll have fairies at the bottom of your garden next. No way. Too many unanswered questions. What happened to Henderson? Where does Harry McGregor fit in? What's the tie-up with the Workers' Militia?'

Ross let out a sigh. 'Well, maybe the trip to Boston will give you some of the answers. It had better; I have to justify my overspend.'

Stewart laughed, but without much humour. 'You think I want to go back to the States? She'd better be worth it!'

The programme safely off the air, Stewart went back

to his desk and started sifting through the files he wanted to take with him the following day. Clare came to help him. She checked the filing cabinet, only to find most of the files empty.

Michael explained: 'I took most of them home at the weekend so that I could sift through them and summarize what I needed to take. I don't want to trail too much stuff around with me.'

They finished off and she helped him carry a couple of boxes to his car. As he straightened up after stowing the files in the boot of his Porsche, Clare – unambiguously, he felt – invited him back to her place for a drink. Tempted, since right now he needed something uncomplicated, he shook his head.

'I can't. I've got to catch the seven a.m. shuttle tomorrow to get the Boston connection at Heathrow. And I've still to pack and sort through this stuff.'

Seeing her disappointment, he bent down and kissed her gently on the lips. His voice was soft as he said: 'Let me work my way through this.'

On that ambiguous note, he left her.

The lurch hit his stomach as soon as he entered the flat. Someone had been in his house. No one else had a key, so it could only be someone who had no right to be there. Dumping his files on the hall floor, he rushed from room to room. No, nothing was disturbed. He went to his desk in the corner of the dining room – everything remained as before, piled neatly at the side of his typewriter. But – too neatly. He had riffled through the papers on his way to work that morning looking for a note, and he remembered his promise to himself to tidy up when he got back. Somebody, though, had done it for him.

Sail boats bobbed on the Charles River as the 747 came in to land at Boston's Logan airport. No one took any notice of the tall handsome man in his soft suede jacket and white polo shirt as he continued to stare out at the skyline of America. His shoulders had a tense set to them; the anxiety twisted his face into a frown. Had anyone looked closer, found the face familiar, they might have recalled the story of the TV star anchorman who had been hounded out of the United States in disgrace over a politician's wife.

Taking a deep breath, Michael joined the queue at immigration, but with little more than a cursory glance from the immigration officer – he was through. His step lightened as he walked through the terminal building to the taxi rank, but he still kept his head down. The traffic jam on the turnpike gave him a chance to gather his thoughts, and finally a more confident Michael Stewart walked across the foyer to the Bostonian Hotel to register.

Settled in his room, bag unpacked, the adrenaline fighting off jet lag, he set to work at the telephone. He dialled a Washington number which answered on the first ring.

'Emma Catchpole please. United Kingdom desk.'

He doodled as he waited to be put through. 'Emma Catchpole please?'

He frowned as he listened to the reply. 'Do you know if she's spending her leave at home in Boston? I'm an old friend and I just happened to be in Boston at the moment.'

He was smiling as he thanked Emma's secretary for her help.

Seconds later he was speaking to Emma herself, his smile showing the relief and pleasure he felt.

'The State Department told me you were here. I couldn't believe my luck. Now I know it's short notice, but can we have dinner tonight?'

A small cloud crossed his face. 'OK, I'll meet you at the restaurant.' Even old friends would be cautious still about seeing him in public.

Displeasure forgotten, he stood up to welcome Emma as she approached the table. A petite blonde with an open, sun-kissed face, she wore white pants tucked into turquoise suede boots and a turqoise silk blouse, knotted at her waist; plain gold chains hung round her neck and gold hoop earrings swung with her shiny hair. She looked twenty, not thirty-five, amazingly carefree for a senior desk officer in the State Department. Despite the obvious warmth and the friendship, the conversation was a little too artificially superficial to start with; the 'incident' that had ended Michael's American career hung, unmentioned. Without warning, Emma broke the ice:

'They're back together again, but word has it she's taken another lover.'

Michael, touching her hand, said: 'I don't want to talk about it. I deserved everything that happened to me for being so stupid. I didn't even love her; it was all about the excitement of an illicit affair. I was lucky to escape with just my career in ruins. I hadn't realized how close some of your senior politicians are to organized crime.'

They passed the meal in small talk, reminiscing, checking up on mutual friends. Emma brought the conversation round to the changes in the British Government.

'Ann Clarke's causing quite a stir here. Have you met her yet?'

Michael fiddled with the salt cellar as he went through the litany of Ann's talents and the effect she was having on the political scene. He only looked at Emma when he asked: 'What kind of stir is she causing here?'

'A feeling that something quite big is happening. There's a top-level committee, much too senior for me or even my boss, that monitors everything that's happening in Britain on a day-to-day basis. Gossip has it the military's represented on it, which is odd given we're still allies, but Britain is definitely getting star treatment from the Secretary of State. My boss told me to prepare for a huge volume of work post-summit.'

Michael looked closely at her. 'What did he mean by that?'

Emma shrugged. 'Who knows! Look, I can't talk too freely about what we're working on, it has a high security clearance. What I can say is that I think Britain is going to be a big issue in the Presidential campaign. I'm sure that's why Horowitz is so involved, it's an open secret he's going to run for the Democratic nomination. What would you think about Britain becoming the fifty-first state?'

Even though she said it lightly, she saw that Michael had taken her very seriously. Emma reached over and patted him on the head:

'Joke, Michael. Joke! We've such a long shopping list of Central American countries to take over, it'll be another century before we start on Europe!' His frown deepened, causing her to say edgily: 'Hey! I'm joking.'

The journalist shook his head. 'I don't think you realize how far things have gone in Britain. We've had more violence in the streets then there's ever been before, and mostly organized by the Workers' Militia, young hoodlums who've been carefully bred to political fanatics. And the more the American presence spreads, the more angry people get. With transport strikes and local government strikes, food is getting short, sometimes the dead go unburied because the gravediggers are on strike. What makes it worse is we all know the country is in huge debt to pay for the nuclear bases your Government says we must have.'

Emma was listening intently. 'That siege at the power plant can't have helped.'

He nodded in agreement, absently twisting his glass. 'You bet! Because of the scare that nuclear material had been planted in Central London, the panic was unbelievable. You heard about the tube disaster? That was caused by nothing other than hysteria, but it cost twenty-eight lives. So you can see, that with things as bad as that, Ann Clarke looks as though she's been sent from heaven to sort things out. Metcalf, they say, is a disaster. And now he has to lead for Britain at the summit!'

'But, Michael, you must see then, why our country is so worried. You're the key to Europe's defences. If Britain becomes ungovernable, we would have to step in to guarantee the defence of Western Europe.'

With a cynical twist he responded: 'Last time I heard that argument it was about Central America – and Libya – and Vietnam, come to think of it. We need to be saved for our own good!'

The conversation was getting too heavy – they returned

to small talk, though Michael remained preoccupied. Soon he pleaded jet lag, and they agreed to leave the rest of their discussion for another day.

As Michael walked Emma to her car, she stopped and looked up at him: 'You're right to be concerned about what the President and Horowitz are up to with your country. They must have a pretty major game plan. Don't forget we can only go on talking sweetly to the Russians about disarmament if we're sure someone else is covering our back, and that's where you people come in. No one's too happy with the socialists taking over, and some of the more sensational talkers here are already suggesting there's a Russian plot to take control of Britain and Ann Clarke's a KGB plant!' She laughed to show she didn't take that seriously.

'But the summit is regarded here as being very significant, and no effort or expense is being spared to make sure we get what we want. Even the London preparations, just the talks before talks, have the most major team I've ever seen working on them.'

Michael looked down at the tiny woman. 'And what is it your people are out to get?'

She shook her head. 'Even if I knew, I couldn't tell you.'

As they exchanged a chaste goodnight kiss, a dark-suited man got out of a car across the street. Michael didn't notice him following in the shadows as he walked the two blocks back to the hotel.

The summer sunshine lit the crystal glasses on the stiff white damask cloth. The table, set for four, had been arranged next to the window in the White Drawing Room. Lace curtains cooled the heat of the summer day; gold cord tied back the blue and gold brocade. Yellow chrysanthemums formed the centrepiece of the table, making the gold rim on the china look dull by comparison.

Sylvia again checked the table with the housekeeper, despite the risk of offending the woman, who seemed to think that the Prime Minister's wife had never set a table in her life.

When the housekeeper had withdrawn, Sylvia crossed to look out on to St James's Park, adjusting the pearl choker at the neck of her turquoise silk suit. She did not have long to wait: her guests were prompt – three women decked in their summer finery in deference to the summons for lunch with the Prime Minister's wife. Kate Thomas, from the *Daily Mirror*, the only one Sylvia had already met, wore a tailored white linen jacket over a plain sunshine yellow linen shift. Huge navy beads lent interest to the neckline, matched to navy earrings peeping out from under her blonde hair. Her shoes and tiny clutch bag took up the navy and yellow theme.

The Women's Editor of the *Daily Express*, Miriam Grey, had gone specially to Jasper Conran for her outfit – a wraparound silk number straining a little over her ample breasts, but camouflaging her less than svelte figure with bright orange sunflowers. Unfortunately the youthful colours only highlighted the worn face. The heat had caused her green eyeshadow to congeal in the creases of her eyes. She greeted Sylvia with respect, but warily.

Caroline Windlesham of the *Daily Mail* was positively hostile. She had been a frequent visitor in the past to Number Ten to lunch with the previous PM's wife, and her brusque greeting revealed a lingering resentment of the 'usurper'. Her temper was unlikely to have been soothed by her obvious discomfort in the Chanel off-white bouclé suit, more appropriate to a spring garden party than lunch on a steaming summer's day. The deeply etched wrinkles on her forehead showed a woman who frowned a lot. Sylvia Metcalf knew that she was not alone in attracting Ms Windlesham's dislike.

The absence of a press officer eased the atmosphere. Sylvia, they gathered, intended this to be an off-the-record lunch, the much tried, and highly successful, setting for dishing the dirt on an enemy. Sherry and gin and tonics were distributed; the four women edged around one another with small talk. Occasionally the talk dried up into embarrassing silence, then everyone spoke at once.

The atmosphere remained somewhat strained as the women settled to their vichysoisse and Chablis, but as the wine flowed, the tension eased. Sylvia had deliberately seated herself between her two hostile guests, taking the initiative in asking them about themselves – their life styles, their families. Soon they struck up a rapport as all recognized the common battles with careers, families, husbands and lovers.

Sylvia had done her homework well. She recognized how foolish it would have been to lay herself bare to these piranha fish without being superbly briefed; the press office had responded with detailed information about all three women, briefing the Prime Minister's wife as fully as they would brief her husband before any such encounter. The real business of selling the strengths of the Government were often more effectively handled in the intimate, almost friendly atmosphere of the social gathering. But it was also the classic, much favoured, setting for destroying the reputation of friend and foe alike. Quickly, she identified the passions of the disparate group, and skilfully she brought them round to her.

Coffee had been served before the real business began. Prompted by the journalists, Sylvia talked about her initial reactions as the chatelaine of Number Ten – the general confusion of having to move house immediately after the hectic and exhausting election campaign; her dismay at the prospect of making the Number Ten flat feel like home – so impersonal, and so constantly close to the civil servants who would disturb the family whether the front door was closed or not; all this mixed with the jubilation at being here at last.

Miriam Grey, with her shrewd, wordly-wise voice, her instincts honed by years of fighting to stay at the top, eventually asked the question Sylvia had been waiting for.

'Well, Sylvia.' She paused. 'May I call you Sylvia? Good. Having got here, how do you feel about Ann Clarke sticking her foot in the door ready to evict you?'

The Prime Minister's wife looked away from the little group, her face clouding over. As she sat, apparently gathering her thoughts, the three journalists exchanged glances. With a raised eyebrow, Caroline Windlesham summed up the views of the others: Now for a cover-up!

Sylvia came back from her reverie. Before she spoke, she looked into the eyes of each woman individually, as if searching for a clue, her face sombre and troubled.

'Do you mind if I speak to you off the record? I know you won't betray my confidence. After all, if you did, how could we become friends?'

The implied threat hung in the air, but she failed to see the grimace on the face of Kate Thomas – recognition that a journalist's confidence was only as good as the strength of the story they were being asked to keep secret. The three women nodded encouragement, anxious to share intimacies. Miriam had a coughing fit, and before taking a sip of mineral water she lifted her handkerchief from her clutchbag, surreptitiously switching on a Sony micro-cassette recorder as she did so.

Sylvia began hesitantly at first, then seemed to gain confidence and warm to her theme:

'I feel sorry for Ann, I really do. Did you know we had been friends since her student days?' The three women shook their heads, their eyes wide to indicate surprise.

'Tony and I befriended her when he was lecturing at Glasgow. She was having a really hard time. Her father had been a high-flying civil servant who was sacked in disgrace, and he used up all his money trying to clear his name. Ann had gone from having everything as a pampered daddy's girl, to having nothing. She hardly had enough money for food, let alone books. We gave her the odd meal and some babysitting jobs. She met Barbara Castle through us, and that's what got her started. In fact Tony enrolled her into the Labour Party. I even fixed up her first job as a researcher over in the House.'

Ruefully, she smiled. 'I suppose I've only got myself to blame for infecting her with the political bug!'

Her audience smiled sympathetically.

'But now she's a woman in a hurry. Desperate to get it all as quickly as possible. She's changed. She used to be so nice, so kind, but now she's becoming eaten up with ambition. It all seemed to start after she'd been in the States. She was glad to get away, her parents were making life hell for her, father drinking and mother playing the martyr – but out there she got into the big league with the Democrats. To be fair, she picked up a lot of good campaigning tricks, and when she came back there was a real gloss and glamour to her. But she was a very different person. I've often wondered if there was a man out there – a rich one. That seemed to be when she got her taste for couture clothes, and take it from me, she couldn't have afforded them on her own. Something must have happened out there to give her this paranoia about the Americans. That, and what happened to her father has made her very bitter and twisted. Affected her mind, I suppose you could say. Funnily enough, Hugh Lawrie was in the States at the same time, they must have met because I remember he wrote to Tony to tell him about this interesting girl he had met. He committed suicide shortly after that, and his blessing must have done some good because Ann got his seat.'

As Sylvia paused, Caroline jumped in: 'But you can't deny she's able. She's worth ten of any of the men around just now.'

As the eyebrows of the Prime Minister's wife shot up almost to her hairline, Caroline quickly continued: 'Except the Prime Minister, of course.'

Sylvia smiled in agreement: 'Of course she's able. That's why Tony offered her the new job. She's one of the best we've got, and it's a real tragedy to see her waste herself in this way. And of course, now that she'll be working so closely under Tony, I'll be able to take her under my wing – try to get her back on the rails. But she's got really rotten judgement. Would you have anything to do with that horrible man Harry McGregor? Everybody know he started the Workers' Militia, but he and Ann are as thick as thieves. Have been since she came back from the States.'

Kate asked the obvious question: 'Anything going on between them? Sexually I mean.'

Sylvia lowered her voice to a more conspiratorial level: 'Who knows! I wouldn't have thought so though, she's got more exotic taste than McGregor. You'll remember Michael Stewart, the BBC man who got caught by the TV cameras in the States having sex with a senator's wife?'

All three nodded their recollection, each avoiding the eye of the other, aware that the excitement was mounting.

'Well, Ann's having an affair with him. It's the talk of Glasgow. I know our Security people are a bit worried by it – could leave her open to blackmail – and of course the story was, when Stewart got kicked out of the States he was told he had got the wrong side of the Mafia. So now people have to rally round and help Ann – sort her out. She could be the Leader of the next generation, and Tony and I are determined to develop her.'

Just at that there was a knock at the door. Mrs Metcalf was already running very late. The women parted, promising to keep Sylvia's secrets, and to make this a regular date.

Once the three most influential women journalists in the country had departed, Sylvia went over to the window to watch them scurrying to their cars, haute couture forgotten in their anxiety to get back to the editor with the story, each aware that two rival papers would have exactly the same information.

Who would break it first?

With a smile of quiet satisfaction, Sylvia picked up the telephone and dialled George Jeffries' private number.

'The lunch went exactly to plan, in fact better than expected. Your friend Warrender is paying for his keep, ammunition like this seems to go down very well. Of course their editors will put the story to the lawyers and they'll demand proof, so all we have to worry about is how long it takes them to get it. A week do you think? And with luck maybe some pictures?'

His reply made her laugh. As she went upstairs, she hummed happily to herself.

As the three excited women journalists were leaving by the front door, an irate Ann Clarke was coming into Number Ten by the back door entrance through the Cabinet Office. Despite the short straight skirt of her green linen suit and her high heels she was striding out, her hair flying behind, far outstripping Jonathan who was almost having to run to keep up. A couple of MPs leaving after a meeting thought about stopping to congratulate her on her appointment, but one look at the anger on her face was enough to make them walk past with a nod. Uncertain of the route to the Prime Minister's study, she stopped a messenger and demanded he lead her.

As she stormed into the den where the civil servants guarded the inner sanctum of the Prime Minister, the three civil servants working happily behind their desks stood up. Ann pointed without speaking but with an eyebrow raised at the two doors. As one man jumped over to bar one of the doors, Ann pushed past him into the room.

Metcalf was sitting on a couch in his shirt sleeves, tie loosened. He had a heavy tumbler of whisky in his hand, and around him lay the debris of sandwiches. His lunch was being shared by a Number Ten messenger, an elderly man whose expression was as grey as his uniform jacket. The intrusion had disturbed him in mid-stream, and he looked in alarm, first at Ann then at Metcalf.

Ann banged the heavy door behind her. She stood in the centre of the room, hands on her hips, ready for a fight.

'What the hell's going on? Why do I have to find out from the TV news that there is likely to be a power strike affecting every part of the country? Is that not considered information important enough to relay to the Deputy Prime Minister – or did you think I'd be too busy painting my nails to be interested in it?'

Metcalf stood up, his face like stone. He marched to

222

the door and held it open for her. 'You can wait out here until I'm free. I'm involved in an important discussion and I will not be disturbed!'

She glowered at him. 'Pschaw! Nonsense! Gossiping, no doubt!'

The messenger, mortified, got up to leave, but Metcalf waved him back to his seat. In a voice barely more than a whisper, the Prime Minister turned to his Deputy: 'I will wait until later to give you a lesson in courtesy. Just get out!'

Astonished, Ann returned to the anteroom where, for the next ten minutes, she paced up and down like a caged lioness. When the messenger did emerge he scurried away, keeping his head down to avoid catching her eye. Without waiting to be invited, Ann pushed open the door and stormed in. Metcalf remained on the couch. Slowly he put down his glass and straightened his tie, stood up and languorously walked round to where Ann was standing. He moved close to her, putting his hands on her shoulders. He ignored her grimace as the blast of whisky from his breath made her recoil.

'Care for the common man, do you? Filled with compassion for the wretched masses, eh? You are a self-centred heartless bitch. That man had just been told his wife has terminal cancer. If you have any human instinct left you'll realize that I've probably done my most significant act today. Now what are you being hysterical about? What strike do you mean? It can't be all that serious if I don't know about it.'

Ann shook herself free of Metcalf's grip. Her hands hung at her sides clenched into fists, the knuckles white. She remained standing close to him, and her voice was low and deadly, but she ignored his criticism, although it had made her colour.

'You stupid fool! It is precisely because this strike is serious that you haven't been told! Don't you realize that nobody trusts you to be sober long enough to do anything constructive about it? And certainly no one thinks you've

223

got the mental equipment to handle solving it even when you're sober.'

Metcalf responded as venomously: 'I'm still your boss. Don't you forget it. Question my judgement and you question the fact that I was the one who appointed you. Was my judgement faulty then?'

The contempt flooded across her face. She tore into him: 'You appointed me because you had no alternative. You realized that you only remain Prime Minister as long as I agree to it. You're a failure, Tony Metcalf, and I want to make sure the country doesn't suffer because of it. You sit knocking back the whisky and being self-righteous about your good deeds when the one strike that could really cripple the country is starting. Do you actually know about the trouble there's going to be in the car industry as well? Do you actually know that we could have stopped producing cars in the country by the middle of next week?'

Metcalf, trying not to recoil, nonetheless stepped back.

Ann gave a shrug of despair. 'Tony, why are you such a fool? This is the only chance you'll get to prove you can sort the country out. You've got the first meeting with the Americans tonight, even if it is only a dinner, and the dock strike will make the Americans even harder to deal with, and here you are locked away in your office with a messenger and getting drunk. It's just not good enough.'

'I don't need you to tell me how to run my life, or my country. I was taking a break from working on the Queen's Speech. Maybe if you took some time to step back occasionally, you'd see that you're part of the trouble. Your obsession with the Americans is playing right into their hands. If we mishandle the summit they'll tighten their grip on Britain even more. Rather than going round the country rubbishing them – and me – you should be trying to build bridges.'

Ann remained silent for a moment, then glaring afresh, she asked: 'Why have I not been consulted on the Queen's Speech?'

Waving his hand dismissively, Metcalf responded: 'The

draft will go to Cabinet tomorrow. You'll get your chance then.'

Her face hard, lips in a thin line, Ann approached the desk behind which he retreated. 'I agreed to become your number two because someone had to get a grip on what's happening to Britain. You patently can't. I have no intention of being marginalized by you or anyone else. If I'm not allowed to make my contribution to the Queen's Speech, I'll create such a backlash that you'll be out of office in weeks rather than months.'

She flung her head back. 'I'm now only one breath away from your job. Don't forget. You take that breath only as long as I allow you to.'

Leaving the sentence hanging in the air, she left as brusquely as she had entered.

A startled Ann stood up as Jonathan ushered George Jeffries into the room. She came round her desk holding out her hand to him.

'George, I wasn't expecting you! Were we due to have a meeting?'

She gestured him to a sofa in the corner. Jonathan hovered at the door, awaiting instructions.

'No, no. I was sitting at my desk getting more and more bored and frustrated because of all the sunshine outside that I fancied a walk, and knowing all about your Scottish hospitality, I decided you were my best bet to be offered a drink.'

Ann laughed. 'Give the Foreign Secretary a drink, Jonathan!'

Orders taken, Jonathan departed. Ann turned to Jeffries and asked directly:

'Now what is this really about? You can't be too thrilled at my appointment. After all, we all knew you had your eye on the number two job. So what's this all about?'

Jeffries settled back in his chair. 'One day you'll learn I proposed you for the job.'

Ann's eyebrows shot up.

Jeffries laughed. 'Oh, I haven't taken to self-sacrifice.

I decided the best way we could get this Government to do some work would be to stop all the skirmishes on the sidelines. Even if I don't have your job, I'm the only person – apart from Sylvia – who can control Tony, so I'll still have the power.'

He watched as Ann's lips narrowed and the warmth left her eyes.

'I'm not here to talk rivalry, Ann. I'm here to talk alliances. What we each want isn't so different. I want a good result from the summit, I want the country run effectively again. And I know Tony is useless, but he's our Leader and we're stuck with him.'

Ann's voice was harsh as she interjected: 'For the time being!'

The Foreign Secretary nodded. 'For the time being. But I think you and I should concentrate on taking the lead in the summit discussions, and I wanted to talk to you about how we play tonight, how we get the measure of the personalities. The people who'll be there will probably be crucial to the summit team.'

There was genuine mirth in Ann's voice as she laughed. 'You certainly don't waste time on subtlety, George. You're really here to tell me not to start World War Three tonight. You needn't have worried, I'm well house trained. I'll smile prettily, use the right cutlery, and leave them wondering what all the fuss was about.'

George laughed with genuine delight. 'I didn't think you'd do anything else. I just want to let you know you're not entirely without allies, and I think if we work on this together we'll stand more of a chance of success than constantly opposing one another. I also think, incidentally, that we could use you much more internationally. I'd like you to represent Britain at the Conference of Major Nations in Nice next month. Do you fancy it?'

Ann nodded, but suspicion hung between them. As he stood up to leave, George put his hand on her shoulder.

'I meant what I said, my dear. There is more that unites us than divides us. Think of it.'

Ann was fifteen minutes late arriving at the American Embassy. She apologized to the Ambassador with her most engaging smile. He graciously accepted the apology, and missed her grimace when he remarked: 'It is a woman's privilege!'

Despite having had to rush to change, Ann looked stunning. Her dress had been made for her by a rising Scottish designer. In a deep blue silk jersey, the padded shoulders were decorated with embroidered and sequined flowers. It was longer than her usual style, stopping just below her calf. She wore silk stockings of exactly the same shade, and matching suede shoes with five-inch stiletto heels.

Her tiny bag was cut to the same pattern as the shoulder detail of the dress, and made of the same fabric.

Ann had brushed out her hair to make it shine, and had coiled it loosely on the top of her head with tendrils escaping round her ears and at the nape of her neck. Her delicate and distinctive perfume enveloped her in a seductive cloud.

The Ambassador was loath to let her move away from him, monopolizing her for much of the reception. But, consoling himself with the fact that she would sit beside him at dinner, he allowed her to be led off to meet the other senior Americans present.

Ann was reintroduced to the Minister, Richard Duncan, a handsome man with a wide smile. An engaging man and humorous, he was the American administration's permanent diplomat in London, surviving political whim to ensure stability in the 'special relationship'.

The senior diplomats brought over on the State Department team included a bright woman a few years older than herself, Catherine Wallace. Ann would have welcomed more of a chance to talk to her, but the senior member of the Administration present, the renowned Richard Horowitz, had been brought over to meet her.

Horowitz looked a real heartbreaker in the American political style. In his late forties, he was well over six feet in height, with the fit, muscled body of a high school athlete who had kept in shape. His tan seemed perpetual, adding even brighter lustre to his unusual hazel eyes. The laughter lines at the corners of those eyes testified to a man who enjoyed life, despite his reputation for toughness on countries he thought were enemies of the American ideal. The elegance of his fine wool suit in dark navy, set against the flamboyance of a shirt in deep pink with matching silk tie, displayed a man of the world, free of the parochialism that had made many of his predecessors dull.

Every British politician in the room knew that this was a powerful man, and one who would push his power as far as he could. His voice was rich as he greeted Ann. If he had changed at all since Ann's days in Harvard, it was only to improve. Here, of course, the greeting was formal, no hint given that they had even met before.

'Secretary of State! I've been waiting all day to meet you, and then I find that we're to be seated too far apart to talk. I've followed your election with interest. I doubt if you realize just how much coverage it got in the States. We're not used to seeing beautiful women politicians accuse us of all sorts of treachery!' His smile took the sting out of his words.

Ann responded in kind: 'I'm surprised people were even remotely interested. I thought the only thing the Americans knew about Scotland was our whisky, and they've not been drinking as much of that as we'd like!'

Tony Metcalf and George Jeffries were straining hard to hear what was going on, but from the expressions of the two politicians from either side of the Atlantic, the talk seemed solely about flirtation. They did hear Horowitz suggest they get together to discuss the Scotch whisky problem just before they were called in to dinner.

The rest of the evening passed pleasantly enough. Both Metcalf and the Ambassador made speeches praising the achievements of the others' country, and certainly among the senior politicians present, the vexed questions that divided them were never raised.

As Ann was leaving, Horowitz approached her again. In the hearing of the Ambassador, he suggested they have a private meeting at some stage, without the formalities of the conference table, so that he could more fully understand her antipathy to his country's involvement in Scotland. Ann gave a noncommittal answer, but as her car moved out of the embassy compound, the driver pulled alongside the Foreign Secretary's car. Ann wound down the window and told Jeffries of the conversation.

'Go ahead, Ann. Informal talks are the best way to break the deadlock. I spoke to him about delaying the start to the summit, and he was more agreeable than I dared hope. With luck the Nice conference will come first. He's going to it, you'll get a chance to talk to him. Let's talk about it tomorrow.'

Both politicians went off home to their ministerial boxes, well pleased with the day's events. In the embassy, a debriefing had begun in the ambassador's study. There, too, there was a sense that everything was going to plan.

As Horowitz stood up to go, Duncan said to him: 'Metcalf didn't touch his wine, he stuck to water all night. Are they getting him sorted out?'

Horowitz laughed. 'Not a chance! He had lunch at his desk today – a bottle of whisky and a chat to a messenger. He's too far gone to be sorted out. We've nothing to worry about there.'

As she left the car, Ann's driver brought the ministerial red box from the boot. He had called back to the office to collect it earlier. It was now fifteen minutes before midnight, and this was the first time today she'd been given the chance to do any real work, make any real decisions.

She wished the driver goodnight and arranged that he should collect her at eight the next morning. When she had first entered Parliament she had rented this house in Roupell Street, near to Waterloo Station and within walking distance of both Whitehall and the Houses of Parliament, from a Foreign Office official, permanently overseas. When the owner got his promotion to Ambassador, he sold the house to his glamorous tenant.

The tiny house had begun its life as an artisan's cottage, but now, a century after it had been built, only the well-heeled could afford to live here. The street that had started life as home for manual labourers now housed politicians with private incomes, bankers and minor showbusiness personalities – the only ones who could cope with London's spiralling property prices.

Inside, the terraced house was an oasis of peace in a grimy city. Ann had told the interior designers that she wanted a cottage atmosphere, someplace comforting and relaxing – not a high-tech showplace. Though her choice seemed out of character, they took her at her word.

Off the narrow hall, with its rickety staircase, a large sitting room had been made from two rooms knocked into one. It ran the length of the house, with french windows at the back leading on to a paved patio. The wallpaper and drapes, in a rich grass green, were in a William Morris print, and Nottingham lace screened the window to the front. Two wicker sofas faced each other across the hearth of a fireplace filled with an abundance of dried flowers. Delicate ceramic bowls of exotically scented pot pourri stood on the pine lamp tables at each side of the sofas next to lamps toning with the upholstery of the cushions. Small authentic Victorian prints hung on the walls, and two silver-framed photographs stood on the mantelpiece: one a happy holiday picture of her parents, the other a copy of the photograph sitting next to her bed in Glasgow. Callers never came to this house unexpectedly, those who did visit would never know that a photograph had been removed.

Ann's work area filled the back of the room. Bookcases covered one wall, and the other housed an antique roll-top desk in rich cedar wood, lit by a green-shaded antique desk lamp, salvaged from her father's study when their house had been sold.

Ann took the red box into the cosy and welcoming sitting room, putting it down on the chair next to the desk while she lit the lamps and closed the curtains. Upstairs, she slipped on an oyster satin robe. Settling down with a pot of herbal tea, she opened the box with the key the driver had given her, and lifted out the large pile of papers inside, groaning as she did so. This would never be finished tonight.

She had been concentrating intensely for half an hour, initialling reports to show that she had read them and scribbling memos to Jonathan, when she heard the key in the lock. Jumping up from the desk, she scattered the papers in her rush to welcome him – she was in his arms before he was properly over the threshold. He held her so tightly she could hardly breathe and his tongue probed her mouth, toying with her own as she reciprocated. Their mouths stayed joined as she loosened the buttons on his heavy Burberry trench coat. He had the advantage over her, easily loosening the satin tie that held her robe in place, sliding it off her shoulders and letting it slither to the floor.

His hands restlessly moved over her body, clothed now only in the sheerest silk bra and pants. As they reached her buttocks, he dug his fingers deep into the flesh; had she been able to, she would have cried out with the pain, but his mouth was still locked over hers.

He forced her back into the sitting room, using the weight of his body to push her down on to the floor. With his mouth, he began to explore, nibbling her neck.

Over and over she kept saying: 'I've missed you, oh God how I've missed you!'

His hands pushed inside the little bra, freeing her nipples. He began to suck at them, kneading them all the time, until she began to shrink away from him, pain breaking through the heat of her passion.

Suddenly, he clamped her right nipple between his teeth, squeezing hard on her left breast. She screamed. She wanted to get away, and called out to him: 'No, Johann! No!'

But it was too late, he was already forcing her legs apart, plunging himself inside her, thrusting, thrusting. Soon he collapsed on top of her, and she sobbed, needing comfort.

He spoke for the first time: 'I've got to go. The car's outside. I can't be seen here, for your sake as well as mine. I'll phone you tomorrow.'

Suddenly, he had gone. He had been in the little house less than ten minutes.

She lay on the floor until the cold began to seep into her bones. As she struggled to get to her feet, she could feel the start of the physical ache. She went into the hallway, slipping a little on the satin robe, and went upstairs to run a bath. Making it as hot as she could bear, she began to scrub at herself. Tears would have helped, cleansed, but they didn't come.

She lay in the bath until the cold drove her from there too. Looking at her body, she could see the first signs of the bruising coming up over her breasts and thighs. Going into the bedroom, she looked in the long cheval mirror to see her buttocks scratched and bruised.

She put on a long fine lawn white nightdress. Now bitterly cold, she switched on both the electric fire and the electric blanket before going downstairs to pour herself a very large brandy.

Curling herself into the downy softness of the bed-clothes, she began to shake, then the tears came. Just before dawn, she fell asleep.

The clear light of dawn streamed into the bedroom through the half open window, teasing Sylvia awake and alerting her to the space in the bed beside her. Still fogged with sleep, she realized she had just had her first night-mare-free sleep since the election: always the recurrent fear – what might happen if it all went wrong. She hadn't heard Tony come to bed, nor had she heard him get up again.

Wearily swinging her legs from the bed, Sylvia pulled on a cotton robe and went in search. The bathroom door seemed undisturbed from the previous night. As she opened the door to the sitting room, the smell of stale whisky and sweat made her recoil. Loud rumblings came from a faded chintz armchair in the corner, where the room, curtains drawn, was lit by a table tamp. Her husband, snoring, lay fully clothed on the armchair. He was out cold. An empty whisky bottle lay on the floor beside him, the contents of his final tumblerful, soaking into the carpet next to the upended glass, adding to the foul smell in the room.

Sylvia shook him, trying to bring him round; he snored even more loudly. She shook him again, more violently this time. His eyes flickered a little. She called his name. He moved his head and groaned, then shifted position, his head coming to rest almost on her shoulder. He was still asleep as the vomit projected from his mouth, covering his wife and adding to the sickening stench that had almost overcome her. Her shakings and proddings became even more violent, but still he slept. In mounting frustration and panic, she even tried kicking him, but he slept as if in a deep coma. In the kitchen Sylvia filled a basin with cold water, and with towels set to work cleaning him up. Repeatedly she wiped his face, still he remained unconscious. Worry gave way to genuine fear. She looked at the clock on the mantelpiece – five fifteen, just over four hours to the first full Cabinet meeting Tony would have to chair with his main enemy present. And as of now he was blind drunk. As she sat on the floor, hugging herself and hoping for a spark of inspiration, the phone rang. Startled, Sylvia picked it up.

'The Prime Minister can't be disturbed at the moment, who wants to speak to him anyway?'

She closed her eyes in despair as she listened: 'Well, you'll just have to tell President Rocard we'll call him back. Soon.'

Putting the receiver down and picking it up again right away, she dialled quickly. After what seemed an age, the phone was answered:

'Graeme, get over here right away. Don't waste a second.'

The hysteria rang in her voice as she responded to his questioning: 'No, I can't tell you why on the phone. Just get here!'

She rang George Jeffries who answered on the first ring. Struggling to keep her voice calm, she asked him to phone the French President, but the inquisitiveness of the Foreign Secretary took her to breaking point. The tears began to flow, and her sobs made her incoherent. Within minutes Jeffries rushed through the door of the flat. The scene needed no explanation.

Jeffries was closely followed by Graeme Jones. The two men looked at one another. Jones shook his head, registering Sylvia's despair and disappointment.

Jeffries spoke first: 'Unless we find a reason to cancel the Cabinet, Ann Clarke will have to chair the first Cabinet meeting she attends, and we'll never pull it back from her after that. I worked on the sums last night. Tony can only count on me, the Chancellor and the Home Secretary, maybe the Lord Chancellor, and if Tony gets him, he'll get the Leader of the House. She'll have Education, Energy, Wales, Environment, Health and Agriculture. The rest will wait to see how Defence jumps before they decide what side they're on. But if she comes out of it today looking like she controls the Cabinet – vote or no vote at Cabinet meetings, Tony will have to defer to her.'

Sylvia Metcalf stood up in determined mood. 'Well, that is most certainly not going to happen. If we can get him sober enough for me to give him a shot of something, then I can get him up and running.' She looked at Jeffries.

'You'll just have to make sure he doesn't do anything silly in the meeting. Especially if Ann has something up her sleeve to bring the doubters on to her side.'

The two men looked at one another. Without a word they went over to the comatose Prime Minister and dragged him from his chair. For the next hour all Sylvia could do was sit quietly and wait for the men to succeed in their ministrations. She tried to listen to the radio news, but her brain was too preoccupied. Cartoons were all that was available on television, adding a surreal quality to the scene being enacted in the Prime Minister's private quarters in Number Ten. She couldn't even get out of her soiled nightclothes, the bathroom and bedroom were the centre of operations.

A little after half past seven the request for coffee came. Pot after pot Sylvia made, closing her ears to the periodic sound of retching from the other room.

A little after eight the two men decided they had done all they could. The Prime Minister was dozing fitfully.

'Give him half an hour, then see what you can do for him. He'll feel pretty ghastly, but if we can get him to lunch time, we'll have won.' Even as he said the words, Jeffries could see from the others' expressions that they despaired of being able to cope with scenes like this for the full run of a five-year Government. It couldn't go on. Tony Metcalf was on self-destruct.

George went over to Sylvia and put his hand on her shoulder. He looked down at her, not masking his pity. Graeme Jones let himself quietly out of the flat. When he heard the door close, George took Sylvia in his arms and held her. When she felt less tense, he held her at arm's length and made her look at him.

'You're a very strong woman, but now you're going to have to put everything you've got into carrying Tony until we get the summit over. After that, he can do the ceremonial, and the rest of us, you included, can carry the Government.'

Sylvia looked far from convinced: 'You've forgotten about Ms Clarke. She'll spot just how vulnerable he is now, and she'll go in for the kill. I'm sure it was a meeting he had with her yesterday that put him over the top.'

Jeffries patted her hand. 'Don't worry about Ann. I've got plans to keep her so busy over the next few weeks she'll have no time for any mischief. And I'm sure we'll find something for the dossier, something to keep her under control.'

As he made to leave, she stopped him. 'Give him time, George. He'll be all right. I know it. He could be a really great Prime Minister. He may have his faults, but they all come back to the fact that he cares.'

Jeffries patted her arm reassuringly, but he avoided looking her in the eye. Without saying anything, he left.

Alone, she sat without moving for a while. Then she went to the telephone and dialled the number of Stephen Robinson's London flat, but she hung up before it was answered. Every step was an effort as she went to clean herself up and return to the job of getting her husband in a state fit to run the country.

It took Ann longer than usual to get dressed. She had forced herself from bed at six to finish her boxes, anaesthetizing herself with work. But when it was time to get dressed for the day, she was uncharacteristically lethargic. She soaked in the bath, the scented oil stinging some of the weals.

She examined hanger after hanger in the wardrobe, rejecting each outfit with growing irritation. Eventually she chose a severe suit of navy linen, matching it to a high-necked Victorian-style blouse. Her only jewellery was a cameo at her neck, and tiny pearl earrings. With her hair brushed severely back from her forehead and caught in a velvet bow at her neck, she looked strong and forbidding – every inch the successful, if unbending, politician. Her face, though cleverly made up as always, looked bleak and sad in repose, and she walked with a certain stiffness.

As soon as Ann arrived at Dover House, the London headquarters of the Scottish Office, Mary could see something was wrong. The click of her heels in the marble foyer seemed menacing in its sharpness. As Ann sped through the outer office, the civil servants all looked to Mary, eyebrows raised, recognizing for the first time that she might have an edge over them when it came to dealing with their new Minister, who might have a more mercurial temper than they had been prepared for. Mary looked as mystified as the rest.

The ever faithful Mary was first to greet Ann. Armed with a cup of tea, she went into the office. Ann sat at her desk and didn't look up as Mary put the tea beside her.

Looking round the room, trying to make small talk, Mary walked over to a painting on the wall opposite the window.

'That's a Stephen Conroy, isn't it? Do you think they got it in specially because you like the Scottish painters, or do you think it's a perk for every Secretary of State?'

Ann was in no mood for chit-chat. 'I didn't pluck you from obscurity to expand your admittedly minuscule knowledge of Scottish art. If you don't have anything to do, get back to Glasgow and do my constituency work. And while you're deciding, and we all know how hard you find taking decisions, leave me alone. I've got a job to do even if no one else has. Get out!'

Since all of this had been said without Ann raising her eyes from the document in front of her, she didn't see the hurt in her old friend's eyes. As Mary retreated to the ladies' room to try to get control over her emotions, the civil servants who had so resented her smiled in triumph. She wasn't going to be so hard to get rid of after all.

The triumph was short lived: minutes later, without recourse to the intercom, Ann called Jonathan into her room. When he emerged, white faced, his voice shook as he told the others that from now on, no Civil Service recommendations were to be put on documents in the Secretary of State's box unless she asked for a recommendation. And arrangements were to be made for the Secretary of State to lead the Employment talks in Brussels the next day. Someone had foolishly put in a note the night before to say that one of the junior ministers had been booked to go to Brussels. The Secretary of State would decide who would represent Scotland's interest, not the Civil Service.

Mary had just put a cup of tea on Jonathan's desk as a kind gesture when the Secretary of State emerged to go to Cabinet. The gesture wasn't missed:

'Mary, you have obviously taken to the Civil Service way of doing things with a vengeance. Not only do you spend every minute of every day drinking tea, you have proved so weak you've now been relegated to making it. Maybe I've made a mistake bringing you with me into the

237

Scottish Office. I want to see you at five this evening when we will review the situation.'

Ann stormed off, leaving Mary to sit scarlet-faced with embarrassment as her new colleagues tried to pretend they hadn't heard. Stephen Robinson had been in the corridor outside, and he beckoned Mary out of the room and led her to his own. As Stephen tried to comfort the woman who had dedicated her life to the career of Ann Clarke, the new Deputy Prime Minister and Secretary of State for Scotland was being photographed on the steps of Number Ten.

Once inside, Ann was treated with deference by the staff of the Prime Minister's Office, but as she was being led along the corridor to the Cabinet Room, her eye caught a little scurry of activity. A secretary peered round a corner, obviously to warn of her arrival. Despite her gloom, Ann felt herself smile; it seemed Tony Metcalf did not want his entry into Cabinet upstaged by Ann's late arrival.

Ann was composed as she entered the Cabinet Room; the rest of her colleagues, apart from the Prime Minister, had already gathered. They stood up as she came in, shaking hands with her as she made her way to her seat. The Cabinet Secretary indicated the seat at the right hand of the Prime Minister, but Ann shook her head, moving instead to the seat opposite him at the coffin-shaped table, evicting the Education Secretary as she did so and disrupting the seating plan so carefully set out to keep key figures within sight of the Prime Minister.

When Metcalf came in he seemed paler than usual, and his eyes were red-rimmed, but nobody could have imagined his condition of a few hours earlier. George Jeffries watched Ann Clarke carefully as she assembled her papers. He could see that she was watching something from beneath her lashes, and when he followed her gaze he saw what had taken up her interest. The Prime Minister's hands were shaking uncontrollably.

Copies of the Queen's Speech were passed round the table, everyone took time to read through it. As she read the text, Ann marked it with bright orange highlighter. Her colleagues exchanged glances. This was going to be a rough meeting.

Meticulously, the Cabinet went through the speech page by page. Points were scored, vested interests defended. Not a word did Ann speak. As they reached the closing pages, her colleagues were openly watching her, their bewilderment scarcely concealed.

As they completed the last page, the time came for the Prime Minister to sum up, the key and subtle exercise of his authority. No vote is taken at Cabinet, the decisions are reflected in the Prime Minister's résumé. A strong Prime Minister can interpret discussion as he or she chooses – the weak seldom survive long enough to learn the technique.

'Well, Ministers, I think we can say that was a very positive discussion. We are agreed then that this should be the programme for our first session of Parliament?'

He looked round the table, where there was much vigorous nodding of heads. Until he came to Ann, who slowly, very slowly, shook her head:

Metcalf stared at her, but it was Jeffries who spoke:

'If you aren't happy, why didn't you speak out earlier?'

'Because the deals have all been struck. A put-up job, the arguments all carefully rehearsed beforehand, and all the little trade-offs worked out – you scratch my back, and I'll scratch yours. Well, I'm not playing that game. I don't accept the Queen's Speech, and I'm going to say so!'

At that, furore broke out.

Again it was Jeffries who brought the meeting to order: 'You are bound by collective responsibility, Ann. You must accept responsibility for the decisions taken in this Cabinet, or resign. It is essential to the maintenance of the British style of government that every Cabinet Minister abide by the collective decision of Cabinet, regardless of any personal disagreement – it is one of the crucial aspects of the Constitution. You knew that when you accepted the job.'

239

Ann challenged him with her eyes. 'That is a convention, and I am not as wed to the British way of doing things as you lot are. I was set up today because you've all been manoeuvring to marginalize me. Well, it won't work. I reserve the right to speak out against the absence of almost all the policies we campaigned for during the election. Who do you think the Party and the public will support?'

The row raged. Minister after Minister attacked her – though not all of them: some bided their time to see who would win. She remained silent throughout, apparently examining the Turner hanging over the fireplace opposite her seat. As their voices subsided, and as the frustration of her irritating non-response threatened to make the room erupt into violence, she spoke directly across the table to Tony Metcalf, who like her had said not a word.

'You can always sack me, Prime Minister. After all, it was to preserve the right to sack me that you decided to do everything in your power to stop me becoming an elected member.'

Her eyes never wavered from Tony's face. He could hardly be heard as he replied:

'There won't be any need of that.'

In the ominous silence in the room, it was recognized that in front of them an exchange of power had taken place. And Ann Clarke suggested they move on to next business.

Afterwards, when only Tony Metcalf and George Jeffries remained in the Cabinet room, George could contain his frustration no longer:

'Do you realize what you did there? Ann can now go around the country disclaiming all responsibility for the Queen's Speech, knowing that when you should have sacked her, you backed down. She has made history by abandoning collective responsibility without you putting up so much as a fight. From now on it will be a free-for-all, and you can forget about the doctrine of *primus inter pares* – no more are you first among equals – you're a lapdog to Ann Clarke. You'll have other members of the

Cabinet going home tonight to work out where their best interest lies, backing you or her. You've signed your own death warrant!'

In his frustration, George had been more harsh with Tony than he had meant to be, but when he looked across at the Prime Minister, he realized he needn't have worried. The PM was slumped in his chair, exhausted, almost asleep after the trauma of the past few hours.

7

Avoiding the extravagances of the hotel breakfast, Michael strolled instead through Quincy's Market, allowing his nose to lead him to good coffee and a Danish. His *Boston Globe* lay unread in front of him as he watched the stallholders set out their wares for the day. Marble slabs were washed down to prepare for an army of lobster, and the smell of garlic grew as huge sausages were brought out for display in the many delicatessens. In downtown Boston the cosmopolitan splendour of a European street market was matched with the speed and vigour of American business.

Shaking off his regret at having been forced to deny himself life in the kind of America he loved, Michael picked up his paper. The lead story, the continuing crisis in Britain, charted the disastrous trade figures announced the day before; financial commentators speculated that the IMF would soon be knocking at the door of the British Chancellor to secure tighter economic controls.

Michael's heart took a leap as he turned the page to be faced with a picture of Ann Clarke – the same one taken on the steps of the Scottish Office and used throughout the British press. A surprisingly glowing profile matched the picture. The conservative *Boston Globe* hailed this mouthpiece of British anti-Americanism as the only person who could possibly lead Britain out of the mire.

Commotion a few feet away drew Michael's eyes from his paper. A pregnant woman had fainted in the growing heat and the myriad smells. Jumping up from his seat, Michael rushed over to help the burly stallholder who had gone to her aid. Together, they gripped the young woman under the arms and hoisted her on to a chair. As they checked that she was secure and comfortable, they caught sight of each other full face for the first time. In the fraction of a second it took for his face to register, Michael saw recognition in the other man's eyes. There was no way to judge if he had been recognized as the key actor in a juicy scandal – or if this man, like the two men who had visited him the night before he fled America, belonged to the Brotherhood. They had seen their stab at the Presidency evaporate when their Senator had been made a subject of ridicule.

Stewart did not hang around to find out. Leaving a generous ten dollars to pay for his half-eaten breakfast, he went out into the bright sunshine and hailed a cab. With every passer-by he half expected to be recognized.

On the trip out to Wellesley, Michael tried to concentrate on the interview to come, but he had to decide what he would do if a furore broke out at his return to the States. To have made a Senator look foolish was one thing; to tangle with a man he now knew to be involved with the Mafia, a different matter. Before he realized it, the cab had pulled up in front of a pleasant white house in a prosperous street shaded with lush green trees. A woman in jeans and T-shirt was sticking a Cookie Monster poster on to the garage door, and bright balloons festooned the porch. The woman turned from her task as she heard the cab door slam shut. Putting down her tools, she walked up the driveway to meet him, her hand outstretched. She smiled as she shook hands with him, her voice a pleasant New England drawl:

'I hope you don't think you get this kind of welcome in every home in the States! We don't usually put out the balloons for guests, but it's my daughter's birthday today and we're throwing a party for her when she gets home from school.'

As he took the hand offered him and looked down at the open, friendly face, he put his anxieties aside. 'All the more reason for me to be grateful to you for agreeing to see me. I do appreciate it.'

As they walked into the house, past bikes and skateboards, this warm engaging woman admitted: 'The mention of Ann Clarke was enough to whet my interest. No

243

one believes that I wasn't always a boring housewife! Once upon a time I went to law school, and my roommate became famous. Without a husband and four kids, that could have been me!'

As they settled to coffee and home-made cookies, Kathleen Caldwell reminisced about her student days with the reserved but very pretty girl who had come from Scotland. The story seemed ordinary enough, two girls studying hard, dating, stretching their allowances. When Michael asked about any interest Ann showed in politics, he began to feel a change in the rosy view the American woman retained of her student days.

'Ann was as interested in politics as any law student, but she was helped by all the letters of introduction she had been given to the Democrats. She got involved with them very quickly, working on one of the congressional campaigns. She even got to cook-out at Hyannis Port, as near to the Kennedy dynasty as it's possible to get. Then she started to change – became more detached. It happened after she'd gone home for a short visit. She'd been in Washington, then she went home and we thought she wasn't going to come back, but she did. She then got very interested in how we run campaigns over here, and she seemed to get on to somebody's candidate programme, because her voice began to change, her hair was different, she went on a diet, she even went to drama classes. That's the usual way the front runners are groomed over here.'

Michael was intrigued: 'Expensive?'

She nodded 'Very. We assumed someone had sent her money. Then a British politician came – Lawrie. She spent some time with him. He seemed very taken with her, but we didn't like him. He was involved in the Communists or something.'

'Were they having an affair?'

Kathleen laughed with delight at that. 'Good heavens, no! She really detested Lawrie. He'd let the side down, embarrassed the British. Everyone was laughing about the way he'd stolen some research, and there seemed to be some other scandal about him. I never found out what it was, but I heard Ann on the phone to someone about it. She tried to cover up for him. But he's the only person I ever heard her be unkind about.'

She stopped to drink her coffee. 'There was a time when we thought she was involved with a man. She had that look about her. Dreamy and glowing. He seemed to have some connection with the Democrats. Money too, because suddenly Ann became very elegant. She abandoned the wool skirts and sweaters we all wore and sprouted little suits and nice jewellery. Good luck to her, but we were all wildly jealous. And a little shocked!'

Kathleen went up to get more coffee. As she came back to the table, still smiling and laughing about the scandal of Ann Clarke having a secret affair, Michael interrupted her:

'Did you ever hear her mention someone called Johann?'

As though the sun had gone in, the sparkle left the eyes of the warm and open American housewife. She put down the coffee pot without filling the cups, and avoided Michael's eyes.

'No,' she said in a wary tone. 'I never heard Ann talk about Johann. I've no idea who he could be.'

From that moment Michael Stewart got no more from Kathleen Caldwell. She fidgeted and he knew she was anxious that he should leave, which he did after another half hour, by which time the atmosphere had become increasingly uncomfortable.

Kathleen had closed the door before Michael reached the end of the driveway. He hung back, just out of sight; then when he looked through the glass sidelights on the door he saw her pick up the telephone.

Johann. A key figure – but who?

The cab dropped him at the offices of the *Boston Globe*. Finding his way to the paper's library, Michael asked for the newspapers spanning Ann Clarke's time in Boston. Slowly and painstakingly, he pieced together the political goings-on that seemed to have captivated her.

Josef Horowitz Senior, an East European immigrant

who had come to the States after the First World War to make his fortune, had been one of the few to steer a cautious path through the troubled years of the thirties. He made a substantial fortune, a multi-millionaire. Everything he touched turned to more money, but it never bought him the respectability he craved. He put his money to work helping to build the Kennedy dynasty, hoping for acceptance, but none came. They took his money – and never even invited him to the White House. As tragedy struck the Kennedys – Jack and Bobby assassinated, Teddy discredited – Josef Horowitz had a willing understudy to go onto the political stage. Richard Horowitz, his son.

Ann had come to Boston just at the point where Josef Horowitz had achieved his dream: Richard had been elected to the Senate, on his way to becoming Secretary of State, en route, everyone thought, to the White House. The fact that Ann Clarke's first experience of US politics must have been about the same time, made Michael's trip worth while. If she and Horowitz had met . . . ?

Even more worth while, he thought, would be information about what had happened to Hugh Lawrie. For hours, Michael searched and found nothing.

Determined to get some lead on the Lawrie humiliation, he had started to go through the papers again when his attention was distracted. Two librarians were talking in hushed tones, repeatedly looking over at him.

Again he knew he had been recognized, it was only a matter of time before someone told the newspaper he was in the building, and his days in the States would be numbered. Quickly gathering up his notes, he left. Out in the street, a depression began to descend on him. Aimlessly he strolled, until he found himself in Commercial Street, near to the home of his friend Emma Catchpole. He took a chance and was in luck.

She welcomed him into the brick and booklined sitting room of her apartment. Seeing the glum set of his face, she poured him a drink without asking if he wanted it, then curled up on the sofa next to him. As he lay with his head resting on the back of the seat, he told her about his day – the recognition, the partial success in finding out about the connection between Ann and Horowitz, the knowledge that Ann had had an affair when she had been here. Something in the way his voice changed when he spoke of Ann's affair made Emma probe deeper into Michael's relationship with Ann Clarke. Soon it all came pouring out.

She had moved to the bar to freshen up their drinks when he stood up and went over to the window. He was looking out into the street when he said to her: 'I've met my match. I think I'm in love with Ann Clarke, but she seems to use me as some kind of stud, I only hear from her when she wants sex, and I think she's got someone else. I'm learning the hard way what jealousy feels like.'

He rested his hand against the rough brick wall. Emma went over and put a hand on his arm.

'Have you any reason to be jealous? You said she didn't seem to be involved with anyone.'

'The last time we made love, she called out the name of another man.'

As he walked back towards Quincy's Market and Faneuil Hall, he paid no attention to the empty streets or the growing dusk. Black thoughts and depression made him incautious. They jumped him from behind – two men who quickly got him to the ground, kicking him hard in the groin. A stray kick hit his head. Before he lost consciousness, his jumbled brain held on to the only words that were spoken.

'Go home, you bastard – we don't want your kind here.'

Stephen Robinson had signalled to the civil servants in his outer office that he did not wish to be disturbed. In her deep distress he had taken Mary into his office and settled her in one of the brown leather button-back chairs in the corner of the room. She wept and wept. 'Humiliated,' she said, over and over.

Stephen stood up and walked to the other side of his desk, looking down at Mary. 'She doesn't need to behave

like that. If Ann is under strain, it's all her own doing.
Let her friends like Harry McGregor help her out. She's
just using the rest of us!'

Mary, vulnerable to the point of breaking confidences,
said: 'He's part of her problem. He seems to think he's
put her where she is, and I think he's trying to get some
reward out of her. As if he hasn't had enough already!'

Stephen looked up sharply at the last remark. 'What
does that mean? She hasn't been in the job long enough
to have kept any promises.'

Mary's face closed in and she turned away from him,
obviously trying to frame an answer. Stephen let the
silence hang. Mary's last vestige of self-control crumbled,
and she slumped again, sobbing even more helplessly.

Stephen unlocked the little bar at the side of the room
and poured Mary a hefty brandy. Holding the glass to
her lips, he insisted the woman sip it. Soon she became
calmer.

'Do you want to tell me what this is all about? Something is obviously upsetting you, and I don't think it's
just because Ann got out of bed the wrong side this morning. What's wrong?'

Mary looked at him for a long moment, then hesitat-
ingly told him of her instruction from Ann to provide an
alibi for McGregor on election night. As she watched the
compassion leave his face to be replaced by shock and, at
first, disbelief, Mary's voice became stronger.

'I didn't want to do it. I've always detested McGregor,
there's something about him that makes me feel unclean.
But Ann said all our plans would come to nothing if it
came out that we knew Roddy Henderson was going to
resign and how that was fixed, and that we knew on
polling night because McGregor was already arranging
Ann's campaign for Secretary of State. But I haven't slept
since I had to lie to the policeman about having been with
McGregor when that poor girl was murdered in Glasgow.'

As he listened Stephen remembered the Glasgow
murder. Even in the post-election chaos, with the fires
and the terrorists, people had still found time to be

248

shocked. And he remembered what he had been told by a Coatbridge police officer! A thousand questions raced through his head. He gathered his senses carefully, tempered his responses.

'Now I need a drink,' he said. 'Can we take these matters one at a time?'

Mary said: 'Ann assured me he couldn't possibly be guilty. She seemed to know about meetings he'd been involved in over that night, and she seemed certain he was innocent. Although she didn't say so, I think McGregor had gone to see Henderson.'

Stephen asked the question that had bothered him since this whole sorry affair had started: 'How did Ann know Roddy was going to stand down?'

Mary seemed surprised by the question: 'He told her, of course. Or rather he told Harry. The week before polling day, Harry had gone to see Roddy about something or other, and when he came back he was closeted with Ann for a couple of hours. Then I was told we'd been given advance notice of his retirement so that Ann could get her campaign organized. Roddy seemed to want to give her a head start.'

Carefully, never aggressively, Stephen put together each jigsaw piece, question after suggestion, inquiry following thought, until he thought he had begun to see the patterns.

Mary said, a hand on his arm: 'I'm sorry, Stephen. I forgot you and Roddy were friends. He probably had reasons for not telling you he was going to resign. Perhaps he knew how fond you were of his wife and didn't want to upset you.'

Robinson said nothing, just shook his head.

As a last effort, pledging his own confidentiality, he warned Mary on no account to tell Ann Clarke – or anyone – the content of their conversation. Mary left him with her step lighter than it had been for quite a few days.

The House of Commons library provided a convenient bolt-hole for Mary to while away the rest of the day, far from the condescension of the civil servants. She left the

Commons at four thirty, measuring her pace up Whitehall so that she arrived at a little before four fifty-five. No time left to linger in the outer office until she had her interview with the Secretary of State. No one spoke to her as she went into the outer office and hung up her jacket.

At precisely five o'clock, Jonathan pressed the buzzer through to Ann and reminded her that she had asked to see Mary now. His expression was totally bland as he opened the door for Mary to go in.

Ann did not look up as Mary came in, but she did say, 'Sit down'. Mary remained standing.

When Ann finally did put down her pen, she looked surprised to see her political assistant standing before her. She looked startled at the expression on her friend's face.

'What's wrong? Why are you glowering at me?'

Her tone was friendly, but her eyes seemed heavy and her fists were clenched in unconscious tension.

'Ann, you humiliated me this morning, and in front of all the civil servants. You told me I could go back to Glasgow to do your constituency work. Well, I am going back to Glasgow, but not to work for you.'

Mary resisted being taken aback by the look of shock on Ann's face. At first the politician didn't reply. Then she stood up and came round the desk.

'Whatever are you talking about? Why should you go back to Glasgow? We haven't been here a week yet, it's much too early to see if it's going to work.'

For the first time in years, Mary's temper snapped.

'You treated me like an incompetent office junior this morning. You've put me through hell today. I know you're very talented, but you wouldn't have got your career off the ground if I hadn't done all the dirty work. You've used me to get where you are, used me as an organizer, used me for my loyalty, and used me because I know more about the people you need to vote for you than you ever could. You've gone too far now.'

Mary stepped back a pace as Ann searched for words. Then the poise and assurance of the beautiful professional politician suddenly crumpled. Her shoulders slumped, and the colour drained not just from her face, but from her eyes as well.

'Mary, don't you abandon me too! I couldn't take that as well.'

Soundlessly, the tears welled.

'Ann, you told me you wanted rid of me. I've been expecting this for a while. Now that you're in the big time, you don't need me around. You even threw away my election gift.'

Ann buried her head in her hands and began to sob; her emotion seemed so intense that Mary's belligerence evaporated.

'For God's sake, Ann, tell me what's wrong. Are you ill? Will I get a doctor?'

No reply. Ann rocked herself, keening incoherently.

Mary bent over the desk to reach the switch on the intercom, to summon help, but Ann reached out and stopped her.

'Oh, please don't tell anyone! Get rid of them, Mary. I don't want to have to deal with any of them tonight. Tell them they can go early, the switchboard can monitor my calls.'

Mary spoke in a milder tone. 'You can't do that. You're the Secretary of State now. You can't hide away.'

Ann moaned: 'Mary, you've got to help me.'

Mary half lifted, half dragged Ann over to a couch and sat her down.

'I'm going along the corridor to see Stephen Robinson. I'll tell him you have a migraine and you have to be left alone until you feel better. I'll ask him to take charge. I'll tell the nosy parkers in the outer office the same. When I go out, lock the door behind me so that you can't be disturbed. I'll knock so hard when I came back that you'll know it's me.'

Ann nodded. Just as Mary was about to open the door, plaintively, Ann asked her to hurry back. Mary avoided looking at the now pathetic figure on the couch.

The civil servants saw a steely side to the political appointee they hadn't known existed. She bundled them

out of the outer office in minutes, almost physically eject-
ing Jonathan who demanded access to his Minister. Stephen Robinson looked at her suspiciously, but agreed to
do as he was asked. As she was leaving his room though,
he stopped her: 'Don't be conned, Mary. Stick to your
guns. Ann is a past master at manipulating people.'

Mary did not respond. Ann had got herself under control by the time Mary returned. As she washed her face
and tried to restore her make-up, Mary prepared her a
stiff drink, which Ann refused, nor did she give any
explanation for what had so upset her.

As they left the Scottish Office some hours later, Mary
could see that Ann had retreated behind her cool professional exterior. But as they got near to the car, Ann
stopped. There was fear in her eyes as she spoke.

'I need to ask a favour of you, Mary, and I know I
don't deserve one after the awful way I've treated you,
but would you mind staying at my place overnight? I
don't want to be alone.'

Mary walked away.

The morning of the State Opening of Parliament dawned
dull and drizzly; a similar pall of gloom hung over the
Labour benches. Ministers, knowing what was in the
speech, acknowledged that it would not meet with univer-
sal acclaim, least of all on their own side. The only festive
atmosphere came from the new Opposition, freed at last
from the trials of government. When Black Rod pounded
at the door of the Commons, Tony Metcalf rose to lead
his Government into the Lords to hear the Speech from
the Throne. Conscious of the TV cameras, he held himself
erect and dignified in his navy pinstripe suit with a white
shirt and bright yellow tie, his hair slicked and gleaming.
He led the way, ignoring the man on his left who weeks
before had been Prime Minister.

As he passed under the cameras, the TV screens cleared
for Ann Clarke who had paced herself immediately
behind, in a green silk designer suit, with a green pillbox
on her auburn hair, diamond studs winking in her ears.

Her compassion as she gave her arm to the oldest MP in the House, her Shadow on the Opposition benches, made a more sympathetic image than the ram-rod straight, unsmiling Prime Minister.

Throughout the Speech, as Ann stood in the huddle of MPs at the Bar of the House of Lords, she held her head erect, her face free of emotion, the cameras devoured her, occasionally flicking to the Countess of Grantham, lined now but as much the English rose as she had been as Margaret Thatcher, Britain's first woman Prime Minister. Unashamedly, the peeress kept her eye on the young woman who had entered Parliament during her period of office as Prime Minister, and a smile played at the side of her mouth, almost as if she enjoyed hugely the fact that she had deprived this determined politician of her place in the history books as the first woman to rule from Number Ten.

As the Speech made its way ever nearer to its conclusion, the commentators, interpreting the code language of politicians for the world at large, dwelt on what was missing rather than what the Government planned; more than one observed the absence of policies so ardently fought for by Ann Clarke.

As the ageing Monarch drew to a close, one pundit told viewers that the speech held little that might not have been written by the previous Government. The cameras spanned the sea of faces of Labour backbenches, some obviously angry, others lowering their heads in despair.

In the silence before the ceremonial began at the conclusion of the speech, the camera's eye came to rest on Ann. For a long second, her face remained impassive, then she bowed her head, running her left hand along her forehead. Straightening up, she slowly shook her head, as if in disbelief. Before she turned away from the concealed camera, the millions of people watching her on television knew – or felt they knew – what she was thinking. The Labour politicians crowding the long corridor from Lords to Commons stepped aside to make way for her, more deferential to her than ever before. It was as if a silent signal was going out.

In the mock gothic splendour of the Central Lobby, a small group of MPs from Liverpool stood in a huddle. As they saw Ann approach, they turned to greet her. The eldest of their number, a loyal MP who had been in the House for twenty years, hardly ever opening his mouth, stepped forward. Ann stopped for the first time since she had left the Chamber.

'We're not happy, Ann. Can we have a meeting with you?'

Silently, Ann nodded her head.

'Committee Room Nineteen at one o'clock?'

Again she nodded. As she was about to make her way to her own office, she caught sight of Sylvia Metcalf, elegant in peach linen, her shiny crop of dark hair peeping out from under a picture hat. The two women looked at one another. Eventually, Sylvia lowered her eyes and turned away.

Ann waited until she had heard the news headlines on the lunch-time TV bulletins before going to the meeting with the Liverpool back benchers. The consensus was that the Speech had been designed with the summit in mind, and pointed the way to a cautious Government, rather than the radical force for reform many voters had hoped for. The tailpiece to the item was the refusal of Ann Clarke to comment.

The next stories flashed on the screen. The dock strike was spreading, car workers in the Midlands had come out on a lightning strike and could remain out for some time; postal workers were taking a ballot on whether or not to strike. Union leaders gave as the reason for the unrest the dissatisfaction with the Government's failure to act to improve living standards.

As Ann came out of the lift on the Committee Room corridor, she could see the place was crowded. More than one hundred and fifty Labour MPs, some of them junior Ministers, had turned up for the impromptu meeting set up to allow half a dozen Liverpool MPs the chance to talk to the Deputy Prime Minister. The buzz of conversation stilled as Members realized she was in the corridor. They cleared a path for her. She looked neither to left nor right, and the sharp tattoo of her high-heeled shoes was the only sound. They crowded into the room after her, standing four deep round the side, some climbing up to sit on the sills of the opened mullioned windows. The little band of Liverpool MPs looked bewildered, except for one. Sidney Lawrence had only just been elected, but he had been a thorn in the flesh of the Labour Leadership for years. He took charge.

Lawrence launched into a lengthy attack on the Government for failing to exploit the 'crisis of capitalism'; his arguments, well known, had been well rehearsed over the years. A low grumble of discontent sped round the room. Some MPs started to heckle. A shout of 'Shut up Lawrence' got a cheer. But the intrepid MP continued, until he noticed that silence had again fallen and his fellow Members were looking beyond his shoulders. He turned round to find Ann Clarke standing behind him. He shrugged his shoulders, bowing to the inevitable, and gave her the floor.

Despite the lack of a public address system, Ann did not raise her voice. She made no opening remarks, just summed up what she could see on the face of every Member present:

'We've been conned. It has all been for nothing. The Government has abandoned everything we campaigned for. No word of Inner City Aid; restarting the National Health Service; reinstating social security payments or repealing the curfew laws. And we're to get more US "advisors", more developments around US bases – "to create employment"! They've sold out again to the Americans. This Government has a majority of only four; from the nature of this meeting we could bring it down tomorrow. If we do that, the Tories will surely win the election and we will be even worse off than we are just now.'

From the back an anonymous voice shouted: 'We know all that, so what do we do?'

Ann smiled. 'We flex our muscles! I expect Metcalf thinks I'll resign. That's something I have no intention of doing.'

She broke off to let the cheering subside.

'But I will need your support to make sure he doesn't sack me. I'll take the campaign into the Cabinet Room – I'll be your voice and the voice of the electors there. But I will not pay lip service to the hypocrisy of this Government. I have already informed the Prime Minister that I will not be speaking in the debate on the Queen's Speech. If Parliament is going to be a sham, then I won't waste my time on it. This afternoon I will go to Brussels to meet with the European Ministers to discuss unemployment, and when I return, I will meet with you here again to discuss an alternative agenda for the American summit. In the meantime, I suggest we all inform the Whips that we will be abstaining on all votes. If they make trouble, we threaten a vote of confidence.'

Again a rumble went round the room – a Government threatened with a vote of confidence tabled by its own side would make Parliamentary history and would be a masterstroke. Power was being restored to the back benches.

'I take it that the lack of dissent means you back me on this?'

A torrent of 'Hear, hear' came from the MPs, ready now for battle with their own leadership. Ann was about to draw the meeting to a close when one wily old MP, a woman who had been in Parliament for over thirty years, spoke up.

'I think we had better pass a resolution, even if we are an unconstitutional gathering. I've been working out some words – how does this sound? "We, the undersigned Labour MPs, fully support the appointment of Ann Clarke as Deputy Prime Minister and Secretary of State for Scotland and look forward to her representing the views of ordinary voters in the Cabinet and at the forthcoming summit with the United States of America. As long as she retains the opportunity to look after our interests, we will take no action to ensure the downfall of this Government." What do you think?'

Ann took a second to think about it, then she shrugged her shoulders and nodded her head.

No one spoke against the proposal.

As the gathering began to disperse, someone shouted: 'What about a collection for the strikers?'

Agreement was unanimous.

As people looked around for something to use to collect the money, Ann picked up the elegant designer hat she had long since taken off her head, and handed it over for the collection. Then she emptied the contents of her wallet into it, earning a cheer in the process.

As she left the room, her woman supporter stopped her, this time joined by a younger woman, a new entrant to Parliament but a seasoned political campaigner. The older woman spoke: 'Don't be naive about what you're letting yourself in for. You're not playing by their rules, and they'll try to destroy you rather than change themselves.'

Ann, who had never cultivated her female colleagues, shrugged and made to move away, but the younger woman laid her hand on her arm. 'You might need us some day. Not just politically. You know where to find us.'

For a moment it looked as if Ann might say something, and a fleeting vulnerability clouded her eyes. But she turned away. A path was cleared for her. Outside even the normally ebullient Commons press corps was sombre and subdued.

The ringing of the telephone penetrated the sound of the running bathwater. Michael couldn't rush to answer it – any rapid movement gave him an excrutciating headache. But according to the intern at the hospital's emergency room, no serious damage had been done. Boston muggers were common, the intern knew his stuff. What he would not have been able to explain, had he known, was why the muggers would leave money, gold Rolex watch and credit cards. Having managed to get himself checked out at the hospital and back to his hotel without attracting attention, Michael was anxious not to let the outside world impinge on his recovery. However, the time was coming when the office would want to know what he was up to.

Ross was in an angry and suspicious mood; his political correspondent, incommunicado for two days, was using the lion's share of the editorial budget in the States and, as yet, had nothing to show for it. The niggles of doubt had come back. What if this man, undoubtedly very bright and talented, really did have the kind of flawed judgement that had caused his hasty removal from Washington? Would he, Ross, have to carry the can for trusting him? It was time to rattle the cage. He might like Stewart, but he liked his career more.

Michael had to convince Donald Ross that he wasn't drunk before he could get out of him what the call was about. He explained away the sluggishness of his speech to pain killers taken for an old back injury – he felt no need to explain that the back injury was only days old.

'What do you mean – the political situation has blown up?' Michael groaned, more with exasperation than pain. 'We always knew the Queen's Speech would be a non-event. Why all the excitement now?'

He let out a low whistle. 'She really is building up the pressure! You want me to come back?'

He flicked open his notebook as he listened. 'I've made some headway, but there's a mysterious character called Johann in her life that I feel holds a clue. And then there was her involvement with the Democrats in the seventies. She was involved with someone who may have been one of Horowitz's staffers at one time. I want to find out who he is and talk to him, but I suspect that means I'll have to go to Washington – although that's one city I'd prefer to give a miss!'

His jaw was tightening as his irritation mounted. 'When the time comes for me to go to Washington, I'll do it, but I don't want to go before I have to. OK?'

Giving a commitment to take only one more day, Michael slammed down the phone. He winced as the sensation jarred his bruised body and reminded him of his headache.

He placed a second call to BBC Scotland, this time to Clare. The vibes of disapproval from Ross had been strong, he needed background. Clare was able to tell him that the Controller had given Donald Ross a bad time; the mandarins were worried that whatever Stewart turned up on Ann Clarke would put them in bad odour with the woman whose power grew with every day that passed.

'What you're saying, Clare, is that everyone is having cold feet. If I didn't think I really had a story here, I'd be on the first plane, but I feel I'm going to get something big soon.'

Despite himself, he smiled. 'It's a long time since anyone was worried about me. I appreciate it, and I will take care.' He hung up.

He had just turned on the taps again when he became conscious of a knocking at the door. Cautious now that the damage had been done, he asked who it was.

'It's me, Emma. Can I come in?'

As soon as he opened the door, she could see something had happened to him.

'How can you be sure it was just muggers? How do you know it's not your old friend the Senator again?'

He shrugged, not answering.

'Have you told the police?' When she saw the strain in his face she relented and sat down on the bed beside him.

'I'm sorry, Michael. I suspect you've had enough. I just came by to say I'm going back to Washington tomorrow, and I wondered if you'd like to go to a concert with me this evening?'

She saw him frown and guessed his reason. 'I refuse to let you hide away! Anyway, I'm stuck for a partner. Pick me up at seven, and we'll be going to a supper party on Beacon Hill afterwards.'

She stilled his objections with a friendly kiss and left.

He paid little attention to the music. On the drive to the supper party, he asked Emma if she knew anyone on Horowitz' staff who might have been around in the seventies.

She nodded vigorously. 'His campaign manager, guy called Mathews. I see him in the market every Saturday in Washington, he lives on the same block. Why do you want to know?'

'I'm trying to track down people Ann knew when she was at Harvard. Ask a few questions.'

She took a long time looking at him. 'Work or personal questions?'

He never answered: she let it drop.

The gaslight on Beacon Hill gave it a romantic atmosphere, and the lights shining in the windows of the tall and elegant house made it look inviting. Michael resolved to put his worries behind him for a little; after all, he could go home tomorrow if there was no chance of talking to this Mathews character.

The butler led Emma and Michael out on to the patio where a light breeze was stirring the warm summer evening. Chinese lanterns added to the ambience. Michael met his hostess, the formidable Polly Westbourne, doyenne of Boston society. A white-collared waiter appeared from nowhere with drinks and canapés. Around him the elegantly dressed company dissected the concert that Michael could barely remember, and his silence earned him the attentions of his hostess.

'Young man, is your European culture offended by our American attempts to emulate it?'

He laughed and got off the hook by asking his hostess about the history of her impressive home. She took him by the arm and led him into the house to show him some of the cornices that had just been restored. As they went into the dining room, there was a commotion. A tall, painfully thin woman whose blue-black hair was pulled back in a chignon caught with diamonds as huge as the stones dangling from her ears, was waving her glass around and demanding another martini. The barman would have none of it – the lady had obviously had one or two earlier.

As Polly ushered him away from this unpleasantness, he heard the high-pitched New England screech of the woman:

'Don't you know who I am? I am Rachel Horowitz. I will be the next First Lady of this country.'

Mrs Westbourne saw that Michael had heard. 'I'm sorry, young man. Mrs Horowitz has a bit of a problem. We all try to be as understanding as possible, but sometimes she goes too far.'

Again Michael smiled. 'Don't worry, Mrs Westbourne. Even European culture has its embarrassments. But will Mrs Horowitz not be a major problem for her husband when the primaries start? All that scrutiny?'

The elderly woman smiled knowingly. 'Not if he gets her dried out she shouldn't. And if he's his father's son, he'll have Rachel all sorted out in good time for the election, and she'll be appearing on chat shows telling us how her husband saved her from the bottle.'

She sat down on a sofa, patting a cushion to indicate Michael should join her – time for confidences:

'Old man Horowitz was quite a man. One of the strongest characters I've ever met. He courted me, you know, but my father would have nothing to do with immigrants, even wealthy ones. Now I'm in my dotage, I often dream about what life would have been like if Josef Johann Horowitz and I had got together!'

Michael almost dropped his drink.

Emma appeared and said to her hostess: 'I think I'd better get him back to his hotel, Mrs Westbourne. He was mugged the other night and I don't think he's as well as he claims to be.'

Michael remained silent all the way back to the hotel.

He shook off Emma's offer to see him to his room. Once there he opened a bottle of whisky and filled a tooth mug. He downed the drink in one swallow

Then he noticed that all his notepads were missing.

The clink of glasses and the waves of polite chatter filled the high-ceilinged rooms of the penthouse flat in the *Daily*

Mirror building. The members of the new Government had been brought together to celebrate for the first time since the election, and although some brave souls put on their party voices and brayed at the most inane jokes, the atmosphere was more like a wake. Groups huddled together talking conspiratorially, furtively looking round to see if there was anyone likely to hear what they were saying.

Stephen moved round the room feeling like a leper. Eyes were averted from him as MPs discussed the significance of the day's events. Two camps seemed to have been formed – those who had attended the meeting in Committee Room 19 – and those who had not. He could smell the suspicion in each camp – after all, he had challenged Ann Clark, but now he was working for her.

Standing with his back to the bar, a glass of wine in his hand, he scanned the room looking for allies. His eyes settled on George Jeffries; the Foreign Secretary's antenna must have been working, he raised his eyes from his discussion and lifted his glass in a silent toast. Stephen raised his own glass in answer, but the effort to smile was too great.

'You look as though you have the worries of the world on your shoulders.'

The familiar voice made him spin round. Sylvia Metcalf, in a plain white sleeveless dress with mandarin collar and gold buttons from neck to hem, appeared young and carefree – but her eyes looked beyond him to where her husband was standing talking to the *Mirror* political editor, tumbler of whisky in his hand.

Stephen's voice was low and intimate as he responded: 'Funny – I thought you were the one who had them.'

They smiled at one another and she held out her hand to him: 'I haven't congratulated you on becoming a Minister. Are you enjoying it?'

His shrug told her 'enjoy' wasn't the word he would have chosen. His eyes became dark and serious as he lowered his voice even further.

'I need to talk to you. Urgently. I've heard a story that

needs a more detached mind than mine to assess whether I'm overreacting.'

Sylvia laughed. 'I'm the last person you should talk to if you're looking for detachment about anything to do with Ann Clarke.'

A rich male voice made Sylvia spin round, George Jeffries had come up behind her.

'Why is it that every conversation I eavesdrop on tonight is about the beautiful Miss Clarke?'

One look at the bitter faces of the Prime Minister's wife and her companion was enough to make him laugh. 'Courage, *mes enfants*. The battle is but starting. We'll win, mark my words!'

Neither seemed to believe him, and Stephen decided to include him. 'George, I've just told Sylvia I need a fresh mind on something. But urgently. Could you both come to my flat in Dolphin Square when this is over? It really is most important.'

Sylvia hesitated, then she saw the worry in his face. She nodded. Jeffries agreed as well.

The late evening sun shone on a deserted Dolphin Square. Sylvia and George scanned the direction signs to the various houses looking for the apartment block Stephen lived in. There was no one around to see the Foreign Secretary and his companion climb the two flights of stairs up to the service apartment that was home to Stephen in London. Both their detectives melted into the shadows.

Despite her anxieties, Sylvia's eyes darted round the flat, looking for clues to Stephen's personality. The main room in the two-room flat was large and sparsely decorated. A sofa and two chairs in a deep blue velour took up the centre of the floor, and a bar table sat before one window, a cluttered desk before another. The curtains were a dull beige, chosen more for serviceability than good looks. No pictures on the walls, no warmth or feeling; no effort had been put in to make this place like a home, or even tolerably welcoming.

Stephen seemed nervous as he made up drinks for them, and when he sat down with his own whisky, he perched on the end of his chair, twirling his glass and staring into its amber depths. No one spoke. Then, without warning, and with no embellishment, Stephen told them his fears.

'On election night a fourteen-year-old prostitute was brutally murdered in Glasgow. The police seemed, for some reason, to take an interest in Harry McGregor's whereabouts. Ann Clarke insisted that Mary Connolly provide Harry with an alibi. Mary thinks McGregor may have been involved.'

Jeffries let out a long sigh, Sylvia's eyes were wide with wonder. Painstakingly, George Jeffries led Stephen through the story he had heard. When there was no more to learn, he closed his eyes and let his head fall back. Sylvia said not a word. The silence grew until Stephen spoke again, this time looking straight at Sylvia:

'Do you remember the policeman who told us the story of the Workers' Militias? The Chief?' She nodded.

'He tried to tell the same story to his superiors – they wouldn't even give him an interview. He's been suspended on full pay whilst an inquiry goes on about "alleged irregularities" in his Division.'

Jeffries opened his eyes a little, his head still leaning backwards. 'Be careful you're not getting paranoid!'

Sylvia and Stephen looked at one another.

Robinson said: 'Point number three. The policeman investigating the murder was forced into early retirement and the inquiry closed almost before it had begun. He decided to freelance it, a totally straight cop. He's just been done for drugs. Denied bail. Until last week. Keeping him on remand was beginning to look bad. And point four – somebody nobbled Roddy Henderson, blackmailed him, or threatened him or something. Somebody with enough clout to terrify him. And all roads lead to Ann Clarke.'

Sylvia spoke: 'I believe you, Stephen. I've felt all along that Ann has powerful backers. It wouldn't surprise me if they were powerful enough to control the police.'

Jeffries opened his eyes and looked at her hard. All he said was: 'My dear.'

Sylvia retorted: 'Don't patronize me, George. What has happened in the course of the past day should be enough to convince you we're not dealing with a normal bit of political mischief, and Ann Clarke wouldn't have been half as effective today if you hadn't had the brilliant idea to make her Deputy Prime Minister. We've got to stop playing at this and find out who really is behind her.'

George leant over. 'I'm sorry, I didn't mean to patronize you. I'm playing devil's advocate. I have to admit I'm not sold on the conspiracy theory, but I do take seriously everything Stephen has said – so seriously that I'm going to leave you now whilst I track down Colin Warrender.'

Stephen looked bewildered and Sylvia said; 'I'll explain who he is in a minute.'

A flicker of the eyebrow was the only sign that Jeffries gave that he had seen the possessive way Sylvia had spoken to the Scottish politician.

When they were alone, Stephen went back to the bar to refill Sylvia's glass with white wine while she told him of the role of the Security officer. He listened carefully as she explained Warrender's mission to find out what was motivating Ann Clarke, and who was behind her. As Stephen handed over the glass of wine, their hands touched, each pulled away. Stephen went to sit at the far corner of the room, but an atmosphere began to grow. Soon words gave way to silences. Stephen moved towards her as she stood up to leave. They barely touched. His lips brushed hers, and neither moved against the other. Gently, Stephen put his hand on the side of her neck. Her fingers lightly touched his chest through his shirt. His hand caught her waist and drew her to him, but she stiffened.

Then the doorbell made them jump apart. Flustered, Stephen went to the door as Sylvia checked her make-up. Within seconds he was back, Government red box in hand, but embarrassment came between them now. Without looking at him, Sylvia took her leave. He walked with her to the head of the stairs, calling down to the detective standing guard at the bottom that Mrs Metcalf was on her way down. As she was about to turn away from him, he caught hold of her again, kissing her on the lips.

This time she did pull away.

'No, Stephen. I love him. I could never hurt him.' The loud clatter of her heels running down the stairs hid the gentle click of the door being quietly closed along the corridor and the disappearing figure of Colin Warrender.

Not a smile could be found on the faces of the two thousand men crammed into the car park. A gaggle, in T-shirts and jeans, stood on the deck of an open-top bus, but even they weren't listening to the man with the microphone as he harangued them. His shouts merely fuelled the rumble of anger that went round the crowd. It reached a crescendo as the man with the loud hailer asked the question they had waited for.

'All those in favour of strike action?'

A sea of hands.

'All those against?'

Not a hand to be seen.

One or two began to cheer, but their voices died in their throats, the atmosphere was sombre. An ominous silence hung over the gathering, as, unbidden, they began to move through the gates, forming a long and menacing column. As the others kept a respectful distance behind him, one man marched in front, head erect, eyes straight ahead. His gaze only deviated as he saw Harry McGregor standing in a doorway.

The numbers swelled as the march went through the grim streets of Birmingham. Urchins with Asian faces and thick local accents danced around the crowd; older brothers and sisters braved parental wrath and joined in. Soon the police were on the scene, but the crowd was orderly, and the numbers too great to disperse with anything less than a baton charge. As the crowd advanced, more or less in silence, the back streets and motorways gave way to shops and offices. Reinforcements kept joining in as if by some prearranged signal; pretty summer dresses of young office workers lent a festive air bizarre in the growing marching column. The silence intensified, adding even greater menace. Bus drivers abandoned their vehicles to add their numbers, often marching side by side with their passengers. Delivery men left the doors of their vans swinging free, keys still in the ignition, as they too joined in. Subtle discipline began to be imposed on the march, now five thousand strong, as they neared the city centre. One column moved off on its own, heading for the Department of Employment headquarters; another made for the town hall. Cars swerved to the kerb side as the column of people moved relentlessly on. Some drivers joined in, others looked bewildered. Even among the onlookers, the silence was maintained, and as the sound of the traffic quietened to be replaced by the rhythmic noise of marching feet, the eeriness grew.

Elderly women stood clutching their shopping bags, some visibly frightened. One tall and elegant woman, her sky-blue silk dress matching perfectly the rinse of her hair, looked with disdain at the tall muscled man who led the march; the column advanced on the street corner she was dominating. She seemed transfixed by his insolent and unwavering stare, picking up the challenge. As he came closer to her, she straightened her shoulders, until, with military bearing, she marched out to confront him. A policeman darted to her side to stop her, but she brushed him off. Horror replaced bewilderment on the faces of the onlookers as they watched the confrontation loom. Then, to their utter amazement, as the woman closed in on the leader, she fell into step beside him; a mutter rippled through the marchers and fell away.

The incongruous partnership – the threatening man and the Lady Mayoress – took possession of the city centre.

Chaos reigned in New Street Station when McGregor arrived to catch the train to London. Railway workers had come out on lightning strike to decide if they would support the other strikers. They joined in, leaving McGregor with a transport problem. He found a pub, ordered a large whisky and settled himself at a table.

Few noticed the insignificant man musing in the corner.

After a while he asked the barman where he could find a phone. Disdainful of the thick Scottish accent, the brawny barman continued polishing glasses, gesturing with his head to a pay phone near the door. The Scotsman dialled a number from a little black book, spoke for a while, then went back to his whisky. He was on his third double when another man joined him. Both got up to leave. As McGregor passed the barman in the now empty pub, he stopped. With his right hand he picked up a heavy brewery ashtray and hurled it at the mirrored gantry behind the bar. By the time the barman had vaulted the bar and got through the door, a yellow car was disappearing up the street.

Three and a half hours later, the car slowly edged its way nearer the pavement in London's Smith Square; the driver tried to find a gap in the television crews milling around the entrance to the former Transport Union head-quarters. As McGregor got out of the car, the hoards of reporters and cameramen made to surround him, but he waved them aside until he had collected his briefcase from the boot of the car. Case in hand, he turned to the driver and shook hands, then he steadfastly forced his way through the scrum, saying nothing.

As he went through the doors, he heard one reporter say to the other: 'I could swear I've seen McGregor's driver before.'

Another enlightened him: 'Donnelly's his name. Three months ago, remember the drugs trial at the Old Bailey? He was the one whose case was dropped.'

McGregor, smiling, let the door slam shut behind him: he had heard the identity of his driver being confirmed. As he passed the security desk, he waved in greeting to the elderly porter manning it. 'Not long now, comrade! We've got the bastards on the run!'

It was dark when McGregor re-emerged on the steps of the union building. His appearance was the first sign to the press that the three-hour meeting was breaking up. The union leader held a single sheet of paper in his hand. Camera crews switched on their lights; sound recordists squeezed to the front. He waited until everyone was ready before he read from the sheet.

'The Executive Committee of this Union today resolved to call all of the union's million and a half members out on strike from midnight tonight, and to call on the General Council of the Trades Union Congress to call an immediate general strike. This action has been taken in response to calls from our membership who are deeply concerned at the failure of the Labour Government to have nuclear weapons removed from our shores, at the growing fear that the Government is determined not to act to end the American domination of our country and at Government refusal to take into public ownership all foreign-owned assets. The Executive Committee also passed a motion congratulating Sister Ann Clarke on her appointment as Deputy Prime Minister and Secretary of State for Scotland. She has our full support in her fight to ensure the Labour Government remains faithful to the socialist principles on which it was elected.'

He stopped and turned away from the cameras, raising his hand to indicate he was not prepared to answer any questions. Two burly men who had accompanied him out of the building, used their bodies to force a passage back inside.

In the general bustle, no one noticed a tall middle-aged man in tweed jacket and checked shirt watching from the door of the Marquis of Granby public house. As a reporter passed him to go into the pub in search of a telephone, he stopped him and in a lilting Highland accent but with the unmistakeable authority of the former police officer, Hamish McLean, asked:

'Is the union meeting over now? Will they all be coming out?'

Absentmindedly, the reporter nodded.

The stranger did not have long to wait. Reassured that they would not get any more information that night, the press pack disappeared. Once the street was clear, McGregor emerged with another man. Together the two men walked towards the Embankment; once there, they separated. McGregor's companion set out towards Pimlico, McGregor to the Houses of Parliament.

A figure stayed close behind him in the shadows of the now deserted road.

The union leader never arrived at the Commons. In the early hours of the morning, two down-and-outs found the crumpled form of the badly beaten Harry McGregor, his face kicked almost to a pulp, his legs twisted beneath him, obviously broken. Incredibly, he was still alive, and his luck held as he was admitted to the Westminster Hospital minutes before a ban was imposed on new admissions. Hospital support staff had decided to join the growing band of striking workers.

8

The first glimpse they had of her was the long sweep of silk-clad leg, as the Jaguar Sovereign stopped outside the Berlaymont Building. The Brussels headquarters of the European Community had never seen a more excited group of photographers since the visit years before of an Italian MP who had moved on from an earlier career as a soft porn star.

An appreciative murmur rose from the pack as they saw they had not been misled about her attractiveness. She wore a dress of peach crêpe de Chine that clung to every curve and stopped just above her knee; the slashed neckline revealed a long swanlike neck encircled by a single strand of pearls. Pearls at her ears nestled in tiny diamonds and her hair, brushed free, was caught behind one ear.

Despite her model-girl height, she wore high snakeskin shoes in pale beige, making her exquisite legs look even longer and lending her an air of feminine fragility. A Gallic wolf whistle made her eyes twinkle with delight although it brought frowns of disapproval from the Community officials present. But even they jostled one another for the privilege of travelling into the bowels of the building in the same lift as the beautiful British Minister. Stephen Robinson and Jonathan were left to bring up the rear clutching briefcases and files. Ann was already flirting with the other European Ministers when they eventually found the conference room; all except one flocked to her side.

She charmed the French Regional Development Minister by responding to him in fluent French; her greeting to the Italian was as faultless. The Spaniard undressed her with his eyes as he listened to her excuse her hesitant Spanish, but to the others present it sounded anything but hesitant. The Greek Employment Minister visibly melted as she apologized for only knowing the ancient Greek she had learned at university, and before he knew it he had invited her to Athens so that she could learn more about his country. He preened with delight as she said she would get her office to be in touch to talk about dates. A flood of invitations followed, and each one she received with interest and an obvious determination to try to accept it.

As she turned away from the adulation in an attempt to get these ageing men to do some work, she caught the eye of the tall German Finance Minister who had kept to the sidelines. She approached him with outstretched hand.

'Hello, I'm Ann Clarke. You must be Dieter Volle.'

The German bowed in acknowledgement, the faint whiff of his elegant toilet water reaching her as his blond hair flopped across his forehead. He held her hand a second longer than necessary, causing Jonathan and Stephen to exchange glances; each noticed the wafer-thin black wristwatch with a tiny diamond where they both had a utilitarian number twelve.

'Miss Clarke, I am delighted to meet you. I hope later we will have a longer opportunity to get to know one another.'

Ann smiled up to him. 'I hope you will come to our reception tonight.'

He held her eyes. 'I had intended going straight back to Bonn, but you've convinced me to stay.'

She lowered her head in acknowledgement of his compliment.

The business of the day commenced. The Ministers seated themselves around the massive circular table, all except Ann and Volle immediately putting on their earphones to listen to the simultaneous translation of the speeches. As the argument began about subsidies for assisted regions with high levels of unemployment, Ann took out the files from her briefcase and began initialling memos, leaving Stephen to do the work. Most other senior ministers were doing the same, having had the foresight to bring juniors to do the actual haggling. Two hours passed in peaceful debate with no progress being made. In the middle of a particularly long and impassioned intervention by the Italians, Jonathan passed Ann a note. As she read it, her face became studiedly neutral. She quickly looked round the table to find that all except Dieter Volle and a Dutch minister who was sound asleep, were joining in the argument with Latin fervour. She caught the eye of the chairman and indicated that she would have to slip out. She was conscious of Volle watching her. Jonathan held the door open and once outside she found the British Ambassador waiting to speak to her. He led her into a corner.

'Minister, I'm afraid the industrial action in Britain has escalated. The TUC has just called for a general strike from midnight tonight, following the Union demands from last night; the country is slowly grinding to a halt.'

Ann thought for a minute. 'Has the Prime Minister sent any message for me?'

'No, ma'am.' The diplomat looked uncomfortable.

'No Cabinet meeting has been called?'

He shook his head. Ann remained silent for a while. Then she looked up at the grey-haired man:

'Keep me informed of developments. Meantime I had better get back to this meeting. I'm sure you realize the importance of today's discussion.'

Thirty years in the diplomatic service wasn't enough to keep the shock out of the Ambassador's face.

'But Minister, I thought you would want to get back home as quickly as possible. We have a plane standing by.'

Her voice was harsh as she responded: 'The Prime Minister has not seen fit to send for me, neither has he called a Cabinet meeting. I see no need for me to abandon talks so crucial to ending the plight of the unemployed.'

At that she turned on her heel. Her hand on the door, she turned to him: 'Oh, Ambassador. Let's give tonight's reception a Scottish flavour. I think we may have a more influential turn-out than we anticipated, and I want these

Ministers to leave with as good a view of Scotland as possible.'

At that she disappeared back into the room, leaving a very perplexed diplomat indeed. He turned to his aide as he walked back to the lift:

'I'd heard the PM liked a drink, but surely to goodness we haven't got a social butterfly as his number two. The least she could have done was go back home.'

Both men were shaking their heads as the lift door closed behind them.

In the conference room, the Latins continued to yell at one another. The volume dropped however as they saw Ann indicate to the chairman that she wanted to speak. Stephen beside her looked completely bewildered, he was sure she hadn't paid attention to anything that had gone before, certainly not to anything he had said, and he looked anxious. As quickly as it had started, the fight between the Italians, the French and the Spanish fizzled out. Ministers sat back in their seats and waited for Ann to be called. As soon as the chairman indicated she had the floor, those who had been working on other things put down their pens and looked towards her, curiosity unconcealed.

Her low husky voice was carefully modulated, and she slowed down to help the translators. All except Dieter Volle and the Dutch had their earphones on.

'Gentlemen, it is crucial to Britain's interest that these talks are quickly resolved and immediate aid given to the unemployed – especially those who have been badly affected by industrial decline.'

She raised her hand again to stop the Latins jumping in – they had been arguing that the true cause of unemployment was agricultural change, and beautiful though Ann was, they weren't prepared to concede a debate that had been going on for decades. But her imperious wave silenced them.

'We all have domestic problems but the scale of the problem in Britain far outstrips anything going on elsewhere. Not only are we fighting against unemployment, but the country is on the verge of revolution – rapidly becoming ungovernable. Today a general strike has broken out.'

She looked towards the Italians: 'I know that some of you have such events regularly, but that is not the British way of doing things. We already have violence and unrest in the streets. Yesterday the mob took control of one of Britain's major cities, and it will only be a matter of time until the Government falls.'

This was too much for Stephen, who put his hand on her arm and said in an undertone: 'For God's sake, Ann, what's got into you? This could destroy Britain for a generation. You're saying the country is ungovernable. For God's sake, stop!'

She shook him off. She was already reaching her conclusion:

'If we are not able soon to show that the British Government in partnership with the European Community is resolving the country's worst problems, then I predict that there will be armed insurrection and that the US Government will annexe the country as the fifty-first State.'

She looked over to the French. 'It is our turn today – can you be sure it will not be yours tomorrow?'

As she stopped speaking a stunned silence rooted everyone to the spot; then they all spoke at once – truly a Tower of Babel. The translators lost control, and the chaos mounted as the press climbed out of their pen and surged towards Ann. But she had nothing more to say. Frantic banging of the gavel couldn't bring the room to order. The chairman closed the meeting.

With Jonathan and Stephen taking hold of each arm, she forced her way out of the room, catching the eye of Volle as she did so. He raised an eyebrow, a slight smile flickering round his lips. She answered him with a defiant smile. Soon she was being hustled out of the building, photographers trying to get what pictures they could, the glamour shots of a few hours earlier already inappropriate.

As she got into the car, she heard someone shout to a friend:

'Have you heard? There's an armed revolution in Britain.'

Ann sat quietly in the back of the car looking out at the fluttering flags of the European Community. Unexpectedly, she laughed aloud and made Stephen look out.

Even in the midst of his confusion he could see that the British flag flew upside down.

The man sitting with his head buried in the *Boston Globe* jumped guiltily when he heard the tannoy above his head.

'Paging Mr Michael Stewart, passenger to London, to airport information for a telephone call, Mr Michael Stewart, please.'

He looked quickly around to see if anyone else was reacting to the call, but the businessmen and families were all too engrossed in their own travels to hear the tannoy, let alone put a name to the face of the pale man in the expensive suede jacket. The signal from the tannoy sounded again, and again he tensed. This time the call was for someone else. Acting as if the second call, not the first had been for him, he got up and made his way to the information desk. The tanned all-American girl looked through a pile of slips on the desk.

'Mr Stewart, your friend rang off, he asked if you could call him. Donald Ross was the name, he said it was urgent.'

He thanked the girl as he moved away from the desk, grimacing as she called after him: 'Have a nice day!'

Thank you, he thought wryly, but I have other plans.

Ross must have been waiting for the call, he answered immediately. Despite wanting to remain as anonymous as possible, Michael's voice began to rise when he heard what Ross wanted of him.

'No, there is no point in me going to Washington. I've got everything I need and it's a terrific story. Trust me, Donald. I've got to come back and tell you about this! I'm already checked on to the flight to London, my baggage is away and I'm in the departure lounge. And anyway, the summit isn't for weeks.'

He held the phone away from his ear as the noise of the tannoy made it impossible to hear.

'Hold on, Donald. There's just been an announcement about my flight, I've got to listen to it.'

He held his hand over the mouthpiece of the telephone and waited for the call to be repeated.

'Urgent call for all passengers to the United Kingdom. All flights are subject to indefinite delay due to industrial action. Passengers are requested to return to the check-in desk where arrangements will be made to assist them.'

With a sigh, Michael went back to his call: 'The gods must be on your side, Donald, they sure as hell aren't on mine! There's a strike in London, my flight is delayed indefinitely. Now tell me why I've got to go to Washington.'

His eyes widened in disbelief as he listened, then he stopped Ross. 'Let's go over that again – she's said that Britain is in the throes of revolution, the country is ungovernable, and about to become the fifty-first state?'

He listened. 'Has she gone off her head? Of course the Americans will insist on an earlier summit. I should imagine the world's bankers might want a summit too.'

He let out yet another sigh. 'I'll need all the help you can give me; send Clare out if you can. I'll be in touch when I get a place to stay.'

Hanging up, he leant back against the side of the booth, his eyes closed, his face grim. He looked exhausted and depressed as he went off to try to unscramble his arrangements.

Getting through the scrum that always greeted the Boston shuttle into Dulles Airport, Washington, Michael again found himself at a pay phone. He was in luck, he could get a short rental in a service apartment block, Sherry Towers, just round the corner from the State Department and near to Pennsylvania Avenue, a quiet part of town where he was less likely to be recognized.

He let himself into the large one-room apartment dominated by a king-size bed, with a window overlooking the buildings of the university. He checked the icebox, deciding what provisions he would need, and unpacked some clothes.

Running out of reasons to delay, he sat down at the desk by the window and picked up the telephone. Clare answered on the first ring. As he listened, his jaw clenched in anger. *Private Eye*, a satirical magazine much used by those seeking to destroy reputations, had carried a story that he had become besotted with Ann Clarke, and was now in the States planning a major profile on her in the hope that this would cause her to look more favourably on his attentions, which she had hitherto ignored. The piece also relayed again the story of the scandal that had made him a laughing stock in Washington. Ross was furious that his senior and very expensive reporter was again an object of ridicule. Michael saw the sense in Clare's advice: to keep out of the way until he had a story so big it would blast his detractors out of the water.

So concerned was he with his problems, he failed to congratulate Clare when she told him her news – she was to be allowed to appear on camera at last, and had been given a couple of minor political stories to cover.

Determined to get this story sorted out once and for all and to get back to perform some remedial surgery on his career, he got out his telephone book, and going through it page by page, came to the name he was looking for. He dialled. The call was expected. 'Come over here then. I'll go out to a liquor store and get some Scotch.'

He laughed without humour at the reply. 'OK, you bring the whisky.' He had barely had enough time to get the ice out of the icebox and unearth some glasses, when he heard a knock at the door. He looked through the spy hole and then opened the door, holding out his hand in greeting. Conway Frazer was a little over fifty with the pallor of the habitual workaholic and the nervous twitch of someone who took his work very seriously. His sandy hair flecked with grey, he was shaggy and unkempt despite the very expensive business suit he wore, his collar frayed and grubby, his tie stained. He seemed nervous as he prowled round the room, looking in cupboards, checking behind curtains.

Michael made a joke of it: 'What have they been doing to you, Conway? You look as if you're checking for bugs. It must be time for you to get out of the State Department. They're getting to you.'

Conway ignored him and went on checking. Happy that all was as it should be, he sat down, accepting a drink as he did so.

'Emma Catchpole told me she'd met you in Boston.'

Michael looked surprised. 'I wouldn't have thought it was a good career move for Emma to tell her boss she'd spent time with a non-person such as me.'

Frazer waved this aside. 'She told me what happened to you.'

Michael shrugged but said nothing.

'I'm sorry things went so badly for you. I've always trusted you, that's why I'm here tonight. I knew if you came to Washington, you'd get in touch.'

Michael moved forward in his seat. 'I should tell you that I'm still a journalist. I'm here to see what I can put together for a piece on the summit. I was hoping you could fill me in on some background. You know what's happened over the past few days in Britain?'

The other man nodded. He sat for a while staring into his drink, his face troubled and his hands shaking. Then he got up and started pacing. Michael could almost touch the tension in the room.

Suddenly Frazer stopped walking up and down and turned to Michael. 'I don't want you to think that I'm a traitor to my country, Michael, but I've been very worried recently and I've got information I think you should have.'

He hesitated. 'I remember Vietnam. I was posted there for a time, and I'm terrified that the hardline attitude of men like Horowitz is going to mean another Vietnam.'

He took a slug of his drink. 'I want you to have these documents. You've got to get them to someone senior in your Government. Miss Clarke is the person I have in mind. This information has to be got into the hands of the people who matter before the summit.'

He almost threw the roll of papers from his inside pocket at Michael and darted to the door. Michael moved to stop him, but Frazer waved him aside.

'Get out of this city as quickly as possible. There's something very bad going on, Michael, and you've got more enemies than most. It's not every day you get on the wrong side of the Mafia. We heard about the mugging you got in Boston. And this document will be the final straw. Take the first flight out of here!'

At that he was gone.

Michael sat down at the desk and put on the reading light. He started to read.

The first document was headed *Managing the post INF environment*. It began with a résumé of the treaty arrangements made between the United States and Soviets which had banned all ground-launched nuclear missiles with a range of 500 to 5,000 kilometres. Both superpowers had made much of the massive progress this had meant for disarmament, each side had sent witnesses to the ceremonial scrapping of missiles amidst a carnival atmosphere. The Soviet and US leaders had both been nominated for the Nobel Peace Prize. But as Michael read on, it became clear that the US Government was already well advanced in by-passing the treaty. And Britain was set to become the central focus of US military activity.

The US airforce was to develop bomber bases all over Britain that would give the Americans the nuclear firepower not just to annihilate the Soviets, but all of Europe as well.

From the deployment of the missiles, it was obvious that the NATO countries of Western Europe, allies of the Americans, were being targeted as hostile countries as well, and the easy deployment of nuclear missiles against them would give the US Government the ultimate threat to control these nations.

Allied to the conventional nuclear capability would be a neutron force allowing 'in a zero situation' the Americans to depopulate all of Europe, while leaving the cities with all their wealth, possessions and art treasures intact.

Page after page, he read; minute detail had been worked out that would mean that Europe would never again be free of US dominance, and would be the battleground in any conflict with the Soviets. It was clear the Americans would have no hesitation in wiping out the entire population of the continent.

Michael moved on to the next document. It was headed *Strategic Plan*.

As he read his whole body stiffened. He read aloud, shaking his head in disbelief as he did so:

The new aircraft and missiles will make Britain crucial to the wellbeing of the people of the United States. In the past the governments – like the natives – have been friendly, but the strategic importance of the country makes it imperative that there be no unexpected political developments.

Furthermore, the proximity of the British Isles to the Warsaw Pact countries means that there is a possibility that the Soviets would seek to annex the country to ensure no land-based missiles could be deployed within striking distance of Warsaw Pact countries. Therefore plans are well in hand to take over the running of the British Government. This is being brought about by ensuring the election of US agents to all the crucial departments of State, rather than by the use of an occupying force. They will destabilize government from the inside.

US companies are also taking control of all the strategically important industries, including the public utilities privatized by the previous Conservative Government on our recommendation.

Absently, Michael stood up, knocking over a glass as he did so. Carelessly gathering up the pieces, he cut deep into the palm of his hand. Ignoring the pain and the blood, he wrapped a towel round and picked up the phone. He could get on the next flight to Paris; from there he would find some way of getting back into strike-hit Britain.

As he threw his clothes back into his bag, he switched on the television to try to take his mind off his fear and loneliness. He was in the bathroom trying to dress his hand when the late-night local news came on. The Potomac had proved cooperative again to yet another troubled soul seeking to take his own life. The newscaster reported that a man, thought to be a senior State Department official, had taken his life by jumping into the river. A picture of Conway Frazer flashed on the screen. It was reported that he had not been involved in any sensitive area of Government but had become increasingly depressed since the break-up of his twenty-year marriage.

The lights were on and the windows open in the Downing Street flat. George Jeffries sat opposite Sylvia on the sofa as Tony Metcalf, at his desk, crumpled paper after paper. He stood up suddenly. 'Sylvia, get me a drink!'

Sylvia remained where she was, staring stonily ahead, the only sign of her feelings the bright glint of unshed tears in her eyes. George watched her, ignoring Metcalf's rantings. The Prime Minister went to the sideboard and knelt down, throwing out table covers and cutlery boxes as he searched for a hidden store of alcohol. He stormed past his wife and Foreign Secretary as he went into the kitchen, Sylvia winced as she heard plates smashed and drawers fall out on to the floor. Suddenly Tony came dashing out of the kitchen, crashing the door to the wall. He dived towards his wife who cowered into the cushions.

'You bitch! Where have you hidden it?'

George Jeffries stood in front of the raging man, using himself as a barrier between husband and wife, trying to sooth and calm him. Just at the point when he thought violence was inevitable, the phone rang. Sylvia picked it up. Putting her hand over the mouthpiece, she spoke to the two men.

'The US Ambassador has been on the phone. He wants to call on you.'

Sharply, Jeffries turned to her. 'When?'

She repeated the question into the phone. 'Now.'

The two men looked at one another. It was Jeffries who spoke: 'This is it, then. We've no alternative. We can't stall him now.'

Sylvia told the desk officer to tell the Ambassador to come right away. Jeffries went back to the Foreign Office to alert his officials, leaving husband and wife alone.

Before he left he looked closely at Sylvia. 'Will you be all right?'

Too brightly she replied: 'Certainly! Nothing to worry about.'

Sylvia kept to the opposite side of the sofa from her husband. He turned to her and she stiffened, but all the belligerence had left his face. Now he was pleading:

'Please, Sylvia! You must see I need a drink. I've got to have something to get me through this.'

She looked at him for a long second, then went into her bag and brought out a hypodermic syringe. Without speaking, Metcalf rolled up the sleeve of his shirt.

The Prime Minister was putting on his jacket when the phone rang again.

'Surely he can't be here already?'

Sylvia picked it up again, turned to her husband and shook her head. He relaxed. As she hung up, she smiled.

'The press office have had a tip-off that there's a story in the *Mail* tomorrow. They've uncovered a sex scandal involving a Government Minister.'

Metcalf slumped down into his seat, dejected. 'What else can go wrong today?' He looked again at his wife, who was grinning. 'Sylvia, why on earth are you looking so pleased with yourself?'

She went over and perched on the arm of his chair, lightly kissing him on the top of the head. 'The story is that Ann Clarke is the mistress of Michael Stewart.'

A range of emotions sped across his face, he didn't know what to think. 'How did they know?'

His wife smiled mischievously. 'I told them. That

should spell the end of her credibility. Not just a journalist, but a promiscuous darling of the gossip columns!'

He stood up to leave. As he spoke his voice was gentler than for weeks. 'You'll stop at nothing for me, will you?' He put his hand on her shoulder. 'I hope you haven't gone too far this time. Sometimes these scandals can misfire.'

He kissed her tenderly on the forehead. He didn't look round as he went out to meet the Ambassador, if he had he would have seen the loneliness in her eyes.

Sylvia paced the flat, then she headed downstairs, going through the front hall and round into the press office. The young assistant press secretary was on the telephone as the Prime Minister's wife came in. She hung up and stood, waiting for Sylvia to speak first.

'When will you get a copy of the *Daily Mail*? I'm anxious to know about this scandal.'

The young woman shrugged her shoulders. 'We're all anxious about it too. They've kept the identity of whoever's involved as tight as a drum. Even the political editor doesn't know and that's made him even more like a bear with a sore paw!'

The two women laughed with delight at the thought of any inconvenience to the unpleasant man who headed the *Mail's* political staff.

'So when will we know the worst?'

The younger woman shook her head. 'Not for a while, I'm afraid. I was just trying to ring you to tell you that the print unions have joined the strike. All the papers are off the streets from now on.'

Ruefully Sylvia laughed and went back to the flat.

Less than half a mile away, the Editor of the *Daily Mail* was making his office secure, expecting that his paper would be off the streets for a while. As he did so he put into the safe the story and pictures he had intended to splash in the next day's paper. He dropped some of the photographs. As he picked them up, he flicked through them.

The first was a picture of Sylvia Metcalf and Stephen Robinson holding hands over what was obviously a breakfast table. The other was of the couple kissing passionately at the open door of a flat. He had the scoop of the decade, and the man who had brought him the pictures hadn't wanted a penny.

A hush fell over the reception room as she walked in. Even without her dramatic intervention of the afternoon, she would have captivated her audience. She had chosen to wear a Frank Usher dress of black velvet, striking in its plainness. The dress hugged her figure and was enlivened only by silk bows at the shoulder, held in place with diamanté clasps. Her earrings were jet and diamond spheres, made all the more effective by the severe but elegant way she wore her hair pulled back into a simple chignon.

The British Ambassador was at her side in an instant. She had remained in her room for the two hours since her return from the conference, spending much of it on the phone to her department, and ignoring the pleas of the Ambassador for a meeting. She even ignored him when he called through the door that the Prime Minister was insisting she return immediately to Britain.

Ann still refused to listen to the tortured bleatings of the Ambassador, but stopped to talk to her exhausted and anxious colleagues. Stephen Robinson told her he was going back that evening on an RAF flight, why wouldn't she come? Her place was back home.

'It's important that there's an authoritative voice in Europe. With no press, we cannot get the true story across to the other countries of the world. Much though I want to go back, I must stay over here.'

Stephen made to protest – she silenced him with a look.

She made her way round the gathering. Every senior Brussels diplomat was present; the only glaring omission was the delegation from the US mission in the city – a pressing subsequent engagement. As she spoke to her opposite numbers from the other European countries, she found the talk inevitably the same – the state of Britain. Each politician who took her off into a corner for a conspiratorial chat was treated to a résumé of the general strike, the unrest, the terrorism. And always she would end on the same note:

'I'll just say one last word for you and you alone: of all the people here tonight, I feel most drawn to you. My Prime Minister is in a sorry state. We've only been in Government for a few weeks, and already he's crumbling under the strain. It's a tragedy, he's such an able and kind man. But somehow we have to fight our way through this.'

And then they would part, each looking into the eyes of the other and shaking their heads. All the British could do was stand back and worry.

The reception was almost over when Dieter Volle arrived. He excused himself to the Ambassador – urgent business had come up, and he had been delayed. He scanned the room for Ann, finding her explaining the merits of scotch whisky to the French cultural attaché. She was animated and her eyes sparkled like the crystals on the chandeliers. She turned to greet him as he came to speak to her, having seen him approach in the mirror over the mantelpiece. He too drew her into a corner for a confidential conversation, but he silenced her as she began her prepared speech.

'Can I see you afterwards? I have a flat here, and my household have prepared a light supper – a change from all the chicken and mussels!'

He saw her mentally withdraw from him, and physically she actually stepped back. There was a wariness in her eyes.

He looked down at her. 'I'm not trying to proposition you. We have a lot in common, more than you realize. It is very important that we speak, believe me.'

He could see that she was being affected by his earnestness, but still she held back. Volle lowered his voice until it was little more than a whisper: 'Ann, I'm a friend of Johann. I knew him when I was a child.'

The colour drained from her face. Her paleness was made all the more dramatic because of the contrast between her black dress and her auburn hair. Her eyes darted everywhere, as if looking for escape.

Again he spoke: 'I know something has gone wrong between you, but there is still work to be done. Even if you can never get back together, you still need one another. Please say you'll come, talking to me might help. I could be your intermediary.'

He saw her hesitate, then she nodded her head in agreement.

'I'll have to make my excuses to the Ambassador.'

He smiled at her and said very gently: 'Do what you have to do. I'll wait until you are clear of here.' With a smile he gestured to the room crammed full of politicians, all watching her out of the corners of their eyes.

As the guests were leaving, she stood at the door to wish them goodnight. Each left with a little sleeve of whisky miniatures and mohair scarves, fine as a spider's web. Last in the line was Dieter who whisked her away from under the disapproving nose of the Ambassador. To ease the man's worries, the official Mercedes of the German mission slowed down to allow the British security car to keep pace. There was nothing sinister in two Ministers having supper together to discuss common problems.

The flat was sumptuous. The central hallway of the penthouse had a marble floor and a huge medieval fireplace dominated the foyer. Brass tubs of flowers filled the hearth and a giant chandelier sparkled as she looked in admiration. Dieter laughed and waved a hand in a deprecating gesture, as he reached to open the door into the reception room.

'Welcome to my little pied-à-terre. Let me show you in here. Make yourself comfortable whilst I go and check with the kitchen – you'll find champagne ready for you on the table by the window.' At that he ushered her into the room, closing the door behind her. She was glad of the chance to look around. Next to this, the entrance paled into insignificance. Her feet sank into the pile of the beige carpet, and her eyes were drawn to a midnight blue Chinese rug on the floor between two massive white

287

leather sofas. Marble tables stood at each side of the sofas holding lamps with black enamelled bases and white silk shades. A marble console table stood against one wall, an opened bottle of Louis Roederer champagne peeping out from an ice bucket.

She was about to go over to pour a glass for herself when she saw the view. One wall of the room was a window and the lights of the city were spread out below. She could make out the floodlighting of the Grand Place, and she was about to walk over to see what else she could recognize, when she heard a sound behind her. A man walked out of the shadows. She grabbed the back of a chair to steady herself, her voice little more than a whisper:

'Johann!'

As he came towards her she looked around, about to take flight, but her eyes were drawn back to his face, more worn and haggard than she had ever seen it. They stared at one another, speechless.

It was he who broke the silence, his rich American drawl hushed. 'I'm sorry, Ann. I had to see you again, even if it's for the last time.'

As she watched him, she saw how grim his face was; her voice shook: 'Why did you do it? Why did you rape me? Did you have to destroy something so special?'

He moved away from her over to the window and looked down at the lights of Brussels.

'Michael Stewart's flat is wired for sound. Our people insisted I listen to a tape of your last visit.' He couldn't go on.

Ann walked over to him, pain, hurt, bewilderment, rushing across her face. But her voice was angry as she spoke: 'You know I couldn't live without you. You've taught me how to think – how to feel. You must know sex with Stewart meant nothing – it's all part of the plan. You trained me, you showed me what I had to do. And going to bed with Michael Stewart was the least you've asked of me. How do you think it felt looking at the mangled bodies of children after the tube disaster? How do you think I felt walking into Hunterston, maybe going to my death? You may have got a warning to me, but you couldn't have brought me back to life if they'd killed me. This is the way it had to be for you to get power and for me. It's a bit late to be squeamish now!'

He turned to face her, cold and unbending. He reached out and put his hands on her shoulders, looking intently into her face. 'But you called out my name. With Stewart.'

The shock registered immediately, she searched for words – none came. She sat down suddenly on the arm of the sofa, shaking her head, mystified.

'I'm sure I didn't! I'm always very careful, and anyway, I'd have remembered.'

He let out a sigh. 'I can let you hear the tape if you like.'

The silence grew between them. 'Did he hear?'

He nodded his head, frowning. 'Remember that day I came to you? I had spent it arguing that you were still of use to us. There were those who claimed you had prejudiced yourself and they wanted to abort.'

She stood up abruptly. 'No! They can't do that! We're almost there. Everything we've worked for, our chance to join our two countries – to give the world peace. It's all about to happen!'

He shook his head. 'They didn't see it like that. The stakes are so high they want everything to be perfect on this.'

Her shoulders slumped in defeat. Her voice shook as she asked: 'So is it all over? What happens now?'

He reached out and touched her face very gently, and she covered his hand with her own. 'You saved yourself,' he said. That little speech today escalated things so much that the summit has been brought forward to next week, so it's too late to abort.'

She clung to him, holding tight in case he should leave, and as he drew her to him – she let out a sigh of relief. Suddenly she pulled back again. 'Can you forgive me! I almost destroyed all the years of work.'

'Of course I forgive you, but now we have to make sure we deliver – then all the work, all the planning, will have paid off, Metcalf will be out of the way, you'll be Prime Minister, and within the year I'll be President. Just as we planned.'

'I promise I'll never take any risks again. Promise me we'll be together!' Her voice was pleading.

In reply he bent down and kissed her.

The foyer of the building was deserted. Only a few weak bulbs burned in their sockets, leaving tiny pools of light; Michael hadn't deliberately chosen to stand in the shadows, but the best vantage point to see the cab as it turned into the street just happened to be in a secluded corner. He leaned against the empty reception desk looking out on the street – to any passer-by invisible.

As he stared absently through the tinted glass doors, his eye was attracted by movement in a car parked across the road. A passing car lit up two men sitting in a black Ford. Intent on watching the men, Michael missed the arrival of the cab, and it was with a start he realized it was there. Quickly picking up his bag with his good hand he rushed out.

The cab pulled away from the kerb, suddenly swerving into a turn to take a short cut to the airport. As he passed the parked car, Michael could see one of the men talking into a radio as the other started the engine. Throughout the half-hour journey he kept looking round, certain now that the car was following him.

Hurrying into the International terminal, he furtively watched what was going on behind him. The car had stopped. One of the men got out, the other drove off. The man who was half running over to the terminal entrance was tall and thickly muscled, his head almost bald. His suit was rumpled, but there was a determined confidence in the way he pushed past meandering passengers.

Michael left the shelter of a magazine rack and made his way to the Trans-World check-in desk. In the mirrored map behind the attendant, he saw the man scan the desks for him. Michael kept his head down, hoping to escape detection, but he knew he had been spotted. He held his breath as the man drew ever closer, ending up inches away, behind him in the queue.

Anxious to delay his departure from the desk, Michael decided to change to first class, and as he did so, a ground attendant looked beyond him to the man behind and offered to assist him. The man grunted, then moved away. The attendant shrugged his shoulders and went back to tidying his desk.

Boarding card in hand, carrying his case as hand baggage, Michael made for the first-class lounge. He tried to absorb himself in a magazine, but his eyes became glued to the door. Only an elderly lady came in after that and Michael waited until the last call for the flight before boarding.

As he went through the boarding channel, he saw the man standing with another, apparently unconcerned, watching the passengers getting on the plane. Neither man showed any particular interest in Michael. Fifty minutes into the flight, Michael got up to stretch his legs. He covered the entire plane – business class, economy, the upstairs lounge – scanning faces, watching for furtive glances. There was nothing suspicious. He returned to his seat and, refusing champagne, tried to sleep.

At Charles de Gaulle Airport in Paris, no one paid him any attention. He travelled along the moving walkways and escalators from the satellite arrivals hall, unaware that ten paces behind him a tall, thickset man kept him in sight, a petite woman, clearly French, at his side. After he had cleared passport control and customs, the man strode out on his own, leaving the woman to follow Stewart.

At the deserted taxi rank a grey Renault approached and Michael ran across the concourse to catch it, but as he reached for the door handle he was beaten to it by the elegant and gamine Frenchwoman. He stepped back, disappointment and exhaustion in his face, but still registering the petite woman in well-pressed blue jeans and a plain white cotton shirt. He saw she was looking at the bloodstained bandage on his hand. Her face puckered in a frown. In perfect English with the faintest trace of a seductive French accent, she spoke to him:

'Monsieur, your need is greater than mine.' She gestured to his hand. 'Please take the cab, there'll be another along in a minute.'

He smiled down at her, indicating that she should get in. 'I'm sorry, I didn't see you when I came across. You got here first.'

She shrugged. 'Are you going into Paris?' He nodded. 'Then we will travel together, *n'est-ce pas?*'

It was the perfect solution. He took her bag and put it with his own in the boot. On the drive into Paris she chattered on about her recent holiday in Biarritz, pouting prettily when she complained about how expensive everything was.

As they neared the city centre, she asked exactly where he was going, but she looked doubtful as he told her he was headed for the Gare du Nord to catch a train for the channel ports. Reaching into her bulky Louis Vuitton hold-all, she brought out a copy of *Le Monde*. The channel ports were closed. He sighed. She looked at him sympathetically:

'Let me give you the name of a comfortable little hotel where you can at least try to enjoy your enforced stay.'

He only half listened to her, but she leant forward and gave instructions to the taxi driver in machine-gun French. Still he was reluctant to accept her help, but as he sat back the waves of exhaustion beat over him. The more she insisted, the more difficult he found it to resist.

She scribbled the address on the corner of the newspaper as the taxi drew to a halt outside an expensive looking boutique on the Rue Rivoli. Michael tried to get out of the car to say his farewells, but she stroked his uninjured hand and pushed him back in the seat, a faint promise in the gesture.

'You've been most kind, mademoiselle . . .'

'Madame. Elise de Meunynck.' She smiled down at the

bandages and tutted and with a cheerful wave went into the shop.

The hotel, in a back street near Nôtre Dame, had all the appearance of a French country house. The reception area, furnished in comforting chintzes, had tall vases of gladioli all over the place. The uniformed receptionist was delighted to tell him they had a free room, and he registered with a sigh of relief. As Michael stood waiting for the antique lift, having disdained the services of a porter, a middle-aged man in the black jacket and striped trousers of a successful hotelier smiled a welcome.

'Welcome to the Hôtel Lion d'Or Monsieur. I hope you have an enjoyable stay. You have been a guest with us before?'

Michael shook his head. 'No, a very helpful lady told me where to find you. Madame de Meunynck.'

The man smiled as the lift shuddered to a halt, held open the gates for Michael and went about his business.

The room was peaceful and comfortable. Pretty furnishings gave a restful atmosphere, and the floor-length windows, thrown open to the summer day, gave the true atmosphere of France. At another time Michael would have been charmed, but as he opened his case and saw the documents Conway Frazer had given him, the enormity of the information he had hit him.

He scanned the room, then picked up the documents and went over to an ornate gilt-framed painting of a group of children playing in a field and lifted it off the wall. Feeling like an amateur spy, he took the documents and stuck them to the back with Band Aid. He returned the painting to its original position, carefully adjusting it so that no hint of the clean wall behind would reveal that the picture had been moved. He had just stepped back to check when he heard a knocking at the door. Elise de Meunynck stood outside; he couldn't conceal his surprise.

'I live near here, and as I was passing I thought I would come in to tell you where you can get a doctor to look at that hand.'

She waved off his protests, handing him a note with

yet another address. Michael accepted it. She showed no sign of leaving, holding his gaze. He fidgeted with the paper, then he said: 'Let me at least offer you lunch for your kindness.'

She shook her head. 'I have an appointment this afternoon. But there is a very nice café on the corner. A kir would be most acceptable.'

He picked up his jacket and followed her. As they sipped their white wine and cassis, Elise prattled on about herself, her apartment, her recent divorce. She asked no question of him. Then suddenly, she looked over his shoulder, stood up and excused herself. Before he knew what was happening, she was gone. Shaking his head in wonder, Michael made his way back to his room. As he went in, his eyes went immediately to the painting. It was askew, a clear half inch of paler wallpaper to be seen at the left side. He crossed the room in a second, lifting the painting off the wall. The documents were missing. Throwing the painting on to the bed, he raced out of the room and dashed downstairs into the street. He looked to right and left but there was no one to be seen. He went to the deserted reception desk, banging on the bell until a flustered receptionist abandoned her lunch. Asked if anyone had been to his room, the bewildered girl shook her head.

'Where can I find Madame de Meunynck?'

The girl claimed no knowledge of anyone of that name. he demanded to see the *patron*.

The commotion brought not the friendly man in the black jacket, but an elegant elderly lady from the back. She drew herself up to her full five foot four and looked imperiously at Michael.

'Monsieur, this is my hotel. What is your problem?'

No one had ever heard of Elise de Meunynck. He had been set up. No one would believe what he knew to be the truth without these documents, and somehow, it was known that he had seen them.

Michael's face turned grey; he went back to his room. The call he made to Donald Ross went badly. He tried to explain the documents, the story he had, but Ross seemed to think him deranged.

Exasperated, Michael yelled at him: 'What the fuck! Don't you believe me, you fool? This is the biggest story this century! Are you so used to your small-time ways with your small-time people, that you don't know a real scoop when you see one?'

He said no more, he was speechless. For the second time in a year, Michael Stewart, the man hailed as one of the most brilliant of his generation, had been fired, this time by a second-rate new editor who thought he had taken leave of his senses. Without the documents, how could he prove the story he knew to be true? Yet again, it was time to pack and be on his way. Now he had to prove his story or he was finished. And he had to tell Ann. She would believe him.

The smell of disinfectant and cabbage pervaded every corner of the overheated hospital. Harry McGregor lay naked except for a single sheet, the only sign of life in his body on the monitor's oscillating screen. She was led into the cubicle by a nurse in green smock and trousers, a cap on her head and dust covers on her shoes. Mary had hesitated at the door, looking questioningly at the nurse. Shouldn't she too wear some protective clothing? But without speaking the nurse shook her head and led her to McGregor's bedside. She brought a chair up to the bed and gestured Mary to sit down.

She sat on the edge of her chair, stiff and tense in her actions. In a soft Irish voice the nurse whispered to her: 'Don't be frightened to touch him. It won't do any harm, and it might help. Speak to him too, we don't know how much gets through.'

Mary reached out and gingerly touched the back of the hand lying inert in front of her, like a pin cushion with tubes and tapes. But as the nurse left her, she swiftly drew her hand away, burying it under her bag. She looked at the grey pallor of McGregor, the blueness about the lips, the bandages. She shook her head.

Mary gave a start at a male voice. She turned round to find that an Asian man stood behind her dressed, like the nurse, in hospital fatigues. She made to stand, he gestured to her to remain seated.

'Are you his wife?' Startled, Mary shook her head. The doctor smiled sympathetically.

'Forgive me, but you're the first visitor he's had. I just assumed . . .'

Mary did stand up this time. 'I'm just a friend, well a colleague really. He's Scottish so he doesn't have much in the way of friends in London.'

The doctor drew her outside the cubicle. 'Could you give us some idea of where we might contact his next of kin?'

Mary thought for a while then shook her head. 'I'll try to find out. He's very bad, isn't he?'

He merely shrugged his shoulders.

'Sit with him a little longer, then come and see me.' He pointed to a lighted cubicle in the corner.

Mary went back to her seat by the bed, looking at the man she so detested. Furtively she looked at her watch. Again and again she looked at it until a respectable twenty minutes was up. Then she stood up to leave. Seeing the nurse watching her, she patted his hand, then hurried out to join the doctor.

He stood up as she came in. 'Would you like a cup of tea?'

She shook her head. 'We weren't that close. I didn't realize he'd be unconscious, I thought he could give me the papers he was working on, I need them to finish off a job.'

She could tell that he didn't believe her.

'I'm afraid your friend is very ill indeed. It is extremely unlikely that he will ever recover consciousness, that's why we need to talk to his next of kin. Can you help us?'

She nodded. 'He's a union official, I'll go round to his office tonight and ask them to get his details out of the personnel files.'

The doctor wrote out his name and telephone number

on a piece of paper. As Mary stood up to leave, the doctor
came round the desk to her, seeming terribly ill at ease.

'My dear, we also need to track down any close friends
he may have had, male or female. I don't want to pry into
your personal life, but there is a perfectly good sexually
transmitted diseases clinic here. I can't reveal details about
my patient, but as you are the only friend who cares
enough to visit him, I've got to suggest to you that you
might like to visit it.'

Mary turned and ran.

She heard the doctor come after her. 'I'm very
sorry . . .' Then she heard his bleeper. The clammy night
air revived her.

The lone porter at the union offices told her she was in
luck, the General Secretary was in and would see her.

Eddie Barraclough was kindness itself, he was fulsome
in his thanks to her for visiting McGregor. She explained
to him she was to meet McGregor the day after his 'accident' to get receipts from him, she had election returns
to file, and if she did not have them before the Returning
Officer immediately, questions would be asked about
Ann's election. They agreed the files were likely to be in
the briefcase McGregor had left in the office that night.
Together they opened the unlocked briefcase. The
receipts were certainly there, but jumbled up in a welter
of other papers, none of which seemed particularly confidential. They agreed it would be simpler if she took the
case away and sorted it out at her leisure.

Mary walked back to Dover House, finding the silence
oppressive in streets uncharacteristically free of taxis and
buses because of the strike. The post-election file in
McGregor's briefcase was quickly put in good order, and
she was able to work quickly, and what she had expected
to take three hours was finished in two. Almost. One
document was missing.

Tiredness seeped through the woman's body; a pile of
letters mocked her from the desk; it would make so much
difference if she could get rid of this tonight. She looked
at McGregor's briefcase, one section bulged with files

297

seemingly unrelated to the election. Could the document she needed have been pushed in there by mistake? Should she? She pulled it towards her and tried to look through it without reading the documents crammed in, but it was no use. Putting the leather executive case on the desk, she emptied it and began to work systematically through it.

When she opened the third folder her heart missed a beat. She pulled the contents out randomly. A pile of photographs fell out; she tried not to look but her eyes would not look away.

The one that fell on to her desk showed the buttocks of a man, an elderly man judging from the flaccid mottled flesh that sagged to his thighs. Beneath him she could see the firm young flesh of a young boy. Even in her solitude, she could feel the colour fill her face, the bile rise in her throat. In the next picture the photographer had used another angle. The face of the man, twisted in ecstasy, was unmistakable – Roddy Henderson.

Locking the door into the corridor, she settled down at her desk and worked her way through the file. A head-and-shoulders photograph came next, but she had to move aside a letter stapled to it. She looked at the face so innocent, so young. Then she read the note. She didn't flinch this time, she almost expected it – confirmation that David Porteous was HIV positive. Henderson had been exposed to the Aids virus. The photographs and the HIV form were dated, the latter before the former. The boy had known he had the virus before having sex with Henderson. She had put the papers down when she saw a note stapled to the back; when deciphered it showed that Porteous had received £1,000 from McGregor.

She put the photographs aside, looking again into the folder. Her face didn't even register surprise when she found share certificates, bonds, two bank books. McGregor was worth almost a third of a million pounds. That couldn't have come just from Henderson. As she searched, she discovered much more than blackmail. No wonder McGregor wore the briefcase practically chained to his wrist. It held conclusive proof that McGregor had been the key to the Workers' Militia, as so many had suspected. She read details of the location of cells, planned raids, and summaries of raids already executed; meticulous plans for the Hunterston nuclear power station siege; other letters proved that money was coming from Libya to finance the terrorist effort, with evidence too of weapons shipments. One sheet of paper confused her, like a balance sheet it tallied up sums of money and quantities in grammes. Then it clicked. Drugs. That was where the big money had come from – and a lot of the incentive to young people to remain in the grip of the Militias. It all became so clear: drugs gave McGregor two kinds of power – money and the potent force of addiction.

Her search continued; huge dollar payments were detailed, stubs from a Chicago bank. Then she found a letter from American Militant – the Revolutionary Socialists had been behind this after all. With the briefcase empty, she ran her hand around the inside pocket. She found one more paper, a yellowed letter from American Militant introducing Sister Ann Clarke to the British comrades, and a copy of a recent note from McGregor to Ann proving how much they had always been partners.

Mary started to laugh; the laughter rose to an almost maniacal pitch. She heard the door handle rattle. Taking a deep breath to calm herself and drying her eyes, she heard the voice of Stephen Robinson.

Mary asked him to go away; Robinson insisted, remembering her distress after the row with Ann.

Quickly she gathered together the papers on her desk, stuffing them awkwardly back into the briefcase, but one sheet of paper crumpled up and threatened to jam the lock. She pulled it out, barely glancing at it, but then she picked it up and read it, ignoring the increasingly angry shouts of Stephen Robinson. Like a robot she went to the door and opened it. As soon as he looked at her, he knew she was in shock. She began to shake, staring at the piece of paper. Stephen picked it up and read it. He sat down.

'Now we know how Ann was so successful so quickly!

299

This must have been written last year, a well-planned strategy to destroy everyone who stood in the way of Ann Clarke and power. Whoever wrote this was cruel and totally ruthless. Who was it? McGregor?'

Staring straight ahead, Mary shook her head. Stephen kept on looking at her, then he groaned, his whole body sagging.

'It was Ann, Ann set this all up. Destroying Henderson, Metcalf, she'd have had a go at me – if she had got the chance. And the Workers' Militia – the violence – the lot. But she must have had money to do it, where did it come from?'

Without speaking, Mary took out the file. 'We need to get this into the right hands, this is too big for us to work out.'

He stood up, helping Mary to her feet. 'Tidy this up, I'm going to phone Sylvia Metcalf.'

The green leather benches were full; even the Opposition front bench had been crammed to overflowing. Only on the Government front bench could space be found; the Prime Minister had yet to arrive.

In the little pen under the press gallery three civil servants huddled. Diagonally opposite, in the matching enclosure under the public gallery, the General Secretary of the Labour Party sat alone, looking worried. Those MPs forced to stand at the Bar of the House jostled each other in an all-party melee. What had in the past been good-hearted banter and juvenile point-scoring now had a distinct edge.

As always, the public gallery was crowded. Tourists and members of the public had been queuing for hours for the twice-weekly public spectacle of Prime Minister's Question Time. Similarly, the press gallery above the Chamber was full to overflowing, some journalists sitting on the floor. The Badge Bearers, House of Commons Stewards in white tie and tails, tried to maintain order, conscious of the watchful gaze of the Sergeant at Arms in silk ruff and gaiters, surveying the scene from the floor.

The Speaker, bewigged and theatrical, gold-buckled shoes encasing silk hose, stretched out in the hooded, throne-like chair.

Into this fevered atmosphere Tony Metcalf strolled to take his first Prime Minister's Questions.

At first his presence brought silence, then a couple of cheers rang out from the Labour benches, quickly stilled by embarrassment. Then the catcalls started from the Opposition:

'Where's Ann Clarke? Have you got her permission to be here?'

There was a commotion in the public gallery as attendants pounced on two women who held up a poster with a cartoon of Metcalf hanging from a gibbet, the Stars and Stripes of America draped around him.

From somewhere – it sounded like the Labour benches – a lone voice cried out above the others:

'Fancy a drink, Tony?'

The Speaker of the House called for order, but order was not given until she stood up – the traditional sign that things were getting out of hand and her patience was wearing thin.

Questions began. The first four were mundane enough – the Prime Minister announced his plans to go to Wigan; He would instruct his civil servants to arrange a visit to Harrogate; he intended opening the new Leisure Complex at Norwich. Question Number Four seemed innocuous enough – yes, the Prime Minister would be visiting Liverpool – but when the Leader of the Opposition got up to ask a supplementary about the Workers' Militia and their new centre of activity in the North of England, full-scale chaos descended.

A distinguished Conservative got to his feet and in ponderous tones asked: 'Will the Right Honourable Gentleman state categorically his opposition to the statement being made by his Right Honourable Friend, the Member for Clydeside West, as she wanders around Europe – that this great nation is ungovernable and near to civil war? Will the Prime Minister take the steps necessary to remove his Deputy from office in response to this treasonable activity?'

A deafening roar of anger rose from the Labour benches, where only the occasional Parliamentary call of 'Withdraw' could be heard. But the rage on the Government benches was all but drowned out by the taunts and catcalls from the Opposition. Scuffling broke out among the Members crammed together in the narrow space at the bottom of the gangway. The atmosphere of anger and chaos was added to by the press, many of whom were hanging precariously over their own balcony above the Speaker to see how she was handling the disorder. Silence descended as Tony Metcalf rose to the Dispatch Box. He seemed to have shrunk, his knuckles white as he gripped tightly the corners of the Box. He opened and closed his mouth a couple of times before he started, long enough for everyone to clearly hear the taunt of one member:

'Not had time for your daily fix!'

The Speaker again called for order, and this time the silence was total.

The Prime Minister cleared his throat.

'I wish to put on record that I deplore the statements made by my Right Honourable Friend, the member for Clydeside West . . .'

He got no further, as the furious mob from his own benches began to surge forward to the Dispatch Box. A Labour backbencher, judging it time for the ritual Parliamentary bovver boy stunt, had seized the Mace and whirled it around his head like a weapon, the veins in his neck sticking out with the force of his fury. Metcalf looked up, his eyes glazing, then he fell backwards to be caught by George Jeffries. It wasn't clear whether or not he had been hit by the mace – there was no blood, only saliva dribbling from the side of his mouth.

As the Speaker rose to suspend the sitting, three of the ex-army Badge Bearers forcibly removed the Mace from the incensed Member as he was hustled out in a shoulder-wrenching arm hold, and George Jeffries, helped by Stephen Robinson, dragged a semi-conscious Metcalf from the Chamber.

Sylvia Metcalf had watched the whole incident on television in the Downing Street flat, transfixed with horror until she saw her husband finally collapse, slumping back from the Dispatch Box. Then she started to run. Her thin cotton skirt tangled round her legs as she hurled herself down the stairs from the flat. She raced through the house and had the door to the street opened before any of the doormen could get to it. Ignoring the cars outside, she kept on running towards Whitehall, but her open-toed sandals caught in the pavement and down she went, saving herself with her hands but grazing her knees as she fell. As she was helped to her feet by passers-by, a Downing Street car screeched to a halt beside her and her detective jumped out to help. As she was bundled into the back, amazed tourists saw the terror etched on the face of the woman they didn't recognize as the wife of the Prime Minister.

As she hurried through the corridors of the House of Commons on her way to the Prime Minister's office, those who saw her, dishevelled and distressed, stood out of her way. No one would meet her eyes.

Graeme Jones threw open the door to the room as he saw her approach. Inside she found her husband stretched out on a couch, his jacket off and his tie loosened. Someone had removed his shoes. Bending over him, one of the House medics – a Tory MP for an Oxfordshire constituency – showed kindness and concern as she straightened and saw Sylvia. Taking her by the arm, the MP led her over to a chair and made her sit down, then she crouched down at her side, taking Sylvia's hand in her own.

'Mrs Metcalf, just take a deep breath and calm yourself, your husband is unconscious and I've sent for an ambulance. He is a sick man.'

Sylvia searched the woman's face for clues as to how bad things were.

'With you by his side, I'm sure he'll be all right. We

303

may not be on the same side politically, but like a lot of my colleagues I admire you. Nothing I've seen here today will be told to anyone outside this office.'

Sylvia hadn't spoken a word since the events had begun to unfold on television. She kept shaking her head.

'Mrs Metcalf, by the time the ambulance arrives I must be able to tell them what he's had today, and how much is likely to be in his system. We can't afford to waste time!'

George Jeffries came over to kneel at the other side of Sylvia. He put his hand on the nape of her neck trying to soothe her:

'It's no use trying to cover up any longer. It's all over. Now the only thing that matters is Tony's survival as a man. You have to tell everything now, it's the only way we can all help him.'

Graeme Jones put his head round the door to say that the House was about to reassemble. George saw the startled look Sylvia cast towards her husband, then she looked up:

'But Ann Clarke isn't here. What do we do?'

'Sylvia, leave the worrying and the plotting to the rest of us now, you concentrate your thoughts on getting Tony well again. I'll take his place.'

As the man and woman looked at one another, Sylvia's face hardened. In less than a second the concern left her, and as her face aged, a look of startled comprehension came into her eyes. She opened her mouth to speak, but George smiled at her and hurried off, back to the Chamber and the Dispatch Box.

As the sitting resumed, a sombre silence had replaced the earlier row. Faces on both sides of the Chamber were grim, and many eyes scanned the assembled throng, memorizing the scene for autobiographies as yet unwritten. The statement by the Leader of the Opposition was delivered in sonorous and measured tones:

'I and my Honourable and Right Honourable Friends on the benches behind me are saddened by the sudden illness of the Prime Minister and wish him a speedy recovery, but notwithstanding that illness, we have a responsibility to Her Majesty and to the country, and for that reason we give notice that we will be tabling a motion of no confidence in the Government.'

A thin hum went round the Chamber. It seemed inevitable that the Government would fall and another general election would only be weeks away, unless Ann Clarke could stem the tide of distrust. But could someone who, even today, was still travelling around telling Europe that Britain was ungovernable, possibly restore stability and international confidence? Why had she not come back? The only possible answer could be that she wanted to use the international stage to make the maximum attack possible on the Government of Britain.

George Jeffries took his place at the Dispatch Box. He let the silence sit for a moment, underlining that he, now, replied for the Government. He seemed to grow in stature, erect, shoulders back, the slight stoop of the academic almost forgotten. A few Members frowned, trying to work out what was different about him, then they realized: George had fortuitously chosen this day to swap his slightly disreputable tweeds for a suit of dark grey cashmere, and he wore a white shirt with his college tie. Suddenly it became possible to see this man at the Dispatch Box as Prime Minister in his own right.

'Speaker, Madam, I and my Honourable and Right Honourable Friends are grateful for the good wishes of the Right Honourable Gentleman opposite, and we share his hope that the Prime Minister is soon fit and well and able to resume his duties. I have been instructed by the Prime Minister to announce that the summit with the United States Government will go ahead within the next week. We will defend any vote of no confidence with vigour, and will instruct our business managers to enter into discussion with the Honourable and Right Honourable Gentlemen opposite on an appropriate time for the debate to take place.'

The House took the news in silence, except for one

Member for whom the respectful acknowledgement of history was too much:

'Who's taking bets on how quickly Ann Clarke will be back in the country now?'

A few knowing looks were exchanged.

As George squeezed past the jam behind the Speaker's chair on his way out of the Chamber, he saw Stephen Robinson in the middle of a group mulling over all the possible outcomes from the day's events. He tapped him on the shoulder and signalled to him to follow.

The two men walked along the corridor in silence. Once in the Foreign Secretary's room, George remained standing as Stephen perched on the arm of a chair. It was Stephen who spoke first:

'I know you must have a lot on your mind now, but have you thought what to do with the information we gave you last night?'

Jeffries let out a sigh. 'Yes, Stephen, I have thought what to do about it.'

He walked across to where the younger MP was sitting. 'Forget it. McGregor is dead. He died this morning, there's nothing to be gained by stirring up more trouble than we've got already. Just forget you ever saw it, and I'll be telling Mary to do the same. In fact my office have been on to her this morning to ask if she would like to join the personal staff of the President of the European Commission, get some glamour in her own right. She's accepted and gone off to Harrod's to blow her first month's salary on a new image, from what I hear!'

Stephen stood up, a nerve twitching on the side of his face. 'You mean you've bought her off! You surprise me. I didn't think Mary was the type who could be bribed!'

Jeffries shrugged. 'There's a price for everything.'

His eyes narrowed with anger, Stephen advanced on the Foreign Secretary, speaking through clenched teeth: 'You really are prepared to cover up for Ann Clarke and whoever she's been in cahoots with for a share of the spoils! That's it, isn't it? And you think we should all do the same. Well what do you think my price is? You must have that worked out! Secretary of State for Scotland when Ann moves into Number Ten? Forget it! My silence can't be bought!'

Jeffries raised an eyebrow and smiled. He walked round the desk and opened a drawer, taking out a large brown envelope. He took out the contents and spread them on the desk in front of him.

'Stephen, you overvalue yourself. But then you men with a mission often do. I don't think anyone will believe anything you have to say from now on.'

He gestured to the desk, Stephen looked down. Spread in front of him were pictures of himself and Sylvia Metcalf – holding hands over breakfast – sitting gazing into each other's eyes in St James's Park – kissing outside Stephen's flat – in the lounge of a Glasgow hotel – on the stairs of Dolphin Square.

Stephen lunged across the desk at Jeffries, a bellow of rage escaping from his throat, but was stopped in mid flight by a savage blow from one of the Foreign Secretary's detectives who had stormed into the room. The two burly policemen frogmarched the yelling man out of the room.

As George Jeffries locked the photographs up again in his desk, he could still hear the shouts from the outer office. He smiled as he heard Stephen's last shout before he was removed from the Palace of Westminster:

'I'll get you, you bastard! You won't get away with this!'

Jeffries phoned through to his secretary: 'Now that the commotion has died down, arrange for me to get an RAF flight to Nice tomorrow. I don't think the airports will be operating normally then so I'm forced into a little bit of strike breaking!'

She could hear the smile in his voice as he hung up.

The sea had a clearer, deeper tint than the cloudless sky, and from the plane could be seen the rugged hillsides, the elegant villas with their azure swimming pools easily identifiable in the pristine light.

As the plane taxied to a halt the stewardess led the tall

beautiful woman from her Club-class seat to the front. In this Mecca of beauty and style, she still stood out, her pink silk dress highlighting the paleness of her skin and the auburn lights in her hair. From her snakeskin shoes to her tiny clutch bag, she was elegance itself; her stride as she walked along the glass-covered corridor beside the Air France stewardess was the walk of a woman confident in her beauty. Only the porter behind carrying the heavy British Government red box gave any indication that this woman devoted her life to something other than her pleasure and her beauty.

As Ann walked into the arrivals hall a woman in the red white and blue uniform of the local tourist office welcomed her to the City of Flowers with a posy of roses, fortuitously in a deeper pink than the colour of her dress. She accepted them with grace, and allowed herself to be led to the official limousine that would take her to Le Mas d'Artigny, and the Conference of Major Nations. This was to have been her introduction to the art of statesmanship, where she would have been given her first showing on the world stage. But she had made her platform for herself when she had spoken at the European Commission and pronounced her country as ungovernable. She had that morning put out a statement saying that rather than return to Britain, she was travelling to Nice to talk with other major political figures in the hope of securing assistance in foreign aid for an immediate emergency programme of reconstruction in Britain. She hoped her first meeting would be with Richard Horowitz, leader of the American delegation. It was, she announced, time to sue for peace, and she called for an orderly return to work as an indication of the willingness of the British people to put the appalling events of the past two years behind them.

The clear implication was that she regarded herself as Prime Minister already – but unlike others who had waited respectfully for the call from the Palace to form a Government, she had assumed the mantle of office herself. As she got into the car, she found yet another bouquet of flowers, this time her favourite white lilies. Attached was a card bearing the crest of the US Government. The message – welcome to Nice – RJ Horowitz II – made her smile. The smile stayed on her face as the car took her along the seashore filled with sun worshippers to Cagnes-sur-Mer, then began the climb away from the coast past the stunning medieval fortresses of Les Hauts de Cagnes and Saint Paul de Vence. Skilfully her driver weaved through the tourist coaches.

As the car sped past the Maeght Foundation, Ann took out a little gold compact and refreshed her make-up, dabbing perfume on her pulse spots as the car swept through the gates of the luxury hotel. Uniformed porters materialized at the side of the car as it glided to a halt under the portico. Ann looked round appreciatively at the paintings and the huge vases in the wide and sunny foyer, the tented dining room and the swimming pool on the next level, and through acres of glass windows, the pine-clad hillsides with the Mediterranean shimmering in the heat in the distance. The receptionist welcomed her, told her a registration card would not be necessary.

'Monsieur Horowitz indicated that you might prefer one of our guest villas to a suite in the main hotel. If however that does not suit, please indicate.'

She smiled an acknowledgement. 'Where is M. Horowitz's room?'

'He is in the villa next to you, madame.'

Ann nodded. 'What's good enough for him is good enough for me! Has he arrived yet?'

Her face fell as she learned that he had been delayed, and was unlikely now to arrive at the hotel before late afternoon. Ann's momentary displeasure disappeared when she saw her villa with its own little swimming pool, nestling in the hillside beneath the pool of the main hotel. She walked out on to the patio and breathed deeply the scent of pine and wild garlic. Inside, the summery wicker furniture seemed to be covered with vases and baskets of flowers.

The maid had left after unpacking, and Ann had wandered outside again, loosening her dress as she did so, when the phone rang. She rushed over to it, but her face fell when she heard the voice of Michael Stewart.

'How clever of you to find me, but I have nothing to say about this conference. There will be a statement at the end, and you will have been told that already!'

She frowned as she listened. 'I can't possibly meet you, Michael. Have some consideration. I need to prepare for the summit and you know damn fine I need to talk to Horowitz . . .'

He didn't let her finish. When she spoke again, it was to agree to meet him for lunch in the Rotonde restaurant of the Negressco in Nice. Sighing with irritation, Ann phoned through to reception that she wanted a car to take her down into Nice, she had a lunch appointment.

She had just changed into a white cotton shirt and brilliantly printed red and orange wraparound skirt, when a large and obviously American gentleman knocked on the glass patio door. From the way he continued to wear a jacket even in sweltering heat, she knew him to be a security agent.

'Ma'am, I have been assigned to your protection. I would propose to accompany you into Nice, if you don't mind.'

Ann hesitated, then she agreed: 'Provided you keep out of sight. I don't want obvious protection.'

He agreed.

At first Ann couldn't see anyone in the Rotonde. Coming in from the bright sunlight, her eyes took time adjusting to the darker light, and the garish colours of the fairground horses that earned the restaurant its name distracted her so much, she didn't realize Michael was there until he was standing in front of her.

Ann couldn't hide her surprise at the change in him. He looked haggard and ill. Michael had fled Paris, catching a slow commuter train to Saint Denis and there stealing a car – learning lessons he couldn't possibly have picked up at Oxford. He had been too frightened to talk to anyone, except for Donald Ross, who had behaved exactly as Clare had predicted and suspended him for dereliction of duty, assuming drunkenness. Michael would have liked to talk to Clare, he knew she was being allowed to do some of the reporting he would have been assigned to, but did not want her to feel compromised by being thought to be his friend. Eventually, Stewart had seen in *Le Monde* that it was still Ann's intention to attend the conference in Nice, so he had made his way to the Côte d'Azur, sticking to the Route Nationale until he could abandon the stolen car and travel on local buses. There was an air of dishevelment about him, and the short sleeves of his shirt served to emphasize the rather grimy bandage round his hand. His face was grim, and he seemed edgy, looking round to see if she had been followed.

The maître d'hôtel approached and inquired if they wanted a table, but Michael shook his head. Without explanation to Ann, he led her back out into the street. She flinched at the tightness of his grip on her arm, and as he hurried her along, she looked round to see if the secret service officer was in sight. She suppressed a sigh of relief when she saw that he was.

Despite her long legs, Ann had trouble keeping pace with Michael as he marched her along the promenade. He only slowed down when they reached Vieux Nice, below the Château. He seemed to know the restaurant he was looking for, and he quickly pulled her past the gingham-covered tables outside and the tanks of lobster in the doorway, into the dark fastnesses of the interior. Once she had been seated and given a cold glass of wine, Ann let her irritation show.

'What's all this cloak-and-dagger stuff about, Michael? I'm much too busy to spend time catering to your fantasies, so will you please tell me why you insisted I see you!'

Michael seemed unaware of her irritation, so great was his agitation:

'It was vital that I talk to you before the summit. And I had to be sure we wouldn't be overheard. I've been given some information that I knew I had to get to you regardless of the difficulty. Once I tell you what it is, you'll see why I had to be so careful!'

And he began to tell her about Conway Frazer and the documents he had been given in Washington. As he told her about the plot to reduce the Government of the United Kingdom to puppet status, and to increase the country's already massive store of nuclear weapons so that there could be an assault on Europe if that should prove necessary as well as the Soviet Union, he could see a veil descend on Ann's face.

'You think I'm mad, don't you? I don't blame you, if I hadn't seen these documents myself, I'd never have believed it.'

Her eyes were as cold as he had ever seen them, he could feel the waves of hostility coming from her. This was the woman who had cried out in his arms. There was desperation in his voice as he said to her:

'Ann, you must know I love you. I wouldn't do anything to mislead you, or make you look foolish. But you've got to take me seriously, I swear I'm telling the truth.'

She stared at him, her shoulders tense, her neck stiff. 'Show me the documents!'

She knew immediately that he couldn't. He shook his head:

'They were stolen. Somebody must have known that I had them, they were taken from my room in Paris. I'm not very good at all this secrets stuff, so I hid them in too obvious a place.'

Ann dropped her head on to her hands, and sat like that for a long time before she raised her head and looked at him again.

Her voice was gentle as she asked him why he had been in Washington. It was his turn to be silent before he replied:

'I was looking for Johann. I know who he is, Ann.'

As he said the words, he knew he had lost her. Her shock gave way to anger, then she jumped up, almost knocking her chair over backwards. Suddenly, she was gone. Although he was only seconds behind her, she

312

seemed to have disappeared when he got out into the street. He looked to right and left, ignoring the stares of the flower sellers in the market anxious for a bit part in what looked like a lovers' tiff. Then he saw the bright swirl of her skirt as she got into the back of a white Mercedes, which screeched off at speed.

Michael raced to a car he had hired, hoping that on a Saturday his credit card couldn't be checked, but the little Renault Five was no match for the powerful German beast. He had his first bit of luck though, he knew Le Mas d'Artigny well. Years before, when his reputation was still intact, he had been invited to attend the Conference of the Successor Generation – a US-organized get-together to introduce the up-and-coming people of Europe to their opposite numbers in the States – which had been held in the luxurious hotel and villa complex. Over the four days he had stayed there he had spent his free time strolling round the surrounding woods and pathways. This time though, he got no closer than the Maeght Foundation where his car was stopped by the CRS – the French anti-terrorist police. He indicated he was from the press, but they directed him into the nearby car park. Getting out of the car, he walked over to the security barricade, fumbling through his pockets for his BBC photo-pass. Despite his schoolboy French and the guards' lack of English, he managed to convince them he was a reporter assigned late to the story who had still to collect his accreditation from the rest of the crew. As they let him through, Michael said a silent thank you to Denis Healey who had proved some years before that even the heaviest security could be breeched: armed only with a London Transport pensioner's bus pass, the former British Chancellor of the Exchequer had managed to talk his way into the Kremlin.

Deprived of his car, Michael began to walk along the dusty road, but soon he saw the familiar paraphernalia of TV crews, obviously given accommodation in the car park of a computer training centre as a temporary home for coverage of the conference. His luck had certainly improved, within minutes he had spotted Peter Watson, his former director, and a BBC Scotland film crew. Watson did no more than raise an eyebrow, still in the grip of a monumental hangover, but Clare, when she turned round and saw him, couldn't stop herself from throwing her arms round him. Luckily the studied insouciance of the international press and the mock affection of even the most casual greeting saved them from any undue attention.

Michael drew Clare inside the stifling camera car. 'I've got the story of a lifetime, Clare. Can you help me get into the conference?'

Seeing her hesitate, he went on: 'I'll give it to you to break, if you can just help me get in there. I know exactly what I need to do to prove it, it would take too long to tell you the details, but I swear it's the big one!'

With a mixture of pity and hurt she looked at him: 'You're sure it's not to get close to Ann Clarke again?'

He shook his head, but she could see from the bleakness of his expression that he had now accepted that he was no longer of any use to the beautiful politician. Clare agreed and went off to negotiate an extra pass – 'for an assistant cameraman'. She was smiling when she returned: not only had she got the pass, but she had been given permission to go into the hotel to shoot some background film of the beautiful location of the conference.

Disguised with a baseball cap pulled down over his eyes and a cameraman's light meter, Michael joined the crew as they piled into the camera car to go into the hotel grounds. Once through the gates and out in the open again, Michael went off by himself, edging his way round the swimming pool, stopping occasionally to check the readings on the light meter and to frame imaginary shots. As he reached the far side of the pool he looked back at the hotel, scanning the bedroom windows, but as he stepped backwards into the shrubbery to 'frame' a better shot of the hotel with its pretty pink roof, he heard voices coming from the garden of one of the villas that nestled in a semicircle beneath the main pool of the hotel. His eyes darted round to see if he was being watched, then he crouched down into the protective cover of the greenery and edged along the line of conifers planted to give the luxury villas total seclusion, and as he neared the perimeter, he could see more clearly. It was Ann, and her words were becoming clearer. She was telling someone he couldn't see what Michael had told her at lunch.

If he had expected to hear derision from her, he was mistaken, she was taking it very seriously. He detected a touch of panic in her voice as she went on:

'And he's been in the States. We know he was asking questions in Boston, what if he's found out how you trained me? All those lessons in statecraft, in media image, in campaigning. He's going to work out that you didn't do it just because we were lovers. He'll put two and two together and know that we had a plan! I tell you, he says he knows you, Johann! He'll destroy everything we've worked for!'

At that the man came out of the shadows. He took Ann into his arms and held her. 'Relax, darling. He's easily dealt with. You're just getting nervous because we've only days to go. Tomorrow, you'll meet all our advisors here and we'll go over the final details. And we'll have won. All the humiliation you've had to put up with, and your father as well, they'll all be behind you, and you can live your life as you want to.'

And then he kissed her possessively. Michael was transfixed, hypnotized yet made desolate by the passion of the lovers. Richard Johann Horowitz was a vibrant powerful man who clearly had Ann under his spell – the man who would shortly lead the free world, and the Secretary of State who had authorized the secret plan revealed by Conway Frazer. Ann was in league with the man who intended to annex the British Isles.

He could no longer pretend it wasn't happening. The realization sapped all the strength from his body, but as he crouched in the shrubbery, he heard footsteps drawing ever closer. Suddenly there was a shout. Abandoning all pretence at subterfuge, Michael got up from his crouch and began to run, heading down into the forest that surrounds the hotel. He heard their yells as they chased him. Twice he heard the sound of gunfire close by.

Sliding and slipping, he got into the dense cover of the trees, slithering on his belly through the mulchy under-growth, trying hard not to sneeze as the smell of wild garlic got to him. He heard the heavy pounding of feet around him, and kept stopping, holding his breath. After what felt like an age, he reached the main road, but there was no question of returning to his car. Losing himself in a crocodile of tourists, he went with the crowd into the hilltop village of Saint Paul de Vence, ignoring the stares at his dirty appearance.

Michael went up the hill into the cobbled network of streets in the village, but the searchers spotted him. He began to run, darting down alleyways and in and out of pretty little craft shops. People shouted as he jostled them in his haste to get past. As he looked behind he could see his pursuers drawing closer – more of them than he had expected – and he could see that they were fanning out to blanket the village.

Every way he turned he was trapped. There was only one way out of Saint Paul, the road he had come in by, and they would have that covered.

But then he realized. There was another way!

Michael darted down an alley through which he could see another clifftop village in the distance. As he ran he skidded, and fell against the rampart at the bottom. He looked behind him – so far so good. He looked over the wall; a sheer cliff face stretched for hundreds, if not thousands, of feet into the gorge, but the rock was pitted and holed. If he could get a secure foothold, he could hide there until they gave up looking for him. Years of rock climbing gave him the skill to save himself.

Turning again to make sure he was still alone, he swung his legs over the wall, his heart beating loudly. He felt with his feet for a secure ledge, holding himself secure with his hands. Above him he could hear the shouts of his pursuers, they had found his alleyway, but he was sure his hands would be well hidden by the craggy wall. All he needed was for his newfound luck to hold.

The shouts died away, then he heard another noise. Someone calling his name. Clare! He was too frightened to call out, but he willed her to look over the rampart.

'Oh, thank God, Michael! Can you stay there just a few seconds longer? Just till I check where they are?'

He grunted a response and she disappeared, but seconds later she was back. With all the strength in her small frame, she hauled him up from his refuge. Holding on to him like a lover, she steered Michael out into the busy streets, pulling his face down to kiss should anyone look closely at them. Ten yards along the street, she dragged him into a little shop with rack after rack of brightly coloured silk dresses. Picking up a handful, Clare gestured to the shop assistant that she wanted to try some on, and holding tightly on to Michael's hand, she went into the back of the shop. She pushed the six-foot man down on to the floor, and threw layers of dresses over him, then pulled her own blouse off, turning so that, bare-breasted, she faced the curtained entrance. Seconds later, the little shop was filled with the shouts of Michael's pursuers. A man pushed open the curtain into the makeshift fitting room, and Clare screamed, not just with mock modesty, but with genuine terror. The man looked at her, taking long enough to scan her full, round breasts, but not looking elsewhere in the room. He muttered an apology and left.

Clare signalled to Michael to stay where he was, then dressed and went out into the shop, where the young Frenchwoman in charge fussed over her, apologizing for the shock she had been given. Clare pushed a bundle of francs into her hands and with the international camaraderie of women, and the historic mistrust of the French for all authority, she secured Michael safekeeping until the search moved elsewhere.

317

EPILOGUE

The early morning sunlight made the water sparkle. With long and languorous strokes she did length after length of the pool. Eventually she hauled herself out of the water and walked naked over to the chair where she had left her robe. He watched her every move. As she came towards him, he reached out and pulled at the knot she had just made in the belt. She smiled at him as the robe fell open. His eyes roved over her, and as she watched, his lips became narrow and his breathing heavier.

His voice was thick as he spoke:

'Take it off.'

She was about to resist playfully when she saw the look in his eyes. She let the robe fall to the ground, then loosened her hair from the top-knot that had kept it dry as she swam. Her eyes were dark as she watched him. Without a word, he stood up and went back into the villa. She followed him.

Later, as he rose up above her to look at her spread out beneath him, she shivered at what she saw in his eyes: he seemed able to see into her soul. To lighten the heaviness of the moment, she giggled.

'You look as if you're taking inventory!'

He didn't reply, just rolled on to his back. They lay side by side for a long time, each aware that the other was replaying memories of the young student who came to Boston to learn about the law, and left having fallen in love; and of the young Senator who had consciously moulded her to become the kind of politician who could captivate her country.

For him.

She had arrived in Boston bitter about the injustices of a political system in her own country that had destroyed her father and protected the guilty politicians he had served. And she met a man who taught her about love – about the joy he could bring to her body and the delight she could bring to his.

He had given her a goal too. His own towering ambition was certain to take him to the top office in his Government. His father had groomed him as he was to groom her, and his father had built an empire for no reason other than to finance his son on the way to becoming the most powerful man in the world. She would be his ally, and in return she could have his love and the most wonderful job in her own country. Together, they would be the world's most influential couple.

At first it was the fantasy of two lovers as they meandered through their private heaven after sex. But then he had introduced her to pollsters, to political scientists, to stylists, voice coaches, colourists. And before she knew it, a new Ann Clarke emerged.

On the day she realized that senior people in his Government were helping him, ambition had become more than a fantasy. She began to believe it could be done. And when a woman had been elected to lead a political party in her own country, then to be Prime Minister, she knew she could do it too.

She worked ferociously to ensure she would. It was the one way they could be truly together. Little by little she had tasted the potent drug of power and become addicted; now everything they had planned was happening.

There had only ever been one flaw. To get the kind of social acceptance an immigrant needed to become President, Richard Johann Horowitz had needed a wife. His father had found him one, the impoverished daughter of a Boston brahmin who sold her to pay off the Revenue.

He had told Ann that even as he walked down the aisle with his bride at their big society wedding, he had hated her. But if he was going to be President, he couldn't divorce her; her uncle was a bishop, and Richard would need the vote of every Hispanic, Greek, Irish, Italian expatriate he could get. All devout Catholics, they hated divorce.

In all the hours they had spent making their plans, they had never discussed Rachel Horowitz. Ann had allowed herself to believe an arrangement would be made. Now they couldn't put off talking about it any longer. Ann got up on one shoulder and looked down at him. She could tell from the way he stared at the ceiling that he was already running over the meeting due to start in a little over two hours. This was to be the first time that all the key figures in the campaign to save Britain – American style – had been brought together, and she sensed his nervousness.

She ran her fingers over his face to bring him back from his reverie. He looked at her, and she bent down and kissed the tip of his nose, her breast lightly brushing his chest. She kept her voice gentle, but it shook as she asked him the question:

'What are you going to do about Rachel, darling? She's a drunk and she'll only hold you back. I know the voters wouldn't let you marry again, but at least we could be honest with each other without you always having to go back to her.'

As he stared at her, she drew her hand away. Her timing had not been right. He moved as though about to get up, but suddenly he pulled her down on to the bed. Without warning he entered her, reaching a climax quickly, then leaving her, not looking round to see the hurt in her eyes.

When he returned to the bedroom, washed and scented and wearing a lightweight business suit, she was sitting at the mirror brushing out her hair. She bent over so that she made a veil of her hair as she brushed it from beneath. As she straightened up, he smiled at her:

'Get the maid to pack for you and I'll make sure your car is ready. I expect you'll have to leave as soon as the meeting is ended. I've got to get some work done now, so I'll go back to my own villa.'

He made as if to leave, then came back. He look her hands, raised her to her feet and drew her to him, kissing

320

her deeply, his tongue probing. He stood back looking at her, then he said, very quietly:

'It has been very, very good with you.'

And ignoring the startled look on her face, he left.

As she dressed with even more care than usual the phone rang – time to join the meeting, everyone had assembled.

Ann checked her appearance in the mirror. Her hair was coiled on top of her head. Her legs were bare and tanned, smooth under the silk dress, gold-painted toes peeping out from high yellow sandals. Gold ball-like earrings were clipped to her ears and she wore a chunky solid gold necklace and bracelet.

On impulse she picked a white magnolia from one of the baskets and pinned it to her jacket. Her eyes glistened, her lips shone, her nipples brushed against the silk. She had never looked more beautiful, and the radiance in her eyes told of the joy with which she was going forward to meet the destiny she had created for herself.

As she swirled round, she couldn't resist saying to herself: 'Well done, Prime Minister!'

Horowitz himself opened the door to her. 'Come in, Ann, there are a number of people here I know you'll be very happy to meet.'

The room was L-shaped, and men were standing around drinking coffee. The group nearest the door were all American. They shook hands with her, congratulating her on her 'magnificent efforts'.

Some of the names she recognized, men she had been in contact with over the years – one was a senior State Department official who had briefed her on a Parliamentary visit years before.

She wasn't really surprised to find Dieter Volle in the room. As she crossed over to shake hands with him, he bowed low and kissed her hand in a chivalrous gesture that made her smile. Richard Horowitz then took her by the arm and led her round into the other part of the room. Two men were sitting there in the shadows; it wasn't until they stood up that Ann recognized them. Graeme Jones came to her first:

'Hello Ann, I bet you didn't know we were on the same side!'

Speechless, she could only shake her head. When she regained her voice it was only to say: 'When?'

He laughed. 'Since about the same time as you! I was recruited at university. I was Chairman of the National Organization of Labour Students. When you were being infiltrated into the Revolutionary Socialist Party, I was busy arranging that they should take over the student movement. I was the guru, when all the time they thought it was that moth-eaten South African, McGregor. Then I moved on – it was my job to get Metcalf into Number Ten, which really meant channelling Sylvia's ambition.'

If she was shocked at Jones' presence, when the other man came out of the shadows she felt herself sway. George Jeffries' grin was puckish as he came towards her.

He held her shoulders and looked down into her face. 'You didn't believe me when I told you we were closer together than you thought!'

Her eyes darted round the three men: Horowitz, Jones, Jeffries. Then she began to get over the shock. She looked at Jeffries:

'And what role did you play?'

He let out a guffaw of laughter. 'It was all my idea in the first place. I've always felt I was born a couple of centuries too late. I wanted to take epic decisions that would change the path of history, and it saddened me that Britain is no longer a superpower in her own right, so I conceived this as the next best thing. You could say – if you can't beat them, join them! And I knew all the right buttons to press. Nothing is so potent as self-interest. The Masons took care of the Establishment, they've been doing that for centuries – they always had a handful in every Cabinet. And as for the Labour Party, the Trots had been digging themselves in there since the forties. Given a bit of sensible leadership and some money, they could easily do a job for us – and greed would make sure everyone jumped at the idea of taking the thirty pieces of silver from the Americans.'

The men had to strain to hear what she said next: 'Then why are you content that I should be Prime Minister?'

The three men looked at her, then Horowitz said: 'We'd better get down to business. Shall we sit at the table?'

Like an automaton, Ann found her place at the table. She had been placed directly opposite Horowitz and Jeffries. The latter went into a lengthy outline of the state of affairs in Britain as he had left it the previous night, emphasizing that the Metcalfs now knew it was all over for them – Tony was in hospital, with cirrhosis of the liver added to all his other problems. Sylvia would take over his seat. Arrangements were being made to end the general strike when the new Prime Minister was appointed. Ann interrupted him. He was in mid sentence when she stood up:

'I've been set up! It was never intended that I should be Prime Minister, I was just a useful vehicle to bring the country into chaos. I've been manipulated all the time when I thought I was the one doing the manipulating.'

Horowitz got up and walked round the table to her. 'Ann, you can be Deputy Prime Minister for as long as you want to be, and when George has had enough – well, you're very young, that'll be your turn!'

She pulled away from him. For a moment it looked as though she might hit him, but the venom in her voice was as searing as a blow:

'You bastard! You played me for a fool all along. The rest – they've just used me politically, but you've invaded my body, abused me for your selfish ends. And I was stupid enough to believe you. But now I'm the one who can tell the world what evil bastards you all are!'

She looked round the table, shaking with rage, a rage that exploded as she saw Jeffries convulsing in paroxysms of silent laughter. She picked up a heavy Baccarat ashtray and threw it at him, but it went wide, crashing through a window instead and setting off the security alarms.

Jeffries stood up. Controlling himself with difficulty, he

managed to say: 'Love, if you come away with some story about a bloodless overthrow of the British Government by the Americans, Tony Metcalf won't be the only one in the funny farm! The only people who know what we've achieved are in this room. Not another living soul knows.'

'That's where you're wrong!' she spat at him. 'Michael Stewart knows!'

His voice was quiet but icy as he replied: 'That loose end is easily tidied.'

The anger drained from her face to be replaced by fear, and she looked from one face to the other, shrinking away from them.

Horowitz put his arm round her shoulder. 'Darling, you have nothing to fear. We know you wouldn't be believed if you told such a fantastic story as this. And the offer still stands. You can remain as Deputy Prime Minister.'

He took an envelope from his pocket: 'But if you don't want to do that, here are the keys and the title deeds to a penthouse in Monaco. There's also a bank account with five million pounds in it. We are very grateful for everything you've done, and if you ever want to join us again in some other role, well – you know where to find us. It would be a pity to put all that talent to waste. And I think you'll agree we made quite an investment in you too!'

She backed away from him until she was up against the wall. She had begun to shake. 'You traitor. You said we would always be together.'

The tears began to course down her face, all the fight drained from her. He went over to her.

'Darling, you know I'm going to be President. You must have realized we could never have a future.'

She was sobbing uncontrollably now, but through the sobs the others could hear her quite clearly: 'But I love you, Johann, I did it all because I love you!'

He and George Jeffries helped her out to the white Mercedes which was sitting ready, her cases already loaded, to take her to her new life.

As the car pulled away she looked round for some last

glimpse of the man she loved, but he had turned away. His arm was round George Jeffries' shoulders as they walked back into their meeting, the problems of the morning already forgotten.

Sylvia, dressed in black and looking thinner and older after the pressures of the past six months, went round the room thanking people for coming. She sat down next to Stephen Robinson and his wife:

'I do appreciate you being here, and it's good to see you again, despite the circumstances.'

It was Elma Robinson who spoke:

'The number of times we've spoken about you since all of this happened. We've had our problems, but for you it must have been so much worse. Bad enough to have Tony so ill, and you having to fight the by-election for his seat – but then to watch him dying, that must have been terrible.'

She put a black-gloved hand on the arm of the other woman. Sylvia looked at Stephen, now with the stoop of defeat about his shoulders.

'How are you coping?'

He smiled ruefully. 'Not bad, considering. I don't miss the House, I had to go. The risk of blackmail from Jeffries was too high. I've been helping Joe Black settle in. He's taken to being an MP like a duck to water. Things haven't been too bad financially, it turns out Elma had been saving like mad all those years in case something like this happened – and thank God for it! I've got an interview next week for a job.'

Elma got up to put her cup and saucer on the table, and Sylvia lowered her voice so that they could not be overheard: 'I'm sorry if I hurt you, Stephen. I know how you felt about me, but I loved Tony, I would never have betrayed him. They say he was a weak man, but he wasn't. His problem was he cared too much, and feared his own inability to do everything he felt needed to be done. But I was very fond of you. If ever you need a friend, you know where to find me.'

Stephen put out his hand as if to touch her, then thought better of it. 'I've missed you so much. I did fall in love with you, and it was wrong of me, but I couldn't help myself, especially seeing you so brave and knowing what you were having to go through. Things are much better now with Elma – she's got me back again – and all the struggling and budgeting is right up her street. I'll be all right – but what about you? Why isn't Jeffries here today – or Graeme Jones?'

She stiffened. 'I didn't want their hypocrisy! Jeffries was betraying Tony all the time he pretended to be his friend. Plotting Tony's downfall, using Ann Clarke to undermine him – all because he wanted the job for himself. And as for Jones! Don't talk to me about him! Now he's got Ann Clarke's seat he's unbearable – and to think he's in the Cabinet, and only in the House four months! To see him toadying to the Americans after all he said about them!'

Her face flushed with anger.

Elma came back and asked about Ann Clarke.

Sylvia responded: 'Living in luxury in Monte Carlo, from what I hear – but locked away, supposedly writing a book, no doubt to damage Tony in death as she damaged him in life.'

'But why did she give up? She'd have been Prime Minister, and I know Stephen always thought that was what she was after.'

Sylvia and Stephen looked at one another. Sylvia replied: 'That is a question no one can answer. I think Jeffries had something on her – blackmailed her into giving up to make way for him.'

Stephen said only two words: 'Colin Warrender?'

'I think so.'

Sylvia got up from her seat as a chic middle-aged woman was shown into the room. Mary Connolly had changed almost beyond recognition in the time she had been in Brussels. The mousy brown hair now had blonde highlights and was caught up in a chignon. The cheap suits had been replaced by a Chanel ensemble in brown and cream check teamed with a simple gold necklace and tiny earrings. Her shoes were leather and unscuffed. She seemed embarrassed as she walked over to Sylvia, who held out her hand.

'I'm sorry I'm late, Sylvia. My plane got held up. But I wanted you to know how sorry I am about Tony. I thought a lot of him, since those days when Ann and I were his students. If I had known what Ann was trying to do to him, I'd have had nothing to do with it.'

Sylvia smiled at the other woman. 'I know you wouldn't have been party to trying to hurt us, Mary. But how are you? You look very well.'

Mary accepted the compliment with a self-deprecating smile that brought back memories of the old days, when only Ann got the compliments. 'I'm well, and very happy. I realize now that all those years, Ann was using me the way she used everyone else. Now I'm free of her spell, I'm beginning to accept that I've got a right to a life and a career too.'

She didn't wait to be asked the question they all wanted answered. 'I haven't seen her since the day she left Britain. She's never tried to get in touch, and I'm glad. I don't ever want to see her again. Although I do see her mother when I'm back in Scotland. She bought a flat in Edinburgh with the money she got from the *Sunday Times* for her story, and she seems very happy, though she's never heard from Ann either. She's left Ann's father, and as far as I know he's still living in the cottage, a broken man, drinking himself to death.' She looked embarrassed as she realized what she had said, but Sylvia merely smiled ruefully and moved away.

The Robinsons took their leave to begin the long drive back to Scotland; soon the house was empty and Sylvia could relax. She had just taken off her dress when the doorbell rang. Sighing in irritation, she put on a dressing gown and went to answer it.

The hair was shorter, cut in a sleek page boy. She was tanned and the slacks and sweater in pale blue, dressed up with gold jewellery, made her look the millionairess she now was.

'Hello, Sylvia. I've come to offer my condolences.'

Sylvia Metcalf was speechless. She stepped back and signalled to Ann Clarke to come into the house.

Both women stood in the hallway, sizing each other up.

'Why have you come?'

'I told you, Sylvia. I wanted to offer my condolences, Tony was very good to me when I was young. I was saddened to hear he had died.'

The smug composure of the woman was too much for Sylvia. 'You bitch! You hypocritical bitch! You killed Tony, with all your plotting and manoeuvring. You undermined him as a man and as a Prime Minister – and you come here to offer your condolences. You're really here to make sure he's well and truly dead.'

Ann laughed. 'Don't be silly, Sylvia. What possible threat could Tony Metcalf be to me, either living, or dead? Now if it had been you – that would have been different. You would have been a worthy challenger. At last you've taken the right decision – gone into the House yourself. You'll make a real name for yourself now, not just as the manipulator of Tony. You should have thrown him aside years ago and built your own career. You failed to see when you should have cut your losses.'

'And is that what you did? Cut your losses? Or did George Jeffries get the better of you too?'

Ann's face was hard, temporarily losing its beauty. 'It was time to move on. Britain under the thumb of the Americans would have denied me the power I want. Mark my words, when Horowitz is sworn in as President, there'll be nothing this country can do to resist him. He's a man who takes what he wants and throws it away when he's had full use of it.'

Sylvia shook her head incredulously. 'To listen to you, who would realize you're living in exile? Discredited here for running away. What possible power could you conceivably get now?'

The other woman smiled again. 'Wait and see, Sylvia.

Wait and see. You of all people should know that when a woman wants something – she gets it.'

At that she turned on her heel and left. Sylvia watched through the open door as the Porsche Carrera swept down the driveway, then spoke to the empty house:

'She's up to something, Tony. Something even worse than she did to you. You're well out of it.'

Tanned almost black and wearing cotton shorts and T-shirt, the grey-haired man with the piebald beard bore little resemblance to the urbane and elegant Michael Stewart of a few months before. As he sat at a table outside a cafe in the tiny village of Atrani, south of Naples, his bleak expression and the slump of his shoulders added to his disguise. Only the repeated tapping of a typewriter, often heard in the middle of the night from the shabby single room he rented above the square, marked this man out as more than a beach bum.

The journey from the dress shop in Saint Paul de Vence had taken him to Italy, Yugoslavia, Switzerland, then back to Italy. The transport was varied: cattle transporter, regional train, stolen bike. He never lost the feeling of being watched, and he feared to engage in even the most casual friendship in case he should jeopardize others. Pursued or paranoid, he remained unsure, but a meeting with Clare, arranged when she left him to return to Le Mas d'Artigny, had brought him up to date with the harrassment she had suffered for helping him to get into the hotel. Only favours called in and a plea that she thought it would help her get nearer to a story, saved her job. She had applied for – and got – an assignment to a more junior job than she was qualified for in Washington – to 'get away from it all'. But it took her nearer to the story she was determined to prove.

There were few breaks, but as the months passed, more and more pieces of the jigsaw fell into place as the relationship between Horowitz and Jeffries became publicly closer. Michael fumed in his impotence and exile, unable to move for fear of exposure, unable to speak for fear of ridicule. The occasional package of information from Clare kept him going, and the recognition that she too shared his crusade. Whatever they had to do, however long it took to prove the story, between them they would do it.

Despite the January day the sun shone brightly outside. The man who sat at the magnificent desk that had once belonged to the Duke of Windsor looked up from the documents he was initialling to watch the television. A secretary came in on an urgent errand, and he got up from behind the desk and walked over to see the set more closely. He was a handsome man, black haired and well built, in his sixties. His body was muscled and fit like a man twenty years his junior. He wore a velvet smoking jacket with a silk open-necked shirt underneath. The rich red of his jacket picked up a colour in the Titian beneath which he stood.

He looked down at the set. Richard Johann Horowitz II had just been sworn in as President of the United States of America. His wife, elegant black hair drawn back in a chignon, wrapped in a red wool cape, looked up lovingly at him, and he bent down and kissed her with obvious passion. The crowd could be heard cheering. Together the President and his First Lady turned to wave, hands tightly clasped, two of their young children at their side.

The President bent down and planted a kiss on the top of the black mop of his seven-year-old daughter, then he turned to shake hands with his old friend, Prime Minister George Jeffries, invited to this prominent position as a sign of the close friendship between the two nations, secure in their joint prosperity.

The buzzer on the desk sounded: 'Your wife is on her way in, Comte Lucarelli.'

He switched off the set and turned to greet her, smiling as he always did at her stylish beauty.

She wore a moss-green velvet dress moulded to her lush figure. Her black stockings drew attention to perfect legs and dainty feet in hand-tooled leather pumps. Diamonds winked at her ears, and a huge emerald hung on a chain round her neck. As she came up to her husband, she reached up to kiss him, touching his face lightly with a hand that carried a large Cabuchon diamond. He touched her close-cropped auburn hair lovingly.

'Cara, I've just been watching the investiture on television. We've been very kind giving President Horowitz his day of glory. Just wait till we announce that you are to be chief executive of the biggest energy consortium in the world. That's real power!'

There was a seductive gurgle as she laughed, and it added to the gentle Scottish lilt in her voice: 'You are so good to me.'

OLD SINS
Penny Vincenzi

An unputdownable saga of mystery, passion and glamour, exploring the intrigue which results when Julian Morrell, head of a vast cosmetics empire, leaves part of his huge legacy to an unknown young man. The most desirable novel of the decade, *Old Sins* is about money, ambition, greed and love ... a blockbuster for the Nineties.

GREAT POSSESSIONS
Kate Alexander

A wonderful saga set in glamorous between-the-wars London that tells the story of Eleanor Dunwell, an illegitimate working-class girl who comes quite unexpectedly into a great inheritance. Her wealth will attract a dashing American spendthrift husband – and separate her from the man she truly loves.

THE WIND IN THE EAST
Pamela Pope

There were two things Joshua Kerrick wanted in the world: one was money to buy a fleet of drifters; the other was Poppy Ludlow. But Poppy and Joshua are natural rivals. This vivid historical drama traces their passionate story among an East Anglian community struggling to make their living from the sea.

FRIENDS AND OTHER ENEMIES
Diana Stainforth

Set in the Sixties and Seventies, the rich, last-moving story of a girl called Ryder Harding who loses *everything* – family, lover, money and friends. But Ryder claws her way back and turns misfortune into gold.

THE FLIGHT OF FLAMINGO
Elizabeth Darrell

A strong saga unfolds against a backdrop of marine aviation in its heady pioneering days before the Second World War. When Leone Kirkland inherits her autocratic father's aviation business, she also inherits his murky past, and Kit Anson, his ace test pilot. She needs him; she could love him, but he has every reason to hate her.

THE QUIET EARTH
Margaret Sunley

Set in the Yorkshire Dales during the nineteenth century this rural saga captures both the spirit and warmth of working life in an isolated farming community, where three generations of the Oaks family are packed under the same roof. It tells of their struggle for survival as farmers, despite scandal, upheaval and tragedy, under the patriarchal rule of Jonadab Oaks.

A BOWL OF CHERRIES
Anna King

A heartwarming East End novel of family life set in post-war London. It is the story of Marie Cowley's working class upbringing, her fight against a debilitating disease which overshadows her childhood, and her passionate determination to survive and find happiness despite everything.

THE SINS OF EDEN
Iris Gower

Handsome, charismatic and iron-willed, Eden Lamb has an incalculable effect on the lives of three very different women in Swansea during the Second World War that is to introduce them to both passion and heartbreak. Once again, bestselling author Iris Gower has spun a tender and truthful story out of the background she knows and loves so well.